Born INTO TROUBLE

Occupy Yourself
Book #1

MariaLisa deMora

Edited by Hot Tree Editing

Cover image by Sara Eirew Photographer

Cover design by Debera Kuntz

First Published 2016

ISBN 13: 978-0-9967486-4-3

DEDICATION

Blood makes you related. Loyalty makes you family.

For a man I saw brought low, who fought his way back.
Tooth and nail, but he made it back. A, you taught me that
when you find something worth fighting for, you hold on
with everything inside you and fight. Your strength amazes
me. I'm proud to be your friend.

Contents

ACKNOWLEDGMENTS

Before I even finished working on Slate's book in the Rebel Wayfarers MC series, I knew Benny had a story to tell. I began jotting down copious notes about his life and everything that happened to bring him to the brink of desolation, and where his life went from there.

Then I worked on *Bear*, and Benny's story evolved in my head. Then *Jase*, and so on.

However, when it came time to put pen to paper for Benny's story, what I found was I had it entirely wrong. So there I ran, back around to the starting line, gathering up all the things I thought I knew along the way, and trying every piece to find where it fit into the new puzzle, discarding many of my preconceived notions.

Benny's path is important. It's important to me, and I suspect will be to many of you. I felt I had to get it right, because it matters. I have friends who died due to their addictions, and this story hits hard at times. In my own way, I wanted to honor not only their struggles, but also the lives of the people who loved them. I have information at the end of the book for anyone dealing with alcoholism or addictions. Please reach out, because there is help available. And until you find the help you need, please...*hold on*.

Thank you to Sara Eirew for the absolutely perfect image you see on the front cover. Gratitude also goes out to the glorious Debera Kuntz, who took that beautiful picture and did the impossible, making it even more gorgeous with her cover design. Thanks also go to Jay Aheer for designing both the logo for the series, Occupy Yourself, and the logo on the back cover for Iron Indian Records, Mason's record label. Exquisite work, Jay. Thanks to all of you for the beautiful wrapping for Benny's story.

Big thanks to Becky and the betas at Hot Tree Editing. I loved reading your comments, and can't wait to work with you on the next book. Muuwah! <3

A special thank you to my brilliant alpha readers and friends who helped me bring Benny's story to life: LeeAnn, Jamey, Kristen, and MirandaPanda. The lengths to which you will go in order to assist me are remarkable, and I don't know what I'd do without you. L&R, ladies.

Shout out to my favorite fellas. Those men who scoff when I call them gentle, my folks who are happier when in the wind, those people who roll two wheels and live the life. Love alla y'all. Straight up. Real words, me to you.

Finally, a thank you to my ever-growing family. Stephie, Petie, David, TobyToes, and West – love you and your kiddos more than you know.

Woofully yours,
~ML

Prologue

CURRENT DAY

Benny scrubbed at his face with his palm, fingernails scratching through his short beard. Frustrated at what felt like a substandard performance, he muttered, "I hate being the one who's always fucking up." He sighed and looked across the studio where Chase sat next to Lucia. He ignored the other people in the booth; they didn't factor for this gig.

With his electric guitar slung low across his midriff, he held it comfortably, almost as if it were a flesh-and-bone extension of himself. Fingers returning to their continuous, steady movements, the music resumed, swelling to fill the air around him. Muscle memory by now, he was always most comfortable when hiding behind a wall of music and his guitar.

"Let's take that section from the top again," he said and waited for Chase to indicate he heard him and was ready before swinging back into the complicated melody. The transition was rough, choppy where he needed smooth. Without comment, he circled the melody again, easing into it better this time.

He glanced up and caught Lucia frowning at him. That expression told him that she had a question, and he knew it because she always had questions. Poking and prodding at things, even things he would so much rather leave dead and buried. Lifting his chin, he wordlessly prompted her to ask and after a moment, just out of sync with her mouth, he heard her voice through his earpiece. "*Dios.* If it's this hard to get right in the studio, how in the heck are you going to play this live?"

Benjamin Jones, guitarist and lead singer for Occupy Yourself, grinned at her through the thick panes of glass separating the control room and the live room. It was what his brother used to call his rock star smile; fake but glorious, plastic happiness hiding all the wrong underneath. She knew what it meant, so when she made a face, he let the smile fall away, knowing the expression he then wore was pained, but truthful. He shrugged, and then closed his eyes, letting the music loose within him. That was how it had always felt, as if the music was this caged and leashed beast inside him, ravening to be released. To be set free.

Three minutes and twenty-three seconds later, the last notes of the song began to die away, and Benny heard the enthusiastic voice of his friend. "Dude, way better. Way. Like so much better. That was dead on, man." That was Chase Mason, his friend and a seventeen-year-old budding musician.

He had met Chase through a series of events so dire that to call them unfortunate would be an extreme understatement. Benny wound up here…well, because he was always the one fucking up. Chase, on the other hand, was the golden boy. The much-loved only son of a wealthy and powerful man, a man who just happened to be a badass biker. Davis Mason was the national president of the Rebel Wayfarers, a motorcycle club with a presence in a dozen major cities. The man was also a Chicago city councilman, best friends with Benny's brother, Andy, and one of the best dads Benny had ever seen.

Lucia was a different kind of friend. Her adoptive dad, Rob Crew, was also connected with the Rebels, and at that moment, watched Benny through narrowed, cautious eyes as he stood at the back of the control room. Not unwarranted, because again, Benny was always the one fucking up.

Luce nodded at him, and he found himself grinning broadly back. *God, I could eat her up*, he thought, imagining the look on her face if he acted on that thought. Little guttural Spanish phrases falling from her lips as he licked and lapped at her while her sweet juices ran down his chin. Instead, he took a breath and shook his cramping hands out at his sides, and, pushing a cocky tone into his voice, asked, "Like that?"

#

14 YEARS-OLD

"*Benny.*" He woke slowly, groggily fighting his way up from a deep sleep. The voice came again. "Benny." Female—one he knew he should recognize. "Ben, you have to get up." Burying his head into the pillow, he slowly rocked his forehead back and forth, feeling an unfamiliar ache behind his eyes. Perfume, thick and cloying, clogged his nostrils, and he lifted his head a fraction of an inch, trying to get away from the thick scent making his stomach roll with nausea. "Benny."

Crap. His lips were stuck together. With some effort, he was able to peel them apart, tasting old blood mixed with new. Running his tongue along the inside of his mouth, he found two tender places where there were splits, blood oozing from the freshly reopened injuries. "Wha?" That was the extent of his ability to think at that moment, a single, slurred syllable which sounded so much like his mother, the sound jerked him entirely from the smothering cocoon of sleep.

"You have to get up. You're going to be late for school." Her voice set him on edge, skittering up his spine with a shiver like nails on a chalkboard, as the woman in the bed with him spoke again and he finally put a name to it. *Benita Owens.*

He moved, rolling onto his side to face Benita as he cracked open one eye. Her makeup was perfect, of course; it wouldn't do for the beautiful Benita to be seen any other way. She'd been up a while if her look told the truth, and he expected it did. You didn't achieve those results without work. Lifting one arm, he was surprised at how sore his muscles were. Arm, back, ass. He moved his legs in the bed. Thighs, calves. *Crap.* Everything hurt. *The fuck did I do?* His stomach rolled again. "Mmhmm. Hey." He got out nearly a whole word this time. "Time's it?" He let his eye sink closed again. The light was too bright; a blade of sunshine pierced through to the top of his brain and set up a fierce pounding there.

"The school bus runs in twenty minutes, Benny. You'll need to leave in time to walk to the stop." That got his eye open again, and he stared at her, then swung his head to look around the room—not his bedroom at GeeMa's place. This was huge in comparison, with posters of actors and movies on the walls and framed cutesy quotes scattered amongst them. He'd been in here before, studying. He snorted because studying was Benita's code word for sucking him off. That was as far as they'd gone: his hand down her pants twice, feeling the glorious mystery that was a woman's private parts, and her hand and lips on his dick. The first time had blown his mind, then he'd blown his load in her mouth, watched in awe as she swallowed, then licked him clean, curling her tongue around the head of his dick like it was a lollipop.

As he lay there looking at her, memories from the night before began to trickle slowly back to him. He remembered her picking him up from school, a wicked grin on her face as she told him her parents were unexpectedly out of town on a Thursday night. *Time to party*, she'd said, reaching over to put her hand on his crotch and squeezing as she sped away from the campus. Her house, a crowd of her friends, and him with an arm around her shoulder so she could put hers around his waist, fitting tightly against him. He remembered booze. So much booze. Faceless hands grabbing his empty glass and replacing it with a fresh, full one. Dancing, Benita pressed up against him, swaying to the music. Everyone listening while he crooned a sappy love song to her, Benita's face soft and affectionate.

He'd watched as couples drifted to private rooms or took up residence in quiet corners, glancing around as Benita led him by the hand up the stairs. That was where it got really fuzzy, and he wasn't sure of the exact sequence of events past taking the first tread upwards. He closed his eyes, thinking hard, trying to remember but he only found confusing feelings and colors, smeared scenes that were so bizarre he wasn't sure if they were real or curious dreams. Chaos in his head, in this bed. Benita naked, chin angled down so she could look at his face as she crawled up the bed on her knees. Feeling suffocated, tearing his mouth away from whatever was covering it. Hard slaps across his face, one which busted his bottom lip, one of the splits still seeping. He sucked that lip into his mouth, tasting more new blood than old. Opening his eyes, he watched as a guilty expression played across Benita's face. Remembering.

She wouldn't slow down, didn't slow down even when he pulled at her hips with his hands. Kept grinding her crotch against his face, covering his mouth and nose, the scent and taste of her filling everything. Nothing he'd wanted, not tonight, and he felt the vodka she'd kept pouring him earlier begin to roll up the back of his throat. Trying desperately to take in a breath to shove the vomit back down, he couldn't get away from her long enough to get more than small sips of air. Choking, he swallowed hard, time and again, twisting his head back and forth. "Be still, Benny." Eyes open, looking down her body at him. Breasts swaying as she undulated over him, hands propped against the headboard. Her voice vibrating with some emotion. "Almost there."

Her hand reached down, brushing past his cheeks, then her fingers worked at her flesh, frantic and fast. Her eyes closed and he felt her legs tense on either side of his head. Dying, he thought, then, heels to the mattress, he shoved hard, gaining two inches when he pushed out from under her. There was a loud cry of anger and pain exploded in his head, his neck whipping sideways and then she had him buried again. A few moments later it was over, and she climbed off him, snuggling into his

side and resting her head on his shoulder, cooing senseless words to him
as he swallowed hard again, still fighting off his nausea.

That was last night. Thursday night. Which meant this was Friday, and he couldn't be late to school, or he'd be riding the pine this evening at the football game. Without a word, he turned away from her to sit on the other edge of the bed. He'd never felt this ashamed before. Not even when the kids started pegging on his ma back in grade school, repeating their parents' overheard conversations. *Your mom's a whore*, the most frequently shouted insult. That was back before Danny Schraff unexpectedly became a friend and supporter, willing to wade into the shouting kids right alongside Benny.

Sitting on the edge of the mattress in the weak light of a Wyoming morning, he looked down, taking stock. Bare knees, scrawny legs, feet too big for his body. Briefs still on, *thank God*, which meant she hadn't touched him last night. In his head, he heard his brother, *No, just used your face to get off*. He pushed that voice aside, because even thinking about Andy seeing him here, like this, was mortifying. He couldn't let his brother down. Andy, who worked so hard to try and give Benny everything he needed, could never know what Benny had done.

"I can't drive you today." The mattress moved and footsteps rounded the end of the bed, heralding her approach. Tilting his chin so he didn't have to look at her, he held his breath against a renewed surge of nausea when she crouched beside his leg, hand on his thigh. "I've got to be in Cheyenne." He knew that. Knew about the trip. Benita was a senior; she had a college visit today that she didn't want. She'd been complaining about it for weeks, and more than once had shared a deep disappointment her parents weren't willing to spring for an east coast university. Benita had scoffed at their arguments, laughing with her friends that behind her mom's back, even her daddy said grades weren't everything. "I can drop you at the bus stop." He nodded, and still without looking at her, he jackknifed off the bed, swaying as he rose to his feet.

Eyes squeezed shut against the pounding pain, he jerked when her hand touched his chest, fingertips trailing across his collarbone, down to his gut, then sideways across his belly, tracing along the edge of his underwear. "I had a good time last night, Benny," she cooed at him; this was her pleased voice. Something he'd worked to pull from her in the past, but today, the syrupy-sweet turned his stomach. "Next time we party, we'll do it alone, so we can spend more time together." Her hand moved, palm gripping his arm and he felt the soft press of her boobs as she leaned in to kiss his cheek. "Next time," she whispered into his ear, "we'll go all the way."

***

"You look like shit." That was Danny's voice, and Benny twisted to watch him pull up a chair at the end of the picnic-style lunch table, squinting at the pain slamming through his head from the metallic racket. Danny Schraff had been Benny's best friend since grade school, the two of them bonding over the knowledge that you didn't get to pick who your parents were, you just had to learn how to put up with them.

That was about five years after Benny's dad died, and his mom had spiraled out of control, becoming the laughing stock of the town, known far and wide by her reputation of being a drunk...and worse. His father's parents had custody, so Benny had basically grown up with his grandparents. While a stable home, it felt like his mom and the situations she created were always drifting around him, threatening to bury him under an avalanche of hometown contempt.

Andy, Benny's big brother, was his rock, always there to push him and make him better. They'd always been more friends than brothers, even with the ten-year age difference, and afternoons spent with Andy were little slices of heaven; something he looked forward to in a big way. As such, Benny's life was decent, not like Danny's, whose father regularly took his fists to him. Danny deflected a lot of the schoolyard bullshit from Benny, and in return, Benny gave Danny a safe place to stay, an escape from a home often filled with turmoil.

The school lunch room buzzed, voices loud and echoing, the noises overlapping in a way that let you be certain no one would overhear anything if you didn't want them to. "Heard about the par-taay. Heard Benita was showing off her hot stud, *stud*." Danny leaned forwards, tipping his head to stare into Benny's face. "Holy shit, your eyes are bloodshot. Any teachers ask if you're sick?"

He shook his head, fingers wrapped around the glass of tomato juice that was his lunch. He'd watched his mother deal with the aftereffects often enough over the years to know food might be his enemy, but tomato juice would soothe things down. Two aspirins, two ibuprofens, one acetaminophen, and a glass of tomato juice. *Breakfast of champions*, he thought, then grimaced. *Or lunch for losers.*

"You know she's using you, right?" Twisting his neck, he stared at Danny, waiting. "She's nineteen, Benny. Five years older. Fuck man, you can't get your license for another two years, and she's off to college in a few months. She's a user, man. Don't let her suck you in." Danny grinned, "Suck you off, yeah. Take all that hot shit you can get, but don't let her jack you up."

Benny waved a hand, "No worries, man. I'm good."

"Keep tellin' yourself that, stud. Coach see you yet?"

Benny gingerly shook his head again. "Hoping to put this behind me before he does." The bell rang, and he winced as it jangled loudly, waking the pain again. "Vodka and beer on an empty stomach do not mix, my friend. Word to the wise from the unwise."

"No doubt about which is which today." Danny's joke fell flat, and he slapped Benny's shoulder, pushing his chair back. "See you in the locker room after school?" The football players held a meeting every game day. The boys dissecting the opponents and laying out planned strategies so there were few miscues on the field. This was independent of the team strategy meeting with Coach because it gave them a chance to focus on the people behind the plays. Benny's idea, which began back in junior high, now carried over to varsity with Coach's support since he was in high school this year. He overheard Coach talking about him not long ago, preening when the words "natural leader" and "talented player" were tossed around.

"Yeah, see you there." Straightening, he stretched his neck backwards, feeling muscles in his back throb. *If Mom is this miserable all the time, I wonder why she'd keep going back to the thing that sets it off.* There was feminine giggling off to one side, and he turned his head, catching the eye of one of Benita's friends. She winked at him and grinned wide, then opened her mouth, waggling her tongue. *Oh no, she didn't. Jesus. Time to shut this shit down.* Turning to face her straight on, he held her gaze and stared steadily, keeping his face impassive, waiting it out. After a moment, her eyes dipped down and to the side, and she avoided his gaze as she turned away. *Fucking Benita and her mouth. Her mouth talkin' about my mouth. Shit.*

Hours later, Benny stood on the sidelines, straps of his helmet dangling from his fingers, huffing in huge mouthfuls of air, eyes to the defensive line taking the field. "Jones," Coach called from behind him, and Benny barely controlled a wince, knowing what was coming. A firm hand landed on the pads covering his shoulder and gripped tightly. "You okay, son?" Typical Coach, worried more about the kids than the game. "You're off, Ben. That last pass should have been gravy." It should have, but the ball had bounced in and out of his fingers as if it were greased, his clumsy fumble forcing a fourth down turnover, the reason Benny was back on the sidelines.

"Yeah, Coach," he offered, eyes still trained on Danny shifting left to right across the field, tracking his man on the opposing team, currently on the move. "I'm good."

"You're sure?" Like most adults in his life, Benny knew what Coach wanted and gave it to him, turning his direction with a cocky grin. He tossed his still-aching head to indicate the stands behind him. Stands that held GeeMa, but not his brother. Andy was always working one of his jobs, but he at least called for a blow-by-blow review of every game. Never his mother, she didn't give a shit about anything except herself. Didn't matter, he played the game because he loved it, not because anyone was cheering him on.

"I won't let them down." Uncertainty still warred in Coach's eyes, so chin down, Benny imitated Andy's gruff way of talking when he said, "And I ain't gonna let you down, either, Coach." Sincerity won the day because the man released him and turned to watch the play developing out on the field. Coach took a step away as he shouted at the defensemen, giving them insights available from his vantage point. Benny's shoulders sagged, suffocating weight holding them down until he forced himself to straighten, ignoring the persistent nausea as he traced the splits in his lips for the hundredth time.

After the game, which they won by the narrowest of margins, Benny and Danny piled into one of the upperclassmen's vehicles, hitching a ride to the after-game bonfire. Benita appeared as if by magic when he stepped out of the truck, moving in beside him and possessively sliding her arm around his waist, pressing an already opened beer into his hand. After last night, he wasn't sure he wanted anything else to do with drinking, but now that she'd made a production out of it, there wasn't much he could do except go along. He wasn't sure about her, either. Danny's words had been circling his head all day, but Benny knew every man and boy present looked at him with admiration so he put a good face on it, smiling down at her and firmly ordering, "Kiss me, baby."

Obediently she rose to her toes to press her lips to his, then slid them across his cheek to respond softly, "Don't demand, baby." She planted a kiss to his cheek on her way back down, and her lips moved soundlessly, forming one word, "Ask." He nodded at her reminder of a lesson learned the first time he'd sat at lunch with her. She turned in his arm to face her posse of girls. "Ben is taking me to the prom this year."

It was the first he'd heard of those plans, and he nearly couldn't control the shuddering physical reaction when he thought of having to ask Andy or GeeMa for the money to rent a tuxedo. *Shit.*

Benita's shoulders lifted in a shrug to a question one of her giggling girls whispered into her ear, and Benita twisted to look up at Benny's face. A disturbingly wicked grin in place, she responded to her friend without taking her eyes off Benny. "I could share if you're nice, Shelby."

***

"Fuck," Benny slurred, leaning against the side of a truck. Benita had walked him out here what seemed like forever ago, propping him up and telling him she'd be right back. She'd held the cup for him to drain the dregs of the last mixed drink she'd brought him, and he was buzzed beyond belief. His dick was still hard from her fondling, and he dropped his head back, watching the stars wheel sickly overhead. *Pretty. Way out of reach, but pretty. Andy won't be happy.* His thoughts circled again, and he remembered the headache and nausea with which he'd started the day. *Pukin' again tomorrow*, he predicted. "*Fuck.*"

"Okay." Footsteps crunched in the dried grass, and he felt her hands at his belt, tugging, shoving his pants out of the way. He tried to lift up, but the weight of his head defeated him, so he stayed in that position. *Pretty stars.* Listening. Feeling. *Benita Owens, suckin' my cock.* She giggled, and he wondered if he'd said that last aloud, the sound of her laughter echoing, gaining an octave along the way, and then her hand was on his dick, tentatively pulling him out into the chilly air. Heat and pressure hit him, and he groaned, the still unfamiliar sensations of mouth and hands overwhelming.

She quickly coated him with saliva and then jacked him, her fingers sliding easily through the lubrication provided. Mouth on his balls, sucking and rolling, and he forced his legs wider, giving her better access. Her mouth on his dick at the same time, sucking deep, brought his head up abruptly. Senses still swimming from the sudden movement, he looked down to see two women on their knees in front of him. Benita's mouth between his legs, gaze locked to Shelby's face. Shelby's mouth around the knob of his dick, eyes turned up to watch him.

Benita changed position, and both women latched onto his cock, one on either side, their mouths kissing around him and he watched as they moved off him, kissing each other in earnest. Benita's hand rose, cupping Shelby's breast through her shirt, and he watched, trying to catalog the smooth and gentle motion and movements, knowing this had to be what Benita preferred, not his fumbling grip and release. Another lesson she might not even be aware of teaching him, so caught up in what she was doing. *Watch and learn.*

They came back to him, Benita's fingers wrapping around his dick and pointing it to Shelby's face. Benita moved behind her, so the women were pressed together, and Benita's other hand moved between Shelby's legs, lifting the short cheerleader skirt, disappearing underneath as Shelby's lips closed around him. Benita, mouth to Shelby's ear, tongue flicking out, whispered, "Told you he was hung." Eyes up to Benny, she hissed, "You do not come." She kissed Shelby's neck in a soft, unhurried way, nibbling her way up, and Benny studied how she did that, too. "Told you I'd share."

The rest of the evening flew past in a blur of faces and mouths as Benita brought two more friends to him before she was done sharing. Between the booze she kept pouring, and the edge they had him riding, he was incoherent by the time she stood in front of him, finally alone. Rolling a condom on his aching dick, she smiled up at him. "You did really well, honey. Let's break the seal." Standing, she turned away and shimmied her panties down before bending over. "Pop that cherry." Reaching between her legs, she gripped him and pulled, guiding him towards her entrance. "Fuck me, Benny."

Pushing backwards on him, she moaned loudly when her round ass met his thighs and it was all Benny could do to bite back a groan of his own. So much sensation slamming him from all sides. The heat of her wrapped entirely around his dick, so much better than his hand, better than her mouth could ever hope to be. The chill of the truck under his hands spread to either side of his torso, pressed flat, fingers wide. Nerves fired all along his spine, and he bowed his hips forward, ass clenching as he drove forwards and into her.

"Oh, baby," she called, twisting her head to look at him. Muscles tightening involuntarily, he thrust forwards again. And again. He was overcome with the sensation of his flesh crawling, balls tightening and drawing up so fast; he couldn't stop any part of it. The orgasm train had already left the station, and he was barely catching up. His hands left the truck and flashed forwards, grabbing her hips and pulling her onto him, hard, holding there as rockets went off behind his eyelids. Stupefied, he could hear himself grunting as he lunged forwards, again and again, buried deep, then deeper, then deeper yet.

If it hadn't been for her ass pressed up against him, he would have fallen. As it was, he staggered sideways, and she shifted with him, looking up with a grin. "Stay hard," she commanded, and he blinked, trying to make sense of the words. Then she was moving again, back and forth under his hands, pushing back onto him and then pulling off, her hands on his thighs, fingers gripping the seam of his jeans tightly, using his legs for leverage as she pounded onto him. He could see the root of his cock in the flashes of moonlight, that cold illumination at odds with the heat surrounding him. One of her hands disappeared from his leg, and he briefly felt her fingers touch him where they were joined, then her head dropped down, and she moaned. A minute later, she stilled, and he felt flutters all along the length of his dick, growing and then gradually lessening in intensity.

Another minute later, she straightened up and twisted her head to kiss him. It was bizarre for her to do that with him still inside her. "Not bad for your first time," murmured against his mouth, the words hit him hard. He'd slept with Benita. He was sober enough to think, *No, not slept. Fucked.* No sentiment involved, just her wanting to get off. Exactly like last night. Not giving one shit about how it made him feel, not caring about anything other than knowing what she wanted and taking it. She glanced down and then, bringing her eyes back up, ordered, "Hold the rubber in place while I pull off."

Reaching between them, he did as directed, hissing when the cold hit his exposed flesh and he felt his dick shriveling up as he stripped off the knob wrapper. At her instruction, he tied a knot at the end before tossing it into the back of whoever's truck he still leaned against. Focused on straightening his clothes, he staggered, not ready when she stepped into him, giving him her weight as she leaned against his chest, her arms going around him in a tight hug. "So good, Benny." She squeezed and then released him. "Come on, time to get my prince home before he turns into a toad."

A half an hour later, stumbling into his grandparents' house, Benny called a garbled greeting to GeeMa, who sat reading in the living room, her chair an island of light from a nearby lamp that he hoped blinded her to his condition. "Good party?" she asked without looking up, and for once, Benny was glad for the distance between them as he responded with a grunt. It wasn't that his grandparents didn't love him because he knew they did. He suspected it was more that she saw a lot of his mom in him, something he couldn't deny tonight, bumping into the hallway walls more than once as he made his way to bed.

Andy had won the gene lottery. He was everything good that had been their father. Benny knew that from hearing grown-ups talk over the years. Strong. Loyal to a fault. A shirt off his back kinda guy. A lot there to be proud of, a lot to look on with love. Benny closed his eyes, feeling the tilt and whoosh in his belly as the bed moved. Swallowing hard, trying to unstick his throat, he heard GeeMa's slippers as she walked up the hallway. *Benita likes me for who I am.* Shifting, he rolled to his side, squinting to focus on the clock sitting on the nightstand. It was three in the morning, which meant Andy would be halfway through his shift at the grain mill. *I'll talk to him tomorrow. Get his advice about Benita,* he decided, scrubbing his cheek on the pillow. *Tomorrow.*

Two

Benny stood by the curb, watching as Andy rode away from GeeMa's house and up the road. It had been barely a week since the fiasco at the bonfire. Today he'd come home from shopping with Benita, to find Andy waiting for him. One thing about Benita, she never was afraid to whip out Daddy's credit card, so Benny now owned a tuxedo, which meant he didn't have to ask Andy for money. Shirts and other items were in bags on the porch, the tailoring on the suit would be done next week and they'd head back to Cheyenne to pick it up before prom. Andy had nearly gotten into an argument with him about the clothes, but Benny had been able to pass it off as not a big deal. He'd played up his relationship with Benita when she let him out at the curb, knowing Andy was sitting on the porch, watching.

Benny had only been home moments before Andy gave him the news. The used motorcycle strapped into the back of Andy's beat-up old pickup truck was going to be his brother's ticket out of town. Andy had finally grown tired of all the shit in Enoch and was doing something about it, which meant Benny would lose him. Benny knew though, that if given the same opportunity to escape the town they both hated with a passion, he'd be gone in an instant. Torn in half with the news, Benny was both pleased for his brother and destroyed, because he would effectively be without a safety net. Sure, their mother still lived in town—*fat lotta help she'd be with anything*—and he had GeeMa and GeePa, but without Andy...he would be alone.

The wind blew steadily, an ever-present entity on the plains, and the way it whistled around the corners of the house reminded him of their father's funeral. Winds so strong that day Andy's hat had nearly been unseated; gusts had rocked the truck side-to-side as their old ranch foreman drove them from the cemetery. Benny had played possum, pretending to fall asleep in the truck and letting Andy carry him inside. Then, as soon as Andy left the room, Benny had crept silently to the doorway to listen as the grown-ups—and he counted Andy in that category—discussed him and his mom.

He'd been five years old. That was the first time he remembered knowing in his gut their mom wasn't going to be able to hack it. Hearing they'd be moving from the ranch into town, leaving behind their heritage to stay in a shoddy rental, and even at that age, Benny knew it was her fault. She couldn't deal, not without Daddy, and Daddy was dead, so wouldn't be coming back to save any of them. He remembered the chill working up his back at the thought. Remembered profound sadness a few years later at his prophecy come true when she fell far into the gutter. The words kids flung at him in grade school became truth because she earned rent and booze money on her back.

The minutes ticked by as Benny stood there staring up the road. Andy'd been gone so long, Benny began to wonder if he'd heard Andy wrong, if maybe the playful banter that passed between them before Andy dropped his bomb about leaving had been their last conversation. Then, off in the distance, he saw a small figure appear. Gradually it resolved into a widely-grinning Andy, seated proudly on the beautiful red-and-white bike. He came back like he said he would, so maybe, just maybe, Andy would do everything else he promised like come back, stay in touch, help out when he could.

Andy pulled up, parked behind the truck and without a word, Benny knew what his brother needed. So he gave it to him. He flooded the air around them with questions about the bike, how it felt to ride fast, what kind of jobs Andy'd be looking for. He would do anything to keep the reality of life at bay for both of them.

***

The morning of prom, Benny stood on the porch with their grandparents and watched Andy ride away again, this time for good. Earlier, while packing the bags hanging on either side of the back wheel, in a quiet voice Andy told him, "Stopping by Mom's rental on my way out of town. One last time." Benny stared at him, not sure what to do with this knowledge. GeeMa would be pissed if she knew Andy was headed over there. She didn't hate her daughter-in-law. She couldn't; hate wasn't in GeeMa's makeup. But she could dislike intensely, and did, trying in her own way to protect the boys from what had happened within their broken family. "Need you to do something for me, shrimp."

"Anything." The truth slipped from his mouth traveling to Andy's ears. He'd do anything for his big brother.

"Check in on her some? Make sure she's eating and shit? I'll send you some money for groceries for her." Andy's forehead wrinkled in a huge frown. "Just make sure she's okay?"

"Sure. I can do that." It was a mile each way to her apartment and, not wanting to deal with Benita's opinions on his family, this wouldn't be an errand he'd share with her, so no lifts. But for Andy? "Anything you need, bro."

Too few minutes later, Andy was a rapidly diminishing dot in the distance, and in only moments, he was gone. Wordlessly GeeMa moved to the front door, waiting as GeePa opened it for her and they went inside, leaving Benny on the porch alone.

He didn't put a stopwatch on it, but knew he stayed staring up the road for a long time, wishing with everything inside him that things were different. That Daddy hadn't died. That their mother loved them enough to fight for them. That Andy could find a different solution. *If wishes were horses*, he thought, turning to go inside only when the sun had traveled all the way across the sky, to rest against the curve of the earth.

Nervously pacing as he waited for Benita to pick him up, Benny stuck his head into the living room to say goodbye. His grandparents were watching TV, GeePa in his recliner, chin to the ceiling, more likely sleeping than actively watching the show. GeeMa had stretched out on the couch, and her eyes never wavered from the screen when she told him, "Have fun, honey."

"I will," he promised. Ducking back out of the room, he turned to look at the kitchen cabinet over the stove. Hard liquor was kept there, and they drank so infrequently they'd never notice if he took a nerve-calming swig from the bourbon bottle. He'd taken two steps in that direction when the familiar sound of Benita's horn came from outside, and he redirected his path with a shouted "Goodbye."

Inside the gym, Benny scanned the crowd. He knew only a few of the guys, mostly from football, but he could see three girls he knew by face— and touch—if not by name. Benita's grip on his bicep never loosened as she guided him to the punchbowl. The junior boy manning the dipper winked at her and nodded, handing each of them a brimming plastic cup filled with red liquid. "Bottoms up," Benita urged, and Benny drank, choking on the alcohol for a moment. *Alone*, the word flitted through his head, and he tipped the cup, drinking deeply of what he hoped would be forgetfulness.

***

"That's amazing." He heard the words but couldn't make sense of them. "How can he stay hard when he's so blotto?" Pressure up and down the insides of his thighs, soft and slow, digging in where it felt good, nearly ticklish in other places. His head lolled to the side, and he wanted to focus to see who it was, but nothing was working right. It felt as if he were no longer in control of his body, and there was a brief moment when a bubble of panic tried to rise to the surface, bursting and disappearing long before it really registered.

"High libido must be something that runs in the family?" From somewhere beside his shoulders, Benita's mocking voice was followed by shrill laughter.

"How'd you find him, Benita? So big. He's just perfect." Feverish excitement in that voice. Weight bearing down, higher now, on his belly, on his hip, heat washing through him as his dick entered something so hot and tight, it felt as if all his awareness focused there. Demanding urges. Pleasure to the point of pain. *Too much.* "Benny and Benita, sittin' in a tree."

"F-U-C-K-I-N-G." Laughter all around, pressure and touch all over.

Benny tried to lift his head to protest, but his muscles wouldn't cooperate, and he let it fall heavily back to the surface on which he was lying, seeing shadowed figures moving around him.

 Three

15 YEARS-OLD

Sweating heavily, just having left the football practice field, Ben sat on the bench outside Coach's office, listening to the raised voices coming from inside. With a thread of fear, he recognized one as GeeMa, and his mind flashed to the mandatory drug testing the team had done last week. Shaking his head, he pushed the irrational fear down, shoving it into a box and locking it up tightly. It had been nearly a year since prom, eight months since Benita left for college and he'd been careful all this time, ignoring the compulsions and holding onto his control with an unyielding fist.

Sure, Benita loaned him her car when she left, and he drove it without a license or insurance, but he hadn't hit anything or hurt anyone. It was purely a loaner, not something he took. On the booze side, the only time he'd gotten blackout plastered since prom was with Danny, and they'd spent the night safely passed out in a field beside Danny's truck. No drugs, no binging on the hard stuff. Not even any girls, since that was Benita's requirement in exchange for use of her wheels.

He would be a junior next year, and based on things Coach let slip, Ben hoped the college scouts might come out. He prayed with everything in him that Coach was right, and having that as incentive helped keep him focused. Toeing the line was easy when there was an exit sign in front of you. *Get me the fuck outta here. Like Andy.*

The office door flung open, and he looked up to see GeeMa standing there. She stared at him a moment, then her gaze cut away, eyes angling down and to the side as she said, "Go change, Benny. You need to come with me." That was not good.

Coach stood right behind her, with a hand to the door he stared at Ben, the look on his face unexpected, filled with sorrow and regret, both of those emotions liberally laced with a broad dose of disgust. The kind of look he'd seen turned his mother's way far too often over the years.

"What's going on?" Ben stood, the clammy pads of his gear sticking to his skin as he moved, pulling away with a silent squelch. His cleats clicked on the cement floor as he shifted from side-to-side, and nervously, he crossed his arms over his chest, fingers clenching tightly around opposite biceps. "What's going on, Coach?" At least the man was still looking at him; GeeMa had moved several feet away as if she could no longer stand to be close to him. Proximity contamination, like a schoolyard game of cooties.

"Ben, hit the locker room and get changed. Put a hustle on it. You need to go with Mrs. Jones." A pause, then with soft emphasis, "Right now, son." Coach didn't give him anything else, only those words before he shut the door, closing Ben and GeeMa out in the hallway.

"GeeMa, what's going on?" He knew his voice was shrill, sounding high-pitched and fearful, but he couldn't help it. "Tell me."

"We'll talk in the car." She still hadn't looked at him, and he took a step towards her, freezing when she retreated, maintaining the same distance between them. "It's going to be okay, Benny. I promise you, baby." That was twice she'd called him Benny. She hadn't called him that name in a long time; he'd graduated to Ben before Andy left town. It happened the first time he stumbled into her house at four in the morning stinking of booze and cigarettes. And GeeMa never called him baby. Not ever. "I'll wait for you in the car."

Not taking time for a shower, he stuffed the gear in his bag, raced out the doors and towards the lot, seeing GeeMa's car parked near the school's entrance. It wasn't until he had closed most of the distance that he realized a cop car sat next to hers. She was out of her vehicle, standing next to the uniformed officer, gesturing. As he arrived within earshot, she threw one hand up and sounded frustrated when she said, "I'm telling you I was bringing him down. There wasn't any reason for you to show up here." She leaned into the officer and lowered her voice, but Ben still heard. "Don't do it here." Leaning another inch, she gave the policeman a low, intense, "Please. You know how this town is."

The man's eyes hit his over GeeMa's shoulder, and Ben automatically straightened. The cop looked uncomfortable, like his uniform wasn't fitting right today, and he put out a hand to steady GeeMa when she spun to face Ben.

"GeeMa?" The same childish fear from before washed through Ben's voice, making it fragile in his throat, subject to wavering echoes as it exited. "What's—"

That was all he got out before the cop stepped around her, asking his own question which was really a statement. "Benjamin Jones?" When Ben nodded, the officer shook his head and then said on a heavy sigh, "You need to come with me."

"Is Ben under arrest?" GeeMa's voice broke through, and Ben cut his eyes over towards her. Just the word was terrifying. The thought, paralyzing. She had a phone to her ear and seemed to be listening intently. "If he's under arrest, tell us now and Mirandize him. Otherwise, he will exit this campus in my vehicle." Not her usual speech pattern. These words were stilted, all legal sounding. "Officer, what was your name? You failed to identify yourself."

"Mrs. Jones," the cop said with a sigh, clearly wanting this encounter to be over just as much as Ben, if for different reasons. "You know me. Don't be foolish."

"Officer." She still didn't give his name, and Ben didn't know if it was because she didn't know it, or she was making a point. "Is my grandson under arrest?"

"No, ma'am, he's not. I need him to come with me down—"

The cop—whose name tag read Simons—found it was his turn to be interrupted. "Benny, son, get in the car." Ben didn't move because Simons' face had turned hard, angry, and the man took a half-step towards GeeMa. Ben didn't want her to get into trouble, but he absolutely didn't want to be put in the back of the cop car. He was frozen, not sure what to do. "Benjamin." She snapped his name, and he swung his gaze to her. "Get into the car and if I'm not there in one minute, you lock the doors."

He glanced back at the cop as he made his way to her car, climbing into the front seat and pushing his bag over and into the back. GeeMa was silent until after he'd closed the door, then through the glass of the window he heard her say, "Lewis Simons. Yes, Darnell's boy." A slight pause and her gaze turned back to the cop. "Right then. We'll meet him downtown." She paused before her face softened into a small smile, but it wasn't directed at the cop. Her next words shocked Ben. "Thank you, Andy. Most helpful. Tell Myron thank you, too. I'll let you know what's going on." Another pause, then, "Love you, too, son." Hand up in front of her face, she peered at the phone and angrily punched a button with one finger. "Lewis," she called, and the cop flung up a hand, clearly exasperated with her. She waited a moment, then continued, "We'll follow you. Okay?"

As she was climbing into the driver's seat of the car, she was already talking. "I don't know anything, really. We'll have to wait to see what they want to know. Coach got a heads-up the police had called to see if you were in school, so he picked up the phone to let me know. I got here in time, and now we're going to see what's going on." She paused, carefully steering to follow the police car out of the lot. "Benny. Son. Is there anything you need to tell me?"

Without hesitation, he answered. "No, GeeMa." Anything to which he might need to confess was months in his past. His act was cleared up, cleaned up, and he'd worked hard to make everyone in his life proud. Coach and his family had been as big an influence as anything else, and as soon as Benita loaned Ben her car, he started taking the roads towards their house at least once a week, finding a mother figure in Mrs. Tynell.

"No girl's daddy is gonna be waiting on us?" He pressed his lips together tightly and shook his head, keeping his gaze on her. "No outstanding ticket you haven't told me about?" Another head shake. "Nothing at all?"

"No, ma'am." Twisting his neck, he stared unseeing out the window. Whispering now, he repeated his words, "No, ma'am. Nothing."

"Okay, then. We'll figure it out, sort it out, and then hopefully be home in time for supper." Her optimism made him snort, and they rode in silence the rest of the way.

Seven hours later, GeeMa had gone home to fix supper, but Ben's ass was still parked on a bench in a room off the cops' bullpen. The cops told her it might be tomorrow before they finished asking questions, but so far, they hadn't even started. Simons had filled out a form on a clipboard and looked at his permit, taking the slip of paper and his keys. Nothing else.

Ben had sat in one position for hours, leaning his cheek against the cold wall, thinking. Remembering the way GeeMa avoided his gaze, avoided *him*, not touching him once. In her mind, he was already convicted of something. Coach knew the cops were after him. And GeeMa had called Andy, which meant everyone who mattered knew he was in trouble. *Am trouble, like Mom. She's the queen of everything*

GeeMa hates. Words teased him, balancing right on the edge of making sense. *Queen of what you hated, smears of fear on your face. Might be something. Face. Lace. Space. Race. Trace. Fuck.* It was gone, escaped from focus.

Not finding anything useful in his thoughts, stiff and sore, he was turning this way and that, trying to find a more comfortable position when he recognized Benita's voice talking fast. He listened as her voice grew louder, she was apparently coming closer. *What in the hell?*

The door to the holding room burst open, and she stood in the opening. Phone to her ear, she glared at Ben as if it were his fault she was here, and if she was here for him, he supposed it was. She was supposed to be in Cheyenne. Already loud, her voice got even more so when she said, "No, Daddy, I *told* you. I *loaned* it to a friend. A *friend*. It wasn't stolen. *Jesus*, Daddy. You could've called me." She snapped her fingers twice, and Ben stood uncertainly, not sure if he should follow when she turned and walked back into the bullpen.

"Lewis?" Her shout could have been heard a hundred miles away. "Keys. Benny's coming with me." Ben slowly walked to the doorway and stood, feet still inside the threshold where he'd been instructed to wait. "Benny, come *on*," she turned and called, snapping her fingers again. A glance at Simons showed he wasn't about to try and naysay Benita Owens, even against what evidently were her own father's accusations.

Ben took a single step forwards, and she whirled, turning back to Simons. "Any paperwork to sign?" The cop shook his head, glanced up at Ben when he handed over his permit, then over towards the captain's office, darkness behind the shutters at this hour. From across the room, Benita called, "Benny, *Jesus*. Will you come *on*?"

Before he really knew what was happening, she had him out the door and into her car; the vehicle miraculously transported from the school, where he'd parked it this morning, to the curb outside the police station in downtown Enoch. He buckled as she pulled out, and then rode in silence for a moment before twisting in his seat to look at her. From fear to anger, his emotions had traveled the gamut, and he was solidly on the side of pissed off now. "What exactly just happened?" She shook her head, not responding. "No, seriously, Benita. What the hell was that?"

"That was Daddy being pissy." Her father was Darren Owens, a man who wielded a great deal of influence in their little town of Enoch, and one wealthy enough to gain the ear of the state governor at will. He and his most recent wife had spent the last six months in South America, and Ben didn't even know they were home.

"Why would your dad be pissy at me?" This wasn't adding up. But it had to be a vendetta against him. First, the call to the school to ensure the greatest embarrassment, and then the maneuvering at the station to keep him there without charging him, ensuring that most folks would have a chance to find out? In small towns, perception was everything, and the town drunk's whoreson being escorted off the school campus and into the station would have made the rounds in about a nanosecond.

"Not at you, silly." Her hand crossed the expanse of vehicle between them, landing high on his thigh. He reached down and plucked it off, putting it on her own leg. "Benny." Her voice was soft and sweet. "Don't be like that. He wasn't trying to hurt you. He was doing this to get back at me."

"Intent doesn't matter. But I'd still beg to differ. It was only me who was hurt today."

"I quit college." Trembling boldness colored her words, but it was undercut by a swath of fear. This was her making a statement to her folks.

It shocked him because she liked what her parents did for her. Money, cars, education, vacations—all paid for as long as she toed the line and maintained a modicum of decorum. They didn't even care about her grades, only how things looked. This act of defiance shocked him enough that he sucked in a breath, blowing it out on a soft "Shit."

"Yeah, shit. Thanks. Eloquent as always." Her words stung because she had no way of knowing what he'd been doing for the past six months. She couldn't have seen the shoebox shoved underneath his bed alongside a guitar case, those two things holding more dreams inside them than anything else in his life ever could.

In the months she'd been gone, he'd made friends outside the narrow circle she'd previously defined for him. Down in Cheyenne, Ben had met a man who owned a motorcycle shop. That shop had become a place where he could hang out, help if he could find something to do, and there was always something to do. A safe place, a haven. The owner was a man who knew his brother, a man who had helped Ben more than he probably understood. *Harddrive.*

Harddrive had handed him an old beat-up six-string one night when he was leaving the shop. In his gruff manner, he'd told Ben to, "Fuck around with that flattop a little, see if you like it."

He had fucked around with it, learning what sounded good, and what didn't. He'd even talked to the music teacher at school and got a chord chart then taught himself fingerings and patterns, listening to songs again and again, dissecting the sounds the guitars and drums made. Fucked around with it, and liked it. Liked how it made him feel, his blood heating when he got it right, feeling a rightness in his bones. Liked how it opened a door inside him, letting feelings and emotions pour out through his fingers. Liked how it felt in a way that made playing it as addicting as anything else.

With the one gift, something that probably cost the old man nothing, taken in trade on a bike or some shit, Harddrive had helped him stay straight. More than he would ever know, the man had impacted his life in so many ways. But, this one? *Profound.*

Part of fucking around with it was coming up with his own sounds, chords, which when played in sequence, pulled words from him. Painful as a horse foaling, but just as natural, things flowed sometimes, and the words strung together helped change the pain and anxiety inside him into something he could hand away. Danny was the only one outside of the folks at the shop who had heard him play. And his grandparents of course, but he tried to keep it to a dull roar inside their house, out of respect for them.

Without knowing anything of what he'd been through since she left town, Benita was calling his pleasure into question, and Ben sat straighter in the seat, coming to a decision. *One I should have made a year ago.* "Take me home."

"Bad idea, Benny boy. Daddy's there, and while he's pissed at me, as you learned today, he will not hesitate to take it out on whoever is in his path." She'd misunderstood him, and he set her straight right away.

"No, Benita." At her name, she turned and glanced at him. "Take me to my house." *I'm done with you*, the words danced on his tongue, wanting to escape.

"I rented a cabin." She didn't acknowledge his request, simply carried on with what she wanted. *Classic Benita.* "We're going there. I've got groceries in the trunk; that's what took me so long. Do you know you can't find risotto in Enoch? I had to go all the way *back* to Cheyenne. Jesus."

Distracted from his demands, he asked, stupefied, "You were in Enoch and then left to go grocery shopping in Cheyenne?"

"Well, yeah. I needed risotto." She said this like it made any fucking sense in the world. "And I know a guy at a liquor store there. He gives me a discount." A flirty grin was thrown his way. "He came through all the way. We're going to party."

"Take me home." With a loud sigh, he twisted so he didn't have to look at her, batting at her hand when it entered his field of vision. "You left me sitting in a police station while you went grocery shopping, knowing all you had to do was make a phone call. Un-flippin-believable. Take me home, Benita."

"Benny." Her voice softened, gentled, reminding him of the first Benita he met. Sweet and kind, she'd claimed to have a need to get to know the kid who had talent on the football field, and wanted to get past the stigma of his mother to know him. He'd believed her. Believed the sweet. Then she'd gotten a taste of his dick, and there had been an abrupt end to the sweet. "I want to spend time together. Just you and me. I've missed you. We haven't had that for a long time." *Gentle, sweet, saccharine lies.*

"No, we haven't. Because the last dozen times you got my cock down your throat, you wanted it with a taste of your girlfriend's pussy. Take me home." *So done with you.*

She hated it when he was crude, and she showed that hadn't changed, snapping, "Benjamin. There's no need to be like that."

"Take me home." The stress of the day was fast catching up with him, knots of tension making themselves felt in his neck and back. *How many people know?*

She turned the car, steering them onto a narrow road.

"Take me home." *Is football still an option?*

Carefully navigating between huge potholes, she said, "Nearly there."

"Give me your phone, then. Let me make a call." *Not Andy, please, God. I'll call Danny.*

"Benny." She shook her head. "Give me a minute."

They rounded the last corner, and there were two cars already parked in front of the cabin. "Oh, hell no. Turn around. Take me home."

"I'll send them away," she offered quickly, and this gave him a glimpse of how much she wanted his cock because she'd never given up time with her friends to spend it with him. They might start out the night alone, but in the end, she always brought in her girls. *She wants it bad. Gagging for it.* Feeling powerful for the first time in their weird relationship, he looked at her, trying to convey his disbelief in a look. She gave him wide eyes and a soft smile. "I will. Straight off. You stay in the car, and I'll send them away. In my head, they're already gone. I will." He curled his lip, and she added, tender and sweet, "Promise, Benny." *Maybe she's changed.* She'd been away at college for a long time, nearly two semesters.

He stared as she parked, and without giving him time to say anything else, she exited the car and ran up the path to the cabin. True to her word, in less than five minutes, two of her clique came stalking out, talking animatedly to each other. Shelly and Hayley separated and got into their cars, driving off without even glancing over to where Ben sat. *She did it. Wonder what else she'd do tonight.*

Benita appeared on the small porch, the unshaded light shining down on her, casting unflattering shadows across her face. He popped the locks, opened the door and climbed out. Standing and stretching for a moment, Benita's hungry eyes on him gave him confidence. *Anything.* Strolling across the small clearing, he paused at the bottom of the two steps leading up to where she stood. He deliberately pitched his voice low and quiet when he asked, "You hungry?"

The question seemed to puzzle her, and she made a small gesture back towards the cabin, the door opening into a flickering light. With a grin, he mounted the steps and wrapped an arm around her waist. "You said you had groceries in the trunk. Thought you might be"—he dipped his head, lips closer to her ear, feeling her shiver when he whispered— "hungry."

It wasn't until hours later he thought to call GeeMa, leaving a brief message on her phone.

18 YEARS-OLD

"Proud of you, Ben." GeeMa's hand wrapped around his upper arm, squeezing tightly. "Papa, get a picture of our boy." Ben stood awkwardly, his hand resting on her shoulder with her arm threaded around his waist. The black fabric of the gown rustled in the ever-present Wyoming winds, cap held pressed to his side for safekeeping.

"Benny," Danny called, and he lifted a hand, giving a half wave. "We did it, man." Benny held out his hand, slapping against Danny's palm and giving it a pump before pulling him in for a one-armed hug.

"We did." Stepping back, he steadied GeeMa when someone jostled past her, rolling his eyes when he saw it was Benita. Watching her, he saw she stopped near a cluster of freshman band members, at the ceremony today to play the small school's version of 'Pomp and Circumstance.' With a frown, he watched as she sidled up to a tall boy, pressing close, leaning into him in a way that screamed intimacy. Without taking his eyes from her, he asked GeeMa, "You and GeePa headed home? Drive safely."

She answered in the affirmative, and in a moment, he knew they were gone because Danny leaned in. "She fuckin' him?" Danny had clearly seen the same thing as Benny, and much as it curdled his stomach, he knew she probably was. "Jesus, he's just fourteen. She's fuckin' a kid ten years younger than she is. Jesus, Benny. Why do you stay with her ass?"

"I don't know," he answered truthfully. "I just don't know anything else. It's always been Benny and Benita." As he watched, Benita's gaze came to him, and she smiled her wicked grin, the one that always preceded all the crazy, fucked-up shit she came up with. Shit he was never quite certain how to take because she made him feel good, and bad, all at the same time. She lifted one hand, pressed her fingertips to her crimson mouth, and then started to blow the kiss to him. She paused the movement, and raised her hand instead, letting the kid take it and bring it to his own mouth, his eyes meeting Benny's over her head in a clear challenge. "Maybe it's time to end the cycle."

Turning, he cut his eyes to a gaggle of senior girls nearby, also still dressed in their caps and gowns, chatting and laughing quietly with their friends. "Laura?" A blonde head lifted, followed by the rest in unison and he had to fight back a grin. "Wanna get a bite to eat?"

"Fuck, man. You're setting her up for shit." Danny's warning was quiet, and Benny gave a single headshake in response. "Incoming."

"I have plans, Benny, thanks. Next time?" Laura Smithfield smiled at him as she spoke, then the expression smoothed away, and she turned back to her friends, who continued watching him over her shoulder. He knew why, and that was confirmed a second later by a hard slap to his shoulder.

"Benjamin." Benita could clip his name out like it was a curse word. This always meant she was pissed. "*We* have plans." She pressed something into his palm, and he looked down, seeing a small paper packet. "Slip one under your tongue, baby. Let's go to our cabin."

He hardly heard Danny's goodbye, staring into Benita's eyes as he worked one of the small pills from the wrapping. Lifting his hand, he offered it to Benita, not surprised when she shook her head. "All yours, baby. It's your day. Celebrate."

 Five

19 YEARS-OLD

Ben sighed and rolled his neck, pushing up on one elbow on the bed. Glancing around the room, there were the usual tangles of tossed clothing on the floor, an overflowing suitcase on the built-in dresser, and—*thank fuck*—his acoustic guitar case in the corner. Every day when he woke up, it was the first thing he looked for. Sober or drunk, so far, he'd always managed to keep the flattop nearby. Retrieved it from a pawnshop more than once before Danny finally realized it was much more than just an instrument for Benny.

Fabric rustled behind him, pulling his attention away, and he twisted his neck to see Benita stretched out behind him. A snore broke the silence of the room, and he glanced at the other bed, seeing, as expected, Danny sprawled corner to corner. *His relationship status should be sleeping in bed diagonally*, Ben thought with a grin. The man never seemed to hook up with anyone.

Blake Downey, their drummer, was another story. He had picked up a groupie tonight who had sprung for a separate room so she could screw him, or there'd be a body on the floor between the beds, too.

Ben and Danny started playing music together in high school. Starting out as a not-bad two-piece garage group called the Enoch Eunuchs, they'd imagined themselves masters of rock and roll. The summer of their junior year, they took their act on the road in Danny's hand-me-down truck, working to get themselves booked into wherever they could. Before they graduated high school, they'd upgraded to a van Benita had scrounged from one of her dad's dealerships in Cheyenne, which meant they were able to travel to more distant cities and play.

After graduation, they'd added Blake, and renamed the band, becoming Occupy Yourself. With four mouths to feed, and one van to keep in gas, Benny and Danny focused on the music, bringing Blake into the fold as needed, while Benita worked at developing a network of venues they could depend on for a good payday. So far, it was working, and Benny felt like things were finally starting to fall into place.

The previous night they'd played a decent bar in Idaho Falls. A medium sized room, but with a rowdy crowd that didn't mind tipping. So in addition to their share of the door, the bills dropped in the tip jar meant they had enough cash to get a motel room for a change. Real rest, a hot shower, and a soft mattress on which to stretch out.

Easing out of bed, Ben pulled on shorts and a tee, then laced up his running shoes before snagging one of the room keys and heading out. Pounding the streets was something he found enjoyable, something he'd picked up while still in high school. It was a way to cope with how everything had fallen apart. There had been no promise of a football scholarship to take him away from Enoch; all through his junior and senior years, he'd been too busy partying with Benita to play with any focus.

The scourge of high school was behind him now, but like Andy had discovered, Benny realized there weren't any jobs in Enoch. While Owens owned half of town, he refused to hire Benny for anything. This meant Harddrive and the music were the only two good constants in his life. He kept trying to hold those together, though some days it felt like a losing battle. The feeling of euphoria at the end of a run was exactly what was needed to help him push past everything else. For hours, the energy and endorphins would feed him in a good way, letting him ride high, like the wave of adrenaline from playing an exceptionally good set at a gig.

This was the third time he'd tried to dry out and stop drinking. Nineteen years old, and he knew he was a full-blown alcoholic. In the past five years, he had burned through relationships with family and friends, much like his mother had. Backing himself into a corner, again and again, always coming out on the losing end, watching as friend after friend fell away. Benita and Danny had stuck with him, at least.

The first blackout he'd had was at fourteen, the night of Benita's senior prom. That first episode of not remembering anything, just vague flashes of faces leaving him feeling so out of control it was like skating on the river before the frigid weather set in. The edges might be stable enough underneath your blades, but if you strayed an inch beyond that surface, the results could be devastating. That blackout was like the first ringing crack of the ice, lapsing into silence, the threat going unrecognized at the time.

He'd woke the next morning, tangled in a jumble of bodies. Sticky limbs draped over him and one girl's hand still wrapped around his flaccid penis. Looking around in disbelief, he'd tried to track which body parts belonged to who, giving up after a few seconds as impossible. Carefully untangling himself from the pile of people, Ben had made his way to the bathroom. Looking down to see something crusted on his belly, he'd hesitated only a moment before crawling into the bathtub. Gross.

The chilly porcelain had felt good against his head. So good, that slowly taking the thought to its next logical conclusion, he'd eventually reached and turned on the shower, setting the water as cold as it would go and sat there with it streaming around him. Shivering violently, he'd tried to reconstruct the evening even as he'd retched and spat, seeing a thin drool of yellow bile hit the bathtub between his feet. Diluted by the running water, he'd watched it circle the drain, eventually passing down and out of sight. Ben stayed in that position, hunched over his legs, the cold seeping into his bones, so lost in trying to figure out what had happened that he'd shouted in surprise when someone had pounded on the door.

"Gotta pee."

"Gimme a minute." Water off, he'd grabbed a towel from the closet and wrapped it around his waist. Unlocking the door, one of the senior guys leaned against the wall, looking about as sick as Ben felt.

"Good party." Naked, the guy pushed past him, and Ben had turned to watch him weave towards the toilet. Jesus.

He'd left the wrinkled and ripped tux on the floor of Benita's bedroom, finding one of his T-shirts she'd confiscated weeks earlier. Looking around, he'd rifled through various after-prom bags to find a pair of jeans which had fit well enough to wear.

All he'd been able to think about was getting away. Away from the press of bodies. Away from the stench of his vomit in the shower. Stuck with the feel of day-old booze in his belly, he'd left the house, picked a random direction and took off, walking. After making it about ten miles, he'd stuck his thumb out once more and finally got a ride. Ben had swung over the tailgate of the pickup and settled in the back. Caring less about their destination than escaping, he'd shrugged his agreement when the driver leaned out the window to tell him they were headed down to the stockyards in Cheyenne.

Ben had leaned against the cab, crossed his ankles and closed his eyes, wanting...trying desperately to turn off his mind. Unable to control his thoughts, they compulsively circled back around the edges of the places he couldn't remember. Blurred images in his head, each of them a taunting fragment of what might be a memory cycling past in rapid succession, overwhelming him. Faces, so many faces, with mouths open in a shout or a groan. Anonymous hands on his chest, fondling his dick, intimate moments shared with nameless strangers.

Gravel pinged off the wheel wells as the truck pulled off the shoulder and back onto the road. The vehicle had then gained speed, and only then had Ben slowly relaxed, spending the next hour zoning out to the mindless droning sound of the tires on the road.

Traffic noise on the outskirts of Cheyenne recaptured his attention, and he'd lifted his head in time to see a motorcycle dealership flash past. Impulsively, he'd pounded on the glass behind the driver's head, frantically signaling to the shoulder. Five minutes later, Ben had stood in the dealership's front lot, looking through the window at the motorcycles. Andy had taught him how to ride a dirt bike years ago, and he'd dazedly wondered if it would be the same feeling of freedom to ride a real motorcycle.

A form moved through the store, a young woman. She'd paused and stared out the window at him curiously. Making her way to the door, she'd pushed it open a few inches and tipping her head to one side, looked him up and down. He knew she was taking in his bare feet, too-big jeans, and worn-thin shirt. "Need a hot meal, honey?" Holding the door open, she'd gestured with one hand. "Come on inside, let's get you fed and warmed up."

She had apparently taken him for a homeless person, and Ben didn't bother to correct her mistake because the honest to God truth was he had needed a meal. Anything he might have ingested yesterday had already come up, and hardly any of that had been solid. Anxious about Andy leaving, he'd been unable to eat the goodbye breakfast GeeMa had fixed that morning. Then the punch at the prom had been so spiked, after a single cup, he'd been far more interested in wrangling more of the drink than hitting the sandwich table. Later, after the dance was over, and after pouring himself into Benita's car in the parking lot, her hand on his dick, there hadn't been any thought of food at all.

The woman, Lauren, led the way up a single flight of stairs to an office area over the showroom floor, seating him at a table while she busied herself in the kitchen. Sitting quietly, he'd listened to her talk about her husband and father-in-law, partners in a multi-location motorcycle sales and service business. She'd had so much pride in the people she loved, and it shone through her every word. I'd give a lot to hear someone talk about me like that. *He shook his head.* Yeah, like that'll happen. Such a loser.

Lauren had kept up the conversation singlehandedly, requiring only minimal input from him to keep things flowing. She'd taken a moment to serve him tomato juice with a splash of hot sauce while she cooked, making him wince at the memories invoked.

Seated across from him, a small grin on her face, she'd watched as he took a first, tentative bite of the sandwich set in front of him. That grin grew to a broad smile when he'd given her a thumbs-up, enthusiastically eating every crumb of what may have been the best fried egg sandwich he'd ever had. His sole contribution to the talk had lit up her face, too, when he'd offered her a quiet, heartfelt, "Thank you." The simple words all he could think of in response to her kindness and generosity.

Once certain the sandwich was going to cooperate with his stomach, Ben had followed her out to the back of the building where she'd introduced him to her husband, Barry, and his dad, an older man weirdly named Harddrive. Effortlessly, the group made room for him in their day as if he were a fixture in their lives all the time. To him, it was a continuation of the entire day feeling surreal, like there was a haze over everything, making the impossible possible.

As if he belonged there, Ben had sat on top of a workbench, dipping a rag into a bucket of solvent and acting as if he'd known how to clean the parts Harddrive brought him. Lunch had come and gone, Ben again seated at the table upstairs, this time listening with a grin as Lauren and Barry good-naturedly argued about the best way to boil eggs, of all things. Surreal.

Six o'clock saw the doors locked and Ben's ass in the front seat of Harddrive's truck, the old man smiling as he'd asked, "Where to, son?" When Ben had recited GeeMa's address, the man had looked at him strangely. His voice gentle when he'd asked, "Enoch, huh? You know Andy? Andy Jones?"

Ben had smiled when he'd responded, "Well, yeah! He's my big brother."

"No shit?" Shaking his head in what looked like incredulity, Harddrive had put the truck in gear and pulled out. With a bag of fast food sitting on the bench seat between them, they'd motored out of town in a comfortable silence broken only by the old man asking for one of the sandwiches, then urging Ben to eat the rest. That soothing quiet lasted until they'd sat along the curb in front of his grandparents' house, listening to the last growl of the truck's engine die away.

Ben had turned to thank Harddrive only to meet an intent stare. His mouth, opened to offer his gratitude, snapped shut when the old man had started talking. "Few people get dealt fair hands in life. I know your brother, so I know all about the shit hand you got dealt. I also know your shit just got yards worse with him leaving town." Ben had wondered how Harddrive knew this, and then belatedly put two-and-two together, realizing Andy had probably bought his bike from Harddrive's shop.

"Andy didn't share a lot, but I did me some pokin' around. I'm old; I can do what the fuck I want, so I did. People look at me, see a harmless old man, they'll talk to me. Found me some people, they talked. Didn't like what I found out, dug a little deeper, tried to sort things as best I could for Andy. But Ben, I'm still going to do what I want, and that want right now is me needin' to make sure you're good when you plant a foot outside my truck." The stare had intensified, and Ben had felt it raking through his head, stirring up the things he'd been able to put to bed for the day. Benita. The drinking. The drugs he knew he'd been given the previous night. The women she'd brought to him when he'd been so plastered that saying no hadn't been a real option.

Andy leaving. Their mom and all her problems. The fact that even after a decade of living with them, he still felt like an overnight guest in his grandparents' house.

Feeling alone. His dad dying, the only real memories left of him tied up in Andy making sure everything was okay. All his life, Andy'd been there, making sure things were good, even when they were total and absolute shit. Until now.

All alone. Nearly a decade of feeling alone, since he was five and standing on the raw dirt surrounding a hole in the ground, knowing life would never be the same.

"Oh, son. You ain't good, are you?" Those gentle words had pulled a sob out of Ben. With fumbling fingers, he'd reached for the door handle and flung it open. He'd jumped out, feeling cold gravel bite the bottom of his feet and then stood there a moment, looking in at an old man who had offered him nothing but kindness. An old man who'd made him feel like he belonged where he'd been today more than anyone in his life ever had, outside of Andy. "You need a place to rest your mind like you did today, you know where we are."

That last bit of gentle was more than Benny could take so he'd slammed the door as tears spilled over his lids. Harddrive turned to face front, and the truck's engine had roared before it pulled away from the curb, made a U-turn, and drove away, leaving Ben sobbing.

Benny gritted his teeth as he tried and failed to stop the flashbacks rolling through his head. *Parties with Benita, her handing him a brimming glass of amber liquid, telling him to, "Drink up, Benny." Upping the game when he'd found out he'd never play college ball, letting her show him how to roll a joint. Holding his hand out for more and stronger ways to forget. Unable to control his shaking hands, he could still maintain an erection for as long as she demanded. Fucking no longer enjoyable; with how Benita wanted it, sex had become his job in her bed. Waking in her bed, in her car, in the beds of her friends, some of the memories impossible to wipe away, while whole days were irrevocably missing in his mind. Coming to in strange hotel rooms, detritus of debauchery all around—hating himself more every time he allowed it to happen. Not knowing how to end things because she'd been guiding him for years. Benny without Benita? Impossible.*

Music had saved him. Music and Harddrive had kept him from the edge of the precipice with their easy acceptance of who he was. Music didn't care as long as he did what it demanded, playing or writing. Letting the beast inside him loose for a few minutes at a time, giving it room to breathe and grow. Harddrive checked in with him nearly as often as Andy did, listening for the things Benny didn't say.

Frustrated, Benny gave up on the run, turning his feet back to the motel. Sweating heavily and panting for air, he swiped the keycard and leaned into the door, shoving the handle down to open it. Harddrive was a long time ago. *Lotta miles under those wheels*, he thought, and then his forward momentum halted in place as the light from the door illuminated Benita's naked form. Straddling Danny, she looked over at Benny and smiled, never missing a bounce. *Fuck.*

Stuck in place for a moment, he was torn between turning on his heel to get the hell out of there and sinking to his ass in tears. Neither were real options. He didn't have anywhere to go for the first, no escape for him. Ever. No schooling, no money, no job—all he had was the music, and to make the music, he needed Danny. Tears wouldn't solve anything, wouldn't change what he saw, what he heard, what he knew.

Without another glance at them, he stalked past and into the suspect safety of the bathroom. Through the closed door, he heard Benita's invitation, taking only a split-second of "Hell no," to turn her down. Shower on, he stepped under the spray, closing his mind to the questions and thoughts flooding through. He slid down the tiled wall, resting forehead to knees, finally taking option number two, but only because no one could hear him.

Six

23 YEARS-OLD

"Hey, man, can you wiggle another two feet outta that cable?" Danny called across the stage to the venue's riggers. A writhing side-to-side whip of the cable in question followed a grunt in response and he called back, "Thanks," as he bent over to plug it into the console. "Ben," Danny glanced up, "get the secondary load stick, this one's tits up."

Bending over to dig through the open flight case in front of him, Ben found the backup memory drive holding the program for their show. Tossing it cross-stage to Danny, he twisted on one knee to evaluate the set-up so far. They had another ten minutes for load-in, and then they'd have fifteen for a quick sound check. *Easy breezy*, he thought, bringing out a microphone and unclamping the cable so he could wind it around the stand. Draping the plug next to the other two he had already placed, he gathered them all up and walked to the console, passing them wordlessly to Danny.

There was a thumping and then a crash of cymbals, and he whipped around to see one of the house riggers had staggered sideways into the already set-up drum kit, setting a snare to a wonky angle. He winced, and didn't even have to wait a breath before Blake was screaming. *Shit.*

Danny jerked his head towards the commotion, mouthing, "HBR." Ben shook his head in response, standing so he could move in and defuse the situation. *Better me than Danny*, he thought, remembering the last time Danny and Blake had an argument about attitudes. Fifteen stitches and two broken fingers worth of disagreement had meant four weeks of canceled gigs.

They still had to finish their load and sound, and then sano the space so the opening act could do their load-in. This carefully orchestrated dance would be entirely fucked if Blake had a meltdown. Fucking it up meant the venue guys would be pissed, the other bands would be pissed, and he would be beyond pissed. This meant he had to manage the 'hassle-to-benefit ratio' to keep things moving along.

He wanted to be able to come back here again. There were fifteen or so venues in the Denver area they'd been playing regularly, and this was a favorite one for all of them. Occupy Yourself had a lot of fans in the area, so as long as they carefully spaced out the gigs, there was a wealth of draw for the shows. "What a fustercluck," he muttered, then forced a smile. "Blake, buddy," he started, and Danny turned back to his work.

***

Seven hours later and covered in sweat, Ben slung his guitar head-down on his back, the strap tight across his chest as he held the microphone overhead, bringing his other hand up, urging the crowd to a rhythmic clapping, maintaining the pose for a planned sixty seconds. Then, one foot lifted to the ego box, he leaned down. Microphone cradled in both hands, Ben stretched out his back leg, carefully accentuating the line created by his body in the super tight, stretchy jeans Benita insisted he wear, like she insisted the muscular and tattooed Blake tear one shirt per show, tossing the ripped fabric into the crowd.

The last notes of that song had faded away but he waited, letting the applause peak before, microphone held to his lips, he flung back his head and screamed, "Fuck yeah! Are you with me, Aurora?" Chin down, mouth open in pretend pleased surprise at the roaring response, he paused a moment and then again asked, "I said, are you fucking *with me*, Aurora, Colorado?"

Grinning wide, he straightened and stood, arms out to the sides in response, embracing the jostling and screaming mob up by the rail, held back three feet from the edge of the stage. Heat hit him from the lights, and he knew the next segment of their program had cued up on time. "Did you enjoy Klatmatch Ends?" Their show openers were a good group of guys who had a killer effect on a crowd. Getting the predrunk attendees riled up and ready took skill, and they'd shown they had it. A lot of that skill was tied up in KE's drummer, Victor Montrose.

Benny had spent time over the past year talking to the guy every show they booked together, finding he had a wealth of knowledge at his fingertips. Born into the industry, Vic's old man had dragged him to gigs and recording studios since he could toddle. Benny couldn't count the number of times he'd stood at the back of a venue, watching KE's opening section because the way Vic played the crowd was amazing. Outrageously talented on the skins, he would build off the crowd's responses until he held them in the palm of his hand. *Kill to have him on board*, Benny thought, his mind going back to the scene during load-in. *Too much time and energy spent on bullshit these days.*

The roar died down, and Ben brought the microphone back up for his next promo scream. "Are you ready for Penapolly?" This response was louder because Penapolly was the main act for a reason. Their fan base here near the military base was unbelievable, and Ben wanted to leverage it every way he could. "I said, are you ready for *Penapolly?*" He knew from where the band sat in the green room, they could hear both his shout and the resulting screams from the crowd, and hoped they'd appreciate it in the form of more bookings.

He glanced down at the setlist taped to the stage, reminding himself needlessly where they were in the lineup. "Those guys are fuckin' awesome, yeah?" Another roar and he nodded, feeding approval back to the crowd, then turned and caught Danny and Blake's attention. Time to roll down the list for another fifteen minutes. This planned four-minute break in the action was a chance for Blake to make any needed adjustments after the first half of their set, and a brief respite for Ben and Danny's hands.

Danny hit his riff once, and Ben watched as the girls nearest the barricade bounded in place, turning to clutch the hands of their also-jumping friends. "Gonna slow it down, Aurora." The riff sounded again, and the crowd surged forward, their fans knowing what was coming next.

"We call this one 'Is It The Blood.' We are Occupy Yourself, and we appreciate every one of you comin' out tonight. Thank you. Matters more than you know to all of us to see all of you. I want to thank Penapolly for having us along on this show. We love playin' the Fillet. Thanks for having us back."

Venue name worked into the patter, he settled the microphone back on the stand and brought his guitar around, his hand going to ensure the plug was firmly seated before he started strumming, automatically looking upwards to verify the flyspace for his speaker leap near the end of the song. Worst thing was being in a place with low hanging pipes or rafters and forgetting. Mouth pressed to the foam windscreen of the microphone, he waited for his place in the song. "You know me best, and that's the worst. Come through the walls, in whispered sighs." Benny launched into the first verse, eyes closed, losing himself in the only safe place he'd ever really known.

***

"Good show." The bar manager's voice came from behind a pissed-off Ben, who was singlehandedly hauling two loaded flight cases down the narrow staircase, annoyed as hell Blake wasn't there to take one of them since they were part of the drum kit. With an internal sigh, Ben turned his head, lifting his chin in response, giving the man his plastic grin while shaking sweat from his hair. It had been a good set, the crowd receptive and responsive, singing and dancing for the full forty-five minutes of OY's stage time. The way the floor cleared after they finished spoke to how mesmerized the crowd had been, saying bladders needed to be drained and drinks refilled before Penapolly took the stage. "Let me help you with that."

This was a startling offer; bar managers didn't help with gear, but Ben shifted to one side, letting the man take one case, leaving him with one. *Jesus, what the fuck's his name?* "Thanks, dude." At the bottom of the metal stairs, these boxes would stack on top of the ones already on the cart, and he'd be ready to wheel everything out to the van. Then he'd finish loading up, lock it up, and come back in and man the merchandise table after Penapolly finished. The manager straightened, and Ben caught a glimpse of the look on the man's face. *Fuck.* Just from one glance, Ben knew something shitty was about to go down.

"Ben," the man said, and Ben was startled at the use of his name. That was odd, too. Usually, the house knew Benita's name, but not the band members. "Blake's," he paused, then continued, his tone showing he knew he was understating things, "a problem." *Yeah, here it is. Shitty.* "We love having you guys here. You have a great fan base. They don't tear shit up, and you boys normally don't rile security. You and Danny, professional to the bone. When I book Occupy Yourself, I know what I'm getting." All kinds of smooth up front to ease the load of shit coming next. "A word of advice, and you probably already know, but Blake is a liability. I had two complaints from the union guys tonight. I'm sorry to say he can't be here during setup or teardown anymore." *Okay, it's not a threat to not book, so maybe not as bad as it could be.* "I want to keep booking you. Think about it." *Fuck.* Veiled threat made, the manager, whose name Ben still couldn't remember, turned to walk away.

"Yeah," he called belatedly, sighing heavily. "I got it." *Shit.* When he and Danny had formed the band, they had no idea the political bullshit they'd have to put up with to perform. Danny had played guitar all his life, excelled on the bass, and when he found out Ben taught himself to play, there'd been no stopping them. Benita named herself manager as soon as they'd gotten paid for their first birthday party back in Enoch, which was okay with Ben, it kept her close, and he liked that. Since her dad had tried to have him arrested, they'd been a real couple. *As long as I overlook her 'mistakes,'* he thought and sighed.

Another case slid into view, and he looked up to see Danny eyeing him warily. "What'd Nigel want?"

"Nigel's his name? Fuck, no wonder I couldn't remember it." Ben bent over to lift one end of the case.

Danny laughed. "Fuck no. I can't ever remember his name, either. I just call him Nigel in my head."

Rolling his eyes, Ben began pushing the cart while Danny steered. They'd executed this routine so often over the past three years that talking wasn't necessary. At the van, Danny fumbled with the keys in the back door for a moment, and Ben wrapped his arms around himself, chilled and shivering. "Jesus, Danny." He muttered this under his breath because the last thing he wanted to do tonight was set his partner off. Danny'd complain to Benita and then she'd be crawling up his ass. *Do without any more of that tonight.*

With a creak, the first door finally opened, and Danny unknowingly echoed him, with a slight variation. "Jesus, Blake."

The other door swung wide, and Ben heard a complaining female voice. Peering through the opening, he saw why Blake wasn't inside helping with teardown. Neck twisted to look over his shoulder at them, his ass never stopped pumping between the spread thighs of the woman laid out on the van's floor. He hadn't even aired up one of the pool floats they used as a mattress when they had to sleep in the van. "A minute, guys." Breathless with exertion, his head snapped back to the woman, and he grunted, "A minute."

Ben caught Danny's eyes and they simultaneously shook their heads. A moment later, there was a loud groan, and he glanced back to see

Blake's skinny cheeks clenching, his back bowing as he came. Bending to offload the cart, Ben told Danny, "Get him to help you load the cases in the van when he pulls his pants up. I'll get the rest of the gear out here. We still need to work merch." *Same shit, different day.*

Three hours later, they were sitting in the van behind a twenty-four-hour diner, watching as Benita counted their take. "Four-thirty," she said with a grimace.

Benny shook his head. "Shit. That's two hundred less than last time here. It was a good crowd, what gives?"

Mouth drawn to one side, she twisted to glance in Blake's direction. "We had to pay three hundred in union fees."

Danny broke in. "You mean in shut-up fees." Benita shrugged, folding the money and putting it into her wallet. She'd hold it until they needed gas or food, then she'd dole it out, bill-by-bill, making them all work for it a second time. "Jesus, Blake. When will you learn to keep your fucking mouth shut?"

"Fuck you." Blake's talents didn't lie in his oratory skills. "Those guys are assholes."

"Assholes or not," Ben shifted uncomfortably on the floor, back to the pile of gear cases, "the manager said he won't book us again if you keep this shit up. As it is, he doesn't want you in the building during load-in or teardown. Which means we'll carry your ass a-fucking-gain." He reached beside him, picking up a plastic jar with a hand-printed sign taped to it. "I saw a good tip hit the gas money jar." Ben unscrewed the lid, reached inside and pulled out a small handful of money mixed with scraps of paper. Dumping the mess in his lap, he quickly picked through to separate out the bills, finding what he was looking for.

While he was counting the money in his hand, Blake reached over and sifted through the remaining contents, picking out the pieces with writing on them. Some people used the jar as a trashcan, but a lot of girls dropped their numbers in, hoping for a call the next time OY hit the venue.

Ben muttered as he counted, "She was a fan, had a shirt on and everything." The first time they ordered cheap CDs from an online store, paying almost as much for the packaging as the CD itself, they'd also printed celebratory shirts which cost more to make than they could sell them for. It had turned into a victory every time someone bought one. "She told me if we'd post our schedule on the website,"—he stared pointedly at Benita as updating the website was part of her job—"it'd make it easier for our fans to find us." Stacking the bills neatly, he ordered them by denomination, then quickly counted again, verifying the pleasant surprise.

Looking up with a grin, he caught Danny's eyes, watching them widen as he laughed and said, "Three sixty-three. She put in three Benjamins." With a laugh, Benny twisted to face the windshield, relaxing into the gear cases. "What can I say?" Laughter in the van broke the tension from before, as well as the knowledge they had more than enough money to tide them until their next gig Tuesday night. "She's a fan of the Benny."

***

Tuesday saw them with a light load-in since the venue lent itself to acoustic. Benny and Danny would both play guitars while Blake sat on a box drum. Benita would work the limited merchandise table, a repurposed four-top from the diner side of the bar. Benny was leaning against the bar, waiting for the bottles of water he'd requested when an elbow hit the edge of the counter next to him. Twisting his neck, Benny turned to see the woman from the previous show standing there. "Hey," he said with surprise. "You came."

She nodded, saying with a smile, "You updated the website. How could I stay away when you took my advice?"

He shifted and stuck out his hand, giving her a wide grin. "I'm Ben Jones."

"I know," she laughed as she responded. "I'm Katherine." She looked over his shoulder, telling the bartender, "I'm opening a tab. Put whatever the band wants on it for me, please." Reaching into her purse, she extracted a credit card from her wallet. "Thank you." The bartender took the card as he placed the six bottles of water on the counter. "May I have a menu, please?"

Benny was mesmerized. Older, but still attractive, Katherine had an innate air of command which might make it difficult to tell her no. He shook himself mentally, breaking free from his contemplation of what it took to develop that kind of manner. Gesturing to her chest, he said, "You wore your shirt." *Yeah, I officially sound stupid.* "I mean, shit. Sorry. You wore the band's shirt. Again." *Jesus, stutter much?* He took a breath, telling her the truth. "Means more than you know, Katherine. Thank you." He reached and picked up the water bottles. "And, thanks for this too." Hefting them in two hands, he gestured first towards the clock behind the bar, then the stage. "It's time for us to start, so I have to get up there, but we'll take a break in about an hour. I'd love to chat with you then if you can stick around that long."

"I look forward to it," she said, hiking her shapely ass up onto a stool. He stood watching her for a moment longer, seeing her ready smile at the bartender, her casual glance around the bar. Confident and assured, she was there to watch them play. Listen to him sing. *Mind blown.*

* * *

Shirt soaked through, he shivered as he settled into the booth opposite Katherine. Wordlessly, she used a fingertip to slide an expensive bottle of sparkling water towards him, and he grinned his thanks. Making quick work of opening it, he drank and lowered the bottle to find her staring at him with a considering expression. Lifting the water again, he held the bottle against his lips as he asked, "What'd you think?" Turning the container up, he kept his eyes on her as he drained it dry.

"I think you're far too talented to be playing in bars like this, or places like the Fillet." Her blunt words caused his gaze to scatter around the bar, ensuring the manager was nowhere close to their table. Thank Christ, he was far out of overhearing range, which meant future bookings were still on the list of possibilities for this place. "Benny, you play and sing beautifully, and when I say play, I don't only mean the guitar. You have charisma and hold the crowd in the palm of your hand. I haven't seen talent like yours in a while, and I've been around the block more than once." Her hand slid across the table and then withdrew, leaving a card in its wake.

He read the name on the card. "Katherine Cutright." He looked up at her and then sighed, glancing back down at the card. *Well, this explains a lot.* "Talent acquisition for some record label I've never heard of. Engel Dari Records." He flipped the card back to the center of the table, tipping his head to one side, watching her. "We aren't interested in signing." Her lips thinned; she'd expected him to at least be willing to discuss the idea. He decided to let her in on a not-so-secret secret. "We've been down this garden path before. Sweet words and promises of money and support turned into a chokehold on our music and a requirement to self-promote in a way none of Occupy Yourself was comfortable with. Thanks for the water." With a stiffened finger, he toppled the empty bottle sideways, the clatter of glass hitting the tabletop drawing a few stares their direction. "But we'll pass on the representation."

"That is, of course, your decision to make, Ben." He noticed he'd been demoted from the friendlier Benny back to Ben. She leaned forwards, placing one elbow on the table, chin in her hand, creating a sense of intimacy with her actions. "I'd rather you hear me out before you reject things out of hand." Palm to the table, she drew the card back with the tips of her fingers. "But, if you'd like me to leave, I'll go." Head dipping to the table, she began gathering her things. "Thank you for the pleasure of hearing you again." Eyes angled his way under her brows. "And, for updating your website." A pointed reminder her recommendation was a smart one. He'd heard more than one patron tonight telling Benita they'd found out about this show from the site.

He leaned back in the booth, elbows hooked over the top of the bench. Head tipped up, he stared at the stained ceiling for a moment. There was a soft clink from the table, and he looked to see another bottle of water in front of him. Katherine still waited in the opposite seat. He sat and stared at her, carefully considering what she'd said so far—none of which he disagreed with—and where he wanted the band to be. It wasn't to keep playing places like this or the Fillet; she was right. He wanted so much more, and it always seemed just out of reach. She didn't seem discomfited by his attention, her gaze swinging back and forth between him and the crowd.

He glanced around. Blake was holding court by the bar, surrounded by full-bodied girls looking young enough to make Ben hope their fake IDs were as good as his had been. Danny wasn't anywhere to be seen, and Benita was seated behind the merchandise table, the sour look on her face promising harsh words later. Normally he'd go and sit with her, sign things, take selfies with fans, urge people to buy CDs, and talk about where they'd be playing next.

Right now, he had other things to do. Things to figure out, leaving the bickering sure to come from Benita for later in the evening. There was a puzzle sitting across the table from him. People like Katherine had a currency they used, and he knew exactly what she wanted from him. Ben let his eyes roam what he could see of her, tits straining the thin tee, hair and makeup carefully calculated to be classy, but not over the top. While this was likely a business deal, still, he'd put money on the fact she was looking to slum a bit. He tilted his head to one side, staring into her eyes. Waiting.

Katherine smiled, full lips shining in the muted light of the bar and Ben's dick woke in his pants as he imagined her mouth on him. Older, powerful, attractive, and into him. *Yeah, there's a lot here I could work with.*

"Spiel me."

Four days later, sitting in another bar on the north side of Denver, Katherine pressed close to her side, Benita signed.

$\mathcal{S}$even

25 YEARS-OLD

"Fuck!" Blake shouted, flinging his bottle of beer sidearm into the wall. Foam and glass exploded everywhere as liquid lashed across the dirty alley. "What do you mean, they've cut us loose?"

Paper rustling in her shaking grip, Benita raised her hands so she could read the letter again. Delivered by courier during their set, she had waited to open it until the band was together. Ben had wondered several times over the past six months if things were souring between the record company and them, but couldn't put his finger on what he was feeling. Nothing specific, just royalties paid more slowly than they had been, less help with the promotion side, not that the label had been much help there, anyway. Then last week they received notification the single from their upcoming CD wouldn't be the original tune the band wanted, but a regurgitation of an at best B-side 70s song to which the label owned rights.

Ben called Katherine when Benita hadn't gotten anywhere with the band's handler at the label, but Katherine said her hands were tied. Scouring the contract revealed the clause giving the label the right to make those decisions. In fact, a thorough evaluation revealed a number of terms they hadn't paid a lot of attention to at first, all seeming so out of reach nearly three years ago that their inclusion in the obviously canned contract language was laughable.

Now, however, Occupy Yourself had worked their asses off and was gaining traction fast. They had been touring steadily during the last eighteen months, and not just the I-70 corridor. Their van had seen miles in more than thirty states, only the far northeast and western states not yet visited. They had opened for more than twenty-five different bands, blending their sounds with whatever options were available, sometimes going from rockabilly one night to metal the next, and landing into acoustic the following. All bands called it the grind, and Ben understood exactly what they meant. It could wear you down if you didn't have something you were working towards.

The label organized studio time whenever they decided it made sense, seldom giving the band more than a week's notice. The studio usually wound up being booked in the middle of a string of shows, which meant Ben had to hustle to find stolen moments in which to write. Something that had seemed effortless since he started jotting lines and words in a notebook rapidly became a chore. No less fulfilling when it flowed, but that roll became harder and harder to initiate. Oblivious to what was around him, Benny wrote in diners, in the back of the van, sitting on the floor behind stages in a hundred different venues with bands and staff strolling past, his head in the lyrics, fingers fixed to the frets and strings. He learned to capitalize on those golden times when the words came easy, writing as fast as the pen would move across the page. Between times was enough to go back and polish, tweak, change word order, find other words, develop the pacing, and find the music.

Sometimes the music came first, and he'd pick out a tune on his six-string, an instrument of torture that, these days, seemed surgically attached. Chance phrases, half-heard conversations, hell, sometimes even road noise—these things would set up residence in his head, and the only way to get it out was to write it. When it was good, when the sound was tight and right, that was when Danny would join him, heads down, eyes closed, picking out and following the tune. A chorus of "What did you just do?" and "Rock it, do that again" would surround them. Listening to the music, feeling it in his gut, Benny loved those moments when you held the crystal of a newborn tune in your hands.

The label organized their online presence, getting them hooked up into all the various platforms by which music consumers found their tunes, something Benita then took over and managed. Made easier by their process, but still something that fell to the band to keep going.

One thing, the only thing the label had done that he knew the band would have never accomplished, was get airtime. Radio stations across North America were adding Occupy Yourself songs into their rotation, and those songs—Benny's songs—were winning fan-voted contests. There were three online fan groups that he knew of, and Benita engaged with the members regularly, usually posing as him or Danny.

Their career was starting to gain traction, finally. It felt good to see the hours and days and weeks of work coming to fruition.

And now the label was dropping them. *Fuck.*

"Why?" At his question, eyes all around their little circle swung to him. Blake, Danny, and Benita. "Why are they cutting us loose, Benita?" Her gaze went to Blake. *Fuck.*

"What does that mean? That look." Blake's face twisted in anger and Ben shifted. "You sayin' it's my fault? Always Blake's fault. Blake's always fucking up." *No, that's my job.* Ben shook his head. "No, Benny, she looked at me. You saw it."

"Let's hear what the letter says." She shoved the paper towards him, and he took it grudgingly as if it were a viper ready to strike. *Fan-fucking-tastic.* Now Blake would associate bad news—and they already knew it was bad news because of Blake—with him instead of Benita. *Fuck.* Scanning the paragraphs, he focused in on one section, reading it again and again, feeling the rage build inside him. "Fuck." That one escaped into the air, surprising him.

Eyes to Blake, he took a step forwards, fist clenching around the papers. "Paternity suit. Lawsuit. Drunk and disorderly. Venue cancelation. They have all kinds of shit here, Blake." His bandmate had the wisdom to look contrite instead of angry, thank God. Ben didn't know if he could have controlled himself if the man—*boy*—tried to pass this off as not his fault. "Looks like you've been keeping secrets."

Blake had never graduated from the initial rush of recognition. Every show was a chance for him to get his nut off. Every girl a conquest to bury the pain of high school rejections.

"Fuck it." Ben shoved the papers back at Benita. He stared at the van, seeing the peeling paint of their logo, the sweeping lines of OY falling in pieces to the pavement at every venue. *It's all shit.* "I'm not feelin' it tonight. Isn't it what you usually say, Blake? Not feelin' it, meaning you're so fucked-up you can't play. Well," he leaned far into Blake, his voice a barely-restrained hiss, "I'm *not feelin' it* tonight. Y'all go on without me."

"What the fuck?" Danny said in a guarded tone, knowing the band could pull off a drummerless show. They'd done it often enough, having to swap over to acoustic about once a week because Blake "wasn't feelin' it," which pissed them off, but they made it work. A show without a lead singer, however? Not as possible.

"No, he's been drunk or stoned for three years, fucking his way through whichever state we're in. It's time for Benny to have some fun." Benita drew an audible breath, and he twisted to look at her, denying her the chance to interrupt and soothe things over. "No. It's my time to fuck off since we're—"—he swung back to Blake, this time unable to control his shout—"fucked straight up the ass."

"Dude." Blake shook his head. "We can't play without you."

"Oh, but we can play without you?"

"Fuck, man. Chill. Y'all do fine without me." Death knell but Blake didn't know it yet.

"You're right. We do fine without you." He grabbed the papers again, shaking them in Blake's face. "We'd do *better* without you, evidently." Moving deliberately, he took a disciplined step back, breaking their circle. "I'm done with you." Another step, distancing himself from them. "My band." Danny's head lifted at those words, but it was the truth. They'd signed papers detailing Ben's portion as 53 percent. Majority stakeholder starting this year, since he'd fronted the money for equipment, vehicles, union fees. *Stolen money.* He winced, remembering the lies he'd told GeeMa, then focused and hissed, "And I say *you're out.*"

Now the uproar bursting from all three mouths was guaranteed to bring security running. *Not my gig.* Ben turned on his heel and walked away from the only good thing in his life. The music.

***

I want to forget. He heard the words in his head, knew how to form the sounds, but activating his voice seemed like an impossibility. His own muscles foreign, unknown. "Jus wana feget." He tried to swallow, succeeding only in choking himself, his tongue seeming far too large to exist inside his mouth. "Wan feget."

"Oh, I know, baby." The woman's voice sounded close to his head. Strains of her drawl echoing down his ear and setting up residence inside his mind. Colors and warmth accompanied those words, the stretching of the tones discordant and painful. "You won't remember anything, baby."

"Goo." Ben barely got the sound out before a narrow prick of pain in his arm surrendered to the broad rush of heat in his blood. That wave picked him up and carried him out to sea, out of sight from land, adrift and blessedly, blessedly alone. No shouting. No demands. No clamoring of people to tear him apart. Just the music in his head, playing sweetly.

#

26 YEARS-OLD

Benny stared in shock at the man seated across the booth from him. Short and heavyset, the thickly accented Mexican had just made a proposal that was too good to be true. But Benny wanted it to be true. Needed it.

Juan had approached him after a gig in downtown Denver a month ago, looking like a fan as he chatted, holding out a poster to be signed. Then he offered Benny a twist of green that would go a long way to letting him sleep that night. Combine it with a cheap bottle and he could even stretch it a couple of nights.

Juan showed at the next show, and the next, the same offering freely extended each time. Next show? Different offering to the rock gods. Also gladly accepted, and Benny found even more peace in oblivion, loving the slow slide into darkness. Hating the climb back out the next day. And so it went, his new friend providing a bliss Benny found himself craving. *Too good to be true, shoulda known. Of course, Juan had an agenda.*

Part of a gang out of Mexico, Juan offered Benny more green, better green and blow, uncut blow and heroin—all he could ever want. All with the understanding he would pay back the value. Eventually. Juan said no hurry. Juan said they were all friends. Juan talked about a lot of things.

After the first taste of the really good stuff, Benny hadn't been able to say no, which meant he wound up owing Juan's friends. One thing led to another, led to another, and he owed even more. A lot of money. More money than Benny could ever pay back in his life, but they'd kept the pipeline open for a long, long time. Now that he was in deep with them, they had an idea how he could pay them back, even things up. *If only.*

Which brought him to now. Juan was part of a biker gang who had picked a fight with a drug gang, both out of Mexico. Juan's gang of bikers didn't want to buy from the drug cartel directly. According to what Benny could understand through Juan's accent, there was bad blood going way back between the two groups. One wouldn't deal with the other, and that was just how it was.

But, one—the bikers—could use an intermediary—like Benny—to make a purchase. They urgently needed to make a purchase. Their Tijuana supplier had failed to provide a needed shipment of product. According to Juan, they needed to offer a steady supply or the buyers would defect. They couldn't have that, so they needed product. All Benny had to do—and this is where it got into the 'too good' category—was make the purchase, hand over a duffle filled with money, and accept a shipment of blow. Bring said blow back to the gang and they would forgive all his debts. All of them. Every dollar. Even if it was too good to be true, he still had to ride the chance to the ground, just in case.

"Benny." Juan shook his head. "You know this gonna be the only way to clear your shit." He tapped the tabletop once, loudly and Benny jumped. "And you *wanna* clear your shit. Trust me, you want that in a big way. So, Benny, you just gotta find a way." He pushed out of the chair and stood. "Call me, but make it tonight, or your debts come due. And that, you do not want."

Fuck. Chin lifted, face tipped up, Benny stared at the man who no longer looked like a fan at all. He nodded.

***

"I'm telling you, I can pull this off." Benita stared at him, lips pressed together, holding back her disagreement. "I can, swear. My brother's got connections, and he can help us make a profit like you wouldn't believe." Ben knew his movements were jerky, a stair step of discordant notes because he needed a drink. He was off the juice, trying to stay sober for the upcoming transaction, but sober was fucking hard these days.

"I make the deal. Get in and get out. No sweat. I've already borrowed the money, found an opportunity and took it. I just gotta turn this cash into product, then turn *that* product into more cash, and we can buy that record label in San Fran we talked about. California, baby. Sun and beaches, all day long." Not quite what the bikers were expecting, but he would talk to Juan after, explain everything. First, he had to make sure the drug guys had enough stuff to sell a bunch to him, too, and then he could do exactly what he'd told Benita. Andy's connections would come in handy, and finally, fucking *finally*, his luck would change.

"Benny." The single word held shadows from a decade of disillusionment and pain. *Jesus, now I get this from Benita.* He had turned twenty-six last month. Just one more day in a blurred string marred only by the expected call home for birthday wishes. That never went well, always leaving him feeling more like an asshole than usual. GeeMa was cordial, friendly, her tone tolerant and loving, and she never brought up his failures or talked about his betrayals. The discomfort was all on his side, because for him, the undercurrent of his treachery threatened to suck him down, never letting him up for air. He had lied to and stolen from his grandparents so many times, and in his mind cutting the ties to them so thoroughly he was certain there'd be no repairing them. Not ever.

Over the years, he watched and listened as his family repeatedly forgave his mother's betrayal of family, labeling her situation extreme. She lost the only man she ever loved, after all. It was understandable she would go off the deep end. Act out to numb her pain. Benny, however, should have known better. Had been raised better. Forget the fact her loss was his, doubled because he'd lost her, too. Tripled with the loss of Andy. Filling in the holes left behind took more than a shovelful of good intentions. Anymore, it took more than a shovelful of booze, too.

He'd been enhancing his numbing concoction with the addition of a few side menu items. Green or blow, he wasn't picky, able to angle either way based on his mood. He'd smoke a 'lil smoke, toot a line of blow, pop a tiny cross, or swallow purple forgetfulness chased with vodka— anything to help oblivion take effect sooner, and let him escape the bullshit always swirling around.

Bullshit aside, Ben believed he'd found a sure-fire solution to the band's current problems. And they had them. Money and opportunity were the biggest obstacles he saw. Money was tight, beyond tight. The last five grand he stole from GeeMa had gone to pay for studio time; overages from their already planned outlay caused by his own behavior, and he knew it. That was why he decided to go all in, hacking his way into her account for what would be the last time. He promised himself. Again. Paying for the final sessions had been his penance to Blake and Danny since it was his stuttering talents that had fucked them all. With the extra cash, they did the studio time and turned out some of the best work ever. Songs sure to get them walking the red carpet, finally.

Dmitri Glass had joined them right before the studio sessions, and he'd augmented the group in a way only Ben had believed in at first. Back when they first began playing bars outside Denver, Ben had heard Dmitri play and loved the guy's talented sound, the phrasing he brought to a song. The fact he could also handle a guitar was a bonus they frequently leveraged, letting his fingers stand-in for Ben's often of late.

Right now, an oblivious Blake and Danny were inside a diner, seated at a table with Dmitri while Ben and Benita stayed in the van. They tended to take things like eating in shifts, first because it made it nearly impossible for thieves to snag gear cases and run, and second because it was easier to get along when they didn't spend too much time together. Or maybe it was easier to get along when they didn't spend too much time with him. *Whatever.*

So he had the band, finally, that he'd dreamed of for so long, and wanted to see if they could take things beyond the next level. Bypassing that stop on the road to stardom, true stardom, where venues competed for your bookings, not the other way around. He had the band, and, thanks to Juan, had an opportunity. Benny had persuaded himself he just had to make his own luck, and get Occupy Yourself the chance to see where they could go.

This meant he had to convince Benita of two things.

One, he had a plan.

Two, he could pull it off.

He smiled at her, shining the rock star hard, knowing he got inside her head when she sighed, closing her eyes.

***

Shit.

That one word hurtled through Benny's head. He was crouched beside group of a tall metal lockers set in the middle of a long wall. His back pressed tightly against the protective structure as he listened to more than one set of footsteps coming closer, leather soles slapping the cement floor in a percussive assault.

Three hours ago, the world had looked different.

Three hours ago, Benita had dropped him off on the side of the road, not too far from the wide driveway leading to this bunker complex.

Three hours ago, he stood and watched her drive off, dust from the gravel swirling up in the van's wake, grit hanging in the air for longer than he'd expected, the rasp of sand between his teeth nearly as annoying as the bite of his need. It had been too long, and he knew it. The thought of a drink or a fix or a snort or a joint filled his head to the point where hardly anything else penetrated.

He knew mentally he wasn't in any place to negotiate, but this seemed a straightforward exchange. *Here, I have money. Give me drugs.* He snorted. Somehow he'd managed to convince Benita. He'd swayed her, and after she gave him her trust, the idea of seeing disappointment written on her face, again, firmed his resolve. Shoving down thoughts of clinking ice and sloshing brown bourbon, he tried to remember which parts of his plan seemed brilliant only minutes before she dropped him off. *Stupid.*

Waltzed in, loaded bag in hand, fully intending to handle the payoff, only to find no one home. No challenges and nobody to even ask him what he was doing. He remembered thinking, *If their security is this lax, they deserve anything that happens.* That became his justification, and for a time, he actually considered what he was doing would be a favor to them, pointing out the flaws in their setup. A security consultant. *Yeah, right. A fully delusional one.* Then there were noises, and shouts, and he ran while fear swallowed him whole, blanking out long moments of time.

Now he was trapped, deep inside the compound in a place where he had no excuse for being, bag of money abandoned in his panicked dash along the way. Voices accompanied the approaching footsteps, and he made out two voices, both speaking Spanish. No surprise there, being as this was a Mexican drug cartel's facility. *Shit.*

"*Nada. Mi esposa es estúpida.*" Guttural laughter. *Talking about his wife, a family guy, a good guy?*

Closer and closer. Benny turned his head, pressing tightly to the wall, wishing he could disappear into it, to meld inside like a science project gone bad, radio waves loosening the hold atoms held on each other. "*Ella quiere más bebés, pero he terminado con los niños.*" Closer still, as tension built inside him.

Fuck this. I'm done with this, he thought, wanting to leap out, put an end to the waiting, knowing they were only steps away. At the same time his stomach clenched at the thought, and he was left wondering if he could really move into view and accept whatever consequences came his way.

A commotion at the end of the hallway nearly had him jumping out and into view, but he managed enough self-control to remain hidden. A distant shout, then another, and far away, he heard what distinctly sounded like the rattle of gunfire. *Shit.* Receding footsteps had him brave enough to peer around the locker in time to see two stocky men running away up the hallway, automatic weapons held in a ready position across their torsos. Benny stood, easing away from the wall for a moment, watching. Then he turned and bolted the other direction, away from the men, away from the gunfire...deeper into the compound.

Herded by frantic sounds of what had to be a shootout, he blindly ran through the maze of hallways. Left. Right. Right. Left. Right. The turns weren't at standard intervals, and he couldn't imagine the size of the rooms they indicated. Huge warehouses built into the side of a mountain; the entire facility was far larger than the outside indicated.

Every few seconds, gunfire would sound in the distance, as fear drove him ever onward.

Finally, a metal door barred his progress, and he halted, pressed against it, panting for breath. With sweat streaming off his body, he cautiously looked through the small glass window set high in the center of the surface and when he did, Benny froze in place. The next area was brightly lit and vast, with tables lined in row after row stretching off to the far wall. On nearly every table was a stack of tightly wrapped bundles. *Jackpot.*

Scanning left then right, he didn't see a single person in that room. *Unreal.* For no one to be guarding so much smack was unbelievable, so he pinched himself, winced, and then checked again. Still no one. He was gathering his courage to open the door when movement caught his attention and he watched as an overhead door on the far wall rolled up, letting in light. Moving fast, a van backed into the building and a dark-haired woman swung down from the driver seat, ran to an empty table and picked up a clipboard. Flipping through several papers, she laid the clipboard back down and then, using a huge button on a device hanging from the ceiling, lowered the door before running out through a normal-sized door set in the wall next to the overhead.

Quiet. Empty. The bundles beckoned. Maybe abandoned. He heard no more gunfire.

He should have taken the money and run from the gang out of Mexico. *So stupid.* But he'd lost the bag, and now, if he didn't get the product, he'd be well and truly fucked. *Sideways. With a crowbar.*

Wrapped packages, lined and stacked. A single brick would be worth enough to keep the band going for a month. This drug gang had all the money. They'd find the bag of money, and then surely they would count it, see it was an even trade. Which just left the biker gang to worry about. Unconsciously, Benny was jittering in place. His desire for the oblivion promised by the drugs laid out in front of him a living thing inside him. This would show them their security was lax. *Look how far I made it inside.* His thoughts splintered, but that wasn't an excuse for what he was about to do. *Band needs this.*

Denial is more than just a river. That was Andy's voice in his head, something he'd heard his brother say to their grandmother. While he'd been talking about their mother at the time, Benny knew the statement could easily be about him now. Not liking how those words made him feel, he ignored it, focusing only on Andy.

Andy was in Fort Wayne, Indiana. A high-ranking person in his own biker gang. Organized crime. That was what the papers called what they did. He'd read all about Andy's gang. Suspicious deaths, racketeering, pimps and whores, gun runners, drug dealers, it read like a laundry list of what not to do. But they did it. All the time. So, this would be normal for them. Same shit, different day. Drugs were normal in a gang.

With the money, he could pay the bikers back. He could pay GeeMa back. Hell, he could even pay Andy back. For years and years, his brother had been pulling Benny's fat out of the fire. Years and years of Benny being the burden. All his life. Born to it. The words teased at his mind, and his eyes slipped closed as he chased the possibility of lyrics into the dark.

Born to be his trouble. Always my brother's burden. Making his life a waste.

Sounds coming from a distant hallway to his right jerked him back to alertness, unaware of how much time had passed while he stood there staring at the darkness behind his eyelids, playing with words. Looking into the room to find it was still empty, abandoned, the van remained standing in front of the now-closed doorway. *I can do this. Andy could use the smack for his friends. Sell some of it for himself. Pay Juan back. GeeMa. Everyone makes a tidy sum. It would make up for so much. He could sell the rest for me. I'd even give him a cut.* These were the arguments he had made to Benita. Sounding reasonable enough to believe, she had stopped trying to talk him out of the idea.

We can get booked into his bar. Show up. He'll be thrilled. I'll ease into it with him, feel him out. See what we can organize. Not something to bring up on the phone as he's in a gang. Their phones are probably tapped. Benny's hands rested on the crash bar that would open the door and almost without conscious intent, he pushed, and the door clicked open. He froze, the door a half-inch away from the frame, held in place. *He has to hate me, that hate growing every year. Lodged in place like a chicken bone choking the life out of a careless diner.*

Andy had been gone for years. All the times Benny needed him the most, his brother had been thousands of miles away, nothing but a voice on a phone. *Gone before I knew him.* Leaving made Andy's life easier, even if Benny learned from Harddrive that it hadn't been an easy decision. *Shit, I haven't thought about that old man in years. Wonder how he's doing?*

Distant sound from the right broke into his thoughts, and he pushed the door wide enough to slip through. The room was cold. Chilled in a way the hallways weren't, and there was a positive airflow that propelled wind out through the doorway until it settled back into place. Drifting towards the van, he trailed his fingertips across stacks of bundles on each table, counting as he went. One hundred on this table, one-twenty on that one, only eighty-five here. *So much money.* In his mind, the bundles were no longer drugs, but blocks of greenbacks. *Benjamins.*

Opening the back doors of the van, he was surprised to find it vacant, the entire cargo area spotless and...empty. Glancing at the tables behind him, he remembered how the woman went for the clipboard and walked over. The top paper held the schematics of a van, showing what looked like voids in the walls. Back to the van, he started feeling around, finding panels held in place with strong magnets. They might be voids some of the time, but right now, they were filled with white bricks, tightly wrapped in paper then plastic, sealed with a hand-written sticker. Everything he needed, right there in front of him, already packaged for travel. A new van. A new start. *A new life.*

He allowed himself one small armload of bricks from a nearby table. *Don't get greedy.* With a grin, he threw the clipboard into the van and closed the doors.

His movements were frantic, and he jittered through the next few seconds, feeling paranoid someone could walk in at any moment, taking all this from him. His drugs, they were an instant way out of the painful evolution of no money for touring, no money for studio, no money for gear. Laid out before him was a way to cut that sequence off, change their luck. *I might have been born into trouble, but I'm gonna crawl out of that cesspit with one short drive.* Finger on the button to raise the door, he paused, thinking. *She opened the door from outside; there's probably a remote in the van.* He knew it was unreasonable, but he couldn't ditch the thought it would be quieter to use the remote. *Quiet is better.*

Crawling into the driver seat, he found a device clipped to the visor. Glancing down, he spotted the keys still in the ignition. *Bingo.* The door clicked into place behind him. Hands to the wheel, he wrung it a couple of times, feeling like his heart was about to burst from his chest. Hand to the keys, a familiar vibration came to life under his ass as the engine turned over. With a finger to the button on the remote, he held his breath and pressed.

Sound and lights assailed him, sirens wailed all around, the volume vibrating the seat under him more than the engine. *Shit.* Loud and piercing, the oougah of the alarm jangled up and down his spine. The door slid up as the bright, rotating lights illuminated the panels. There was a hissing sound and he looked into the outside mirror, seeing a thick mist beginning to gather in the room behind him. *Shit.* Gearshift jammed down, he stomped on the accelerator and rocketed forward, the top of the van scraping against the overhead as he went, the door not having reached enough height to allow escape.

Outside, the gate he had avoided on his way in was right there. The length of a football field in front of the van, standing wide open, the road only feet beyond that. There was a rattle from the van's side door, and he looked in the mirror to see a man with an automatic gun running alongside, hand grasping at the handle. In the distance, more men were flooding towards the warehouse, and Benny saw smoke pouring out through the doorway he'd left open behind him.

Foot to the floor, Benny bounced in the seat as the van rocked through a series of potholes, each jarring jerk conspiring to keep the man's hand off the handle. *Ping.* Something like a stone bounced off the top of the van, but he knew intuitively it wasn't a rock. *Shit.*

The gate loomed, moving, and he saw it was closing, slowly, still ample room to slide the van through. Another ping, and another, and the man stopped running, planted his feet and pointed the gun at the van, mouth open in an impotent scream before turning to face a second flood of men rolling from the other side of the compound. *Shit.* Van tires sliding sideways as he hit the road, shimmying and shuddering, he whipped the wheel back-and-forth, forcing the vehicle to straighten out as he smashed the accelerator to the floor again. "Your security ain't worth shit," he shouted, the words followed by a rash of hysterical laughter.

***

"Jesus, Benny," Benita breathed, staring into the back of the van from the passenger seat. She could see the dozen bricks lying scattered across the floor, but held the clipboard in her hands; the treasure map.

"Told you I had this." He grinned. No pursuit meant he was in the clear. He'd fled to downtown Denver, trailing through the alleyways he knew well, watching for anyone following. Nothing. After several hours, he'd called Benita, told her to ditch the guys and meet him here.

"And no one questioned the trade? They threw in the van?" she repeated the lie he'd told her and he grinned.

"Yeap. Easy as pie, just like I said." He reached for her hand, ignoring how she pulled back. "No sweat."

"The news said there was a warehouse fire." Her face held doubt, but no disappointment. Doubt he could win over, change that expression to pride. *Easy as pie.*

"I don't know about that. Everything was quiet when I drove out. All good." *Liar, liar, building's on fire.* "Baby, you see what this does, right? We go to Fort Wayne. I get my brother to unload this through his channels, and we're rolling. Suites and champagne, take my baby dancing."

She smiled, then that disappeared into a frown. "What do we tell the guys?"

"I worked a deal, got a new van. The Klunkster"—he used the nickname for their band van, so named for the noise their transmission had been making for the last fifty thousand miles—"needed replacing and I worked a deal. I'll pack these few bricks into the spaces on the paper." He pointed to the clipboard lying in her lap. "We get to Indiana, unload and then get loaded." At the grimace on her face, he laughed. "Not like that, baby. Loaded as in moolah." So far, he had resisted the siren call of oblivion, running on adrenaline alone. He could hold it together for now. *Forever.*

"Seems too easy, Benny. You bought drugs from a gang." Mexican cartel, but he wasn't one to split hairs. "Can we really do this?"

"Yeah, we can." He shook her hand. "Just to make sure we're clean, I'll swap the plates. It's the same model so unless we fuck up, no one will ever know. The ride is cleaner and doesn't stink, and the guys won't give two shits which van is driving our asses down the highway. I need you to call that bar in Fort Wayne and get us booked, though. That's step one. You do your part." She frowned, and he knew it was at the suggestion she wouldn't pull her weight. *Shit.* "I'll get things tidied away in the back, then load the gear. We can park the Klunkster in a mall lot or something, leave it to be towed and then junked. Everything is going to work out, Benita. Promise." Lifting her hand to his mouth, he trailed kisses across the backs of her fingers. "Love you, baby."

"Yeah?" Her tone had deepened, gained the suggestive note that preceded her taking control of...everything. *Shit.* She glanced out the front window, and he followed her gaze, for the first time seeing the woman in the van Benita had driven. "How much do you love me, Benny?"

He stared at the blonde for a long minute. Short hair, curvy cheeks, her mouth moved as she popped her gum, blowing a bubble. *Jesus. She can't be more than eighteen*. He couldn't make it without Benita. She'd told him that a thousand times, and he knew it was true. Without her, he was nothing. "As much as you need me to."

Nine

From where he stood on the small, raised stage, Benny let his gaze sweep what he could see of the bar. Nicer than he'd expected, Marie's in Fort Wayne had a classic feel to the place, which was surprising considering who owned it. *Bikers and elegance. Whoda thunk it*. He grinned. Load-in was done, sound check complete; now, time for a little reconnaissance. They'd been in town for a day, and he hadn't yet laid eyes on Andy, that avoidance only partly by design. From a brief conversation with GeeMa he knew his brother should be here, but he wanted to have a good feel for the lay of the land before they reconnected in the flesh.

Through the years, he and Andy kept in touch, mostly via phone. Not frequently, but since their conversations were mostly about him fucking up, he didn't think anyone would blame him for not calling often, and keeping it short when he did. They'd chatted a couple of weeks earlier, an uncommon occurrence, not because they talked, but because it was a real conversation. Benny had worked the band into the conversation, nearly laughing aloud when Andy mentioned a band with the same name was performing soon in his bar. It wasn't until after they hung up that he realized Andy truly didn't know Occupy Yourself was *his* band. Then, instead of seeming funny, it pissed him off. Just one more way for Andy to show how little Benny really mattered in the grand scheme of things.

Gypsy, the bar manager, stood near the door, wearing the ever-present biker's leathers, talking to two men who wore the same patched vests. Waiting for the man to finish his conversation, Benny timed his own trip to the bar, meeting him near the cash register. Time for a little info digging.

Thirty minutes later, he knew more about his brother than he expected to learn. And every word of it fucked with his plans. *Shit.*

Not only wasn't Andy in a gang, they got offended at the word. Deeply offended, to the point Gypsy suggested Benny clear the band's gear. That made him backpedal fast, earning him a gruff, "Fuckin' watch your mouth, punk."

The *"club,"*—in his mind he enclosed the word in air quotes—wasn't into dealing drugs. What Gypsy said backed up everything Benny had learned yesterday. The Rebel Wayfarers MC was in the middle of a war against a group of drug dealers, trying to get them out of town. It seemed bizarre that a gang—*club*, he corrected himself—was policing their turf against drugs, and not so they could control the flow of product and money associated with moving and selling the stuff. Not Andy's guys. Nope. It was all in an effort to keep it at a distance from where they lived. Altruistic bikers.

Shit.

He had a stolen van with thousands of dollars in drugs and hadn't thought much past getting to Fort Wayne. In expectation of a big payday, he'd talked Benita into checking into swank suites at the downtown hotel last night. They'd earned good money on their way here, but three nights of cash upfront for the suites had nearly cleaned out their stash of funds. *Shit.*

He made his way backstage to the bar's joke of a greenroom. Three steps down from the main level, it was a small, concrete enclosure with poured cement benches scarcely padded with cheap cushions meant for patio furniture. Windowless, it seemed more a bunker than anything. *I wonder what it was used for before the bar had a need to put musicians somewhere.*

Stewing, he sat and propped his feet on the opposite bench, fingers plucking at the strings of the guitar cradled in his lap. Mindless music flowing, his thoughts turned in a dozen different directions, trying to find a way out of this mess.

"Benny." Benita's voice startled him, and he looked up, suppressing a groan as he moved his legs, knees locked into position from sitting God knew how long. She stood in the opening that led up to the hallway. "Fifteen minutes." Once sure he'd heard her, she turned and walked away. *Shit.* He'd sat there for nearly three hours. Stupid, because he hadn't eaten lunch and had since missed dinner. With a three-hour gig in front of him, he knew he'd be severely flagging by the first break, and totally gassed at the end of the night. At least they didn't have to tear down; they'd be back in Marie's the following night.

He stood and stretched. *So little time before the show, where are the guys?* Hands over his face, he scrubbed hard, pressing the heels of his hands into the sockets of his eyes, squeezing through the pain. *God, I want...something.* Benita's voice came again, this time her tone edged towards annoyed. "Got a visitor, Ben." Blinking at the two forms filling the opening, he jerked when he recognized Victor Montrose standing next to Benita. *Shit.*

He'd totally forgotten he and Danny had finally decided to get rid of Blake. Danny had called Vic, a drummer they'd watched grow in stage presence for several years, but Benny didn't remember Danny saying the kid was joining them here. From the look on Benita's face, she might not have known about the call at all.

Pulling on his performance persona like a second skin, he stepped forwards, reaching up with one hand. "Hey, Vic. Good to see you, man. Wasn't sure you'd make it." Time to bluff until he knew enough to steer things. "You talk to Danny today?"

Vic's hand closed around his, callused fingers rasping roughly across Benny's own. With a shake of his head, he offered, "Hey, Ben. Last talked to him two days ago, before I climbed on a bus. We still on for tomorrow night?" That meant Danny had talked to him right before they got into town, probably at the diner in South Bend after their show there. Tonight would be Blake's last performance with OY, and he expected Danny planned it that way so their volatile drummer would be exhausted and less likely to explode when they told him.

Benita cleared her throat, looking to her left and Ben heard a shouted, "What the fuck?"

Head tipping backwards, he stared up at the ceiling. *Fuck.* Seemed Blake would be learning about his replacement now, instead of after the show. "Get Danny," he told Benita, who was already pulling her phone from her back pocket.

"Montrose? What the fuck you doin' here? Saw a kit being carried in, wasn't mine. Figured these assholes were pulling something." Blake was still out of sight, but Vic had turned to look up the hall past where Benny could see. Mouth shut, Vic stared, and Benny had no doubt Blake was putting on a show.

Time to enter the fray, he thought, hearing Benita talking to Danny on her phone. Two steps up, he leaned out of the opening, putting himself between Blake and Vic. Two more steps and he stood in the way as Blake tried to push past him, two—*barely, but please, God, let them be legal*—girls standing behind him. *Shit.* With an audience to impress, their drummer would be even more of a blowhard.

"Vic," Benny said without turning around, "hit the door behind you. Take Benita with you, yeah?" She didn't need to deal with Blake, and the less Vic saw and heard the better. He stiff-armed Blake back two steps, following and quickly shoving him again. The door behind him thudded shut, and he stopped, hands clenched into fists at his side. "Not how we wanted you to find out, Blake." The man's eyes were jerking side-to-side, trying to map a route around Benny to get to the man he thought was the problem here, the source of his embarrassment. "Vic doesn't know anything. We wouldn't do that to you."

Private arguments were best kept that way because bands talked. Groupies talked. Sound engineers, guitar techs, tour managers, merch booth gals—everyone talked. Gossip ran rampant in the community, and Benny had never seen a group of people as ready to be happy about another person's misery. Breakups, letdowns, heartbreaks—all fodder for the gossip gristmill.

"Been comin' a while, Blake. You know it." Benny shook his head. "We've stood together for a long time, but this is the parting of ways. Last show."

"You can't fucking do this to me." Blake started with bluster, but he knew the score and Benny could see it in his eyes. "You can't replace me like this. No warning. What the hell am I supposed to do?"

"You'll get what's coming to you," Benny promised, not having one fucking idea how it would happen since they were nearly broke. "It's time to move on, Blake."

The door behind him opened, and he heard Danny telling the pair outside, "Why don't you both head to the hotel. Get Vic checked in, baby." The door closed, and Blake's eyes cut over Benny's shoulder. "Been a good run, Blake." Benny stepped to one side, letting Danny move beside him, the two of them filling the hallway side-to-side. "We'd like to go out on top, having a good show tonight. Can you do that with us? Can you play tonight? Hold it together and be professional for one fucking time in your life?" Blake opened his mouth, and Danny talked over him. "Don't fucking give me shit, man. You knew if you jacked your shit one more time, you were out." Leaning in, he hissed, "South Bend." Blake's face went white, and Ben turned to look at Danny, wondering what the fuck that was about.

Whatever it was, those words were enough for Blake to back down entirely, all his bluster deflating and the next two minutes were him saving face and pretending to be gracious. Retreating towards the stage where Benny could hear Dmitri warming up, Blake walked away without Danny or Ben having to say another word.

"What the fuck happened in South Bend?"

"Same shit, different day." That familiar refrain was all Danny said before walking away, stalking up the hallway after Blake.

"Shit." *I'm awake now*, he thought. *Nothing like a little drama to get the blood flowing*. He was edging towards anxiety, with thoughts of the product in the van slipping through his head. *Just a taste*. He shook if off, wishing he could turn back the clock. Hat in place, shades on his face, he stretched tall before grabbing his guitar and slinging it over his shoulder.

Heading up the hallway after Danny, he glimpsed a figure walking through the door to the bar and even without seeing him for years, knew who it was. "Andy," he called as the door closed and then watched with disappointment as it stayed that way. He was thinking, *Well, shit, maybe I was wrong*—then the door moved, and his brother stuck his head back through the opening, a searching look on his face.

"Hey, man. Are you with the band?" Andy's question took him by surprise. There was a casual curiosity, but no recognition. Andy seemed to have absolutely no idea it was him.

And that, my friends, is how little I count in the lives of those I love.

Fighting back tears, he tipped his chin to one side and slapped Andy's shoulder as he moved past him. Footsteps paced him, and he kept his face averted, not wanting his brother to see the hurt rolling through him.

Shocked, he listened to Andy's next words, a request that bordered on him playing a game with Ben. "My little brother is a big fan. Is there any way I could get you to sign something for him?"

Ben came to a standstill and turned, automatically reaching for the autograph material offered, then he stopped and lifted his hand to pull off his sunglasses. Waiting for the joke to end, for Andy to give him a "gotcha," instead, he saw a shocked disbelief. *Fuck, he honestly didn't know it was me.*

Arms enveloped him, and a fist pounded his back as Andy held him tightly. "Baby brother, what the hell are you doing in Fort Wayne? Ben...Benny, oh man, it's good to see you, shrimp. God, it's good to see you. How long have you been here?" Words gushed from the man, and Ben grinned to hear his childhood nickname mixed into the flow.

Ben laughed, returning the embrace, finding himself near tears for a second time that night, this one due to joy. "Andy, I've missed you." He pulled back, staring into his brother's face, seeing age and a hardness he didn't recognize, lines etched in the corners of his eyes and a set to his jaw which said you didn't fuck with this man. Glancing down at the leather vest his brother wore, he saw something that startled him. Even Gypsy hadn't said who the gang's leader was. "You're a fucking president, man? That's hardcore." *Jesus, if I sold the stuff here, I'd be placing myself against my own brother. Shit.*

Setting him apart with a little shake, in a serious voice Andy asked, "Does GeeMa know where you are?"

With shaking hands, he pushed his shades to the top of his head. *Time to lie outta my ass.* "Yeah, yeah. She's the one who told me about you being in Fort Wayne, where to find you. I started looking for gigs out this way, and then heard about this place." Andy wrapped his arms around Ben again, hugging him tightly at the affirmation he'd talked to their grandmother recently. *Liar, liar, pants on fire.*

At odds with himself, ready to both get away from the brother he hadn't seen in years and stay close, Ben chose the path of least resistance, saying, "I gotta get to the stage, man. You gonna come watch us?"

Andy frowned at him, looking puzzled at his words. Lifting an eyebrow, he asked, "What the fuck you mean, 'get to the stage'?"

Ben stared at him a minute, disbelieving. *Annnnd, we're right back to how little I count in the lives of those I love.* "You really didn't know, bro? Even after I talked to you on the phone, you never, like, Googled the band to listen to some of the music?"

Andy was slow to respond, holding his gaze for a long minute. Caution colored his voice when he did speak. "Know what? What don't I know? What's going on, Benny?"

Rather than assume Andy meant the insult, he decided to adopt a teaching tone. "Andy, Occupy Yourself is my band; we're playing here at Marie's for the next week." *I am so over this shit.* He sighed. "Enough talking for now—I need to get to the stage." He assumed a theatrical listening stance, exaggerating the fact he heard the crowd in the main room, the growing rumble of conversation music to his ears, a group that would welcome him with open arms. *Unlike my own family.* "Because the crowd is getting restless, and believe me when I say drunk, pissed-off people can get really ugly. We'll talk after the show, Andy. Okay?"

Even in this, Andy had to correct him, letting him know his brother had moved farther from their family than ever before. "Slate...that's what everyone calls me now—Slate, not Andy."

"What the fuck ever, bro, just come listen." Ben laughed, the sound rough and jangling in his own head, his anxiety ratcheting up a dozen notches. *A fucking drink would smooth those edges.* He shook the thought off, again trying to push down the need.

Striding to the stage, he was mollified to see Blake on the stool at his kit, scowling but clearly ready to go. Danny and Dmitri were in their spots, angling towards the front on the small stage. In his head, Benny ran through the show changes they'd put into place during sound check. This venue didn't lend itself to some of the larger movements, so he would have to dial it back, be more controlled.

Mentally he reminded himself of the set list, unchanged for the past dozen shows. Tomorrow they'd have a different lineup, but this was the first time in weeks they'd booked into the same venue on back-to-back nights. Glancing down, he read Benita's neatly written list taped to the stage near his microphone stand, and after checking with the guys, grabbed ahold of the stand and whirled in place, greeting the crowd with a shouted, "How the fuck are ya, Fort Wayne?"

Listening with half an ear to the screamed responses, he leaned over to pick up his water bottle. In his head, he saw Andy's face again, questioning why anyone would want to listen to him sing. *Fuck it*. On the fly, he changed trajectories, grabbing the glass of unwatered whiskey Benita had set out for him during sound check. Already half empty, he drank down a slug, once more thinking of the stash in the van and how easy it would be to pry open one of the packages. *Just a little bit*, he thought, then slugged another drink of whiskey back instead. *Only a taste.* "I said, how the *fuck* you doin', Fort *Wayne?*" Louder than before, the roaring response came, and he grinned at Danny.

"Now that's what I'm talkin' about." Dipping to a conversational tone, he said, "My first time here at Marie's, but I'm looking forward to our time with you fine folks." Shifting back to a roar, he leaned backwards, face lifted to the ceiling, microphone to his lips, shouting his question, "Are you ready for some rock and roll?" With that, they were off, and the first half of the set went by quickly, every man on the stage in sync and rolling, playing like they hadn't done for a long time. *Shoulda threatened to can Blake a long time ago*, he thought, waiting for the next intro to play him in.

Looking down, he saw his whisky glass was empty, so he grabbed the still-full bottle of water, downing more than half of it in one go. Lifting the tail of his shirt to wipe his face, a gaggle of girls at the front of the stage glanced up, giggling and grinning, and he smiled back, pushing his rock star grin as he launched into the next song. There was one, a pretty Hispanic chick, who smiled at him and he held her gaze, singing to her as if they were alone in the greenroom. A private show. He watched as a dark blush crawled up her cheeks, but she kept the connection, her brown eyes bright as she sang along. *Beautiful.*

A scowling leather-clad guy came from behind and latched onto her arm. Benny stumbled into the next verse, watching as she followed the guy old enough to be her father to the back of the bar. *Just my luck.*

Lifting his gaze, he caught Benita's attention across the crowd and raised his empty glass, waiting until he received a nod in response. Setting it down, he continued on with that song, then the next, and the next, earning two more glasses from Benita. *At least, she loves me*, he hazily thought as she was bringing him another drink. Anger filled him when Danny met her at the edge of the stage and sent her away with it. "The fuck?" Benny questioned Danny as he walked past, fingers working hard on the thick strings of his bass.

Danny leaned in, mouth close and yelling over the music he continued to play, "You're drunk, asshole."

"Fuck you," Benny said, turning to face the audience again. *Three more songs*, he thought, *and we'll have a chat about his motherfuckin' motherin' techniques.* Mouth to the microphone, he shouted, "What's a man gotta do to get a drink in this place?" As he knew would happen, a dozen hands lifted half-full glasses of beer or liquor towards the stage. Grabbing the fullest container within reach, he slammed it back, four forced swallows later he was handing the empty glass back to the owner with a grin. "Thanks, man. Vodka's my favorite. Wets my whistle. Y'all ready to go?"

The crowd roared and laughed, and Benny took a step backwards, that step turning into two before he caught himself. "Let's fuckin' go!" A bit more patter for the crowd and he turned to Blake, mouthing, "One more time." With a nod, Blake counted them down, and they started their final songs of the evening.

That was the last thing Benny knew for a very, very long time.

***

Voices sounded far away but seemed to be appearing in the air right over his head, the sound waves of their words compressing unbearably against his skin. "He gonna die?" A different voice, softer, smooth and sleek where the other had been ruined with pain. Mountains of emotion in every word. "He's stable for now, Mr. Jones, but things are still very uncertain at this point." Clouds of agony swallowed him whole, white-hot electricity shooting through his body, fusing his bones into glass, grinding him into dust. Mists and wisps of him lifting on the swirling words surrounding him. "He's seizing again." Shouts. Blood in his mouth. Wrenching grunts that held an immense depth of misery, his chest rattled in a complex rhythm of sympathy. *Catch the beat, man. Follow the sound.* "*Clear.*" Urgent movements, jerking him this way and that, then a sudden and profound blessed silence, disconnecting from everything weighting him down. Soundless harmony. Words came to him, dropping into his mind like crystals falling from a ballroom chandelier. *Look at me now. There's nothing left to lose, only a leap away from forever, castaway.* Ruby lips sang along with him, brown eyes sinking into him, forcing the verses rushing through his head to shift course as he made room for her. *Look at us now. We've got everything in our arms, holding tight onto forever, masquerade.*

7 WEEKS LATER

"I don't know? Why don't you tell me why I'm here?" The doc scribbled something on the paper in front of him, and Benny knew it was probably a buzzword of the day like denial, or noncompliant, or combative. "Jesus. I know why I'm here, doc. We've only been over this a thousand times." Shaking his head, he lifted a trembling hand to swipe across his lips. "I'm a drunk and an addict, and my brother doesn't want to see me die."

When he came to after the show, tied to a bed in the hospital, every muscle screaming at him, the first person he'd seen was Andy. Looking like he hadn't slept, his brother was seated right at his side, waiting to tell him those exact words. A rushed, one-sided conversation informing him that Andy had once again cleaned up after his mess, the anger in his brother's voice telling him how close it had been. Benny found out Benita had been keeping secrets, talking to the Mexican biker gang he'd borrowed the money from, talking to the drug cartel, talking to everyone, helping all those folks he'd fucked over to keep tabs on him. She'd fucked that up, and pissed people off even more, making it so the whole band was a target.

Andy, though? Benny scoffed at the idea, *Super Andy*—he fixed everything. He knew a guy, who knew a guy, who knew a guy, who peddled the heroin out to the gang Benny had borrowed the cash from, that gang who then used the product to fuck the cartel in the ass. Now Benny was free and clear, escorted from the hospital and put on a plane for Arizona. Fucking Phoenix. For at least ninety days.

He wanted to spew threats every time he talked to Andy on the phone, hating those twice-weekly supervised calls spent on his brother. Family calls, but Andy was his only family now. GeeMa was done with him. She'd seen his mom travel the same path, had no desire for a repeat session, and Andy told Benny he wouldn't be going back to Enoch. As in, ever.

The first time he heard the phrase sober companion, he'd laughed. Men had drinking buddies; they didn't have non-drinking buddies unless they were twinks. Andy didn't seem to be joking around about this, though, and Ben realized this when the first three contenders were shipped out to meet him only a month into his stay in rehab.

None of them was a fit, and not only on Benny's side of things. He suspected they all took away a different view of him. He had been first an asshole, then a flirt, then a flirting asshole, based on the attractiveness and gender of the candidate. Now, he knew he was stuck at asshole, because even after more than a month clean and dry, he still regularly got the shakes like he had right now. And the need? Yeah, even with chemical assistance, that bitch was still gnawing a hole through his head, calling and calling, teasing him with ideas on how to find oblivion that never came.

"Is that the only reason you're here, Mr. Jones?" This doc steadfastly refused to call him Benny, even after repeated requests. Always Mr. Jones, like Benny was an old man.

"I can run through the list again if you want, Doc." Benny looked down, shaking his head. "I'm a habitual liar. I lied and stole from family, lied and stole from a gang, then stole from a drug gang, then lied to my brother. I lied to my band, my friends, my lover. I'm in danger of self-harm. I nearly killed myself unintentionally a dozen times over the past five years, the most recent of which was less than fifty days ago, when I made my brother watch as I took a nosedive and face-planted off a stage, drunk off my ass." Benny shook his head.

"I can't go home. Don't have a home anymore. Hardly have a family, except the brother I already mentioned. The band I worked for years to build is disbanded, which is a terrible play on words, and you should shoot me now for letting that slip out." The joke fell flat, and he took a breath, then another. Consciously slowing his words, realizing the rapidly increasing speed of his speech was telegraphing his anxiety.

"My career is in ruins, and even the music, which has been my saving grace whenever things got bad, has now abandoned me, too. I can't write my way out of a wet paper bag these days."

Holding up his palms, he reached out, exposing small, non-descript red marks on each wrist. "Fifteen days ago I got a pair of scissors from the nurses' station and tried to cut my wrists. I did a shit job of it because I'm stupid and didn't think about dismantling the scissors first, but there you go. I'm a suicidal alcoholic homeless junkie loser." He laughed. "And yet, my brother claims to love me."

"I spoke with your grandmother yesterday, Mr. Jones. I'd like to know why you think you don't have a home." Implacable and unmoved, the doctor looked at him with a carefully level stare.

"My own brother told me I'd never go back to Enoch. I don't have to talk to GeeMa to know how she feels." Rolling his eyes, he flung himself backwards in the overstuffed chair, resisting the urge to sling a leg over the arm like a child in the grip of a tantrum. "I know."

"Mrs. Jones indicated you would always be welcome in your childhood home."

Benny exploded from the chair, walking to the door with fast steps, leaning his heated forehead against the cool wood. With closed eyes, he stood there a moment, waiting. Sure enough, the question came at last.

"Why did that statement upset you, Mr. Jones?"

"Can you stop it with pretending I'm an old man? Can you? Huh? Stop pretending you give a shit? Can you stop? Jesus, you pick and pry until you find something so you can scribble a note down, make sure your time is well spent in here with the drunks. Can you stop it? Just stop with the lies." He didn't move, head bowed.

"Why do you believe I'm lying to you? What part of my statement was a lie?"

"Jesus." Twisting in place, he leaned his shoulders against the door. "Everything. If you knew me, you'd know better. That's what tipped me, man. Lies."

"What's a lie?"

"Her house isn't my childhood home!" Teeth clenched together, his jaw ached painfully with the pressure. "My home doesn't exist anymore. It got wrecked by *her*."

"Your grandmother wrecked your house? I don't understand. I was under the impression she still lives there, Mr. Jones."

"Fucking shit. Can you just call me Benny?" Shaking his head, he twisted to one side, turning his back to the doctor as if that would hide his reactions in the too small room. "GeeMa lives in her house. My home got sold, and then seven years ago, it burned to the ground. Burned and gone. Wrecked and ruined. If it weren't for *her*, we'd have lived out our days on that place."

"Who?"

"HER!" Benny jerked his body around, facing the doctor again, and seeing the fucking compassion in the man's face unraveled his control. "*HER!* She ruins everything she touches. Always has. Daddy, then Andy. My whole fucking...life. She...my entire life."

"Tell me who, Benny."

It was the use of his name *finally* that did him in. One word, two syllables, and when the doc said it, completely took his legs out from underneath him. Back to the door, he slipped to the floor, sobs racking his body. There were noises in the room, footsteps scarcely audible over the rushing breath in his ears, then arms around him, a solid chest under his cheek. It reminded him of Andy and all the times his brother had held him in the middle of the night. Back when he would wake in the grip of a nightmare and two boys far too young to be alone were the only people in the house because she was out whoring around. "Mom. My *mom*."

***

"Heard you had a breakthrough, man. Congrats." Beans, the resident long-timer, greeted him at supper. Mortified, gaze fixed to his plate, Benny didn't respond. The man leaned close and quietly, for Benny's ears only, said, "No, man. This ain't me raggin' on you. We all advance at our own pace and I'm envious. When you know part of what's fucked-up in your head, you can find a way to fix it, man. That'll lead to you figuring out more, fixing more. Before you know it..." He sighed. "You having a breakthrough, and nobody knows what it was but you and Doc, is a thing to celebrate." Straightening in his chair, he said, "When you're ready, you'll find the person to celebrate with. Until then,"—picking up his fork—"congrats."

Through supper and beyond, Benny turned Beans' words over in his head. It seemed absurd. First, to assume he could fix himself by uncovering things in his past that might have had a hand in shaping who he became. Second, to believe he wanted to be fixed.

The need never stopped. That bitch was riding his shoulders every day, pointing out how much easier this or that situation would be with a drink in hand, or a spoon at the ready. Some days worse than others, like today. Every time he thought about what happened inside Doc's office, he cringed and reached for a drink that wasn't there.

Tossing and turning, his sleep was restless, and he spent most of his time staring up into the darkness. Thinking. Remembering. Scenes playing ceaselessly through his head, underscoring every failure. Full color, on repeat, Coach couldn't have done a better job putting together a highlight reel of fuckups. He knew daybreak was waiting and for once, he prayed the night would speed by, but like with most things in his life, his desires had no place in reality.

When the afternoon rolled around, he was early, waiting in the hallway well before appointment time. Doc had to note this change in routine, but didn't point it out, simply unlocked the door and invited Benny in. Even before they took their seats, Benny had started talking. Asking questions about how this worked, why it worked, how he could speed it along if it *was* working. Before Doc got an answer out, he had already segued into a story about Benita. Dredged up in the middle of the night by his restless brain, it was something he'd never told anyone. One of the sessions where she basically pimped him out to her girlfriend while he was so wasted, if he'd been older than fifteen, there was no way he'd have stayed hard.

"It was like she hated me, but couldn't get enough of my cock. Always fallin' on my cock. And nothing I did was enough. I wasn't enough because she's layin' there on top of Hayley, grinding her pussy into the girl, and having me dip between them. I had a condom on. Yeah, early on I got real good at self-preservation, but in one, then the other, nothing there good for me. Not the first time I didn't get off," he scoffed, "not the last, either."

"When did you realize she was using you to fulfill her own fantasies?"

89

"I'm stupid, so it took longer than it should have. At first, I liked the attention. An older woman," he scoffed again. "Older, right. But in the little world of Enoch, she was a big fish. Her daddy was a bigger fish, owned half the town. She wanted me. Out of all the boys in school, she wanted me. Something prideful in there, because of who my ma was, and she wanted me anyway." His words slowed as he found something there that bothered him.

"But, she didn't want me. She immediately set about changing me. Different clothes. 'Talk like this, Benny. Hold your fork like that. Come to this party. Do that thing.' It wasn't a control thing, but more a veneer she needed to paste over the prairie kid to make me into what she wanted to show off." Shaking his head, he dropped into the chair finally. "She whittled me down until I matched the picture she had in her head. It was never me at all. The only thing that was me was the music. The band. She latched onto that, and I still don't know why because we sure weren't lush with success, but she stayed, and nothing ever changed. Nothing changed."

That talk led to another the next day, and the next, and finally Benny's calls with Andy became anticipated rather than dreaded. Between Doc and Andy, they eventually talked him into taking a call from GeeMa, and that led to him sitting on the floor in the office again, shaking with tears as she told him what was in her heart. "Always loved you, boy. Didn't like what you did. Those are different things. Always love you. Always will, Ben."

Then he set to work trying to separate the acts from the man. It was hard work, and he would never have believed it to be work before now, where he found himself in all of this. Found the heart of who he needed to be, and the things that had concealed him falling away. The music still wasn't flowing, but he hoped that was a piece he would again hold at the end of the day.

***

Wordlessly, he stared at Beans. The man held his stare for a minute, then the most beautiful smile Benny had ever seen spread across his face. "You did it, man. Graduation day."

At the reminder, Benny broke the stare, looking down and away. "Scary shit. The world out there."

"Yup. You got this, though. Know what you need to do. Remember what Doc says. You can do anything a minute at a time. Just break things down into sixty-second slices, and you got this whipped." Those words were similar to what his brother had told him last night, calling from the hotel near the rehab center, killing time until he could pick Benny up today.

"Yeah, I got this." Self-doubt worried around the edges of his certainty, but he had the doc's words to fall back on, and Andy was committed to helping him keep it together. It sounded like his brother had a steady girlfriend now, and that was good. Benny hoped he hadn't met her in the few hours he was in Fort Wayne, but even if he had and given her the worst first impression in the history of first impressions, even if she hated him, he'd work his ass off to turn her opinion around, for Andy's sake.

Turning to face the door, he squared his shoulders, guitar hanging down his back. Feeling like a nomad troubadour, Benny walked out the door and into what he knew would be a better future.

Eleven

Seated at the end of the breakfast bar, Benny continued softly strumming the strings on the guitar in his lap, his eyes downturned while Andy and his red-haired beauty walked up the stairs to their bedroom. Her shorts left little to the imagination, and he was afraid if he looked up, he'd know if the carpet matched the drapes. *Fuck.*

He needed to get his own place, but there were a few impediments to that plan. One, it was Fort Wayne, and he didn't know many people here. Two, he was essentially flat fucking broke because his brother held the purse strings tighter than an old lady at the end of the month. There was money, because, through his connections, Andy had pedaled the product and admitted he'd gotten more than amnesty for Benny from the buyer. But half that money went to Andy's biker gang, and even Benny couldn't fault the reasoning.

He'd brought trouble to their door, using his family. His gaze flicked to the top of the stairs, hearing Andy's low murmur, and then the bright laughter of the woman, Ruby. Her name as pretty as she was, but Benny thought Ruby seemed like a nickname because one of the ladies in the gang had called her Melanie.

Club, I gotta call it a club, he reminded himself. He'd brought more than trouble to the club. It seemed he'd brought it directly to his brother's feet, too. *Kidnapping.* He shook his head. What the hell kind of people would kidnap a cute thing like Ruby? *The kind of trash I dragged into town with me.* The house phone rang, and he waited, hearing Andy's voice again as he answered. After a couple of minutes, his brother called down the stairs, "Shrimp, pick up."

Leaning the guitar against the wall, he reached over and snagged the handset. "Hello?"

Silence for a moment, followed by a voice he didn't recognize. "Ben? Ben Jones?"

"Yeah. What can I do for you?" Echoing on the line, then into the silence he prompted, "Hello?"

"Hey. It's Vic." Shaking his head, Ben leaned one elbow on the counter, lifting a hand to rub the back of his neck, moving to a rolling massage when the man spoke again. "Glad you're feeling better, man. Real glad." A pause. "Um. Wanted you to know I've got all the gear. Well, not Blake's kit, he took that. But the rest. Mitty,"—Benny must have made a confused sound, because Vic elaborated—"you know, Dimitri. Anyway, Mitty and I got it all loaded into the van your brother loaned us since ours broke down." A hollow click on the line and Ben realized Andy had been listening. "You there?"

"Yeah." The word hurt to say, cut through him like ground glass in his throat. He didn't remember a lot from the night he'd nearly died. Andy had filled in some of the gaps on the plane ride home yesterday; filled in a lot of holes, but only a few had to do with the band.

Vic Montrose was one of the things he didn't remember, not really, but Benny was glad to hear he and Dmitri had stuck around. Benita and Danny were back in Wyoming, as a couple, which surprised everyone except Benny. He heard both of them were working for Benita's dad at a car dealership in Cheyenne. Blake was done anyway, so Ben didn't give a shit either way about him. He hadn't thought about the gear, though, so it was good to know it hadn't disappeared. His hand convulsed around the neck of the guitar at the surge of hope that whooshed through him. *Maybe there's a chance at rebuilding.*

Footsteps descended the stairs. He watched Andy stop about halfway down, bending his knees to sit sideways, settling in with his legs dangling over the side of the stairway.

"Where are you guys staying?" *Maybe I can move in with them.* Even as he had the thought, he saw Andy grin and shake his head, reading his mind. *Fuck.*

"Hanging with some friends of your brother. Bear's a cool dude. We've been jammin' with him." Vic's voice dipped, and Ben suddenly felt like a teenager, far younger than his twenty-six-years, standing there with a hand cupped around the phone to keep anyone from overhearing a conversation. "He's good. Like totally good. Outrageous. Dude, you *need* to hear him."

Excitement burned through him at that. There were few things better than playing with someone who could actually play. Someone you could bounce and grind your skills against, honing both your talents to a fine edge. Someone who could match and play with you, tying a song into a tight bow no audience could escape from. Best feeling in the world.

"Sounds good." *Understatement.* "I could meet Bear anytime. Wanna pick me up tomorrow?" Andy's head moved side-to-side, and Benny gestured to him with his free hand. *Jesus.* He fumbled, then suggested, "Or, I could get my brother to bring me to you?" An up-and-down movement that time, and Benny looked down, staring at the toes of his shoes. "Why don't I do that? It's probably easier. I'll see you tomorrow."

Vic was still talking when Benny hung up the phone, glaring at Andy. "Why does it feel like I just made a playdate?" He swallowed hard. "Andy, I don't mean to...what I want to say is I know how—"

Andy cut him off with laughter. "Fuck that noise. I'm lovin' this, shrimp. You bein' excited about meeting Bear is awesome to see. You bein' excited about anything." He grinned. "If this works out? Worth everything." Andy scooted back, standing, his voice trailing after him as he made his way back upstairs. "See ya in the morning."

"Night," Benny called and then picked up the guitar again. After not playing much for so many weeks, it would take his fingers time to toughen up again. Walking to the couch where a pile of blankets waited for him, he strummed and hummed quietly far into the night.

***

"Wakey, wakey, eggs and bakey." The too-bright voice buzzed alongside his ear—soft, girlish tones luring him up from sleep. "Come on, beautiful boy, time to get up." Benny reached out a hand, found a feminine wrist and clamped tight, pulling her into bed with him. "Hey. Let me go." *Too petite to be Benita, I must have hooked up with a groupie last night.* "Ben. Let me go." *Got me some strange.* He grinned but then the woman's tone registered. Trembling, her voice was small and frightened. "Please."

He released her and opened his eyes, seeing a flash of red as she scrambled to her feet. *Fuck.* "Ruby, I'm sorry. I didn't—"

"Breakfast is on the stove." There were tears gathering in her eyes as she turned away, then she paused in place, keeping her back to him. Taking a deep breath, seeming to steady herself through willpower alone, she quietly asked, "Coffee or juice?"

"*Jesus*, I'm sorry." He sat up and realizing he'd slept in his jeans, threw off the blanket and stood. She turned around at the noise and stepped backwards, away from him. Retreating. From him. *Shit.* "Ruby—"

"Don't worry about it, Benny." Gaze to the floor, she was the picture of an abused woman. *And I put my hands on her. My brother's woman. Fuck.* "No worries," she lied to him.

My big brother. "Do you have brothers or sisters?" Not sure where the question came from, he ran with it as she shook her head. "Baby brothers are supposed to be a pain in the ass. That's me. I'm your new pain in the ass." A flickering smile danced on and off her face. *Fuck. More.* "Thing is, you get to torture me in return. Ask Andy, he has a million ways to make me pay. Today, I'd say your best option is to demand I do the dishes in payback for my deed just now. Later, you could tell me to mop the bathrooms, but I also might decline. That's where the fun starts. Means you get to badger and pester, and I can't do anything about it. Gotta put up with it. My big sister gets the last say, see?"

He must have hit the right tone, because when her eyes met his, a tiny but real smile curled her lips. *There we go.* In that instant, he saw exactly what his brother had in Ruby, and hoped like hell he'd find the same one day. "Deal?"

She took a shaky breath, and then responded on the exhale, her voice still soft, "Deal." Head tipped to one side, she laughed, that sound strong in comparison. "The guys all call me little sister a lot of the time. It's kinda fun to think about being someone's big sister for a change."

"All day long. Bossy lady gets to boss the baby brother." His phone rang, and he laughed as he pulled it out of his back pocket, connecting the call while listening to her answering laughter. "Hello."

"Who's that?" Benita's voice was loud, shrill, and pissed off. "You sound like you're doing a lot better, laughing it up like that. Who's that with you?"

"Hey." He still wasn't sure how he felt about her leaving everything in the dust like she did. He'd been angry at first, then when he heard about her and Danny, Ben wondered about all the times he'd left them alone in hotel rooms. That pissed him off even more, feeling the fool because he knew they'd hooked up at least once. But, hearing her voice now, he thought back to everything she'd put up with from him and guilt settled in his chest. "How's Wyoming?"

"You ruined absolutely everything, you know?" That beginning let him know she wasn't calling for an update, but to make sure her message was heard loud and clear. "All our plans. Ruined my life." Gaze to the toes of his shoes, he listened, offering no argument. "Ruined everything. And now I feel like people are watching *me* to see when I'll mess up. *Me!*"

There was a long pause, one he felt compelled to fill even as the need welled up inside him. "I'm sorry."

"Well, sorry doesn't go far anymore." She huffed, and he imagined her raking her hair back, frowning as she said, "Daddy told me you shouldn't bother coming back to Enoch because no one there will hire you. Cheyenne, either."

His gut cramped. "I don't know what else I can say. I am sorry. Truly and deeply sorry." He should have called her earlier. Should have reached out while still in Phoenix. Should have done things differently. "I just—"

The phone was pulled from his hand, and Ruby scowled up at him, green eyes glaring out from under her tousled mop of hair, daring him to try to retrieve it. "Who is this?" A pause. "No, I asked who you are. I didn't stutter." Another pause, this one accompanied by a roll of her eyes. "Whatever, honey. Listen, you don't get to talk to Benny like you were." She straightened, and he watched her eyes narrow. "No, *you* listen to *me*. You don't call him. You don't talk to him at all. Ever. As in *ev*-er. If he wants you, he'll reach out. Until then—and if he takes my advice, it'll be a cold day in hell before that happens—you don't call. You don't exist for him. Stopped existing when you hightailed it out of town."

Hand to her hip, she turned away, and he could see her chin jutting out in profile. "Ruby," he called softly, reaching out only to have her swat at his hand.

"Listen, bitch. You think you're all hot shit, I can tell. But from what I heard, you ain't all that. He can do better. Will do better, he finally gets rid of you." A pause, her head tilted to one side as she listened. "Well, if you ever make it back to the Fort, you'll deal with me." She twisted, glaring at him again, hissing, "God, Benny, could you have picked a bigger bitch?"

Her attention returned to the phone. "Shut up. Just shut up. He's my family, and you don't want to fuck with him. Because if you fuck with him, it means you're fucking with me, and I won't put up with your shit, honey. Not a bit of it. And I have a hundred brothers who can back me up on that."

She snorted indelicately, tossing her hair. "Well, I think *you* are trash. Doesn't matter what your daddy owns. Trash is as trash does, and you faded. Left our sweet Benny high and dry when he needed you the most. That's not how a friend acts. Especially not a *girl*friend. That kind of fade in the clinch? Tells the tale of the person, and that tale shouts trash about you. That's on you, and that means you're not anything we want in our family. You can shut up, and go fuck yourself. Fuck off."

Disconnecting, she tossed him the phone, and he roared with laughter when she said, "Man! *That* felt *good!*" With a grin, she asked him, "She's a piece of work, Benny. What did you ever see in her, anyway?"

***

Benny sat, fingers nervously plucking at the seam of his jeans, listening to some old school rock coming through the speakers in Andy's truck. They were headed over to one of the places Vic and Dmitri had been staying for the past three months, a span of time Benny found impossible to wrap his head around. He knew how long he'd been in rehab, but to have his brother's friends put two strangers up in an apartment for that long smacked of crazy. A good kind of crazy, but still crazy.

"Don't worry about it, shrimp." Andy downshifted as he steered around a corner. Not taking his eyes off the road, he said, "Bear's cool. You're totally going to love this dude. He's all about the music." They were rolling through a comfortable complex, large apartments on either side of the street and Benny was surprised when Andy slowed, turning into a driveway and pulling up behind a small car. "Bear's old lady is cool, too. This is her house. They've been splitting time between apartments, getting ready to move into a bigger home. You'll like Eddie. She's rocking right alongside him most days." Truck in park, Andy looked at him. "His kids are cool. Bear adopted them. We had a brother who didn't clean up his shit, died from it." Shaking his head, Andy popped the driver's door open as Benny stepped out on his side of the truck. "Bear adopted his kids."

The casual way Andy talked about the death of his friend shook Benny. *Would he have been so cavalier if I'd gone toes-up in the end?* His thoughts were derailed by Andy's next words. "Kids' dad was the dude who took Ruby." The chill in his voice froze him in place as Andy's eyes stayed fixed on him, conveying the weight of what he was about to say. "I didn't kill him, but would have if given the chance." Standing beside the truck, he slammed the door with more force than was necessary. "I'd have done it. No qualms, no hesitation. Shot him dead, Ben. He took her, nearly killed my Ruby. I'll do anything for the people I love. Anything."

On that declaration, Benny watched him stride up the sidewalk and open the door to the apartment, walking in without knocking or announcing himself. *Shit.*

Inside there was a kind of controlled chaos that seemed comfortable and energizing all at the same time. Two Hispanic kids were running around, and a dark-haired woman stood with her arms wrapped around Andy, grinning up at him. Without looking away, she yelled, "Bear, baby? Slate's here." Ben still couldn't get used to people calling Andy that name. In his opinion, it didn't fit. A rumbling response came from deeper in the apartment, and she tipped her head, looking at Benny. "You're Ben, Slate's brother, right?"

He nodded, walking forward and extending his hand. "Yeah, I'm Benny."

She met his palm with her own, before adjusting the grip so she managed to cradle his hand in hers. Squeezing and tugging, she pulled him a step closer and then, lifting to her toes, she pressed her lips to his cheek, fingers of her other hand cupping his jaw. Grinning up at him, she said, "I'm Eddie. Want you to know, Slate's brother is always welcome in this house."

Footsteps in the hallway heralded the entrance of Bear, and Benny watched as the big man scooped an arm around Eddie's middle, tucking her to his side, holding out one hand for a wrist-clasp with Andy. The two men didn't speak, but a bond deeper than friendship was written on their faces. His gaze cut to Benny and he lifted his chin, then said, "Bear."

With a nod, he introduced himself. "Benny."

"Boys, cool it." That was to the small boys running through the room, the older of the two hitting the couch cushions at a run, planting a foot and vaulting over the back. "Come on, Miguel, can we not try to kill ourselves today?" Then, on a shout, Bear called over his shoulder, "Vic, Mitty—Benny's here." Lifting a hand to Eddie's face, he tipped her chin up and leaned down to brush his lips across hers. "My heart, I need to talk to Slate outside for a few. Can you help the guys get set up?" Gaze back to Benny, he said, "Club business, I'll come jam after we settle shit, yeah?"

Hand nervously fiddling with the case strap over his shoulder, Benny nodded, relieved he'd get a chance to talk to Vic and Dmitri without much of an audience. Moving his gaze to Eddie, he saw her watching him and wondered if she'd seen his relief. "No worries, me and the guys can catch up while you talk to Andy."

Snorting a laugh, Bear echoed him softly, reaching out to slap Andy's shoulder. "Andy. Hilarious, brother. Buy him a clue." With nothing more than that, he and Andy turned and exited through a door leading to the parking lot, neither man looking back as the two band members strolled down the hallway and into the room, skirting the boys now energetically wrestling on the floor.

"Hey, man," Vic greeted him, hands stuck in his pockets, looking unsure of himself. Dmitri circled close, silently thumping him on the back as he swung to face Eddie. "How...you doin' okay?"

"Sober ninety-eight days." The doc said it was okay to count the hospital stay before he was shipped off like a misbehaving dog to corrective school. "I'm cool." Hand to the strap over his shoulder, he jostled the guitar case. "You guys ready to play a little?" Vic nodded enthusiastically while Dmitri gave a shrug. "I'm a lil' rusty. You'll have to cut me some slack."

Dmitri's neck twisted, head turning to face him and Benny braced when he saw the anger burning in his eyes. "Thinkin' you got all the breaks you're getting for a while, man."

"Fair," he returned instantly. "More than fair." Holding out his hand, he showed the tips of his fingers. "I'll play until I can't, then I'll play some more. I want OY back, man."

Eddie spoke up, her voice casual, even with the emotions swirling between the men. "Slate know you want that?"

Arms out to either side, he bumped into Dmitri, who stepped sideways. "He brought me here, didn't he?" Not really an answer, but then again, he didn't want to lie to her, and he hadn't talked directly about the band. Andy had to know he wanted it back, though. Gaze to the closed door separating his brother from him, he considered. "Gotta count for something."

She nodded. "Might do so. Let's get you set up." She preceded them up the hallway, calling over her shoulder, "Miguel, Roderigo, don't forget about practice tonight. Gather your baseball stuff." To the three men following her, she said, "Youth league, takes a ton of time, but will be worth it if those two learn to be teammates." Her tone was loving and casual, tolerant of the steady riot of noise from the two boys.

"You've adopted them, right?" Andy had said as much, but since neither she nor Bear were Mexican, the lack of birthparents was glaringly evident.

"Bear did. It was final about a month ago." Even from behind he could see her head tipped down, hear a tone he couldn't decipher enter her voice when she said, "They are his family. Those are his boys." Framed pictures on the wall captured Benny's attention, and he stopped stock-still in front of one. An image of his brother was on the wall. Andy, a broad grin on his face, sitting astride his bike, what looked like a dozen kids piled on with him. In front, behind, hanging from his shoulders, in his lap—they were attached to every possible location. The two boys he'd met today, a taller girl, half-hidden behind Andy's shoulder, and a whole slew of others who all had the same look to them. Eddie's voice carried amusement when she said from beside him, "Slate looks good with them, yeah? It's good he loves kids."

"He wants kids?" That was something he'd never thought about, being an uncle to his brother's children. It seemed weird asking her a question he should know the answer to, but thought she probably already recognized, like everybody else did, how the two brothers weren't really friends.

Eddie giggled. "Ruby's preggers, so I hope he does."

Twisting to face her, he stared in shock at her brilliantly happy face. "No shit?"

"Shit free." Leaning in, she gave him a quick hug and then backed up the hall towards an open door. "Barely, but this is good." A serious expression hit her face, and he grimaced because he knew this was about Ruby getting kidnapped. "She didn't get pregnant until after everything, so she and Slate can just be happy about it. And they are." Gesturing to the door, she waited. "Come on, play your guitar for me. I love music." She grinned and teased him as he hesitated. "Sing to me, kind sir. Regale me with one of your, no doubt, many talents."

An hour later, his fingers had a steady, deep burn stinging the tips, but he and the guys had an audience of four smiling faces he wouldn't trade a full venue for. The oldest brother, Rafe, wandered in early during the session and sat on the floor next to Eddie, who was leaning against a bed. She already had Miguel's head in her lap, so Rafe took possession of her shoulder, angling into her. Roddy, the middle boy, was lying on his back, head pointed towards where Benny, Vic, and Mitty were seated on the second bed, chin tipped to the ceiling so he could look at them upside down. Eddie seemed to have forgotten baseball practice and Benny didn't remind her, not wanting to break the moment. He and the guys were jamming and flowing, rolling the lead back and forth between the guitars; Vic showed himself a taskmaster, pounding on the beatbox and sounding out the rhythm, keeping them marching ever forwards.

The door opened to show Bear with Andy walking in behind him. Eddie startled and looked at her watch, wrinkling her nose. Bear went to her first, stooping to ruffle Miguel's hair and then cupped her jaw, lifting her mouth to his. It wasn't sappy or stupid, didn't make him look pussy whipped or foolish, simply a natural action that let you know this couple was affectionate like this all the time. It looked good, sweet, and beautiful. She whispered to Bear, and he grinned, kissing her again, a quick reassurance for whatever worry she'd shared.

Grabbing a well-worn six-string off a stand by the closet, Bear settled onto the bed near where Eddie sat while Andy leaned a shoulder against the doorframe. Looking at Bear, Benny asked, "Anything in particular?" Vic and Mitty laughed, and Bear grinned at them before turning back to Benny. "What?"

"Dude can play anything," Vic said, starting a distinctive beat using the heels and palms of his hands to improvise the bass lead-in for a hugely popular song. "Check this." Looking at Bear, he grinned, bobbing his head in time. Eyes closed, Bear listened for a minute, then he smiled, fingers moving on the strings, and he rounded the corner on the melody, picking up where Vic was in the tune. Mitty—Benny had adopted the nickname already—grinned, also falling into line.

Benny listened for a minute more, then found his place. Support to Bear's lead, counter to Mitty's adaptation of the bass line, Vic taking over the percussion. Perfect. Seamless. As if the four of them had been playing together forever. They went from that to an 80s classic, which got Andy's fingers snapping, and then to a different decade, followed by another current popular selection. Eyes closed, Benny followed the lead of whoever felt moved to pull them into a song.

A discordant twang pulled Mitty's playing to a halt, and Benny opened his eyes to see his friend nursing a finger, pulling it from his mouth to see blood welling from a cut caused by a broken string. "My cue," Eddie said, sliding Miguel to one side, the deeply-sleeping boy not waking. Andy moved to one side, as pushing to her feet, she walked out while the musicians all stretched hands, which seemed to be painfully cramping all of a sudden.

Benny glanced at the window to see only artificial lights outside. *Jesus, we've played all afternoon and into the night.* A noise at the hallway caught his attention, and he twisted in time to catch the barest glimpse of what might be the most beautiful woman he'd ever seen. Dark hair trailing over her shoulders and down her back, she walked past the doorway and down the hall, calling in a musically accented voice, "Eddie, I'm home."

Benny ripped his gaze away from the door to see Andy watching him closely, eyes narrowed. *What now?* He shivered, the beauty of the woman moving through him in a way he felt might mark him forever. Memories of dreams from rehab washed over him, and he closed his eyes.

Dark eyes, red lips, smiling up at me. Singing.

Fingertips touching the strings of the guitar, gliding over the frets and stopping, then moving, stopping, strumming. Humming, he sang in his head, *If you'd told me I'd see her once and be hooked, I'd laugh at you. If you'd told me her beauty would call to me in the night, I'd laugh at you. If you'd promised me a lifetime of beauty like hers, I'd laugh at you. Knowing nothing is as sweet, nothing is as pure as the promise of love.*

"What's that?" Bear called across the narrow space between them.

Benny shook his head, fingers already digging for his phone. "Nothing," he lied, and Bear laughed, clearly understanding what was going on.

"Gimme a sec," Benny muttered, then froze in place as Bear's fingers picked out the song as Benny had played it, then added alters to make it better, embellishing and changing phrasing in a way that made Benny's fingers itch to play. "Wait up. Jesus. Hold on," he said impatiently, then hit record on his note app, frustrated because when the music had him in its grip like this, wringing his heart in his chest, nothing moved fast enough to keep up. "Okay, go."

Picking up the main melody, Benny held it steady, repeating the verse phrasing until Bear and Vic were with him, Bear adding in the alters again, changing it up even more. Then Benny opened his mouth and softly, so softly it felt like he was in church back in Enoch, whispering on the back bench with Danny, he sang.

When the last notes died away in the room, he looked up to see Bear grinning at him, lips stretched wide in his face. "Exquisite, man. Honored. Nothing more beautiful than the birth of a song."

Benny grinned back and was looking down to save the file on his phone when he heard Eddie coming back up the hallway. Eyes to his phone, he didn't see the two women walk into the room, so was startled when he heard the musical voice again, so close he could feel it against his skin. Looking up, he had a brief glimpse of her face before she angled away to talk to Rafe. He focused on her eyes first. Luminous and brown, they fit perfectly in her beautiful face. Then he saw her mouth, generous, full lips. Lips he wanted to feel moving under his.

She lifted her chin, and he had a flash, like a memory, but knew he'd never met her before. He was sure he'd remember her. If there were a million women lined up, he would pick her out if he'd ever been blessed to see her before. In his head, music and lights surrounded her, and he could swear he saw her crimson lips moving, smiling as she sang along to an OY song. Shaking his head, he finished with the file, tucking his phone back into his pocket. "Feels good." He belatedly responded to Bear's statement, picking the guitar back up, hissing through his teeth when he set his fingertips back to the strings.

"Give it a rest, Benny. You don't have anything to prove to me, man." Mitty scowled at him over Eddie's head as she wrapped tape around his finger. "That was a good one to end on if you want." Shaking his head, Mitty looked at Eddie. "Well, doc, am I gonna live?" Benny shivered at the words, not sure why they bothered him.

Laughing, she tucked his finger into his palm, closing the rest of his fingers around it. "I think so." Twisting to put one knee to the floor, she looked up at Benny. "This is Bear's daughter, Lucia. She's Rafe and the boys' sister."

Lucia. He would definitely remember her name. Still filled with the unsettling thought that he'd met her before, he smiled and stuck out his hand. "Benny Jones." With her chin tucked to her neck, she gave him a quick smile before lifting one hand in a wave, keeping her distance and leaving him hanging in a way no one in the room could miss. Shifting to a similar wave, he said, "And you're Lucia. Pleased to meet you." Definitely not a fan. *Shit.*

It felt as if every person in the room were staring at him. He had performed in front of hundreds of fans, lit up like a Christmas tree by spotlights, and never felt as exposed as he did at this moment. *Time to run away.* Jerking his gaze from her, he looked at Andy, feeling more like a kid than ever when he asked, "Ready to go home?"

Twelve

"I can't believe you're still living with your brother," Vic said on a laugh.

Benny leaned over to pick a glass off the floor, downing the last of the tea Ruby had brought him an hour ago. He grimaced at the watered-down taste of melted ice. "Me, either," he responded finally, tucking a strand of hair behind one ear. "Andy's still on his trip, though, and he wanted me to hang out here so Ruby wouldn't be alone."

"I heard that," a feminine voice called from upstairs, and Vic laughed. "It's a small apartment, baby brother. I can hear—everything." She giggled, and he cringed. "But, you're in luck." Quick footsteps descended the staircase and Benny looked to see her approaching the couch, her beautifully rounded baby bump preceding her. Giddy with happiness about the pregnancy, she had been the perfect housemate. Their friendship had grown strong, and he felt close to her, closer than he'd ever felt to a woman, and Benny realized he did think of her like his sister. Bossy and sweet by turns, she hassled and managed him, making life better because she was there.

Ruby was never up in his face about his recovery, helping smooth things instead of making them harder. Once she learned his routine, he would find her patiently waiting for him at the door, keys in hand, so she could take him to scheduled meetings. Without him having to ask for favors, or having to put a difficult and embarrassing request into words, she saw the need and handled it. Like she handled his brother.

Against the doc's express orders to get Benny into an organized treatment plan, Andy had listened to Benny's promises about staying straight. He swore to Andy all he had to do was remember the last few times he laid eyes on their mom, and he'd turn away from anything mind-altering. Their deal was he'd attend at least three meetings a week, find a sponsor, and not slip. All threats aside, if he fucked up, he knew Andy would have him back in rehab so fast his head would spin. Just the thought of that Arizona desert wasteland was more motivation not to ever do it again.

So he hit the meetings and tried to make the available programs work for him. Some weeks saw his ass in a folding chair more than three times. Just trying to stay straight, keep his tally going in the right direction. Two hundred and fifty-three, and counting. But, every day saw him still struggling to hold in the wanting, that need so huge in his head, pounding and echoing through his thoughts, begging to be fed. The desire eating through his belly in a way he knew he needed help to beat it back. His sponsor was a cool dude, a local photographer who needed to stay sober so he could keep working. Sometimes all Benny had to do was text him, and when the response came in, simply seeing it would steady him, making it so he could breathe through the next sixty seconds.

One minute at a time. Still sober, he thought, looking up at her. "Why is my luck turning?" Pushing his lip out in a pretend pout, he whined, "I like my luck. Don't turn it. Stop touching my luck! Imma tell Andy."

"Silly," she said, flopping on the couch beside him, hand on the side of her belly. "Slate called." Grinning, the happiness poured out of her in a giddy flood, and he found himself smiling back at the petite beauty. "Guess who's going to New Mexico?"

"My brother finally wise up that if he left you alone here much longer, you're gonna pop before he sees you again?" He made the sound like a champagne cork, and her laughter bubbled out again, echoed by Vic's. "I take it you're headed out to see him?"

"Yeah." That one whispered word held a lifetime of longing, and he thought there might be something there. Closing his eyes, he tried to follow it, frustrated when nothing surfaced. *Nothing*. He'd written nothing in months. *Unless you count Lucia's song*, he thought, then dragged his fingers across the strings randomly, breaking the silence with the jangling noise. He and Vic had worked on the song he'd started calling "The Promise of Love," but it wasn't quite right yet. *We'll get it.*

Mitty had headed home to Michigan for a break, leaving Vic and Benny behind, but promised he'd be back in a heartbeat when they were ready to start performing.

Benny just wasn't ready, yet.

The idea of getting onstage gave him chills, making his insides shake as much as his fingers did a dozen times a day. He'd talked to Bear about it, learning how music came into his life, listening as his friend talked about losing his wife and daughter to a terrible accident. Loss that changed the fabric of his life in a way he was still struggling to recover from.

Bear said the music had saved him, was saving him still, and Benny hoped for the same outcome. Pushing himself every day to play longer, harder, take on different styles of music, force himself to sight-read and play by ear and utilize a dozen different tactics to make himself better. Mold his talent into a skill that would stay with him forever. Form himself into someone who could hold his own against Bear, or any other talent on the market here in the Fort.

A hand closed over his on the neck of the guitar. "Stop it," Ruby told him, glaring at him, nose scrunched. "You're doing fine. You're going to be fine." She shook her head, letting her hand fall away. "I'll be back in a week, tops." Leaning back, she propped one slim ankle on her knee, her belly filling the space created by her angled leg. "Vic can keep you in line." She slapped Vic's thigh with her palm, grinning between the two men bracketing her on the couch. "I gots faith in the boy."

***

Two days later he was seated in the exact same spot when his phone rang. Picking it up off the table, Ruby's info was on the screen. Concerned, he quickly answered, putting it to his ear. Before he could even get out a greeting, she was shrieking, half her words lost in her eagerness. "...osed, can you believe it? I didn't hardly get off the plane, and he's all, marry me, and I'm all, okay. And so there you go, it's good, right, Benny? It's good?"

"He asked you to marry him?" *Holy shit.* He knew Andy loved her—the emotion was plain on his face every time he looked at her—but to get married?

"More told me than asked." Ruby giggled, and he heard voices in the background. "I gotta go, Benny. I wanted to tell you first." She sighed, and he knew she was looking at whatever ring Andy had put on her finger. "I'll be your sister-in-law."

"Sister-in-truth," he countered, then asked, "Is it pretty?" She'd called him, not one of her friends. Not someone from the club. Him and that kind of sharing told him how much she'd grown to care for him. "I'm your brah now, Ruby mine."

She giggled again, and he heard Andy's voice in the background, calling her name. "Yes, it's beautiful. He did good, brah." She giggled again. "Nope, can't bring myself to call you that. I'll pick something else." Her tone was teasing. "Gotta be something you hate. I'll give it some thought, come up with a good one. You wait and see."

Rolling his eyes, he told her goodbye and then, because she started talking to Andy before the call disconnected, got to listen to her speaking animatedly, clearly communicating her love for his brother, the cadence of her speech rising and falling, flowing into something that made him smile.

Hmm. Fingers to the strings, he strummed slowly, the song taking shape in his mind. Music first, it rolled through his fingers, notes finding their place next to each other effortlessly. Then, once the music was firm in his head, the words came with the same simplicity. Complete and whole nearly from inception.

Ghost of love no more, you brought my desires into the sunlight. Passionate and strong, your love braces me, laces me, in places worn to pieces. Phantom pain erased by your hands, gold band joining us feels so right. Head lifted high, your love braces me, places me, in your hands, cradled.

He strummed through the melody again before he lost the thread, then he tapped record on his seldom-used phone app, working his way through the lyrics slowly.

That doesn't suck, he thought, and then his gaze caught on the cabinet beside the stove. In Andy's efforts to cleanse the house of booze, he'd missed one stash. A small pint of black label whiskey sat on the shelf behind that thin piece of painted wood. It stood next to a container of salt and a bottle of olive oil, and Benny knew it was probably a cooking additive, but still...the need whispered, *whiskey.* In his mind, he heard Ruby's giggle, happy and light, telling him her good news first. He mattered to her. "My sister-in-truth." Repeating the words he'd said to her helped give him strength when he was ready to pull his gaze away from the cabinet door standing between him and pleasant numbness. "Make her proud."

***

Walking into the club's base of operations the next day, he nearly crashed headlong into someone as they ran out the door, stumbling and dodging to one side to avoid the collision. "Whoa," he clipped, settling his guitar case on his shoulder again, then took a second look and realized it was Lucia. Their paths hadn't often crossed since that first day at Eddie's, but when they did, she seemed easygoing and sweet, a quick smile on her lips, even if she didn't say a lot. Today her eyes were red and tear-filled, hair tangled around her head like she'd been tearing her hands through it.

"Luce," he called, reaching out to steady her with one hand. "What's wrong, honey?"

Frozen in place, she jerked and shuddered, trying to hold the tears in check. Staring at him, she seemed frozen, saying nothing, so he tried again. "Luce, tell me what's happened?"

"Miguel." Her voice husky with emotion, she offered nothing more than her baby brother's name and Benny's gut clenched.

"What happened?" She needed to tell him Mickey was okay. He'd come to love the little turd. Mickey and Roddy both, Rafe, too. Bear's blended family. Benny suddenly remembered what happened to Bear's wife and daughter, and his grip on her arm tightened involuntarily. "What's happened to Mickey?"

"He…" She pulled in a breath, visibly steadying herself. "He broke his arm."

"Oh, thank God," he said, taking a huge breath, feeling relief washing through him, spilling side-to-side, coating and calming the terror gripping him tightly. "Is that all?"

Pulling away, she slipped from his grasp, and he missed the touch of her immediately. "Is that *all?*" Her question hissed through the air, and he watched as her mouth twisted, her head shaking side-to-side. She sniffed, fingers wiping her cheeks as her eyes flashed with anger. "I guess if you're a famous star, a little boy's pain isn't much to worry about. *Soy su hermana.*"

He was hurt by her tone and without thinking, snapped, "It's a lot better than what happened to Bear's family." When her face went white, he wished he could suck the words back down, bury them underneath anything he could find in order to ensure they'd never break free. "Honey, I'm sorry. I like the little shrimp a lot. I'm sorry he's hurt, I am. All I meant is a broken arm will heal." He stepped closer, not surprised when she took a matching step backwards. *Make it right.* "Are you headed home?" He knew she hadn't held her license for long, and didn't want to think of her driving in this state. "Let me give you a lift. We'll get there faster, I promise. Get you wherever Mickey is, yeah?" Intentionally, he echoed Bear's speech patterns, hoping to drive home the idea quickly.

"I'm sorry, Ben." She looked at the ground between them. "I wasn't thinking."

"Neither was I, Luce. Water under the bridge. The important thing is Mickey's gonna be okay. Now, let me get you home." Reaching out, he held his breath until she slipped her palm against his, holding on tightly as he led her to his borrowed car.

***

Leaning sideways, he whispered to Lucia, "I think he likes having two grandmas." It was six hours after he'd literally run into her at the club's place, and Miguel was finally installed on the couch in Bear's apartment. An apartment that was coincidently in the same building as Andy and Ruby's apartment. Lucia had been that close, and he never knew.

They were laughing at Bear's mom, Maggie, and the kids' grandmother, who everyone called Abuela, as they good-naturedly dueled to see who could give the kid the most prizes and treasures for being so silly as to get hurt.

He turned in time to see the smile Lucia turned towards the couch. Fond and affectionate, it softened her face in a way that accented her beauty. Everything he'd discovered about her, he liked. Nearly of a height with him, she had her hands tucked behind her back, shoulders against the wall they were sharing. Out of the way, but available in case Mickey needed her, she waited with a patience that spoke of deep love. Her lips parted, and his eyes dropped to see the tip of her tongue glide across her bottom one, his cock waking up at the sight. *Fuck.*

Jerking back to face the room, he saw Bear was standing in the opening to the kitchen area, watching Benny, an appraising look on his face. Fighting getting hard in a way he hadn't done for a long time, Benny gave him the wordless chin lift so many of the Rebel Wayfarers seemed to use as a covers-everything greeting. After a moment during which his contemplation of Benny stayed heavy and focused, he returned the gesture, turning to speak to Eddie where she was fiddling with the coffee maker.

"Yeah." This came from Lucia and pulled his attention back to her, seeing the expression on her face had softened even more, but now she was looking at him, and he didn't know what to make of that. Eyes falling to her lips again, he watched her pull the bottom one between her teeth, letting it slide out slowly, glistening with wetness, which made her already plump lips look even more so. Now his dick was doing a lot more than waking up, and he was afraid he would be looking for a pillow to hold in a minute.

"Benny." His name came from Bear across the room, and he jerked his head up, erection effectively managed with a single word from Lucia's dad. "Talk to Slate lately?"

Shaking his head, he decided he would share Ruby's news. "Talked to Rubes yesterday morning." He wouldn't have been able to derail the grin on his face if he tried. "He met her with a ring when she got off the plane." Bear started grinning back at him. "She was a little...excited."

"What?" That shriek came from Eddie, who pushed Bear to one side as she forced her way into the living room. "DeeDee," she turned to speak to the redhead coming out of the kitchen behind her. "Did you know about this?" DeeDee might not be Ruby's birth mom—that bitch was as poor an example of motherhood as his own was—but she had effectively raised Ruby since the girl befriended her daughter in grade school. Her daughter died in a car accident alongside DeeDee's husband. Benny cut his eyes to Bear. Like his wife and daughter.

"Slate showed me the ring," DeeDee murmured, her face holding as much love for his brother as Lucia's had for Mickey a moment ago. "Glad he decided to take the leap." Her gaze turned to Benny. "She called you?"

Uh oh, this might be tricky, he thought. With a slow up-and-down movement of his head, he said, "Yeah, she's turned into my big sister. Gonna be my sister-in-truth we decided." That should explain the relationship he had with Ruby, without making it seem odd she called him and not the woman who might as well be her mom.

"I'm glad she's got you." DeeDee's words were honest and filled with joy, not upset Ruby hadn't called her, hadn't picked up the phone, more than a full day later.

***

Baby. Benita's voice drilled down through the drunken haze engulfing him. He liked it here. He didn't want to wake up. Didn't want to lose the fog that gave space between himself and the pain that seemed to be his entire life. Baby.

The voice held more than a hint of an accent, and he found himself squinting up at the unsmiling face hovering over him. "Benny."

Blinking up at the beautiful cocoa-colored skin and warm brown eyes, the first thing he thought with any clarity was *Fuck*. His mouth wasn't connected yet, wasn't working. Mute, not enough synapsing connections working right now to drive the engine behind his most useful deflection weapon. "Benny."

His stomach revolted, and he turned his head sideways, trying not to vomit on the woman seated on the edge of the couch. Even with Andy and Ruby gone, he still couldn't bring himself to sleep in their bed. That was theirs, nothing to do with the trash that was his existence. Trash he'd proven wasn't far away with his decisions last night. He moved, and a loud clunk announced the heavy-bottomed, but now entirely empty black label whiskey bottle had fallen to the floor.

"Get out." Face to the back of the couch, he squeezed his eyes shut, waiting to feel the weight leave the cushion at his hip. He swallowed convulsively, still trying not to vomit, knowing from his vast experience, he'd be losing the battle within a few minutes.

"Benny." Could a voice carry the weight of disappointment and sadness? Seemed so, because hearing Lucia say his name again pressed against him, forcing him deeper in the couch, keeping him where he was. Mired in his decisions. Again. "What happened?"

"Get out." He repeated his words, but with less conviction than before. If he had to open his mouth again, he'd lose what little control he had over his body, even now feeling his hold slipping away. His stomach jerked, and lurched again, and he jackknifed to sitting, feeling the room sway in a way that would not assist in achieving a settled stomach. A bowl appeared in front of him, and he grabbed it away from the small, feminine hands, dropping his head into the opening as he heaved. And retched. And gagged. Dribbles of bile the first thing to make an appearance. Burning yellow globs of acid setting his throat on fire, the familiar pain telling him how bad this was going to be.

Two hundred and seventy-four fucking days.

Back to zero.

Fuck.

Now the retching produced more quantity, this burning no less because the alcohol following the bile always bit deep. Loud groans coincided with each splash, his body moving involuntarily to purge the offensive substances. A clunk. Water running in a nearby room. The cushion settled at his back, and he hadn't even been aware she'd moved away. A cool cloth draped across the back of his neck, pulling a different kind of groan from him because it felt so good.

Silence accompanied her care of him. Hands changing out the too quickly heated wet cloth for a cool fresh one every few minutes. Exchanging the stench- and swill-filled bowl for a clean one. Fingers gliding soothingly up and down his back, gripping his biceps gently when he bent deep, wracked by cramps and shuddering in the grasp of his addiction. Because even now, right this moment, vomiting in front of the woman he'd been trying to deny he wanted, he wanted a drink so fucking bad it was all he could to do not beg her for a ride, for five dollars, for a bottle of booze to help him push back the pain of remembering.

"I'm sorry." He finally had enough breath to push the empty fucking words from his mouth. *I don't know what else to say. I don't have anything else to offer.* A clean bowl appeared, and he gave up his grip on the soiled one without argument, without lifting his eyes.

"I know." Her response was curious. Normally people would rush to tell him not to worry. That it wasn't his fault. That he could be better. Be more. Be stronger. If only he would do this one thing. That one thing. Every one thing. "My dad was an addict."

Better and better. Now he was as hopeless as her father, who'd died because he'd laid hands on Benny's brother's girlfriend. It reminded him he had a question, though. "Why are you here?"

"Your sponsor called Ruby. You didn't pick up, so she called me." Swallowing hard, he felt the burning in the back of his throat increase, knowing it was from tears rolling down his throat, forced back. "Since she left, you missed group, missed meetings, missed a call from him, but then you reached out last night. He wasn't available."

Benny barely remembered picking up the phone, bottle in one hand, the amber-colored liquid whispering promises and lies, phone in the other, a dead end, offering no connection to hook his anchor on this time. "When he got free and called, he said you didn't answer." Good news. If his sponsor didn't know Benny slipped, then he couldn't have told Ruby. If she'd known, she wouldn't have sent Lucia. She'd have told Andy, and he'd have flown back. Dropped everything as he always had to do to clean up Benny's messes. Or he'd have called someone else. Like Bear. *Fuck.*

"Bear." Not even aware his mouth was moving, he heard his voice, quavering and sounding stupid with badly hidden tears. "Did you tell him? Anyone?"

"Not yet. I wanted to make sure you were okay first." The too-hot cloth changed out for a cooler one, and he tipped his head sideways, trapping her fingers for a moment against his shoulder in silent thanks. "You know what triggered this?"

Her question tugged at his memory like a fishing line. Andy on the phone, telling Benny he and Ruby had spent the day with their mother. Saying she'd changed, pulled her head out of her ass, finally. Twenty years too late. "Andy called. He's mending bridges with our mom. She wasn't the best…influence when I was growing up. It was just us, most of the time—me and Andy. My dad's been dead for years. Since I was five." She shifted on the cushion, and he turned to look at her for the first time since she woke him. "I'd say it gets easier, but I think this proves that's a lie people tell to make themselves feel better when they stop talking about things." He groaned as another wave of nausea broke against his throat, causing him to sway in place on the couch.

"My dad's been dead nearly nine months." He remembered that part, counting by months because as they racked up, it became more bizarre that the person was gone so long. That you'd experienced so much without them being around to see. Andy gone, never seeing football games, driving lessons, prom night. Months morphing into years. Time marching on. Ever onward.

"Andy told me what happened." He shook his head, then stopped when she turned a confused look to him. His eyes swam for a moment, then settled, the two Lucias gradually resolving down into one.

"What happened? What do you mean?" Shit, now he'd put his foot in it. Of course Andy and Bear would protect her from that. No way was she aware of what her father had done. "What did Slate tell you?"

"That he was dead." Play the ignorant card, see if she believed a minute of it in his state. "What happened?"

"There was a break in." Her voice quavered, and he hated being the reason she was reliving this pain. "He got shot. At least he went fast." His stomach was slowly settling, along with the room around him, ceasing wavering and circling as things clicked back into place. Now, time for damage control.

"I'm sorry you had to deal with that. And then to have to help your brothers through his death, pushing past your own sorrow. Amazing. You must be so strong, Luce." She shifted, uncomfortable with the praise, faint as it was. "I can see how they all depend on you." Rafe needed her more than Benny had understood at first; his autism masked by the boy's silent and withdrawn personality. After seeing Roddy and Mickey with her, he had noted the differences between the boys were more marked than he realized. "Bear, too." Since taking on an entire instafamily, Bear leaned on her a lot. "You're stronger than you give yourself credit for, honey."

Now the glance she flicked him was annoyed, and he didn't know why. "I do what's needed." She stood, taking the bowl out of his hands, stripping the damp cloth from the back of his neck, leaving the spot feeling wet, vulnerable, and cold in an uncomfortable way. "I'll be back with food in a minute." Not asking what he wanted, which was good because he didn't want anything. Would have turned down all options right now. But knowing he needed to eat, he nodded. No doubt she'd show up with the perfect thing for a tender stomach ill abused by a drunkard. Ten minutes later, she did, rousing him from the half sleep he'd dropped into as soon as he got horizontal.

Grilled cheese and strong coffee. Just greasy enough to taste good, and perfect to absorb the rest of the shit in his gut. Wordlessly he struggled upright, accepting the plate and putting it carefully on his crossed legs. Staring at the food, he pulled a bite-sized piece off the sandwich he bemusedly noticed was cut on a diagonal. *Totally a chick with little brothers.* She settled onto the couch at the far end from where he sat, resting comfortably against the cushions as if she'd been there a million times. He asked, "You know Ruby well?"

"Yeah. Not friends, but friendly. Not like her and Lockee. They were really close. But, yeah, I've known her for a while." Lockee was DeeDee's daughter who'd died.

"Ruby talked like they were more sisters than friends." All he could do was talk about dead people today, it seemed. He stuffed another small bite of sandwich in his mouth, frowning.

"They were." No jealousy or anger there, simply an acknowledgment of what was. "Daddy wasn't a..." She hesitated, and he wasn't sure why. After a minute, she seemed to gather her thoughts, leaning forward to sit straight. "Daddy wasn't a good member. He didn't understand how Rafe was, always believed his behaviors were a choice, not a...disability. We didn't go to events with him because he was afraid Rafe would embarrass him...us. I'd usually stay home to take care of the boys." Still no anger, which seemed real, but he found himself hating what her statement said about her growing up.

"My mom's an addict. A drunk. Alcohol is her drug of choice." As he spoke, Lucia's hand appeared, snagging a small piece of bread crust he'd pulled free. *Stealing from my plate like we're friends.* He liked that. A lot.

More than was prudent, given who her father was. "Andy called last night." He swallowed, the edges of a suddenly too-dry bite gouging ditches on its way down his throat. "I already told you, I know. It's just weird. We've hated her for a long time. He saw her yesterday. And now he's gonna invite her up here for his and Ruby's wedding." Twisting his neck, he chanced a glance at Lucia to see her studying him. "I haven't seen her in years. Hate her. Hate what she did to our family after Daddy died. I lost everything when he died. My home, my family. Everything."

Unfolding a leg, he toed the empty bottle, shifting it to one side, hearing the echoes of his retching in the grating slide of glass on wood. "Got off the phone with Andy. Remembered there was some whiskey in the house." Pulling his leg back, he kicked the bottle, sending it rocketing into the kitchen where it ricocheted out of sight. "I tried. Swear to God, I did. But the more I thought about not drinking the more I wanted to drink." He shoved another bite into his mouth, furious with himself for saying anything. *Weak. So fucking weak.*

"Sucks you didn't have the tools you needed." No censure in her tone, no disappointment at his failure. She leaned close, and he shivered when he felt her fingers working under his thigh. That was a surprise move, intimate in a way he wanted but was afraid of, so he lifted and pulled back in reaction even as he wanted to push forwards. She grinned as she came up with his phone, fingertips dancing across the screen before she paused. Her ass buzzed, and he realized she'd called herself from his phone. "Now you have my info. If you can't get in touch with your sponsor, you can call me." She dropped his phone to the cushions next to his ass. "That sandwich gonna stay down?"

He nodded, watching her face intently. She wiggled to the edge of the couch and paused there. "Call me if you need me, okay, Benny?" He nodded, and she stood. Turning, he watched her walk out of the apartment without looking back. *That*, he thought, *felt like a beginning.*

Thirteen

"Why did I have to wear old clothes?" Luce was laughing up at him, trying to match his running strides, his hand clasped around hers pulling her along with him. They were racing through the big park near Andy's apartment, Luce having come over when he called with a wild idea, luring her in with a promise of fun. He had two things with him, both important to this plan.

"Because I said so," he yelled back at her, smiling to see the wide grin on her face in response, her head shaking in dismissal at his silliness. "Hurry." They were nearly there, and he took the four steps down to the splash pad in a single jump, feeling her flying through the air beside him. "Here."

Quickly he positioned her, shushing her questions as he assumed his own place nearby, their heads nearly touching, shoulders side-by-side, feet pointed in different directions. "Wait for it." He urged patience, even as he wanted to go faster and faster. They'd spent a lot of time together over these past weeks. As often as he saw her, it was never enough for Benny, and he hoped he hid it from Luce, but more from Bear. *Never enough*. It could take a lifetime to explore every nuance of joy on her face. "Wait for it." A nearby clock pinged, and he took a breath, then on the exhale, whispered, "Now."

A clicking rumbled under their backs and then the air was filled with water. Arching over their heads, crossing their bodies. Big fat droplets were cascading down onto her face and, eyes closed, chin tipping to the sky, she lay drinking in the sensation. With a flick of his wrist, he opened one object in his hand, settling the umbrella over their faces. Water tumbled down the sides and created a curtain separating them from the world. Phone in hand, he quickly shot picture after picture of her laughing face in close-up. Right there, so close he could touch, could kiss were he brave enough.

Since the unfortunate beginning of their friendship, tied up in her brother's pain and his failure, they'd spent part of nearly every day together. Most often just being quiet, she soothed him and brought a deep peace with her, so that sitting beside her on the couch became moments free from the bite. When they were out, they talked, chattered at each other, and probed the edges of the attraction they both felt. Soft touches, glances weighted with meaning neither were ready to act on yet, but every moment with her built something inside him. Something good and right.

In those times, Benny often found himself surging forwards, then reining himself in, pulling back, because she mattered. Mattered to him, and to his brother, because of who her dad was. He wanted her, felt her confusion when he edged them back from the line that would change things.

Turning to face him, she reclined on her side, pillowing her head on one arm. Slow blinks of her gorgeous browns. Spellbound within the illusion of privacy created by the water raining down. "Perfect." That was all she said and all he needed. Relaxing, he let his head fall to the metal and cement underneath them, hand clutching the phone that would carry his memories of this moment. Another reason he could use to not fail. *My Lucia.*

Eyes closed, he listened to the sound of her breathing over the splashing water, the echoing space under the umbrella making it seem as if she'd moved closer. Then he felt the heat from her on the side of his face, the sensation freezing him in place. "Thank you, Benny," her whisper hit his skin like a brand, followed by her lips pressing to his cheek, burning the moment deeper into his memory. Indelibly marked. *Forever.*

Without conscious thought, he lifted the phone and blindly pointed it at their heads where they lay curled around the other like a yin-yang symbol.

"Anytime, honey." Her lips touched his cheek again, and he breathed in air she was making richer simply by being there. Repeating himself softly, he whispered a promise. "Anytime."

***

Benny held a smile in place on his face, the same one the radio DJs saw whenever they'd ask for an unscheduled acoustic performance on-air while they were on-air, leaving him with no good way to decline. "Sure, DeeDee," he lied through his teeth, "I'd be happy to go to the party store."

"Great," she said, turning away from him to stare at the lists she had taped to the kitchen cabinets. Why she decided she needed to do the wedding planning in Andy's apartment, he'd never understand. She had a perfectly good condo and a man who could help with whatever running around she had to do, but no, she'd picked here and him. "Luce can go with. She'll have a good eye for color. You're doing me a huge favor, kiddo."

Well, if I'd known Lucia was going, I would have been more gracious. "Sounds good." Keys in hand, he turned to leave when she called his name.

Looking back at her over his shoulder, he noted her expression was serious and concerned as she asked, "You doing okay, Benny?" She stood in front of the cabinet where the whiskey once resided, and he felt a swirl of fear that she knew about his failure. Luce had promised not to tell anyone, but still, it was a big thing to ask a girl whose recited memories of her father held more than one incidence of her performing exactly the duties she'd done for Benny. But she promised, and he got the feeling she didn't lie, so he pushed down his fear, readying himself to lie to DeeDee. Again.

"Right as rain, DeeDee. I'll head out." He leaned back and snatched the list she'd been writing and waggled it at her. "Gonna pick up Lucia. We'll do some shopping." He walked down the stairs, his preferred mode of transit these days, doing his best to avoid the elevator since the day he was trapped on a tour of three endless floors with Bear's mother. Maggie was nice enough, but she had a million questions about everything and didn't mind asking any of them. Groupies, drugs, crazy parties. Every story she'd ever heard about a touring rock band birthed a question.

Phone in hand, he made his way to the landing on the floor where Bear's apartment was. **U up 4 shop trip?**

A moment later, his phone vibrated in his hand. **Y**

On lndng. He waited, eyes to the little window that looked out into the hallway, watching as the beauty of Lucia filled his vision. She walked out of the apartment, turned to look over her shoulder, laughing, and even without hearing her, he knew the laugh was beautiful. A sound he could make a mint on if he could bottle it and release it to the world a little at a time. Shoving the handle down, he pulled the door open just as she got to the opening, losing sight of her for only a moment before her eyes hit his, crinkled at the corners, echoes of laughter in her voice as she asked, "Wedding shopping?"

He rolled his eyes and nodded, and she reached out, grabbing his hand in a movement that was so natural it would feel odd to walk with her and not be hand-in-hand. *Her touch is so perfect. Just like she is.*

She grinned. "Let's go then. *Vamonos!* Procure the goodies for the happy couple's pending nuptials." He let her lead him, mostly because it caused her to glance back and up at him frequently, so he got to see her face as she rattled on brightly about her day. How much better Miguel was doing, how Eddie and Bear were, how things were good in her world right now. It also gave him a bird's eye view of her glorious ass. *Best of both worlds.*

***

Three hours later, he walked her into Marie's. Not a place he wanted to be, but not one he could avoid due to the association with his brother's friends. It was still not somewhere he was overly comfortable. These days he had mixed feelings because it was the location of his most embarrassing failure, but also the place he'd first seen Lucia. He knew that much, even if he didn't remember anything else from that night. Luce was laughing and talking as he led her through the room to a booth near the back, waving to get the waitress' attention as they made their way through the crowded tables.

"I'm starved," he said, letting Lucia slide into the booth, waiting to see where she settled to take his cue on where to sit. She slipped far over, leaving three foot of room on the end, so he turned and sat next to her. Elbows to the table, he reached for one of the menus propped against the inside wall. "What do you want to eat?" When she remained silent, he turned to see her staring fixedly down at the table. *What the hell?*

Twisting to look at the room, he found there were a half a dozen men glaring holes through him. Every one of them had on a vest similar to Andy's, so he assumed they were all Rebel Wayfarers. As Luce's dad had been. *Shit.* "Honey," he turned back to her, "let's go somewhere else." They hadn't ordered yet; it wouldn't be awkward at all to slip out as they'd slipped in. He figured it would be far less uncomfortable than her sitting here wondering what those men were thinking of her being out with the drunk.

As he moved to slide out, a body blocked his way. "You're stayin' right here, boy." The big man leaned around Benny to look at Lucia. His voice was gentle when he said, "Luce, honey, give me five minutes with Ben." She scrambled into action, pushing at Benny's ass, shoving him out of the way as the man muttered, "Thanks, honey." A hand hit his chest, and he rocked backwards, the edge of the booth catching him behind the knees and his legs folded up. Suddenly ass to seat, he didn't say anything as the man wedged himself into the booth opposite, and Benny's attention was captured by a group of men who had moved closer. They were now standing with their backs to the booth, facing the room's occupants in a loose half-circle. Guard dogs for whatever was about to go down.

"You don't know me." Not a question, the man led with the obvious, propping an elbow on the table, one finger pointing to his own chest. "Mason." He paused for a moment, staring hard at Benny's face, then gravel-filled laughter swelled and faded, his mouth hardly moving, features caught in an expression which was mostly scowl, but also part disgruntled amusement. Shaking his head, he said, "Nope, you don't know shit."

Leaning back, Mason stretched out, hooking his elbows across the back of the seat on his side, eyes drilling holes in Benny, who found his skin covered with sweat, soaking through the pits of his shirt like he was sick with the flu. Daunting didn't cover it. The dude was fucking scary as hell. "Slate say much to you before he left? After he hauled his ass to Arizona to bring your ass home?" Benny shook his head, pleased when he could stop the shuddering movement after only four or five wild swings. "Fuckin' figures." Mason shook his head. "He's always protected you best he could."

Movement in the group of men around them caught Benny's eye, and he looked up to catch a half wave from DeeDee's man, Jase, before the man turned around, fitting himself into the circle as if there had been a space waiting on him all his life. Gaze back to Mason, he waited. What this man had said meant he didn't truly know Andy, not the brother who'd left Benny alone for so long.

"Ruby got taken." Mason's words were blunt. With a wince, Benny nodded, because he knew that much. "Man did it was Rabid." He'd heard Andy talking about this, knew Rabid was Lucia's father's club nickname. He nodded again. "Luce don't know it, can't know it. I'm probably stupid as fuck to tell you this, but I wanna see if the man your brother loves is in there. Trusting you with this, so you better fuckin' keep your lips zipped, but it was me. I killed him."

This was stated so baldly, so matter-of-factly he couldn't help his reaction. His eyes widened, and he muttered, "What the *fuck*?"

"I killed him. Popped a cap in his fuckin' head. He put his hands on something he shouldn't have even looked at, shoulda never taken his hands to." Mason shook his head. *Jesus.* Leaning forward, Mason unfolded his arms, propping elbows to the tabletop, palms clasped in front of his face as he peered at Benny around those powerful hands, fingers adorned with silver rings. Covered in tattoos, he was the definition of biker and unbelievably imposing. *Oh, hell yeah. I totally believe he shot a man.* "Do it again." Mason focused on Benny, their gazes locked together. *And Luce doesn't know. I can't tell her. He's trusting me with this.* "Anybody fucks my brother over, I'd do it again."

That didn't make sense. Ruby wasn't his brother, not even in the way these men used the word. "What?"

"Slate." *Oh, fuck.* "My brother. Known him a longass time. Trust him more than nearly any living being on this earth. I'd do anything for him." Mason leaned in, lips pressing against the side of his clasped hands as he paused a moment, then he sighed. "Even take out his own family's trash if it's needful. You gonna get this one warning, boy."

Benny's breath had frozen. His lungs seized in his chest as the weight of the threat crashed in on him. Mason would kill him for Andy. *Kill me.*

"One warning. All you're gonna get, Benny boy. You fuck your brother over again, you're fucking with my family, and I'll tell you this: Blood might make you related, but loyalty makes you family. Right now, you're nothing to me but a bug running from dung heap to dung heap, spreading the touch of shit along the way. You work at it? Put your mind to it? You might become something to me." He leaned in deeper and Benny felt himself pressing into the bench cushions at his back, trying to gain another inch of distance from this man. "You don't work at it? Your brother won't ever give up on you, but you're rippin' him up with small doses of your shit, plain as if you killed him outright. I won't tolerate it."

Mason leaned back, and Benny began to feel as if he could breathe again, so he tried, but his intake of air was as jittery as a meth addict's fingers holding a pipe. In and in, seeming never to end, his chest expanding with the release of pressure and he wondered if his muscles would be able to support him, if he could even move. Mason's next words froze his breath again, threatening mode still fully engaged. "You fuck over our girl, I'll own your ass in a different way. She's had enough shit in her life, too. Don't need you shoveling any on top of her own family's more than ample contributions."

"I never meant to..." His voice trailed off as Mason's expression sharpened, focusing back on him so attentively he felt like a rabbit with a hound arrowing straight at him.

"Intent matters, but only if you're honest about it. Meaning doesn't count when you know full well it's the doing that fucks people over." Mason shook his head. "Slate won't tell you this. He loves you and wouldn't want to lay the burden on you of what mighta happened, but you need to know, so I will. Your brother leveraged himself for you. Him against all those fuckers you owed. Nearly a war, and if it had gone one single fucking inch to one side or the other, it would have been war. I'd have been required to bring the entire weight of the club in behind him, having his back when it counted. Because family watches out for family. All so he could clean up your drunken-assed shit."

Mason gestured to the backs of the men standing silently, and Benny knew they were close enough to hear every word of his humiliation. That didn't hurt as much as knowing Lucia had seen him drunk and vomiting into a bowl while she held it. But it still burned.

He shook his head and focused back on Mason, who was eyeing him curiously. Once Mason knew Benny was listening, he spoke again, "Your brother loves your ass, man. Loves you. Loves the club, but he loves you, too. He would have hated it, but he still would have pulled the club in with him. Half the men standing here would be dead right now if we did that. Would have been a war like no one's ever seen." Leaning back towards the table, Mason rested a hand between them, finger tapping the top of the table in an insistent way. Thudding like a heartbeat, racing faster and faster. "Men with families. Wives. Lovers. Kids. Hell, brothers. Dead because of you." Benny felt sick, thinking about DeeDee's face this morning, knowing she'd already lost so much, thinking, *What if Jase had been one of the fallen?*

"I see that's sinking in." The weight of Mason's stare didn't lessen. "See a lot of what I said sinking in. You let it get in there deep where you can't ever question the rightness. Because I ain't foolin' with you, boy. You fuck up, fuck Slate over, you'll be history in a way he can't set right. Slate'll hate it, but in his gut, he'll know I did him right. Might hate *me*, but that's something I can live with, knowing I done my brother right." They stared at each other for a long time, the noise of the bar muted, seeming to not exist beyond the patched circle of men's backs, men who might have died because of him. "We're done here."

With a sigh, Mason shifted and stood, looking down at Benny for a long minute. His expression lightened, and he said something so ludicrous Benny's brain arrested for a moment. "Get the tenderloin. It's good."

Bitter laughter burst from Benny and the corners of Mason's mouth tipped up, but his eyes stayed cold, evaluating. "Advice is free, boy. So's the sandwich. On the house. It's all on the house tonight." A pause. "My treat." Mason's finger tapped on the table, echoing the rhythm from before. A reminder. "Take it or leave it." Benny knew Mason was talking about so much more than the choice of entrees, and he didn't mistake the look that sliced through him before the man turned on his heel and walked away.

With a scuffle of boot soles, the men retreated to the tables they had previously occupied, and Benny watched as they sat back down with friends and family. Groups of men all around the room, as Mason had said, dining out with wives and children, brothers and sisters, even what looked like parents or grandparents sitting with one man. Benny watched as he leaned in, kissing the older woman softly on the cheek, her eyes lighting as her cheeks lifted in a smile.

Lucia hurried up, gaze locked on his face and he stared as she slid into the seat opposite him. Same seat same position, but her presence not carrying nearly the fear factor Mason's had. Luce's presence pushed him past the threat, and reminded him of something Mason said. *He trusted me enough to tell me his secret about her dad. He thinks I can do this, stay sober, stay straight. He wouldn't have warned me if he didn't think I could do this. Mason strikes me as someone who'd act instead of talking, so maybe he wants me to succeed. For Andy. For Luce. For me.* "You okay?" She smiled, the expression strained, and he was glad when it quickly faded. "Mason's *muy* intense."

"Yeah, he is. But I'm okay. He's got some good points, savvy advice. And recommendations." Carefully replacing the menu between the wall and napkin holder, he said, "I'm gonna have the tenderloin."

"Good choice." She grinned, slotting her menu alongside his, reaching out to slip her fingers under his and he accepted the offer, curling his hand around hers and holding tight. "I'll join you."

 Fourteen

6 WEEKS LATER

Benny sat on a log near a roaring bonfire, listening to the music lifting into the air all around him. Some from boom boxes and speakers, but most came from a variety of instruments including dulcimers, flattops, mouth harps, and the beauty that was an a cappella song. *What a perfect day*, he thought, making a mental note to thank DeeDee again for all her hard work. Andy and Ruby were on their way to the Georgia coast for their honeymoon, leaving all their worries in the cloud of dust that lifted in a rooster tail behind Andy's bike. Now it was dark, and the Rebel Wayfarers celebratory party had swung into high gear once the sun went down. Even with that, the mood was mellow and sweet for the most part. Benny grinned into the darkness as a loud shout and splash sounded near the lake. Some groups might be a tad rowdier than others.

"Fuck." The muttered curse came from behind him, the voice one he recognized. Benny twisted in place to watch a young man making his way across the grounds. Benny frowned when he saw Chase, Mason's son, carrying a partial six-pack of mixed beers in his hand. Andy had brought Benny up to speed on the relationship between the boy who desperately wanted to fit in anywhere, and the man who threatened Benny's life in a local restaurant. Not that Andy knew a single word of what went down with Mason, but it would be an encounter Benny would never forget. *Another reason to stick to the straight and narrow*, he thought, shivering as he remembered the weight of Mason's displeasure. *An extremely compelling one.*

"Heey." Only the slightest of slurs marred Chase's voice as he stumbled over absolutely nothing, staggering the last couple of feet to the log. "Benny." Chase leaned over to set down the lop-sided cardboard container of bottles; his body elaborately angled to keep his balance, and Benny felt a sadness sinking inside him. He was this kid at fourteen, drunk but holding tight to the illusion that no one noticed.

Benny had been able to fake things for a long while because the people who surrounded him either didn't give a shit or wanted him wasted. He liked Chase, liked how the kid worked hard at learning how to play guitar. Worked hard at things his dad never knew about, like blending so as not to embarrass. Benny knew he could give Mason's boy more than he'd gotten as a kid. Could give him better, let him know people gave a shit. *Call it like I see it. Like Andy would.*

"You're drunk." His words dropped into the stillness like a rock into a pool. "Not stupid drunk yet, not blackout drunk, but well on your way. And it shows if you look close enough. I'm looking, Chase." Chase straightened and stared through the darkness at him, shadows hiding his expression. "I get it, the wanting to grow up and be what you see around you." Chase's head shook the slightest amount, and Benny wondered if he'd gotten it wrong, deciding to try a slightly different tactic.

"I get wanting to block shit out, and booze? Oh, man, booze is great at that." Chase didn't react to this gambit, and he knew he was probably hitting closer to home now. "Shit happens in our lives, and it's easier to numb the shit out of it than think about it. Numb becomes a go-to response. Shit happens? We drink it out, pill it down, snort it away. Numb ourselves until we can be convinced that shit doesn't matter. Nothing matters. But it does." He leaned forwards, trying to emphasize his next words. "It matters even more at that point. This,"—he gestured to the beer—"it ain't the right way, Chase."

Benny paused, trying to compose his thoughts. *Make it real. Tell him what he's got.* "You got a dad who gives a shit about you, Chase. Cares what happens to you, what's happening in your life. He's here, and he's giving you room to be the man you need to be, but he gives a shit. More than gives a shit, he's all over trying to be what you need. And he cares." Mason did. Benny had seen the truth with his own eyes more than once. "If you're struggling with something, you should talk to him." Finally out of words, Benny sat quietly, waiting.

Tipping his head backwards, Chase stared up at the sky for a moment, staggering a step before he caught his balance and looked down at Benny again. Chase's voice was tight when he muttered, "Mason. All I hear is Mason. I've only known him a couple years, did you know that? I saw him forty times total before my old lady dumped me on him. A man who never wanted kids, stuck with me, and I'm always just..."—he staggered again, dropping his ass to the log, finally—"in the way. Just in the fucking way. I'm a loser dragging him down. Not smart enough for real school because my ma kept me out almost all the time." He leaned over, pulling a bottle from the container positioned precariously next to his foot. "I ain't got nothing to offer him.

Chase struggled with the lid on the bottle, voice dropping to a near whisper. "First time I fucked up? He kicked me to the fuckin' curb." Chase's head came up, and he abandoned his efforts to open the bottle, inclining his body towards Benny, yelling, "Right to the mother. Fuckin'. Curb. Muthafuckin' curb." Clapping his hands together, he lost his hold on the beer, and it fell to the dirt, the condensation on the sides turning it to mud, a thick layer covering the bottle. "Fuck." Chase looked down at the bottle as if it were unfamiliar. "One strike and I'm out? That's jacked, man. I wanted back in so bad, do anything. Tried hard. Got beat down every time. Jacked. Muthafuckin' curb." He gestured wildly with one arm. "Well, fuck that. And fuck him."

"Chase." Benny leaned over, picking up the bottle and wiping it casually with his fingers before slotting it back into the six-pack holder. "I think you've got it entirely wrong." Chase shook his head, but Benny continued. "Lemme break it down for you. You might not remember it all tomorrow," he grabbed a bottle of water from the stash Lucia had brought him earlier and pressed it into Chase's hand, "but if you remember even a little of it, you'll be better off than you are now." He nabbed the beers and put them on the other side of the log, away from the fire and light. *Out of sight, out of mind. Yeah, right.*

"Mason thinks a lot of you. So much, I'd have never known you weren't raised by him. He's so easy and comfortable with you. Loves you, man. Clear as day. I don't know what kind of relationship he had with your mom, but I know what he has with you." Cradling his guitar, he strummed the strings softly. "I don't think he sees you as a fuck-up. Certainly not a loser. He loves you. Your mom doesn't sound like the sharpest stick, man. You sure she got the details right?" He fell into a well-memorized rhythm; an old Occupy Yourself song he'd written about himself.

Humming, he picked up the melody's thread, nodding when Chase started mouthing the words. "Queen of what you hated." All his life, his mother had been the queen of hearts in the hand dealt him by life. "Life gone wrong, no room for space." She'd never had room for him. Not since he was a kid. Not since his daddy died. "Heels tottering in the nighttime." Benny bowed his head, having seen his mother this weekend, even keeping his distance, he knew the words no longer fit her, but things were what they were when he was a kid, and that was what this song was. *The legacy of my childhood.* "Smears and fears of living, written on your face."

Moving with jerky motions, he set the guitar aside, surprise on Chase's face at his abandonment of the song. "That song's for my mom, Chase. How she made me feel for a long time. I held onto the pain for...ever. Things happened, and she's ashamed of them, and I'm ashamed of what I did, too. But my behavior isn't her responsibility. It's mine. And your mother doesn't have one thing to do with you being drunk tonight."

Anger twisted Chase's mouth to the side, and Benny knew he was losing whatever tenuous hold he had on the kid. "But for me, writing it out helped. Putting it to music helped. Singing it a million times? That helped, too. Until now." He picked the guitar back up, threading the melody with his fingertips again. "Not anymore. Those words don't hold any power over me." Changing the melody, he gave it an upbeat rockabilly sound, the lyrics bounding out of his mouth.

"Because I was born into trouble. Oh yeah, I was born to be trouble." Arm effortlessly strumming, he moved through the song. "My brother's burden." A voice lifted from the darkness, joining him and he grinned when he recognized Bear. "A burden no more. What's the matter with trouble, brother?" Bear and another man walked into the clearing, carrying six-strings, playing the song, following the alters effortlessly. "My brother's a beast, never gonna make his life a waste. Because I wasn't born to be trouble. No, oh, no I wasn't." He grinned when Luce followed her dad into the clearing. Benny felt his chest get tight when she had eyes only for him. They'd gotten so close over the past weeks, and now she was as important to his life as breathing. Maybe more. "Lines were drawn, oh yes, they were. Plans were laid. My plans, they changed, because I'm a burden no more."

She smiled broadly at him, then looked at Chase and made a face. Benny segued into another song he knew was a favorite for Bear and then let him lead their playing from there on. Lucia walked past him, fingertips trailing familiarly across the nape of his neck and he tipped his chin up, waiting until she leaned in and brushed her lips across his, glad that he had stopped trying to push her away. *Need you*, he thought, savoring her touch. Lifting an inch, she stared into his eyes for a moment and then, apparently satisfied at what she saw, moved to sit next to Chase where the boy immediately leaned into her, head on her shoulder. When she wasn't watching, Chase's eyes stayed fixed intently on her face, and Benny frowned, wondering what that was about.

Fifteen

"Beautiful, Andy." Benny's whisper was quiet, soft in the hallway outside Ruby's hospital room. The heel of Andy's boot held the door propped open; Ruby lay asleep in bed with two bassinettes full of babies next to her. "Twins? That's crazy." He knew his grin was crazy, too. Seeing how happy his brother was had bent something inside him clear over, making him grin like a loon at everyone.

"I know." Andy's answering whisper was just as soft. "I had no idea. Her belly was big, but I've never been around a pregnant woman before. How was I to know she was eatin' for three? She wasn't talking to me about it. And with her determined to keep the secret?" He sighed heavily, exhaustion and a deep joy playing across on his face. "Freaked me right the fuck out, I'll tell you. Glad they all came through okay." Shaking his head, he lowered his already soft voice more, barely even a whisper when he said, "If anything happened to her again, Benny? I don't know what I'd do."

"Nothing bad's ever going to happen to her," Benny spoke the words he most wanted to be true. Ruby had more than grown on him; she had quickly become a stable factor in his life, and like his brother, he couldn't imagine life without her around. *Sister-in-truth.* "Your brothers will all see to that." Andy turned to look at him when he spoke and Benny grinned. "Even me," he hesitated only a second before continuing, "Slate." It was past time to acknowledge the change in his brother, the depth of loyalty he'd found, building on the foundation he had with the Rebels.

Grinning widely, Slate tipped his chin down, staring at the floor for a minute. When he spoke, his voice was still quiet, but now thick with intensity, giving Benny a glimpse of the emotion he had deep inside. *Like my music.* "Proud as fuck of you, shrimp. You've done a hard thing and stuck with it." *Shit.* He hadn't lied to his brother about slipping yet, and his insides quivered as he came to a decision, unwilling to utter that lie now. Especially now, standing in the open doorway to Slate's entire future.

"You were in Colorado." He kept his voice quiet, and took a step back and to the side, trying to ensure his words wouldn't carry in to taint the air where Ruby and her two babies were sleeping. "I fucked up. Only the once, I *swear* it was just once. But, big brother, I won't lie to you. Not even by omission." He swallowed hard. "I fucked-up."

"I know." At his brother's flat tone, Benny lifted his head to see Slate staring steadily at him. "It was the night I called about Mom. I knew it. Had a feeling. Then your sponsor called Ruby, and I *knew*." Slate's voice rose, anger taking over as he said, "First taking Ruby away from you, and then talking about Mom? Knew I'd tipped you right the fuck over the edge. *Knew it.*" The expression on his face was twisting away from the joy infusing it only moments ago, rage beginning to spin inside Slate. Not at Benny, but at himself. *Shit. I need to make him understand.*

"Stop it." Benny's words were firm and drew his brother's gaze to him. "Just stop it." He stuffed his hands into the front pockets of his jeans to hide the shaking. "Not your fault, brother. Not yours. Don't do that. Doc taught me people have to let me take responsibility for what I do. GeeMa always blamed Mom. I blamed Mom, too. Blamed you. But it's not right, and you know it. It's on me. I took a step back down the ladder, only a couple of steps. Then I caught myself, set my feet on the rungs, and climbed again. That is *mine*. If you let me own those wins, then you can't take responsibilities for the losses from me, brother." Slate stared at him, his eyes still tortured.

More was needed. "I had a chat with Mason a few months ago." It felt odd to characterize the nearly one-sided conversation as a chat, but he still couldn't pass Mason's words on to his brother. Not now, not ever. Or at least not the entirety of the conversation. "He said something that stuck with me. Blood makes me a relative." Slate grinned, apparently he knew the other end of the statement, but Benny forged on anyway. "Loyalty makes me family. Your brother. I haven't earned that. Not yet. But I'm trying. I am. Swear, I am. Every day. Every meeting. Every breath I take sober, I do it for me. For you. For everyone I love." He gestured towards the hospital room. "Everyone. Even the little peanuts I haven't yet met. Every day. One step at a time."

"Fuckin' proud of you." Intensity back in his voice, Slate reached up and gripped his shoulder, shaking him back and forth in place. Then he blew out a hard breath. "We're done with this topic. You're doing good, shrimp. Love you, man. You're right. Put it behind you, behind us, move forwards." He reached out, pushed the door open wide, and called out softly, "Baby, got a visitor wants to meet Allen and Dani."

Benny peered inside to see a sleepy Ruby lifting her head from the pillow, staring at them groggily before looking around. Her face softened when she saw the babies sleeping peacefully. "Don't wake 'em." Her words were slurred from exhaustion, not meds, and Benny knew by her unclouded eyes, barely suppressing a shudder of relief for something he didn't know had worried him. *Everywhere I look*. "'S tiring stuff, being born." With awe in her voice, she told Benny, "I'm a mommy, Ben."

"Yeah, you are, Rubes. A beautiful mommy." Leaning in, he brushed her cheek with a kiss. "Most beautiful one I've ever seen."

***

Benny was walking towards the elevator when he recognized Eddie in the hallway. She was being escorted by a big biker wearing a Rebel patch, his arm around her waist, hustling her along. Luce had been busy babysitting a lot over the past couple of weeks as Bear took a trip out east, but he hadn't heard about anyone being hurt or sick, certainly nothing that would give him an inkling of why they were rushing around in the hospital. *Shit.*

"Eddie," he called, but they turned the corner before he could catch up. Forcing his legs to long strides, he startled when a hand gripped his arm, pulling him to a stop. Swinging around to berate whoever it was, he stopped short when he recognized Mason. *Shit.*

"Bear's out of surgery," Mason said, walking fast and pulling him up the hallway in the same direction Eddie had gone. "He was bad when we left Cali."

Surgery? Cali? California? What the hell, he was out east, not on the west coast. Benny held his tongue, instinctively letting Mason say what he needed to, impatiently waiting until the end to voice his questions. Trusting he would tell him. After what Mason had said to him, the loyalty he'd witnessed time and again, he did trust Mason.

Benny had found out just what kind of man Mason was in a conversation with Slate before the wedding. Learned how fate had brought his brother to a bar in Chicago at a time when he needed something to believe in, someone in whom he could place his trust and faith. Found out in a way that cut deeply how Mason had been the only person in his life that Slate could lean on with full knowledge that the support would always be there. Unwavering. Love so deep, Mason would take it on himself to tear away a parasite like Benny when Mason saw the pain being inflicted on a man he called brother. *Loyalty makes you family.*

"Worse when we landed. Doc rushed him out of the ER and into surgery about three hours ago." They turned the corner, and he saw a large cluster of black leather in the hallway outside what looked like a waiting room ahead.

"Luce...she's holdin' it together. Barely. Needs a strong shoulder right now." *Why didn't she call me?* Mason pulled him to a halt, looking down into Benny's face, seeming to search for something. Finally, he found it and pulled in a deep breath. "Trusting you to do this right, brother." At *that* word from Mason, he froze in place. Instinctively he knew it meant something, even if he wasn't sure he fully understood Mason's use of it now. *Loyalty.* "Trusting you to do her right. You take care of her, Ben. She needs you."

Stepping back, Mason gave him a shove towards the room. "I need to go back, be there for Slate. For Ruby." Shaking his head, Mason closed his eyes for a moment. "Fucking lies. I need to be there for me, see the promise of goodness born today. See the joy in our brother's eyes. Need that." Pointing up the hallway, he gave Benny's shoulder a push. "Go find what you need, Ben."

Quick steps taking him the rest of the way, he paused in the doorway, seeing Maggie holding Eddie, both women crying, but in what seemed like relief rather than sorrow. Taking a swift look around the room, he caught sight of Luce at the same time she saw him, and he stood stock-still because the moment she laid eyes on him, she was on the move, running to him. Long legs eating up the short distance, still she gained speed with every stride until suddenly she was there, right there, in his arms, hers wrapped around his neck, her face buried in his shoulder. Folding herself around him, even as he wrapped her up, feeling the sobs shaking her frame. "I got you, honey. I got you."

It was hours later when Eddie finally walked out of ICU. Lips curled in a small smile, arms wrapped around herself. She was bruised and battered, looking like she'd been days without sleep. Through listening in on the conversations swirling around him as they waited for word, Ben had found out she'd been kidnapped and taken to California. Bear, Mason, and a bunch of the Rebels flew out and organized what sounded like a recovery mission coordinated with the Navy *and* local cops. Benny shook his head again, thinking about how absurd it was to imagine the bikers being avenging angels. *Black leather riding to the rescue. And how bizarre, Ruby and Eddie, how many people know* two *individuals who have been kidnapped?*

Arm around Luce's shoulders, he pulled her to her feet, steadying her as she swayed in place facing Eddie. The boys had headed home with Maggie a couple hours ago; even Rafe so tired he hadn't argued.

"Doc says he's out of the woods. They're going to keep him sedated for a while, so he can get past what will be the worst of the pain. They want to make sure his lung stays inflated." She held a hand out, palm up, and one of the bikers gripped it, holding on tightly. "He's going to be okay."

Luce turned and buried her face against Benny's chest, shoulders shaking as she wept. Benny felt muscles all over her body beginning to loosen and relax as she leaned into him. He waited until her tears slowed before asking, "Ready to go home, honey?" She nodded, and he turned her, pointing her first towards Eddie where she got a long, close hug, the easy affection between the two women a clear indication of how deeply they had bonded.

Benny reached across once they were in the car, gathering up Luce's hand and pulling it over to rest on top of his leg. "You okay, honey?" From the corner of his eye, he caught the movement as she shook her head. "He's gonna be okay, right?" A nod, her hair rustling across the collar of her shirt. "Wanna talk about it?" Back-and-forth her head went—a definite no. "Okay. We can be quiet if you'd like." In response, her hand squeezed his tightly, silently conveying her thanks.

He pulled off to the side of the road in front of Bear's new house, seeing there were a few lights still on in the bottom level of the house. The location meant the living room, so it was probably Maggie. He held Luce's hand while they moved up the walk, and opened the door as she called a soft greeting to the silent house. Maggie appeared in the doorway to the large living room, a smile on her face. "Eddie called," she said right away, letting Luce know she didn't have to do a debrief, and he smiled his thanks at her. She asked, "Want something to eat before you hit the hay?"

Luce shook her head, letting go of Benny's hand to move forward and embrace the woman. Resting her cheek against Maggie's, she stayed there a moment, both women holding tightly. When they released each other, Benny slipped his palm around Luce's hip, tugging her backwards so she could lean against him. "Let's get you to bed," he said softly, and she nodded. Trudging up the stairs, he let her lead the way. The Crews hadn't lived there long, and he'd never had occasion to see her bedroom, so other than it being upstairs, wasn't sure where they were headed.

She passed three closed doors before opening the next one on the left, not pausing as she pulled him inside. He froze when she shut the door firmly behind him, but she didn't even glance at him, moving to put her purse down. Using her toes to push off her sneakers, she gently kicked the discarded footwear to the side and then, with a huge sigh, dropped to the end of the bed, falling to her back, hair swirling around her head. Arms outstretched, she was staring up at the ceiling, and Benny was left standing awkwardly by the door.

"He's a good man." These were the first words she'd spoken since before leaving the hospital, and the sound of her voice startled him. There was sorrow and sadness weighing down every word. "A genuinely good man. Honorable. Kind. Decent. Everything a father should be. Look at all the things he's done for the boys and me." Her head rolled on the light-colored comforter, and she looked at him. "You don't know what it was like before he came into our lives. *Papa* wasn't home a lot, and he...well, his focus wasn't on us, most of the time. We lived in a cockroach-infested apartment complex where we had to sleep on the floor if the weather was good." He must have looked confused because she laughed and rolled up to one elbow, curling her legs up onto the bed.

"If the weather was nice, it meant the men would be outside. Them being out of their apartments meant a chance of stupidity in the form of fights." She yawned, eyes closing as she hid her mouth behind one delicate hand. "Fights meant guns. Bullets don't care where they go. You point a gun, the bullet leaves it in a rush, and finds whatever target is in front of it." She changed position again, moving to her back, heels to the bed, tucked up against her ass.

"So we slept below the line of fire. Drug dealers, pimps and whores, fights, murders—we saw it all. I kept my head down, didn't make waves, tried to be invisible as much as I could." She yawned again, relaxing even as Benny grew more tense with every word. He had no idea what her life was like before he met her, hadn't asked even though he knew about her dad. "I escaped as often as I could, which wasn't enough. Went through a wild-child phase." Blinking slowly, she continued, "Rafe had the worst of it, since if *Papa* was gone, he had to put up with me." Glancing at him, a brief smile curled her lips. "I'm a bossy one."

"Nah, you're just right most of the time. The boys hate that. Lucia's righteous rightness." He pushed away from the door, taking the four steps to bring him to the edge of the bed. Squatting next to her, he lifted a hand and brushed strands of hair back off her face, threading the silk between his fingers. "You communicate forcefully." Cupping her cheek in his palm, he felt her skin heating under his hands and saw the darkening of a blush coloring her skin. "Beautiful orator, you could be a senator or something. You don't argue. You convince people of your ideas. Be anything you want to be."

"I'm tired." Her eyes didn't blink, didn't waver as she gazed at him. "I don't want to be alone tonight, Benny. I don't want to think about the past, don't want to think about tonight. Don't want to think about what we nearly lost, the boys and me."

"I'll stay, honey." An immediate response held his hopes she would know he wanted to be here for her. "Of course. I'm here." He wanted to reassure but wasn't certain how to say what he was thinking. "If I can hold you." Thumb brushing across her bottom lip, he stayed locked on her eyes. *Danger.* "Help to make it better. I'm here."

This was a bone of contention between them. As their friendship had developed, so had the attraction, grown stronger every day. He wanted her, *God yes*, but wanted to take it slowly. For her. For him. Because Doc told him not to start something. Because she'd already seen him fail.

So he took it slowly. So slowly it was killing him, and Benny had to work hard at ignoring the signs she kept tossing his way, shouting she wanted things to go faster. He'd kissed her until they'd been both gasping, teetering on the edge of losing control before reeling himself back. In an embrace, he'd found his hand sliding up her side of its own accord, thumb grazing across the bottom curve of her lush breast, heard the hitch in her breath when she'd felt that touch, knowing she'd give him that when he was inside her for the first time. Wanting her with every breath he took...denying himself, denying her.

On a late night call, in a whisper she'd admitted she wasn't a virgin, something he hadn't been certain about. Shyly, as she did often, she asked in a mix of broken English and Spanish if he could still want her. Benny'd spent the next hour soothing and convincing her that not only did he still want her, he wanted to be something important in her life, wanted to be someone she needed.

The next time they'd been alone in her room, he'd taken things farther, touching her intimately for the first time. He'd worked up to it, starting with sweet kisses, nipping at her plump lips, drawing the crimson to the surface. Hand to the inside of her knee, he'd lifted, bringing her thigh up to press against his rock-hard cock, slipping his palm to cover her, he'd eaten her gasp down with a rough, demanding kiss.

She'd opened for him beautifully, moaned into his mouth as he'd worked his hand, bringing her to orgasm. Felt like a king as he cradled her afterwards, ignoring his too eager cock, losing himself in the whispering sighs she'd given him.

God, he wanted her, wanted to be between her legs, wanted to work her over with his mouth, taking everything she had to give. But he'd never felt like this about a woman before. Not Benita, maybe especially not Benita. He could finally see how fucked–up that relationship was from the beginning.

Lucia was...different, special, and he wanted her to know how exceptional she was, wanted her to understand what she meant to him. More than a way to get off, so much more than that. From the first time he saw her, he knew she was special, meant something, and every glimpse and interaction since firmly reinforced the knowledge.

Over dinners with her family, he'd watched as she effortlessly managed the tempers and needs of her brothers, helping balance everything Eddie and Bear did for the boys. She took on anything asked of her with a smile and happy heart, glad when she could make a difference. Happy when she was needed. *That's what I have to do*, he realized, *make sure she knows how much I need her*. More than just someone to have sex with, so much more. Instead, she might hold the key to the rest of his life.

"Lucia," his voice was soft when he called her name. "I want..." He trailed off. There were no words for the want coursing through him when she looked at him like that. As if he were the most important thing in her world. "Get ready for bed, honey." Pushing to his feet, he stood, looking down at her. "I'll be here."

***

Lying in bed beside her, comforting her...torturing himself, he lifted the arm not curled around her waist so he could push his fingers through her hair. Sliding like silk across his skin, he smiled at the ceiling, knowing the darkness masked his expression. She fit him perfectly. Curved into him as she was, even with the covers between them, she had crowded as close as she could. Soft breasts pressed firmly against his side, covers tugged up, she had one leg on the outside, knee resting across his thigh.

Her arm firmly tucked around his belly, head resting on his chest, Luce was still, but her light, even breathing told him she wasn't sleeping.

"Gypsy asked me to play Marie's." He took a breath, feeling his stomach dip and sway at the thought of taking the stage again. There, of all places. "I'm thinking about it." Luce knew his fears, knew nearly everything that had happened to him since he got to Fort Wayne. Even knew some of the family drama that happened in Enoch, and then various parts of his years with the band. Not everything. *Hell, no.* He couldn't burden her with shit that horrendous. Shit like his life had been.

"You should do it, Benjamin." Her breath gusted across his skin. With thoughts about having her hands on him, he'd shucked the shirt before lying down. But, in what he now knew was a wise move, knowing the temptation she would present, he'd kept his jeans on and was lying on top of the comforter. Double barrier to paradise, and even now she was all he could think about. "I bet if you get the first show out of the way— *boom*—you'll be right back to where you were."

Not a chance of that happening. Losing their manager and two key members left the band down not only in numbers, but talent. Chase was learning fast. He was determined to master the guitar, and in playing with him, Benny had found he could carry a pleasing harmony. When Benny had mentioned performing, however, the kid had looked sick to his stomach even more than Benny felt. *Fine group we'd make, puke buckets to either side of the stage for the nervy musicians.*

"We've lost nearly everything." Radio airtime, online rankings, fan base—all the work it took to keep a band in front of the public eye—gone. They'd be starting from scratch when they relaunched. Vic had never toured with them. Meant he was an unknown as far as their fans went. He was good and so charismatic he'd win them over, but an unknown for now. Mitty would be back; Benny had faith, but he wasn't core. Not like Danny had been. Danny and Benny had always been the public face of the band. *Now just me.*

"No, you haven't." She sounded so certain of herself he couldn't stop the laugh from escaping. She didn't know, not really. "Benny, stop it. You haven't lost anything." Lifting her head, she stared at him, and even in the dark he could tell her eyes were fixed on his face. She raised the hand tucked around his side, bringing her palm up to place it over the center of his chest. Patting softly, she said, "The music is in here. You haven't lost that."

A flash of white teeth signaled a smile pointed his direction. Raising his hand, he pushed his fingers through her hair again. Pure silk.

"I've heard you when you don't think anyone's listening. Might be my favorite thing to do. I lurk." Her head tilted to one side. "Did you know?" He shook his head; a movement she must have been able to see because that flash of teeth came again. "I'll sidle into the hallway by your apartment, drop to my butt, and sit there. Just listening because, when you think you're alone, when you don't realize there's an audience, you let things go, and *Jesucristo*, Benny," she took a breath, pressing deeper into him, "what you do then is amazing. If you give an audience half of what you have inside you, you're going to win back every foot of progress you lost by getting sidetracked like this." He watched her head dip, but even with that warning wasn't prepared for what she did next.

Lucia's hair draped around her face as, lips to his chest, she brushed her way across side-to-side, then the tip of her tongue traced around his nipple, teeth nibbling gently. He was hard in an instant, imagining her lips on him in other places. Her heated breath rushed across his skin, and he opened his mouth, preparing to say something, but before he could find his voice, she had retreated, resting her head in the hollow of his shoulder, curving into him again. "You're amazing, Benny. Never doubt it."

Wordlessly, he stroked her shoulder, down her back. Soothing himself as much as her, he lay awake long after she finally found sleep. Turning her words over in his head, he felt the beginnings of a plan. He had to earn her belief in him. *Marie's.*

Sixteen

"Are you fucking kidding me, Ben? What the fuck?" The frustrated shout woke him, and Benny lifted his head, looking with bleary eyes towards the stairs. *Shit.*

The pounding in his head was sickeningly familiar. So was the sight greeting him. A disappointed face. Andy's. "Shit." He muttered this, but his voice was loud enough for Andy to catch it.

"Yes, shit. Shit again. Mighta shit on yourself, from the smell of it." Andy—*Slate*, he tried to remind himself to call his brother Slate. *He likes that.* "What the fuck did you do last night?"

He'd played. Gotten onstage and played, pushing through the terror-driven shakes threatening to derail the performance even before they'd started. Bear and Chase took the stage with him—Bear's presence promising to help make it easy, Chase's making it better because Benny was able to focus on giving the kid his own brand of reassurances. Lucia in the audience, front and center, sitting at a table near the stage so he could see her every time he looked up from his hands. Belief and love so clear on her face he nearly froze at first, from the full knowledge of what she was giving him.

While Bear had been recovering at home, they hadn't been able to take much time for themselves. Quick lunches in the family kitchen instead of leisurely dinners out, stolen moments on the phone. With Luce out of the picture a lot of the time, he'd dialed in on Chase, working with the boy every day, bringing him along faster than he'd believed possible. Vic and Chase formed the other two legs of his musical tripod at the moment, and he let them balance him as often as they could all be in the same room. So they played, and the music flowed from his fingers, if not his head. Lyrics were still a scarce commodity, but when they did come, they were good. The kind of curl-your-toes, make-you-shiver, raise-the-hair good.

Last night had been good, too. The last half of the set was rocking, the bar filled to capacity in a party for DeeDee's man, Jase. A music lover, if not a musician, Jase had sat in with them one night at Bear's place. Proving while he could carry a tune, he couldn't be trusted with an instrument, he had broken four strings on one of Bear's guitars before the guys could wrestle it away from him.

The gig had been so good, Benny let it go to his head. Thinking to himself, *If I can get back on stage, then I can handle anything. Right?*

Wrong. So fucking wrong.

After they finished playing, he was only three swallows into the first beer and had already been thinking how he could get another without anyone seeing. Three beers and he was in the alley out behind the bar with a different gang of bikers passing a joint around, accepting the jug of moonshine when it made it to him, hooking a finger through the handle and lifting it to his lips as if he did it every day. Laughing men loaded him into a van with shouts of a party, and vaguely he remembered seeing Lucia standing on the walk in front of the bar as they drove past, looking side-to-side. Another bar, another back alley. Another drunken night ending in a blackout.

Now was now, and he was on his brother's couch with no memory of getting there. Focusing on the floor, he found the remains of the night in the form of a single empty bottle on the floor next to the couch. *If he doesn't know how bad it was, maybe I can bullshit him.*

"What?" Quiet, so he didn't wake the babies, he flipped over on the couch, pretending the movement didn't set his stomach churning. "I'm up. Was there something you needed?"

Standing close, so close Benny could see every detail of the seam stitching on his jeans, Slate glared down at him. For several long minutes, he bore the weight of that stare, and then Slate shook his head. His brother's eyes slowly closed, and Benny watched as Slate made a visible effort to get himself under control. Voice vibrating with anger, Slate hissed, "You fucked up."

"I slipped." No chance of lying now, not if his brother already knew. "That's all. Just a slip."

"Fucked." Slate leaned down, shoving his scowling face into Benny's. "Up."

"I'm sorry."

"Save it." Slate whirled, hands to the air, fending off something Benny couldn't see. "You." His voice rose to a shout. "*Fucked up.*"

On cue, the cry of a baby trailed down the stairs, and Slate turned to look that direction, the expression on his face so torn it twisted something sideways in Benny. For a moment, it felt like things were unbalanced, on the cusp of something huge, and then slowly Slate turned to look at him. Eyes bleak, he said, "I got kids, brother."

Benny nodded, shoving to a seated position on the couch. "I know you do."

"Want them to have an uncle they can love." Benny knew Slate saw the flinch his words caused, watched as matching pain moved through his brother's face. "Want them to have a family who loves them."

"I love them. You know I do." *How do I make this right?*

"Love the booze more." Slate looked down, hand to the back of his neck, fingers kneading and rubbing. "You need more than I can give you, Benny." His words came slowly, seeming forced out. "Time to go back to Phoenix."

"No, Andy." Benny was near tears, hating the disappointment in his brother's voice, wishing he could turn back the clock to before he got in that van, took the first drink, climbed the stairs to that goddamned fucking stage. "Please, God. I can do better. I will. I promise. It was just a slip." In his head he heard Chase's words from the darkness around a bonfire, *"Right to the mother. Fuckin'. Curb. Muthafuckin' curb."*

"You slip then you use whatever you need in order to get your feet under you again so you can stand strong. Rehab is a tool. You need to work it." One hand shoved deep into his pocket, Andy pulled out his phone and placed three calls.

Two hours later, Benny was on a plane. Seated on the aisle next to him, boxing him in, his silent escort, was none other than Davis *fucking* Mason. *Jesus.*

Seventeen

"Ben, how does it feel to be back here?" New doc for group, but he'd seen this one around before.

"Hey, Doc." Benny waved one hand as he flopped into the thinly cushioned chair nearest the door. "Feels like shit. How you doin'?" No laughter from the group, but he didn't expect any. There weren't any faces he knew. All his rehab cohorts had gone on to graduate, moving on. They wouldn't be back as failures. *Not like me.*

"Well, let's see what we can do to ensure this is the exception, shall we?"

Cup of coffee in hand, he lifted it to her in salute, letting the movement be his only response. Smoothly, she picked up the thread of the topic her group had been discussing before he walked in, and he listened as she covered strategies to recognize when a behavioral or environmental trigger was in play and how best to sidestep it, keeping to the sober side of the track no matter what. He found a way to contribute to the conversation when she asked for additional triggers they might think about. He snorted and raised a hand, waiting patiently as she worked her way around the semi-circle of occupied chairs. When she pointed to him, lifting her arched eyebrow in a question, he responded with one word. "Success."

***

"Hey, shrimp. How's it hangin'?" There was noise in the background, and Benny heard Ruby's voice, then the cooing of a baby.

"I catch you at a bad time?" He had a favor to ask and didn't want to rush to it if he didn't have to. Ease into it as it were. Stealing attention from needy babies would not be the way to go.

"Naw, Ruby just took Dani to lay her down. Allen's already snoozin'." Slate laughed softly, affection thick in his voice and Benny knew he was watching Ruby walk away. "It's never a bad time to talk to my baby bro."

"You...you talked to Mom, right? About before, back when she was in Enoch?" The words came tumbling out, and Benny was already off script, not having meant to dive in so deeply from the start. "About before you...went looking for work." He choked out the words, the phrase "left me" so close to escaping, he had to clamp his lips shut for a moment.

"Yeah, I did. She had it tougher than we knew, but we were kids, Benny. What the hell did we know?" Benny knew if he could see him, Slate would be standing with one hand wrapped around the back of his neck, pulling and massaging, trying to ease the decades' worth of weight he carried for everyone around him. "She landed in Colorado. Found a program she could work, kicked her habits. Came out the other end stronger."

"Did she tell you what worked for her? Doc says different things work for different folks. We were talking and she said not to get discouraged, because different doesn't mean bad." Now the words were coming faster, and he didn't think he could stop the flood if he tried. "Like group seems to click for me. Better than the confessional of a meeting podium." Meetings left him frustrated. Most people didn't appear to want to talk about what was working, only about where they were in the program, or what the response had been from their families. Which worked for a lot of people, but not him.

"I feel like I need people to bounce things off, people who will give it to me straight, but all the time. Not only when I ask what they think. If I'm talking and what I'm sayin' is shit, then I don't want to spend time chasing a dung heap." Mason's face swam up from his memories, and Benny once again felt the weight of piercing grey eyes holding him in place as Mason made Benny's situation clear. "I...you were talking once...about a...talking about...you know. A different thing."

The words dried up; he was left with an incomplete statement, and he didn't know if he'd given Slate enough to figure out what he thought he needed. As ever, his brother surprised him. "Sober companion. I'm way out ahead of you, shrimp."

Air whooshed out of Benny, a breath he wasn't even aware he had held in. "Yeah." The single whispered word seemed to reassure his brother.

Sounding confident, Slate said, "I've talked to folks who've done this. The person has to be a fit for you, but also not. Because they need to have enough of their own brand of tough to stand against you if you need it. Not a pushover, not a friend. A paid companion on your path to staying sober." Now he sounded relieved, and Benny was glad he could hand this to Slate, at least. "I have a few applications that came in yesterday. I'll sort through the mess, and we'll interview when you get home. But, Benny?"

Slate paused, and it seemed his name was a question because he didn't continue until Benny said, "Yeah?"

"They work for me, not you. They report to me, about you. And it's just how it's going to be." Iron and steel didn't have anything on the strength of purpose populating Slate's voice. "You understand everything upfront, we won't have any problems."

"I got it. I get it." He swallowed. Words that once had come so easily now sticking in his throat. "Slate...Andy?" It was his turn to wait for his brother's response, and he wasn't left hanging long.

"Yeah, shrimp?"

His voice, strong in the beginning, trailed off to a barely heard whisper by the end. "I love you. You know that, right?"

"I know you do." He could hear the smile in Slate's voice. "I love you, too, shrimp."

Eighteen

Benny looked up to see Bear walking through the bar towards where he sat waiting, guitar in hand, up near the stage. Bear had called earlier and set up the meet, a call Slate didn't screen, so he must have known about it ahead of time. From his tone on the phone, Benny hoped Bear wanted to jam, because he was ready to get back to it. Friendly, if brief, their conversation gave Benny hope things would be able to continue as they'd been before. Playing, jamming and collaborating on music. Right now, however, from the look on his friend's face, he feared the purpose of this meeting might be very different from his expectations.

As he reached Benny, Bear reached out and snagged a chair, flipping it so when he sat so he was straddling it, with the small barrier of the back between them.

"Hey," Benny said, plastering a sheepish smile on his face. "How are you doing?" He was expecting a lecture like Mason had given him as he dropped him off in Phoenix. A reminder he didn't want to fuck Slate over. Everyone had their eye on him, watching and weighing his actions against his brother's reactions.

For a long moment, Bear sat silently and looked at him. Benny's smile faded as the pressure in the room seemed to double, then triple, increasing the longer the silence went on. Then Bear sighed and without preamble said, "Lucia likes you. She likes you a lot."

Benny gave Bear a small shrug, feeling his lips twisting to the side with the flood of anxiety that swelled inside him at this start to their conversation. "I like her, too."

The full weight of Bear's glare landed on him, and Benny felt his stomach clench. *Shit. Shit shit shit.*

"Don't matter. Ain't happening. Not now. You seriously think I'm going to let you in there with her?" Bear shook his head. "Ain't happening."

Not something he'd expected. His brain stuttered, making it so he had no response. Couldn't think of anything but the look on Luce's face when he kissed her. How she leaned into him whenever she was near. How it felt to sleep innocently next to her, waking early just to have time to drink his fill of looking at her relaxed, beautiful face, her arm still claiming him even in her sleep. The feel of her hand on his heart when she reassured him that the music was inside him. Stunned, Benny sat and stared at him, hearing his mouth stammering, "What? Wh...why?"

"Do you not know where you spent the last four weeks? I do." Bear leaned in. "She doesn't. And she won't. Because she likes you." Bear shook his head again. "But you aren't the guy she likes. You're an asshole who thinks his shit don't stink. Who doesn't know good when it's standing right in front of him. You're a user. I ain't talkin' drugs and you know it. And my Luce"—Bear flipped out a hand, pointing to Benny— "liked what she thought she saw. What she hoped was there. So I'll allow her to keep the illusion. That nice guy. That sweet guy who takes her for ice cream, the guy who makes her laugh, the guy who plays fucking beautiful music. But, it's all you get of her. She keeps that, and you get shit-all because you fucked up one too many times. You'll let her go. Let her go, take your goddamned hooks out of her, and let her find a decent man. One who can love her how she deserves."

Benny sat for a minute, frozen. Hearing the seconds loudly tick past in his head, frantically considering and discarding what he could say that would change Bear's mind. He had to. *I can't do that. Can't glimpse what might be and have it ripped away. Never have the promise of her love.* He went with honesty. "I love her."

His words were met with a quick, resolute headshake. "No, you don't. You love booze. You love yourself. You even love the music. Got that whole rock star thing going for you. You do not love her. You take your hooks outta her, unlatch however you gotta do that, but you take care with my girl. Leave her with the memory of the man she thinks you are."

"*But...*"

With a roar, Bear came off the chair, turning it over in his rush to get at Benny. And in his movements, Benny saw what his friend had been holding in check. Gone was the laughing and affable man. In his place, a dangerous, protective father, set to make the world better for his girl. In a silent, quiet corner of his brain, he was glad she had that, wanted to be the one to give it to her. To do better for her, to make things right. Bear pulled him back into the moment, wrapped his hand around Benny's throat and picked him up, pushed him against the wall. Held him there on tiptoes. Leaning close, Bear hissed, "You do not understand me. This. Is. Not. Happening." He shook Benny. "Not today. Not tomorrow. Not fucking ever."

***

"You are not my favorite person right now," Ruby told him. "You need to go away. I'm tired. I'm grumpy. I'm a milk machine. And the babies are sleeping, so I'm taking advantage by napping. Go away, Benny."

Benny sat on the edge of her bed, looking down at an exhausted-looking Ruby, who lay there with resolutely closed eyes. She was his last hope, but seeing the look on her face, he felt a wash of despair and desperation move through him. "Ruby," he said, "please. Please, God. Please, you gotta help me. Luce..." He paused for a moment and took a breath. "She means everything, Ruby."

Ruby abruptly sat up, pushing her hair away from her face, frustration and fatigue making her look a little crazed. "No. I won't. I can't. You can't do this, Benjamin. You can't. I know what happened, what Bear said. And honestly, I get where he's coming from. What you gotta get is your brother and Bear are *brothers*. Bear doesn't want you for his girl. He doesn't. He's seen the devastation you leave in your wake. He doesn't want you for his girl. He's her dad now. He gets to make that call. Do what he has to do to keep her safe, sane, and healthy."

Benny looked at Ruby, confused. He thought she liked him, but saying he left devastation behind him didn't say, *I like you*. It said something entirely different.

She continued. "You cannot set your brother against *his brother*. You can't do it. Slate has given up enough for you. Don't up the cost to something he can't pay. I know you love him." She reached out and grabbed his hands, shaking them to make her point. "I know you do. Do not"—she shook his hands again—"make him make this choice."

It was at that moment Benny got it. He experienced an epiphany so piercing, it felt like something ruptured inside him, and he bled understanding and loss.

All these years, he thought Andy had left him behind. He hadn't understood. He couldn't. He didn't have the same kind of loyalty inside him. Now he saw, Andy had always loved him. Had done what he could his whole life to try to make Benny a better person. Someone who would make the world a better place in turn. His brother had never failed him, but now he could see how time and again, he'd failed Andy. Hadn't cared what his brother had to set aside for him, only taking in what he wanted from their interactions, never seeing the price Andy paid. Like Ruby said, this one would be huge. Crippling. Because Andy without the Rebels wasn't Andy. Wasn't Slate. Asking him to intervene with Bear would break something inside Slate. *Found it, finally. Here's the line I won't cross.* Without another word, he stood and walked away.

***

Benny sat on the floor, back pressed to the front of the couch, phone in hand. Flipping through pictures, his thumb swiped across the screen, again and again, each motion revealing another smiling image of Luce. Gorgeous. Sweet. Kind beyond belief. Bear said she loved him. No, Bear had said she loved a false image of him. Something he wasn't, might never be. A lie.

He loved her, though. Loved her so much. The words escaped, hanging in the air, the pain in his own voice slicing through him. "God, I love you, Luce." He swallowed hard, then looked at the picture frozen on the screen. Touching it, he made it come alive in his head, feeling the water soaking into his clothing, the sounds of the fountains shooting streams into the air, the tumbling racket the water made when it hit the umbrella. Captured at an angle that put his face out of focus, Lucia was front and center. The softness of her expression revealed even then she might have loved him. Lips to the side of his face, her eyes were closed, lashes drifting to touch her cheeks. *Love.*

A reminder popped up and he stared at it for a moment before dismissing it. Group would begin in fifteen minutes. He looked over at the counter where a still-full bottle of failure taunted. "Not this time." His voice surprised him, and he shook his head. Opening his phone app, he poked some buttons until the call connected, then waited for the person at to pick up. Glancing up at the clock on the wall, he decided this was worth being late. "Set it up," he said, and disconnected before the party at the other end could respond.

Nineteen

Fingertips to his forehead, Benny attempted to rub his headache away, but it was being stubborn and refused to leave the hangover party taking place in his head. It felt like a hangover, which it couldn't be. He cut a gaze to his right, taking in the tiny woman seated next to him, her ass scooted far back from the edge—because his fucking sober companion wouldn't let him have even a single drink tonight. *Thank God.*

He leaned back, putting both elbows to the roof, stretching out. Legs crossed at the ankles, he stared past his feet and out at the Fort Wayne skyline, what there was of it. Fort Wayne was nice, decent sized for the Midwest. But a Denver, it wasn't. Not even a Cheyenne, not when it came to what he wanted. Craved. Every single fucking day. *Again, thank God.*

Twisting slightly, he looked over at Mercedes. *Who the hell names their kid Mercedes?* That thought flitted across his mind for the hundredth time. Over the past few weeks, she'd proven herself an adept companion, talking him down and through several episodes of a craving so hard and painful he didn't know how he kept breathing, much less walking and talking. Petite, her angular face was partially hidden behind the fall of green-streaked yellow hair.

Benny wasn't sure what to think when she'd showed up for the interview, apparently without giving one fat fuck about what her appearance screamed about her. Eyebrows, nose, septum, and lower lip pierced, gems and metal glittered in the overhead lights. Big, fat, shiny flat disks in her ears, huge gauges stretching the lobes. Beyond casually dressed, it looked like her style was stuck deep in boho-cheap. She'd sat there across the desk from Slate and, after the initial greetings, waited.

Serene, she rested, at ease in the straight-backed chair. Giving the impression there wouldn't be any end to her brand of patience, she waited in silence, without fidgeting or moving. His brother was a bigass biker dude, who had worked his way up and into the higher echelon ranks of the Rebel Wayfarers. They were in Slate's office at the house the club owned in town, which meant she braved a gated and razor-wired parking lot as well as any number of other bigass biker dudes to get inside. Then she sat, unruffled and quiet, waiting for the interview to start.

Her quietness ate at Slate. His brother was used to negotiating with so many different kinds of folks, he wouldn't let it show for the casual viewer, but Benny caught glimpses of it in his posture changes, the cadence of his speech. That very stillness that disturbed Slate stirred something different inside Benny. For months, he'd felt like a gigantic watch spring that had been overwound, sprung and tight, driven nearly to breaking. Been held in a single, strained position for a long, long time, and in the reflective silence of her waiting, that spring began to ease, uncoiling.

Benny was always in motion. If he weren't playing the guitar, he would be walking, talking, even jittering in place if he had to be still for too long. Always in high gear, his GeeMa used to say, back before he fucked her over and quit talking to her, ashamed and embarrassed by his own behavior. Benny winced at the thought, and the chick's eyes swung to him. She tilted her chin slightly, so slightly that if he hadn't been looking at her, he would never have seen it. But she'd seen his pain, and her movement acknowledged it.

The tension in his gut eased the slightest bit more, and he drew in a long, slow breath.

"I like her," he said, propping one thigh on Slate's desk, leaning against the edge.

"What's to like?" his ever-blunt brother asked, stretching backwards in his chair, putting his muscles and tattoos on display in the sleeveless vest worn over a bare chest. "She ain't even talkin' yet, Benny. How can you figure she's someone you want to spend a lotta time with? And make no mistake, little brother, whoever I settle on," he emphasized the pronoun, making his point this wasn't under Benny's control, "will be spending a fuckton of time up your ass."

Using a mocking tone, Benny said, "She sees things." Her lips twitched the barest amount, then settled back into the neutrally pleasant position they'd occupied since she seated herself. I could be a fan of someone who didn't go for over the top all the time, *he thought. "So many things."*

Slate sat forward, elbows to the desk and twisted his neck to look up at Benny so he could ask, "What kind of things?"

Benny studied her for another moment, thinking about the instant she walked into the room, how she had assessed him in a second, figured out his brother in another one, and then effortlessly made herself a safe place inside what should be a frightening situation. Safe enough she could sit there without speaking, listening to them talking about her. "Everything, I think." He sighed, "Doesn't bode well for any possible renewed partying, tell you that much. I think she can handle me, Andy."

"Slate." His brother said this idly. The same correction he'd made every time Benny said his name over the past six months. In Benny's mind, Slate was Andy's biker persona, the man who busted everybody's balls all the time, who ran this whole enterprise here in Fort Wayne, the one who would hire Mercedes if they came to an accord. Benny hadn't found it in himself to give in to the nickname for a long time, and was still on the fence at times, and today, he felt like once again ignoring his brother's

wishes. Poke the bear. *He winced at the unsubtle reminder to himself of why he was doing this as Slate continued,* "She can handle you? Can you even handle yourself, brother?"

The blonde's mouth opened, and she said, "She has a name." *Pointing to the application and resume lying on top of a folder on Slate's desk, she reminded them,* "Mercedes Gruffudd."

"Griffald? Griffwald?" *Benny laughed aloud, continuing his absurd pronunciations of her last name.* "Griswold?" *She was shaking her head, but he powered over whatever she'd been about to say.* "Please, God, tell me that's a maiden name. Tell me you didn't pick it. Griswold is a terrible name, and if you have chosen to bear that particular burden of your own free choice, then it's a deal breaker on my side of things. Plus, you're named after an ostentatious car." *Shaking his head, he said,* "Sorry, toots. Deal breaker."

Enunciating slowly, as if she were speaking to a child, she said, "I took my wife's name when we married. And it's pronounced grih-fith. G r u f f u d d. Grih-fith. Mercedes is unfortunate, I agree, and have told my parents so repeatedly. However, I will not refuse the gift of the name given me, because I was named after the Virgin Mary, our Lady of the Mercies. And I wanted to make my wife happy, so I chose to let her know I was all hers, something I reaffirm daily." *Without seeming to need breath, she continued, segueing into a frontal attack.* "Benjamin is an interesting name. Do you know what it means?"

He shook his head, wanting to laugh but she seemed to be taking this all seriously, so he was afraid he would offend. A year ago, he wouldn't have given a fuck, but Mercedes seemed to be nice. So there you go, already a good influence, *he thought.*

"Benjamin is a biblical name. Benjamin founded one of the twelve tribes of Israel, the youngest son of Jacob and Rachel. It means son of the right hand. You're intended to be someone's right-hand man, supportive and strong. You simply haven't found your way, yet." *The top of her head tipped to one side, and she stared at him. "Hebrew, good strong roots. Wyoming, good strong roots." Proved she'd done her homework, at least. Most people thought he was from Denver, where the band had spent so much time. "I don't like Benny for you, it feels...throwaway. You're not a throwaway person. To me, you're going to be Bibi."*

"You start now," Slate stated firmly, pressing bunched fists to the desktop as he pushed to his feet. "Paperwork will be emailed to you by end of day. I'll need it back soon as you can find time, but you begin now."

"What? Just like that?" Benny's laugh was abrupt, and he hated the way the loud sound echoed around the room. He liked being smooth, had made an art form out of smooth, dealing with fans and managers, sponsors and venue promoters. That laugh, like most of his laughter lately, was not smooth.

"He said I got the job. You said I could handle you," Mercedes responded, turning to face him, effectively dismissing his brother. "Therefore, I'm your new sober companion."

He thought she wouldn't last a week, and because she didn't miss seeing anything, within a day had hoped she'd quit even sooner. She didn't, and that brought them to here.

Breaking the silence, Mercedes asked him, "What will make it better? What do you need?"

"Booze. Blow," he responded immediately. "Or, smack. Smack would numb things. Sting and bring tears, then make me feel alive and buzzing for a moment. Music blazing through my body. And, after the first magnificent flash, the numbness is bone deep and satisfying. Smack would fix everything." He shook his head, rejecting the idea. "Wouldn't fix anything."

He shifted to his elbows, lifting his gaze to the nighttime sky. Stars twinkled overhead, and the flashing lights of jets crisscrossed the sky. Different trajectories and heights, taking the same pathways but never meeting. *Hmm*, he thought, *might be something there.* He muttered, "Pathways...our pathways are so different, but the journey is the same. Awash in the beauty around us, immersed in the same pain. Same, pain, strain, plain, chain, insane, mundane, chow mein..."

With effort, he fell silent, attempting to quiet his train of thought. The lyric idea was on the cusp of escape, and he knew from experience one wrong breath would send the thought skittering away.

Humming, he softly sang, "The pathways are so different, be they high above or down below. Unsettled changes steal our dreaming, saved memories in faded photos. Our gazes never meeting, but our journey feels the same. Awash in beauty surrounding us, drowning in a maestro's pain."

He sucked in a breath, scared. Excited. This was something that hadn't happened for a while. A while being weeks, maybe even months. He'd been locked in his own mind, unable to find a way to put to words anything he was feeling. "That doesn't suck," he whispered, lying on his back and pulling out his phone to tap the words into the notepad program.

"No, Bibi," Mercedes' voice came from the dark, but he could hear a smile in her words. They'd talked about this, how the writing, which had been a part of his life for so long, had stopped. Dried up like a wet weather spring in the hot summertime. When he tried to force it, the flow wouldn't come. It became stiff and awkward. The unbearable agony of something that at one time, was so effortless, had become impossible. "That doesn't suck."

"Nope," he muttered. Locking his phone, he slipped it into his pocket, lying flat on his back on a slightly sticky rooftop of the apartment building his brother's friends owned. Now, if he could manage to stay on track, keep things under control. "I want Slate to be proud of me again."

He winced, not intending those words to be spoken, but the dam was cracked, and words kept spilling out, the breach growing wider with every word. "I want him to be a brother, not a caretaker. He's taken care of people his whole life. Still is. Look at him with me. Did you know he basically learned how to be a nurse? Back when Daddy was dying of Hep-C, we couldn't afford home care. So Slate learned how to start a fucking IV. He wasn't old enough to drive, but he nursed our daddy as he lay dying. I remember looking up at him, thinking he could do any-fucking-thing we needed. My hero.

"Daddy died, and Slate stayed larger than life. He never let me down. Not once." Closing his eyes, he hid in the blackness behind his lids, letting it cocoon him. *Safe.* "Mom did, fuck. But not Slate. Then he had to take care of our mother." He shook his head, bringing his arms overhead, shoving his hands underneath his neck, fingers tangling on his too-long hair. "She's an alky. First one I ever knew. Most influential one, too."

He laughed, the harsh sound echoing off the buildings around them shocking him. Eyes open, he stared at nothing, looking up into the darkness hovering overhead, barely pushed back by the streetlights. "She'd come into my room, stinking of booze and cigarette smoke. Sweaty and stinking of men's cologne, some nights." A softer laugh this time. "Hell, most nights.

"She'd lean over my bed, talking to me. Talking to me like I couldn't see what she'd become. Like I couldn't see my big brother behind her, steady hand on her arm so she didn't fall down on top of me. Like I didn't see the stagger as he guided her out." The laugh came again, tearing out of him in a way that left pain lodged deep inside.

"I hated it for him. Hated her. I was relieved when GeeMa got custody of me. I was about seven. It meant I lost my mom, and I was okay with that. But, I lost him in the mix, too. He stayed with her, and I never understood why. Not until now, at least." He gestured to himself, a self-deprecating sneer on his lips he hoped Mercedes couldn't see in the darkness. "Look at me. He never gives up on people. Never. He'll bend and break himself, ripping who he is into smaller and smaller pieces to make sure the people he cares about are good.

"Did the same for Mom. Gave until he didn't have anything left for her. Gave until she sucked him dry. Ran him out. Not only out of her life but out of town. Meant I lost him for good, then." Digging his fingertips into his scalp, he tried to work the pain out that way, pressing and rubbing. It was too deep, ran through him like blood and he knew it. No way this kind of pain could be eased from the outside. So he went with it, letting the flow of words continue, talking far into the night. "I found my own way to cope, though. Booze and Benita."

***

"You sure he's gonna be cool with me showing?" They hadn't discussed it, but Benny knew Slate had learned about the situation in Marie's, when it took five men to pull Bear off him. Not that Benny had fought back, but Bear wouldn't let go, couldn't seem to once he locked onto Benny, so Gypsy and some of the other Rebels in the bar got involved. Bear ignored their questions, shook off the restraining hands and gestured brusquely towards the door. Then he'd stood, arms crossed over his chest, watching as Benny slunk out to the parking lot. Which meant Benny had put Slate into another position that might have set him against his friends. His brothers. His real family.

That had been the turning point, though. The kick in the ass Benny needed, the push to sort himself and figure out how he wanted to proceed. So he wasn't simply moving forwards as he had been, pursuing movement for the sake of movement. Instead he had been setting and working towards a goal, not giving up, not playing a scam or game to shortcut his way around the rules. Weeks of working for and achieving that first goal. Then the next. Another, and another, building on success as he went.

Benny had one real objective. Sure, there were sub-goals in there, things that would help lead up to what he wanted. Perquisites so he didn't—*slip, backslide, fail*—he shook his head, rejecting these gutless ways of telling the truth. *So I don't fuck up again.*

First up was getting his ass back into the groove of playing. Playing sober, for the first time in his life. From the beginning back in Wyoming, he realized he had always paired the two things. Motivation and reward tied up in music and oblivion. Now when he played without having a drink, the idea was never far from his mind, like his brain believed he needed the advantage of a fogged brain to make music. Doc called it a behavioral trigger.

It was also exhausting to play sober, without the expectation of a buzz on the horizon. He wasn't sure why but knew this was the hardest thing he'd done so far. A different mindset, far more mental than physical, forcing him to pay attention to technique and making him strategize transitions and chromatics like never before. Rewiring his playing into something better. Good work, but hard.

Next, would be to see about getting the band some gigs. The Rebels had been cool about everything, putting Vic up in a room at the house they had in town. He'd been helping out on odd jobs for them, too, whatever they needed a hand with. Chase said Vic had taken to working out with some of the bikers, and they were bonding. Chase was working with Vic, too, but on instruments. Their drummer had the ability to play nearly anything he could lay a hand to, and he was teaching Chase all he knew. Chase was eating it up, loving not only the attention but also the challenge of mastering a skill, having learned from his old man the power having knowledge provided.

Finally, please God, Lucia. He'd only seen her twice since coming home. Both times Bear was in the room, standing close, and the look on his face so murderous it drove his point home, forcing Benny to keep his distance. Something he could see hurt Luce. Nothing good there, not for either of them. Not until he could win Bear back over.

This might be the first step. No way of knowing, but Bear had asked for a meet. Unlike the last time, routing this request through his brother. Benny turned back to Slate, cocking an eyebrow, waiting for a response to his question.

"His suggestion, shrimp. Probably be more pissed if you don't fuckin' show." Slate yawned, groaning and stretching his hands far over his head, the tattoos on his arms writhing and moving as the muscles under the skin flexed and strained. Benny had studied those over the past months, reading and re-reading them, wishing he could ask about them, but they awkwardly pointed towards a time where he once thought Slate felt relieved to be rid of him.

Knowing now that wasn't the truth, today he felt brave enough to ask. "Do you remember all your tattoos? Like where you were, what you were doing?" Slate's head swung around, and quickly Benny ducked his chin, dodging whatever look might be aimed his way. "You've got a lot of ink, for sure."

"Yeah." Slate's voice was thoughtful, solemn in a way he didn't understand. Like so much about his brother, this was a mystery. "I remember them all. Every piece is important to me. Ain't got no throwaway trash on my body. Every tattoo means something." Slate unbuttoned his shirt and shrugged it off his shoulder, the movement registering in Benny's peripheral vision. His voice held a note of intensity when he said, "Benny."

"Yeah?" Aiming for nonchalance, gaze steady on his hands, Benny rubbed his thumb across the still-building calluses. More work to do there, making it so he could play an entire set without killing his fingers.

"Benjamin," Slate called his name in a way that meant this was important. Benny looked up and into his brother's eyes, surprised to see they were wet.

"This one, the first one, was for you." Benny's eyes dropped to Slate's shoulder, seeing an angel with bowed head, naked sword in one hand, gun in the other, arms and body flexed and tense. Ready to react to whatever threat was coming its way. Wrapped tightly in its own gossamer wings, the sentinel was gazing down at the words positioned under its feet, *My Brother's Keeper*.

"All my life, I wanted to make yours better. I never got over the need, shrimp. This"—he pointed to the tattoo, the inked angel seeming to move as his muscles flowed underneath it—"was how I reminded myself so I didn't stray from the path. So I could be what you needed." He pulled his shirt back over his shoulder, covering up the other tattoos he wore on his body. "So when you needed me, I could be in a position to help." He paused, staring into Benny's face, intensity building in his expression. With emphasis, he said, "All I am, I owe to you."

Quick laughter bubbled out of Benny; he couldn't help it. "That's absurd, brother." Shaking his head, he watched as Slate began to button his shirt, hands moving in quick, angry movements. "I mean, I always wanted to be you when I grew up. The idea I had a hand in making you the man you are? Total crazypants."

"Not so crazy when you've been my focus this long." Slate shrugged, turned away and Benny saw him swallow, squeezing his eyes shut for a second before he very intentionally changed the topic of conversation. "Get your stuff. I'll run over with you. Bear and Chase should be there, and they'll be ready to go, waiting on your skinny ass." There was a muffled noise from overhead, and both men froze in place. Ruby hadn't been feeling well the past couple of days, and every member of the household was waiting on the twins to come down with whatever stomach bug she had. "Hold on," Slate muttered, already moving towards the stairs, "be right back."

Ten minutes later, Slate was walking down the stairs with a baby on each arm. "Ruby's sleepin', kiddos are up. You're on your own tonight, shrimp." He tipped his head towards the couch, where their silent observer had been waiting. "Except for Mercedes, of course."

***

"Bibi," Mercedes launched into her interrogation before he even got the car door closed behind him in the apartment parking. "How do you not know these things about your brother?" She shifted in the seat, seeking a more comfortable position. "You told me he was your hero, and has been from the time you can remember things clearly. How does he not know this about you? Why are there so many unspoken things between two people who love each other so much?"

"For God's sake," he muttered, neck twisting to check for traffic. "Goin' to a bar, Mercedes. Wanna focus on that with me?" Going back to Marie's would be far harder this time. Three times, three failures, two of those requiring a stay in rehab. "Hard doesn't begin to cover it." *I'm not going back just to crash and burn*, he thought, frowning through the windshield, determined. *Not happening.*

"First, tell me about Andy." *Fuck, she's persistent.*

"He prefers Slate." Turning left, he pulled smoothly into traffic, watching as the cars moved around them. Flowing like a river around rocks piled on the bed, fast and quiet. *Life moves fast, till I can't see things clearly. Bends and curves, they obscure me. Find me, and pull me from the river. Save me, from myself.* "Grab my phone." She knew the drill now, having argued successfully against him being the one to work the phone while driving. When she had it up near his face, he recited the lyric possibilities into the phone, knowing she would have already launched the notes app he used. "Not great."

"Doesn't suck," she offered, and he knew from the lightness of her tone she was smiling. "It doesn't suck, Bibi." A little pause, then in a voice hardened with resolve, she asked, "Why doesn't your brother know he's your hero?"

"Because I never had occasion to tell him. You know the story, Mercedes. He was gone, well before I would have been comfortable sharing." *Two more blocks.* "And pretty much since I dropped back into his life unannounced, he's been subject to me fucking up in one way or another. Not a lotta time for heart-to-hearts." Pulling into the parking lot, he slotted the car into a spot near the back door, already considering he might need to make a quick retreat if he couldn't hack it. *Environmental trigger*, he thought.

"First time I saw him—after years, mind you—the first time I saw him, within six hours I was seizing in the ER from alcohol poisoning." He twisted, reaching over the back of the seat to grab the guitar. "I nearly died. They had to shock my heart to get it beating right." She ducked to the side to avoid being hit by the instrument.

"While I was gone, he got a girlfriend, and they got serious. Then he had to rescue her from a terrible situation, all while dealing with cleaning up the massive pile of shit I left behind when I skipped away to rehab." Voice rising an octave, he finished with, "La-di-dah, fix it for me, big bro. You got this, right? *Jesus.*" Pausing a moment with the case held awkwardly in his lap, he looked at Mercedes, who was watching him, silent and undemanding, her nonjudgmental demeanor exactly what he'd come to depend on.

"I get out. I'm in his way but useful for the first time in my life. He left on a trip, was supposed to be gone three weeks. Turned into months and months. He got back, got married, got a honeymoon trip out of the way, and then got to be a father. His life has been moving forwards at light speed, and me wanting a minute more than is absolutely needed is wrong." He shook his head. "That's one of the things fucking with my head. Knowing he's giving so much to me when he should be focused on Ruby and their babies. He makes room for all my shit, and I just let him."

He pushed his door open, watching as she did the same on her side. They stood facing across the top of the car for a moment, and he said, "I'll talk to him soon." She didn't move, her expression didn't change, nothing gave him indication she was anything other than mildly interested, but he felt her disapproval as clearly as if she were shouting it. "I will. I'll talk to him tonight."

She lifted an eyebrow, and he laughed. "Promise." With a slow nod, she granted him a reprieve before taking it away along with all the air in his chest when she quietly asked, "What is the name of the beautiful woman who is looking as if you hung the moon, Bibi?"

***

Fingers working on the strings, Benny quietly warmed up, trying to be unobtrusive in the corner near the stage. God, he'd missed this. Every moment he spent not playing, he missed the music without realizing why he felt crippled. Half the man he needed to be; without music it was as if someone had ripped away one of his senses, and left him alone. Music had been such a constant in his life for so long, all the way back to when he met the old man. "Harddrive."

"What?" The question came from behind him, and he jumped, shifting position to see an older biker standing behind him. "What'd you say, boy?"

"I was thinking about back when I learned how to play." Benny strummed across the strings, flexing his fingers for a moment before clamping down on the frets, sliding to the first chord in one of the first songs Harddrive had taught him. It was a terrible tune called "An Irish Ballad," one specifically designed to capture the attention of a totally fucked-up desperate-for-attention kid first learning to play. He softly crooned the lyrics, downplaying them because the topic matter was harsh, satirical, about a girl who murdered her entire family, never seeing what she'd done as wrong. Interrupting himself, he told the biker, "An old man in Wyoming taught me. Took me under his wing. I went to his bike shop every Saturday for more than a year. Good guy. Harddrive."

"Fucking shit. You gotta be fuckin' kidding me." Shaking his head, the old biker twisted his torso and yelled across the room. "Bingo, get your ass over here." He waved a hand over his head, then called, "Dixie, you too, darlin'." He turned back to Benny, "I grew up with Harddrive, we served together overseas. Bingo's his blood brother."

Within a minute, Benny was surrounded by Harddrive's family, and found himself sharing every story he could dredge out of his memory and pass along. They were eager for news, thrilled with this new connection with their brother and father, however tenuous it was through Benny. More Rebel members came over, joined in the conversation, and they shared their stories, too. Turned out the man was a legend, which meant with Benny knowing Harddrive and these men knowing them both, Benny found himself drawn a little deeper into the fold. Harddrive's daughter, Dixie, gave Benny the sweetest, tightest hug before she went back over to sit with her husband, whispering in his ear she couldn't wait to hear him play tonight.

Bingo slapped his shoulder with a hard palm, told him to break a leg, then turned and walked away to meet Bear, who was approaching their little group. Reaching out, Bingo clasped Bear's upper arm in a tight grip, pulling him close. Benny couldn't hear what words passed between the two men, but Bear's look his direction was searching as he nodded sharply once. Bingo shook Bear, then pulled him close again for a moment; whatever he said this time caused a wave of grief to pass through the man. The sorrow a nearly physical thing you could watch move over his face, and he nodded again, more slowly.

Dropping his eyes immediately to the toes of his boots, Benny didn't watch his friend finish walking his direction. Didn't want to see whatever new look Bear wore like an ill-fitting skin. Simply tipped his head towards the stage, waiting. Waiting for Bear to deny him the opportunity to take those few steps up to the platform, waiting for this to be stripped away as a mistake. "Benny." Bear's voice was rough, hoarse with an emotion Benny couldn't place, but didn't dare look to see. "Son, look at me." Benny let his head rock back and forth twice, trying to stall, still wanting to wait and find out what Bear intended for tonight.

"Son." Benny lifted his head slightly, only until the headstock of Bear's guitar came into focus. Seeing the wood, worn from years of constant playing in uncertain conditions. A used instrument, but still capable of bringing forth music beautiful enough to break your heart into pieces. Tatty and tired, but infused with a fierce strength through the artistry that created it, with durability enough to carry on for years more. Like Bear. Like Slate. *I hope like me.*

"I was wrong."

Bear's words caused Benny's gaze to jerk up, eyes locking to his friend's face, seeing sorrow and regret there, not the blame and disappointment he had expected. "Slate, man. He's got the right of it. Came and talked to me last week. Told me what you've been doing. You and I, we know why you're doing it, even if he doesn't. But he knew other things. Asked me how in the hell I got to be the one to decide how many chances at redemption were enough. Asked me how did I know exactly when to pull the plug." Bear reached out, wrapped an arm around Benny's shoulders, tugged him to face the stage and pushed him up the steps. The hesitant sounds of his sneakers so different from the bold slaps of Bear's leather boots. "I realized I don't. Can't. If people had given up on me...well, let's just say I'm glad they didn't."

Benny's mouth wasn't working, but he thought, *That doesn't make any sense, what would Bear have to forgive?*

A shadow crossed the stage in front of Benny, and he looked up to see Mason putting a stool in front of a microphone, dragging it slightly to one side before he seemed happy with the placement. Bear was crowding behind Benny, forcing him forward one step at a time. Looking up, Mason stared at him, and Benny felt caught, pinned in place. As it had before, a weight began to gather on his chest, pushing hard against his lungs, keeping them from bringing in enough air, gluing his feet to the floor. Then one corner of Mason's mouth tipped up, and he gestured towards the stool, saying in a low, gruff voice, "You've put the work in. Proud of you, son. This is your time, Benny. Your time to show us what you can be. Show us what you dream of, brother."

Mason's words hit him hard. If he was going to show anyone, he wanted his brother—

A slow clapping started near the front of the stage, and he turned to see Slate standing there with Ruby in the crook of one arm. She was grinning mischievously at Benny over the bands of muscles and ink surrounding her and he remembered her quiet faith in him, her adoption of him as a family she wanted...maybe even needed. A touch on his arm pulled his attention away, and he looked to see Chase standing there, shoulder-to-shoulder with him. Benny shifted to find Bear had taken a step back, flanking him on the other side.

Overwhelmed, he tipped his head down a moment, listening to the growing applause in the room, fear and relief warring for space in his chest. Throat tight, he swallowed hard, pulling in a breath that shuddered its way into his lungs, beating back the fear. *They're here for me.*

Clearing his throat, he lifted his head to stare at Bear. *Go time.* In a barely audible whisper, he asked the familiar phrase, one they had used to start every practice session, back before he fucked it all up. "So, how do you see this going tonight?" He stayed fixed on Bear's face, waiting for the response. Surprised when it came worded as it did.

"Your call, son." Bear motioned to someone in the audience, and Benny saw Vic climbing the stairs, but he hadn't seen a kit and wondered at the two guitars in his drummer's hands. Benny was shocked to see Mitty walk onto the stage behind Vic, holding out his hand to take the five-string he preferred.

He came back from Michigan. For me. They're all here for me. With a grin, Benny said, "We're gonna need a bigger stage, man." Bear's mouth stretched in a grin, then he strummed his guitar once, twice, urging Benny without words to get things moving. "Okay, let's do a couple of OY songs we all know, then we'll...wing it, yeah?" Twisting, he saw nods coming at him from every person on the stage so he moved to the stool, knowing it for the honor it was, placed there by the hands of the man his brother loved most in the world. *Just maybe, except me*, he thought, seeing Slate's proud face watching him. *He loves me.*

Leaning forward, he put his mouth near the microphone and in what he desperately hoped was a low, steady voice, filled with the confidence of knowing he was finally—*God, finally*—surrounded by people who gave a shit about him, he asked the crowd, "Are you ready to hear some rock and roll?"

The answering whistles and shouts made him grin. Mouth to the microphone again, he said, "Sorry to disappoint, we only have folk songs on tap tonight." Boos and hisses, good-natured catcalls sounded, and he grinned again, mouth still to the mic. "Bluegrass, I mean. We got bluegrass."

Mason's voice rang out in a loud and raucous shout. "Fuck *yeah*, love me some Kentucky down-home music." *Crap, now I gotta remember what fucking bluegrass songs I know.*

"Well, that's for later. Guess we'll have to play some rock and roll after all. Y'all ready? Ready for some music right here and right now?" He settled himself on the stool with his heel propped on one rung, guitar balanced on his leg, other foot planted on the stage as he waited out the applause. "Here we go." Without additional preamble, heel bumping against the stage floor, keeping time, he swung into the first song he could think of, "Born Into Trouble," and as the men on stage with him found their places in the melody he looked straight at Slate, willing him to understand the meaning behind the lyrics were so different now. Promising himself he would tell his brother outright, make him understand.

Mouth working automatically, words flowing easily, singing a song he had performed so many times he had literally done it in his sleep, Benny's heart skipped as he watched Mercedes make her way to the table he'd been trying to ignore, the woman seated there looking at him, watching him. Waiting for him to claim her. Lucia's face swung to the side, her attention taken from the stage when Mercedes planted herself in the chair next to her. *Shit.*

Twenty

Benny played onstage for nearly three hours without a break. There were moments where he spoke into the microphone, talking to the patrons around the bar, speaking to his friends and family. Mercedes kept him supplied with water, and along with the rest of the band, he found himself upending bottle after bottle, the lights taking a heavy toll on all the musicians. The other men had gradually collected stools and chairs, and they now sat in a rough half circle reminding Benny strongly of group, an intimate collection of people who shared a force in their lives that drove them to great lengths to feed their need. In this case, it was music and the joy they found while creating it.

After each run to the stage with an armful of bottled water, Mercedes retreated back to the table she seemed to be permanently sharing with Lucia. Moments after she replanted her ass in the seat, the two women leaned in close, having what looked like a lengthy heart-to-heart. Bonding over a sticky bar table listening to the oft-changing music led by a man who felt more broken bard than band front guy. But it was the role cast for him tonight, and he led his friends from song to song, even dredging up a bluegrassy tune Mason approved of, if his smile and bobbing head were any indications.

All night the music had held him together, and when he felt like he'd fall apart, Bear took over, nudging their playing to some of the songs he knew best, the angel playlist he'd shared with Benny. What Bear had first started out with. Playing and singing along with him was surreal, knowing the man had lost everything and then worked his ass off to find there was more to come. More in his future, waiting for him to be ready to claim it. *He never gave up.*

Benny's eyes drifted back to Lucia, thinking about the claiming part of things. It wasn't until this last trip to rehab that he'd spent much time talking about the things that happened with Benita. He'd opened up to Doc about all the shameful things he'd done at Benita's urging, but if he were honest, and honesty was surely demanded when doing the kind of soul searching he'd been conducting, it hadn't been hard to talk him into any of it. Doc argued strongly that all blame rested on Benita's shoulders, but Benny knew differently.

At first, yes. Maybe. He'd been too young and vulnerable to reject anything she wanted, his need for acceptance so strong that even her brand of fucked-up felt good. But, even after the power in the relationship shifted, he scarcely refused her anything. Couldn't find it in himself to turn down a blow job, or a wet dick and Benita liked it. *I liked it.* Collusion disguised as acquiescence.

Doc had explained how things had gotten tangled up in his head. Desire and drink. Booze and bustin' his nut. Tied up together in a way that meant he didn't have a good chance at ditching one without the other. Thank God, that was the one thing he seemed to have known instinctively, not been able to put a label on it before the doc talked him through, but knew in his gut. So, since arriving in Fort Wayne, all those months ago, he'd unconsciously abstained from sex.

He and Lucia had played around a little, and when the need reared up inside him, it scared the shit out of him. So even before going back to rehab this last time—*please God, let it be the last time*—he had kept things slow and low-key as much as he could, suffering her touches and teasing, giving her what he could. Knowing what she needed was more of the same. Tender caring, from someone who loved her. *Someone like me.*

"Hey, you in there?" Bear's voice came from beside his ear and Benny jerked away, pulling his head around to find him standing close. "You've been staring at my Luce for a good ten minutes, strumming the same tune. We're tired of playing that one, dude. Pick something and go with it."

Nodding slowly, he let his hands rest on the strings, waiting as the others did the same, Vic using the moment to set his guitar aside and make his way off stage. Without giving himself time to think about what he was doing, Benny shifted his grip, readying for the first swing across the sound box.

Turning to look at Lucia, he found her eyes on him, and the steady, loving look took his breath away. *Even now, she cares.* A D-minor slipped to a C-major, then back again, and again, weaving through the sounds into the melody. Bringing Bear, then Chase in, setting their roles in the song, Mitty bleeding along the edge with them until they settled, then Benny swung off to the counter, holding and holding, then the bridge, holding a moment, then back around to the melody. They took one full tour through the music before he let himself lean into the microphone, every eye turned towards the stage as the spotlight focused on him.

"This is a song I wrote a few months ago. We've been working on it, polishing it up, waiting for the right time to let it shine. This feels good. Feels right. Full circle here tonight, playin' in Marie's with friends and family. I hope you like it." He paused briefly, then, pulling all his courage together, said, "Luce," his voice fell to a whisper as he finished, "this is for you, baby." Bear's indrawn breath was audible, but his hands never wavered on the strings as Luce's lips parted, waiting. "I call it, 'The Promise of Love.'" Then Benny, for the first time in his life, sang a song to a woman he loved. A woman he prayed knew every word had been written for her, meant for her, and she was meant for him

If you'd told me I'd see her once and be hooked,
I'd laugh at you.
If you'd told me her beauty would call to me in the night,
I'd laugh at you.
If you'd promised me a lifetime of beauty like hers,
I'd laugh at you.

Knowing nothing
Nothing is as sweet,
Nothing is as pure,
As the promise of love.

There's a moment in time where your heart knows,
Mine beats for you.
Never making peace with the hollow left behind,
My heart weeps for you.
Finding you again grants my dream come true,
It's always been you.

It's you for me and me for you
Nothing is as sweet
Nothing is as pure
As a promise come true.

Be my promise, baby.
My promise of love.
True love come to me.
My promise come true.
Love me, like I love you.
Be my baby, be mine.
My baby.
Mine.

As the last notes trailed off into silence, the bar erupted in applause. Stomping boots, slapping hands, piercing fingers-in-the-mouth whistles—they gave him one of the loudest ovations he'd ever received. But most important was the woman who made her slow way towards the stage. Dark hair swinging around her shoulders, brown eyes only for him, he waited, and she came to him. *Mine.*

Twenty-One

Benny stretched, rolling to his side on the couch, hearing voices in the kitchen. *Fuck.* He needed more sleep. Sounded like Ruby had company, and since he was still staying with them, camping out on their couch, she couldn't entertain in the living room, so she made do. Never complaining, that wasn't her way, she simply made things work. Shushed laughter told him she was watching out for him. He stretched again, then rolled to his back, shoving one hand behind his head, as with his eyes closed, he considered his night.

Best ever, was the first thought to pop into his head. Finding the music, finding his way through to being able to bring that out in himself, felt like he was flying high over everything. A better high than he'd ever had before, and he made a note to call Doc and tell her he got it. How tied up music and sex was with the booze and drugs for him. Harddrive had been the first person to see he needed something other than what he was getting, but over time, even the music had gotten warped somehow.

Not anymore, he vowed, then grinned. Being part of a productive, creative, sober band would be a change. A huge one, one he knew wouldn't be easy, but it was a challenge he welcomed. Bear was a big part of what happened last night, and he couldn't believe the change in course there. In the weeks since he'd been thoroughly put in his place by the man, Benny had come to realize some hard truths about himself. The work he'd been doing wasn't for anyone this time. Wasn't for Slate, or Ruby, or even Lucia. *All for me.*

He sighed. *Luce.* These past weeks of seeing her, knowing she was out of reach, never to be his, never anything more than a friend had been harder than anything he'd ever done. Knowing it was through his own behavior and actions he'd lost her? That tore his heart out of his chest, every time he woke and knew he wouldn't be seeing her that day. Or the next. Or ever, if Bear had his way.

Then to see her last night, looking at him with such hurt in her eyes, but still showing up to support him. For all she knew the distance between them was entirely Benny pulling away, needing space. Intentionally being busy. Having other plans. The million and one excuses he had come up with in response to her calls and texts, her inbox messages, and dozens of questions passed through Ruby. *I love her.* This affirmation was as rock solid now as he had been when he told Bear. A statement he knew would only grow stronger every day. No matter what, even if he never got to tell her. Then last night happened.

Her in his arms last night? Amazing.

She walked to the edge of the stage, and he laid his guitar down, jumping off the raised platform. As he had so many times in the past, he reached for her hand, but she slipped through and into his arms. He held her, then, as if they were in a private room, as if there weren't a hundred bikers and their women watching. Blocking out the words, the shouts of laughter, the rumbling questions. Holding his Luce close, wrapping her up in everything he had to give her, face buried in her hair, hers pressed tightly to his neck. Arms secure around his waist, she held on, and when the men on the stage behind him began playing a slow song, he swayed with her, breathing her in. Beginning to believe this was happening. She was real.

When the music ended, he led her to a quiet corner of the bar, sitting beside her on the bench seat of a booth. "Benny," she began to speak, then faltered, halting when he lifted a hand and curled his fingers into her hair, tugging her mouth closer to him for a kiss, the soft brushing against her lips torture when it ended so quickly. Then, in a rush she said, "We need to talk." Now his heart was seizing in his chest, but for an entirely different reason. Terrified. Those words didn't say "we're building something here," they didn't say "I cannot wait to be with you."

She couldn't have missed his silence, but she forged through, making certain all was good with him as he found his fears weren't based on anything. Mouth open, he stalled, not knowing what to say, but she made it all right, as he knew she would.

"With Bear's stuff, and whatever it was that crawled up your butt, we haven't had much time to talk. Everything happened when we were barely getting used to each other." She took a long, shaky breath. "But, I want you to know I understand you need to work on your sobriety." Chin tipped down, she hid from him, and he reached out to lift her face, needing to see. There were tears in her beautiful eyes, but she bravely moved forward in the resolute way he'd come to expect from her. "Just don't shut me out again, okay? I need to know you're all right." Gaze locked on his, she pinned him in place. "You...matter so much to me, Benny." There was the tiniest hitch to her voice when she continued, "I need you to know that what you said? Up there on the stage? It meant everything."

"It's all true, you know that, right?" He heard the pleading in his voice, willing her to believe him.

"I know, Benny. For a long time now, it's been you and me." That tremble was again present, and he leaned into her, resting his forehead

against hers. "And what you gave me up there? You gotta know it comes back to you tenfold. A hundredfold. So much, Benny. Promise."

DeeDee shook him from his thoughts when she walked into the living room, holding Allen, pausing in the doorway with one hand on her hip. "You're finally up." With a grin, she padded barefoot towards him, and Ruby appeared in the doorway behind her, Dani in her arms. Eyes to DeeDee, he stared up as she stopped in front of him. "Got a favor to ask you, kiddo."

***

Standing in the Zamboni tunnel just off the rink, Benny shook his arms out for the thousandth time. Bouncing from foot to foot, he tried to shake the nerves wrecking his composure. Wireless microphone clenched in one fist, his fingers were hurting, the flesh bloodless and white from clamping so tightly around the plastic. The sound of the crowd rose in the arena, swelling into the space, chatter and conversations lifting to the rafters as people filtered in, finding their seats. *Hockey.* He shook his head.

The Tridents were in the playoffs, but if they didn't win tonight, it would be the last game of the year for the team. *Sudden death,* he thought and had an unexpected memory of ceiling tiles split by bright lights, flashing overhead as the surface he was on racketed down an endless hallway. He shook it off. Jase's team had to win to keep going, and a loss would mean immediate elimination.

DeeDee had organized this, him being here, giving him a chance to perform without the pressure of performance. One song, one minute and fifty seconds by his watch. No music, pure voice; he would be singing the national anthem a cappella. He'd joked with Slate earlier about taking book on the length, telling him he'd throw short or long if he got a sign. *Like I'll ever make it big enough to worry about that.* Chin lifted, he hummed a scale, stretching his neck to one side and then the other, trying and failing to block out the sounds around him.

Feet planted wide, face raised, eyes closed, he let himself grow still, calming his thoughts, and just breathed. Simply...breathed, soaking in the knowledge he was about to sing again. Sing for people who didn't know him, and who, for the most part, could do without his performance entirely because it would be lodged midway between the team taking to the ice and when the referee would drop the first puck of the game. A necessary annoyance for some, a patriotic celebration for others, but not entertainment. That would be the guys with sticks. Realizing he wasn't the draw, an even larger measure of the stress and nerves dropped away.

And then it happened. As it so often did, trying to take him unawares.

The craving flooded in around the edges of his mind, swamping him, taking him under. He was drowning, carried off in a tide of hunger for something. Anything. Cramps curled in his belly, gut and muscles revolting, a riot in his body for a demand that must be met. His chest seized, lungs refusing to work. No air. Nothing. Pure need.

Heat hit his skin. A small hand to his arm captured his attention, and he tipped his head down to see Mercedes looking up, her hair blue and purple this week. "Bibi." All she had to do was say his name, and he took a breath. Another one. Her belief anchoring him.

An arm circled his waist, and he looked the other direction, seeing those beautiful brown eyes shining up at him with love. He stared, breathing, wondering if she knew the miracle she performed every time she looked at him like that. He had everything he needed, right here. *Everything*.

Mercedes' hand flexed on his arm, and he felt her push him, hearing the introduction coming from the announcer, "...Jones, lead singer for the chart-busting band, Occupy Yourself."

Lucia smiled, and he dipped his head, brushed his lips across hers and took a deep breath, giving himself a final moment of peace before he stepped out onto the rug the arena crew had dragged onto the ice.

Wouldn't do for the loudmouth guy to fall on his ass. "Please rise, and gentlemen, remove your hats…"

Microphone lifted to his lips, Benny swept his gaze across the people crowded into the rows of seats stretching far overhead. As he opened his mouth and took a breath, there were only a few faces turned his way, most of their eyes were fixed on the flag hanging from the rafters. *Perfect.* Strong and proud, his voice flowed out, mastering the notes, rising and falling, until two minutes and three seconds later his lips closed, cutting off the final word. Applause, ringing so loudly his chest shook with it. An unfamiliar noise, the slapping of wood on ice and he looked over to see Jase and the Tridents looking at him, yelling and whistling, tapping their hockey sticks against the boards and ice, congratulating him.

Two fingers to his brow, he saluted Jase, gaining a chin tip in return, then he was off the rug and back into the tunnel. Stepping to one side, he, Lucia, and Mercedes waited so the arena workers could quickly clear the ice, close the doors, and ensure everything was ready for the game to begin. "Well done, Bibi." He flashed Mercedes a grin intended as thanks for her quiet praise. Lucia received thanks of a different kind, his mouth working against hers, her giving back to him at the same time, arm tight around his waist, squeezing.

"Let's go watch the game," he said, tugging on Lucia's hand. The club had rented a clubhouse suite for this game, and he knew Slate would be there. He thought Bear would likely be there, too, and while that thought made him nervous for reasons far different from the singing he had just done, he was determined to show everyone he could change. Had changed. His arm tightened around Lucia, pulling her into his side. Still totally a selfish bastard, he was fixing himself so he'd be better, and so he could have what he wanted.

Walking into the suite, he stopped dead in his tracks, Luce, still connected to him, jolting as she was jerked to a halt. His throat closed, bile boiling up into the back of his mouth as he swallowed convulsively. *Shit.* Nearly every legal-aged person in the room had a drink in their hand.

A year ago, he would have never noticed the scent, but now, after so long fighting the pull of alcohol, he could nearly taste the yeasty flavor of the many beers scattered around the room. A presence on his other side, hand to his arm, then her soft voice, "Bibi, this is no different from playing in the bar. People who don't have a problem with alcohol drink. You cannot." She got closer, crowding him and he stepped out of the flow of traffic, half-turning away from the room, using both Lucia and Mercedes to block him from view. "If this is too much, we can walk to the rooftop patio, get some air. It's only a three-minute stroll." Mercedes proved she'd again done her homework, figured out what the triggers might be and then looked for ways to help him manage his responses. *What would I do without her?*

"I'm good," he lied, the tightness in his throat making speaking painful. Shaking his head, he said, "It...caught me off-guard. I wasn't thinking about there being booze." She rolled her eyes at him, and he laughed. "Yeah, I know, right? Wasn't thinking. I expect it in the bar, do my pep talk thing. Get ready. There, it's not a surprise. Here—"

"Benny." His name called from across the room, and he looked up to see both Slate and Mason bearing down on him, and was grateful for their empty hands in a way which nearly pissed him off. *They shouldn't have to worry about me.* "Hey, shrimp." Slate thumped his shoulder, and he acknowledged both men with a chin lift, standing in place, glancing at a TV screen over their shoulders. Trying to look anywhere except at the booze in the room. Avoiding their empty hands pointing out his failures. *Fuck.*

It looked like the game was already underway, and he wondered how much Jase would get to play. Benny listened to his brother and Mason for a few minutes, accepting their praise of the anthem as graciously as he could, still feeling as if his skin was crawling, that brief flash of success wiped away by his failure to cope.

DeeDee stood alone near the open front of the suite, arms wrapped around herself, hands cupping opposite elbows. Luce was busy chatting with one of the women and Mercedes had made herself scarce, but he knew she was likely lurking close by, waiting for him to ask for a beer, so she could jump out like a sober ninja, knocking the drink from his clutching hand. He snorted at his melodramatic flair, made what he hoped was a graceful exit, and moved to stand next to DeeDee, stretching his arms out to lean against the railing.

"Wanted to thank you." He kept his eyes on the players skating up and down the rink, the swirl of colors and motion hypnotic, soothing until they crashed to an abrupt halt against the edges. "I get you put yourself out there for me tonight. So, thank you." Surprised when a strong arm circled his waist, he looked down at DeeDee to find her face turned up to his. He didn't move, not sure what she wanted, but not wanting to cause offense.

"Didn't do it for you." Her voice was hushed, like this was a secret and he stared at her, not sure how to take what she'd said. "Love my girl." Ruby wasn't her daughter by blood, but this was an example where family didn't necessarily mean related because even if they weren't mother-daughter, their bond was as tight as any he'd ever seen. "She likes you." He knew Ruby did, but it felt good to hear her affection confirmed like this. That he hadn't fucked everything up with her. "She loves your brother." She did, too. So much, you could see it on her face every time she looked at Slate. "Wants him to have whatever he wants. She'll put her ass on the line for that, anytime, any day. That was her ass on the line tonight. She pushed this with Jase." Her arm gave him a squeeze. "And it all came out right, yeah? You did well, and Slate got something he needed." There was a shout from the arena quickly buried by the blast of a horn, and she looked away quickly, then the warmth of her grip dropped away, and she lifted both hands to her mouth, shouting, "Way to go, Spencer! Go, Tridents!"

She looked supremely happy, and he had to ask, wondered too much not to. "What happened?"

Head back, she laughed so hard it drew the attention of several people nearby. "Jase scored a goal. This is his last game, and he scored a goal. That's"—she leaned closer, speaking quietly, another secret—"a big deal for him." Patting his chest with her palm, she told Benny, "Watch at the intermission. He's going to announce the foundation."

"Foundation?" Benny realized he'd been so soaked up in his own misery over the past months, he'd missed out on a lot with the people in his life. Looking around, he saw Ruby seated in an armchair, Allen in her lap holding onto her fingers and standing. Wobbling, sure, but still supporting his little baby ass with his own two legs. "What foundation?"

"My old man is retiring, you know about that. Last game and all. He needed to keep hockey. It's been his life for so long, I can't imagine he'd be good without it. He wouldn't be. The game makes him happy, and I don't mind sharing him with something that makes him so happy. So he cooked up an idea to do a charity, raising scholarship money to get kids into training camps and stuff. Started down that road, decided he didn't like some of the camps available. They were all about gear and schools and who your daddy was. Charity cases were treated like...charity cases. Kids whose folks couldn't afford the expensive training got left behind because even raw talent needs a chance. An opportunity to learn, to push, prove themselves." *Like musicians*, he thought. She turned to look down at the ice as a buzzer sounded. Benny watched as the other team skated off the ice, but stayed in their bench area while all the Tridents lined up on the centerline.

"So he came up with the idea of creating a foundation which would do both. Raise money to cover costs, so every kid gets a chance to love hockey like Jase does. And find a facility where he could do classes, lessons, workshops, training camps...everything a player needed, right here in Fort Wayne. Make it a mecca for hockey. That's been his saying for the past couple of months. Level the playing field. Smooth the ice." She leaned against the railing. "It matters so much to him, and he's done it. Got the paperwork filed, found a place and bought it. It's being gutted now, renovated for the kids. Rink, changing rooms, media room, training equipment. He's got it all lined up. Making the announcement now." She pointed, and Benny watched as an unhelmeted Jase skated to the center of the rink with a wireless microphone in hand.

"So proud of him." An arm circled his waist, and he looked down to see Luce standing there, eyes to the man on the ice. "Him and Bear, Bingo, they all work so hard to make things better for kids."

Benny's neck twisted and he looked around the room. Almost all eyes were aimed at the ice, these men and women here to support one of their own. A man they loved without hesitation because he deserved it. *Not like me.* Someone had rested their drink on the counter next to where he and Luce stood. Five inches from his hand, what looked like a bourbon waited. As the room erupted in shouts and clapping, boots stomping to add to the din, he caught Mercedes' gaze trained steadily on him. Fingers curling into Luce's waist, he anchored himself, giving Mercedes a sharp nod she slowly returned.

Twenty-Two

"Dude, gimme." Chase's voice came from behind him and pulled him from his thoughts. He'd arrived early to their practice room in the back of Marie's and grabbed his guitar. Anything to fill his hands, keep them busy, keep his mind busy. Mercedes would be stationed in the hallway outside, book in hand and ass to the floor, legs sprawling sideways. "That's sick. Go again, brother. I want that. Gimme."

Benny grinned, hands moving across the strings. He'd been messing around with something over the past couple of days, working on it and working it until the music was flowing through him like it used to. It didn't suck, he knew it, could feel it and now hearing Chase's response solidified that knowledge. "Good, yeah?"

"Hell yeah. I want it. Gimme." Chase slung his guitar strap over his shoulder, eyes and his full attention to Benny's fingers on the strings as he fumbled with the other end, attaching it to the base of his guitar. "Want. Want. Want." On a chant, Chase picked up the melody, their standard process for jamming on new songs. "Want." He steadied the song, kept it moving forward, freeing Benny's fingers to wander and find the counter, find the hook to drive it harder, farther. "Want."

An hour later, they were both covered in sweat, but the song was blocked and notated, a recording on each of their phones. *Good*, Benny thought, with a shiver. No lyrics, but that was okay. It happened both ways for him. He'd find a phrase and follow it, lacing the words together and finding the music as he went. Or he could latch onto the music, rolling through the process and then the words would come. Benny shook his head, flinging his wet hair wildly as he grinned. Both he and Chase laughed, fingers staying in motion, tunes popping into their playing and they'd play by ear, chasing those notes, the results ranging from cartoon theme songs to loose variations on classics.

The door opened, and Mitty walked in followed closely by Vic. Benny stood, fingers moving on the strings, up and down, back and forth, watching as his friends and bandmates greeted each other, sliding into their customary roles for a practice session. He had something that would shake them up today, and he hoped like fuck he was doing the right thing.

Vic stepped to his practice kit, a sprawling amalgamation of percussion pieces so he'd have anything he wanted at his fingertips, a way to refine songs and determine what would be needed for any particular song setup. Benny watched as the drummer touched the rims and edges of the equipment reverently, the action telling in a way he didn't think Vic knew. This was a man who loved music, loved making music and Benny felt a twist of pain and guilt that he'd been the reason Vic had gotten derailed. *If I hadn't lined him up for OY, he'd be playing right now, not stuck in a backroom of a bar, about to roll into practice again.*

Shoving that regret to the back of his mind, he tried to focus on where he hoped they were headed. *I can't change the past.* Something his sponsor had told him but hadn't sunk in circled through his head. *Make amends for your wrongs, unless atonement would cause further harm.* The only one here he hadn't harmed was Chase, except by extension. He had undoubtedly hurt his brother, and his brother was Chase's dad's closest friend. *Zero degrees of separation for my shit.*

He shivered, dreading this while at the same time anticipating what would be happening in about thirty minutes when the door opened the next time. "Hey, guys," he started, keeping his fingers moving. *My security blanket.* "Got something to say." Three sets of gazes turned his way, but they followed his lead, staying in the music.

Vic's leg pumped, softly pounding the bass, muscled arms working effortlessly to stroke the heads of his toms and snares. Thrashing out the heartbeat of the band in a way that pushed them to be better. Quiet faith in the music, in his friends.

Mitty plucked at the keys of the board on stands in front of him. He did so much, worked alongside Benny as tech for whatever was needed, could and did pick up the bass when they needed him, but his love was built around black and white. With a classical background and training, he could deconstruct songs and help put them back together in a way that made everything he worked on special.

Chase, fingers moving across the frets, arm strumming tirelessly. His gaze was trusting and open. Seeing it, Benny was reminded the boy looked to him for a lot of things. Another reason to stay sober, hand back to Mason a little bit of the goodness that man had given Slate.

"I fucked up so much." Mitty's gaze sharpened. He'd been around the longest, seen the most of Benny's fuckups. "I'll never be able to thank you for what you did." Each of them knew what they gave him, what they'd done to help him come back. "We've been in a holding pattern for a while." Nods from the two professional musicians, and a grin from Chase. The boy'd been on stage a handful of times and had the bug, but hadn't played for a crowd that wasn't plump with friends. Still, his kind of easy enthusiasm could fire a crowd in a way that was infectious. "Time to break free." Unconsciously, he'd picked up the pace, shifting to a driving beat that Vic snagged back and drifted a little sideways, forcing them down to steady. *Yeah, I know I'm not in control*, he thought, grinning at the drummer making goofy faces at him.

"Time to settle in, get serious." Chase looked confused because to him, this was what making music was, playing with friends until your fingers bled but loving every minute. "I've talked to that downtown place." Mitty's eyes sharpened more; he knew where this was leading. "Booked time. Two days." Now Vic was the one leading them into a drive-by, shattering the rhythms set so far, Benny putting his head down as he tried to follow. Tried, found it, fed it to Mitty and Chase, and minutes later, the four of them were on the same page again. "Three weeks from today, we're layin' tracks. A demo."

"You looking for representation?" That was from Vic, probably the savviest of them all, having been raised in the industry. Benny nodded, and Vic glanced around the room, sweat starting to shine on his shoulders. *Finally, he shows he's working.* "We're missing a key part, friend." Vic halted in place, resting his hands on the skins in front of him to still the remaining vibrations. "I don't want to blow this vibe, but we need a fucking bass."

"Yeah, we do. Guys, I asked a local to step in today. Totally sick, man, seen this shit on stage in a dozen places, with a dozen bands. Blending bass line, stand out solo—this one does it all. I think I found us a fit." On cue, as if this had been rehearsed, there was a knock at the door, and Mercedes' head rounded the edge. She caught Benny's nod and stepped to the side, opening the door wide. "It's our first go, and we'll see, but you're right, Vic, we need a bass." He pointed to the doorway as a woman stepped through. "Guys, meet Bonnie Dupont." There was a brief, discordant clash of wood on rims and his gaze shot to Vic in time to witness an unsettling emotion twist through the man's features. *Shit.* He hadn't thought about possible previous encounters, even knowing Vic had been stuck here in town the whole time Benny was in rehab. *Shit.*

Bonnie angled her head, dark hair shot through with shimmering blue sweeping across her shoulder. She had a case in hand, and stood there a moment, feet apart, hip angled out, exuding confidence. "Victor," she murmured just the one word, holding Vic's gaze for a moment before she turned to the other two. "Dmitri, heard good things about you, man.

Can't wait to rip it. Thanks for the chance." Tipping her head to one side, she grinned at Chase. "Chase, dude, I got brothers about your age. You'll have to cut me some slack if I treat you like shit, yeah?" She was hitting the right note with each of them, and Benny twisted to see Mercedes grinning at him through the narrowing slit as she closed the door. "Benny." Bonnie pulled his attention back to her. "Thank you, man. Glad to get the call."

"Okay." He clapped his hands and then rested his elbows across the top of his guitar. "Set up, let's see what we can do together. We're gonna get started. I've put some music over there." He pointed to where she'd be standing in their group, and she nodded, walking over to pick up the pile of papers. He heard the intense tone in his own voice and knew it revealed how much he needed this to work. "Let's make some fuckin' music, all right?"

***

"You gonna be cool with me if this works out, Victor?" Benny started to open the door to the bathroom and paused, locked in place as he listened to what he hoped was his new bassist and the best drummer he'd ever played with, talking. "I nearly called, but figured you'd not let me pass through to this point unless you were down with the idea." A shuffling sound and Vic sighed. Softly, Bonnie said, "Never thought he would spring me on you."

Silence for a moment, then, "Yeah, Bunny, I'm cool." At the nickname, Bonnie sucked in a breath that sounded wounded and painful and Vic made a strangled noise. "Sorry. I just…I'm…it's okay, no worries."

He absolutely wasn't cool, that much was clear from the sadness in his voice, but before Benny could fuck up and reveal himself to them, Bonnie said, "Right on. It'd be boss if you can do that. This means a lot, Victor." A grunt, then light footsteps moving away up the hallway and Benny sighed. He'd fucked up even trying to do right. *Shit*. Stepping out into the hallway, he found Vic still leaning against the opposite wall, eyes to the door, revealing he'd known Benny was there all along.

"Know you heard. Need you to know this is cool, you doin' this for Bonnie. She's killer, and I couldn't have picked better." Vic swallowed hard, glancing away for a moment. "Small world, ya know?" Benny nodded because he did. There was one point in his career where nearly every night he played with people he'd fucked over, been fucked by, or simply fucked. "She's a fit."

"Yeah, she is." Their session had lasted hours, far longer and better than Benny had dared hope; Bonnie sliding into place as if she'd always played with them. Done her homework to prepare, so she knew their songs, even knew their variations from watching online videos shot by fans. The only things tripping her up were the new layers added by Vic and Chase, but she'd found her way around those, too.

"Fuckin' kills, man." Vic's eyes were on the toes of his boots and Benny waited, knowing Vic needed something from him. "Finding the one," he paused, then continued, "then finding out you aren't hers." With that, Vic turned and padded up the hallway as the end door opened, the light silhouetting him, isolating his form from everything around.

***

Benny woke to trailing fingers down his ribs. Without opening his eyes, he smiled, changing position so he could wrap an arm around the woman sitting on the edge of the mattress, pulling her into bed with him. He moved her, shifting her form around, fitting it close to his. Cock swelling, blood was pounding through his veins and he wanted to be buried deep inside her. "I'm naked, baby," he murmured against the hair on top of her head, pressing a kiss there. Her palm smoothed up his arm, curling around his shoulder and he grinned when she pulled, holding him close. Nails pricked his skin and at that, his eyes shot open, seeing blonde hair instead of dark brown.

With a shove and a shout, he pushed from the bed, jumping out on the other side and whirling in anger.

Shaking his head, he stared down at the empty mattress. Nothing. *Fuck.* Swiping at his face with one palm, he shook off the dream. Chin to his chest, he closed his eyes, feeling sweat drying on his skin, chilling him to the bone. "God." He'd spent the evening with Luce and her family, hanging out on the couch, helping Eddie in the kitchen, jamming with Bear. Then, as had happened the last hundred times, Luce walked him to his car where they had a long, but controlled make-out session, ending with her panting against his neck as she trembled in his arms. And he'd driven away, leaving her waving in the driveway. Went to the apartment Mitty and Vic were renting, stalked in, and heard a chorus of laughter about his bad mood blue balls, turned on his heel and stalked back out, headed to his own place.

The closest he'd gotten to pussy in months was on the phone with Luce, listening as she fingered and stroked, making cute as fuck whispery gasps when she came. She got off on him talking to her, got off in a big way when he told her what he was doing, how she made him feel. *"Would you like that,* Papi," *her pet name for him spoken quiet as she listened to his groan. "Want my mouth?" Hand sliding up and down his cock, arm moving faster as she panted. "Want me to—"* He pulled his thoughts from those moments, shoving the memory away.

When they were together, like last night, she made it clear she was ready for more. But he'd been honest with her, so she knew both his doc and sponsor had counseled against starting anything. Their recommendation: No major changes for at least six months. Then, once he blew past the not starting, thanking God that it fell by the wayside and he had his Luce back, they had joined forces and strongly advocated going slow. *Fucking snails move faster*, he thought in frustration, willing his erection to deflate.

Just one drink. The whisper threaded through his brain, and he froze in place, every muscle seizing in response. Then he relaxed a bit, thinking,

Too right. Just one, I can handle just one. His new apartment didn't have any booze in it, but his neighbors wouldn't know he was a drunk, probably handed out beer like candy. Benita's voice, *Little boy, want some candy?* That caused bile to roll up his throat and he swallowed hard.

Chin down, he closed his eyes. Lucia's image suspended in his mind, his anchor. *I could take the edge off. Free my mind.* His hands turned into fists. *No.* Out of the blue, this time, going from thinking about loving and loving on Luce to needing *something.* Hundred miles an hour in the time it took to pull in a single breath. "I'm a fucking adult." *I can have a drink if I want.* "Grew up a long fucking time ago." *No.*

Grabbing his phone from the floor, he unlocked it, hit one button and waited. In fifteen seconds his door opened, no knocking, no pretense of privacy here. Mercedes stood there, looking at him, taking in the state of the bed, the room, the man, and knowing immediately what he needed.

Closing the door, she dropped to her ass in front of it, preparing to be his...protector or custodian—it was hard to tell. His sentinel, guardian angel. *My brother's keeper.* "How bad is it?" He didn't answer, knowing she'd see it in his face because the shakes had started, fingers jerking and trembling. Heat gathered along his skin, sweat beading on his upper lip. Naked, he felt the swirl of air along his back and shivered. "What do you need to make it better, Bibi?"

"Blow." He could taste the bitter flowing down the back of his throat, numbing everything in its path. White powder caking his nose, clouding his brain, taking the music away. "No, not blow." *I can't lose the music again.* If he had known then what it took from him, he would never have...*LIAR*, his head screamed. Knowing the way Benita introduced it, he would have taken anything she gave him.

"Booze." Next morning heaves, rooms tilting on their axis, sending him staggering from side to side, giving up and puking where he stood, or laid, uncaring of what he soiled. Waking to find bodies of strangers draped over him, find himself still inside faceless women. Lucky as fuck he hadn't caught shit that couldn't be cured. A real threat since the crew he hung with weren't too particular who they fucked. *Hell, they fucked me. Shows how low they fell.* "Not booze, no. *God.*" *I'd lose Lucia. Can't lose her.* He turned and pressed his face to the wall, the cool seeping into his overheated skin. Too temporary, like everything in his life, the minute he moved away, he'd lose even that faint comfort.

"I don't know." He shivered, skin rippling like waves on a river. "I don't know. I don't know. Don't know." Nothing close, nothing to hold onto, nothing to anchor him from being swept away again. Down and down the river, the madness of his addictions surfacing alongside him, stripping his joy and love and even his fucking breath. *Alone.* "I don't know. Don't." Sucking him under again. Out of control, nothing he could hold onto. A memory surfaced, his brother's broken voice asking, *"He gonna die?"* He slid, body giving way to the need, pressing harder against the wall, the chill all along his side now, his hip, and arms flat out, a sacrifice on the altar of something that would kill him, eventually.

"You do know, Bibi. Tell me, what do you need?" Mercedes spoke quietly, certainty infusing her voice in a way that made it impossible for Benny to deny her request. He hated her at that moment because she was so self-assured, strong. Never weak enough to fall as he had. Hated the very strength he needed. Hated she could be unaltered by life, hated she saw him like this, hated she knew him so well.

"Luce." Whirling, he put his back to the wall, eyes looking all over for his phone, finally finding it already in his hand. "I need Luce." Staring at Mercedes, he swayed as he waited for her to caution him, waited for her to tell him not to make the call. Lifting the phone to his face, he recognized the text he'd sent Mercedes nearly four hours ago, their signal he was falling out of control so fast he couldn't breathe. **SOS**.

"I need Lucia." Hands trembling, he tapped the screen and waited. She never made him wait. No games, no playing with his head. No coy persuading him to be anything other than what he was, Luce accepted him as he was. He stared at Mercedes.

"*Hola*, Benjamin," a laughing voice answered, saying his name in the Spanish way, but this voice was male, adolescent, and it took him a moment to place. *Roddy, up late, probably against orders.*

"*Hola*, Roddy." God, his voice was hoarse, sounded like he'd been screaming songs at a festival for hours. "Is Lucia around, buddy?"

Concern clear, Roddy responded immediately, all humor gone from his voice. "Yeah, Benny, she's up. Sec." Older than their years; all those kids were. Grown up in a world Benny didn't know existed, even if he'd been scraping the underbelly of a similar one far too long.

A moment and then Lucia was there, her voice making him feel steady and sure, at least, more than he had five minutes ago. He could nearly smell her perfume, feel her hair, her hand in his, sharing her unyielding strength. *Holding on.* "Benny? Roddy said...is something wrong?"

For a second he stood there, letting the rightness of this wash over him, not dragging him out to sea, the knowledge of her was enough to give him a firmer standing. With her, he felt like he could do anything. Be anyone. *Anchored.* "Benny?" There was an edge of fear to her tone, and he rushed to fill the silence.

"I need you, Luce." Raw urgency filled his voice, and he didn't care how much it gave away; with her he didn't need to be worried. She'd never take more than he could give, never ask more than he could offer. She'd drive him beyond what he thought he could do, or take, but would never leave him hanging. "I need you."

"Five minutes." No questions, no hesitation, she gave him what he needed. He could hear noise on the other end of the line, Eddie's sleepy voice, then quiet followed by a mechanical racket. Garage, overhead door. "I'm on my way, Benny. Hold on, honey." A car door slamming, then an echoing, her voice at a distance now. "Hold on. Is Mercedes with you?"

Eyes slipping closed, he sank down the surface of the wall until, heels to his ass, he sat on the floor. "Yeah. She's here."

"Good, honey. Hold on." Anything he asked for, she'd give. *Everything.* "I'm on my way."

Phone tight to his ear, unaware of how much time had passed, he heard the sound of her unlocking the apartment door. Mercedes was on the move, footsteps traveling away even as other ones made their way his direction. Through the speaker, Mercedes said, "Hang up now, Luce." Quiet in his ear, hushed voices in the hallway.

The phone remained clenched in his hand. A lifeline he couldn't let go of yet. With his lids pressed closed, he still knew when the lights were turned off in the room. Darkness surrounded him, cocooning him. He smelled Lucia before she made it to him, the scent of her sweetness and goodness rushing over him, beating back the damnable need, that living beast which gnawed at him all the time.

Fingers grazed across his side; a palm brushed his bicep, his shoulder. She was real; here and real, not a phantom in the night. Her arm curled around him, pulling him close. He shifted so he could wrap Luce up, fitting himself to her. She pressed deep like she wanted to absorb the things that were killing him. Like she could feel his pain. Her knees wedged under his legs, she curled tightly. "Hold on, honey." The words he wanted to say were trapped in his throat, so he sat there, holding Lucia, uncaring if she knew he was weeping because he called and she came. "I'm here."

"Hold on." He forced the words out around the choking lump seated deep in his chest. "Please, baby. *God.* Hold on."

"I am." Pressure as she squeezed him, firming his footing in these still uncertain waters. "I will, *Papi.* I'm here."

The last thing he saw before his eyes closed again was the shadow of soft, dark hair as she pressed her cheek against his chest, lips murmuring her message again and he prayed she'd never get tired of him needing her. "I'm holding on, Benny."

Twenty-Three

"Are you fucking kidding me?"

Benny held the phone slightly away from his head and rolled his shoulders, trying to shrug off the tension that had ripped from the phone and into his body at Slate's shout.

"You are not going out there alone, shrimp. Ain't happening." A sigh.

Benny waited, knowing from experience his brother wasn't done.

"Give me a day. I'll sort my shit here, go with you." Ruby's voice lifted in the background, questioning. *Fuck.* "Let me make a call or two, Benny."

"I need something from you." He was learning. It took a long time; he was a slow study at these things, but the lessons were beginning to sink in. Giving people the chance to help him gave them power, but it also provided them a sense of satisfaction he couldn't deny. "Can you help me out, Slate?" While he still called his brother Andy in his head sometimes, Slate was a badge of respect, so Benny had to give it to his brother. Having heard a dozen slightly different stories about a gunfight and how he came to the name, after getting over being terrified that he could have lost

Andy, Benny never tired of it, through it learning so much of what made his brother what he was. Strong, honest, dependable, loyal. Benny used another phrase he'd come to understand, trying to ensure his brother listened to him. "Love and respect, man."

"Fuck me." That was muttered, and given the tone of voice, it wasn't a bad thing this time. He'd heard those two words used in so many ways by Slate, a go-to phrase of anger and love, rebellion and acceptance. "Whatcha need, shrimp?"

"I need to do this. Need to talk to her. If you aren't comfortable with me going there, and I get it, totally get why you'd be hesitant about me doing that, Slate. But, I need to talk to her. It's part of what I need to move forward, and given what I've learned of this whole fucking process, it's going to be something she needs, too. Amends, brother, gotta make amends." He drew a breath. "So let me bring her here."

This conversation was a result of Chase calling him the previous day, when they'd talked far into the night, the kid letting go of a lot of bad memories about his mom. It wasn't until the call was nearly done that he'd learned Chase's mom had been killed in a single-car accident a few days before. Chase, only now learning about it, had reached out, picking up the phone instead of the bottle, which was a good decision. Lying there in the dark after he'd disconnected, Benny had thought about his own mom, and how he might feel if she died without him being able to talk to her. The idea didn't sit well, and Benny had come to a decision. He just had to get Slate on board.

"Benny." The pain in Slate's voice ripped through him. "The last time she was involved, you nearly wound up back in rehab." Guilt colored the next words. "I wasn't even here to see it happen, was in fucking Kansas. *Fuck me.*" That was an unhappy version of the phrase, and Benny flinched to hear it. "I'm not down with bringing her back into your life like this, bro."

How to make him understand? Benny thought for a moment, and then hit on an idea. "Remember the ranch?"

Startled laughter, then Slate said, "Yeah, I remember it." It had been in their father's family for generations, was supposed to be the boys' legacy. That was before their dad got sick; before their mom sold it.

"Were you...do you miss it?" Closing his eyes, he could see the endless stretch of the plains, feel the wind whipping past them as the two boys rode double on one of the ranch horses to the top section to check fence. "Was a lot of work, and I remember how you wore yourself stupid tired trying to do everything." A grunt he took for agreement filtered through the line, so he forged ahead.

"You put yourself between me and that bull, remember? Mean fucker spooked the horse. I fell off, busted my knee open. You could have stayed up in the saddle, safe. But you didn't. You got off, right then, no question in your mind. I wasn't going to face it alone. And I knew," he put stress on the words as he repeated them, "*I knew*, you'd *never* let anything hurt me."

"Love you, shrimp." Slate's voice was thick with emotion and he hated doing this, but he had to make him understand.

"I know you do. I've always known it. I used it, brother. Took advantage. So fucking selfish. I hate looking back and seeing everything I've done to you. The lies. Fucking lies, everything out of my mouth a lie for the longest time. And all you ever did was try to make things right." He swallowed, trying to compose himself. "I need to hear her. Hear what she wanted to say at the wedding, but I was too much of a pussy to listen. I need to know what tripped her up, what trips her now. Help me figure this out. It's the next step in my path. I get not going out there alone, and won't take you from your family. I'm done being stupidly selfish. I'll be smart about it." This got him a snorted laugh, which was good; it meant his brother was still listening, not planning how to word a careful refusal. "Help me."

"I got this, baby brother." A heavy sigh, then Slate told him what he needed to hear. "I'll call, set it up. Let you know when it's going down, yeah?" A pause, then a question. "You still there?"

"Yeah. Just basking in the submission of my favorite big brother."

"I'm your only brother, assbag. I'm thinking I need a video game session soon, shrimp. Need to whup your skinny white ass. PWN the noob." Benny could hear the grin and knew it matched the one on his face.

"You're white, too." He laughed, then Ruby's laughter rang in the background, and he knew she'd told Slate the same thing.

"Fuck me." This one was the best, happiness reverberating down the call and Benny smiled.

***

Waiting in the airport lobby, his attention was focused on the toes of his shoes. The rubber tips were scuffed, needed cleaning, and polishing if the sneakers were to last much longer without looking like total crap. Footsteps echoing through the building brought Benny's gaze to the escalator beyond the security checkpoint, where arriving passengers entered the unsecured world again. He'd finally won an argument with his brother, and it had to be about who would be picking their mother up. He scoffed. Not that Slate was happy about it, but he'd given Benny what he needed. This was a button he didn't want to push too often, but right now, he needed this meeting to be on neutral ground, wanted to see and talk to her without Slate around. Needed it, and it wasn't a bullshit line he'd fed Slate.

When he'd seen her at the wedding, he had been shocked in a good way. She wasn't back to the beauty in the pictures papering GeeMa's walls, celebrating the marriage of her son to Susan, but she was far from the haggard specimen of addiction he remembered from his last years in Wyoming. She'd looked the part of mother of the groom, older and conservatively dressed, deferring to the bride's mother. He remembered thinking what a lie it was, what a lie she lived, every day, pretending to be a decent human.

Gaze to the steady stream of people moving down the stairs and into the hallway, he watched and waited, finally spotting her. Thin. Thinner than she'd been at the wedding and he wondered what it meant. Hair in a ponytail, scraped away from her face, leaving nothing for her to hide behind. She was looking through the airport, clearly nervous, her head swinging in short arcs back-and-forth. The greeter at the door offered her the airport's trademark cookie, and she paused a moment to accept. This was when Benny took a blow he wasn't expecting, his heart clenching so hard it might jump out of his throat. She smiled at the older man standing there beside the display, mouth moving to thank him, and that smile was everything good he remembered about his childhood. Every good thing that happened to him bracketed on either end of the experience by his mother's smile, missing from his life for so long.

Turning to the main lobby, smile fading, she swept the room again with her gaze and he knew when she saw him. When she recognized him in spite of the shades and hat worn in a shabby disguise against the scant fans he had in this town. Knew it when she stumbled, catching herself but not before the misstep gave her away. Slate said she sounded good on the phone, was happy to come to Fort Wayne, pleased at the chance to reconnect with her youngest son. She might be all those things his brother said, but she was also scared as fuck, and her face had been stripped bare in that instant, showing him all her cards.

He waited, feet planted wide, letting the mass of people part and move to either side of him, the clicking of their roller bag wheels sounding like playing cards pinned to his bike's front wheel. *Clickity, clickity, clack.* The sound her heels made as she walked up the hallway towards his room in the middle of the night, stinking of booze and men. *Click, click, thud.* This last the sound her shoulder would make as she stumbled sideways, catching herself against the wall. He stared at her, seeing her face pale as she approached and he didn't move. Didn't speak. Didn't give any indication he gave one shit about her being there. *Jesus, give her something. You asked for this, asshole.*

Stopping several feet away, she looked at him, and her bottom lip disappeared into her mouth, nervous fear oozing from her in a way he could never miss. Modulating his breathing, making it so the sound of it surging in and out through his nose was the only noise inhabiting his head, holding that moment until echoing through the years he heard her heels again. *Click, click, thud.*

Benny shook his head and then allowed himself to smile at her. Not a real smile, but his rock star one, and he knew she knew the difference when she flinched. "Susan." He used her Christian name, pulling another flinch, but not wanting to offer her the thing he wanted most in the world, a connection to his mother. He reached out and took the handle of her bag, clasping it tightly.

"I'm parked right outside." She was staring at him, not having said anything yet and he waited for a beat. "Do you have any checked bags?" Chin dipping to her throat, she shook her head. "Hey," he called and got her eyes for a moment before they fell away again. He didn't know what she'd expected, but she wasn't getting it from him, that much was clear. "Let's go where we can talk, okay?"

A nod and he watched her swallow. *Shit.* Without saying anything else, he reached out and grabbed her hand, turning her so they walked out through the wide sliding doors together. He couldn't miss the way she clamped tightly, couldn't miss how her cold fingers trembled. "Was it a good flight? You want some coffee or what? Breakfast? Maybe lunch?" Now that his mouth was moving, he couldn't seem to make it stop, deciding to roll with it. "Packed light for a week, didn't you? Didja get a cookie? You came in for the wedding through here, right? So you knew about the cookies? Best part of hitting the Fort, I swear." *Fucking mouth, I can't shut up.* "So are you hungry?" Determinedly, he clamped his lips closed, still pulling her along by the hand, not giving her time to pause or probably even think.

"I could eat." Her voice was low, trembling with what he thought were nerves until he chanced a glance her way to find her lips tipped at the corners. *She's amused.* "The cookies are good, but not enough to sustain." He watched as her mouth tightened, that tiny smile slipping away. "Your brother asked the same questions the first time he came to pick me up."

"First time?" *She's been here more than once?*

Her tone turned cautious as she said, "For the wedding, yes."

"When else did you come?" *And why didn't anyone tell me?*

"Uhm. A couple of months ago. I was here for a couple days to see the babies." *Explains that*, he thought, knowing the timing would have been his last trip to Phoenix.

He clicked the trunk on the car, followed by the door locks. Pausing a moment, he opened her door. "Hop in. I'll toss this into the trunk. Be thinking between Greek, Italian, and American." Pointing to the woman in the backseat, he said, "This is my sober companion." Leaving the women to introduce themselves, he walked to the back of the car and stood there a moment, shaking his head at his own reaction. "Asshole," he berated himself on a mutter, slamming the trunk and swinging into the driver seat. Logically he knew why Slate hadn't told him of her visit, but it still pissed him off because it spoke directly to what he hated the most about what this whole fucking head trip had done to him. Made him vulnerable, someone to be protected.

Weak, like Mom.

That thought froze him in place, halfway backed out of the parking space, hands on the wheel. After a moment, he carefully finished the maneuver and drove them downtown. "Did you pick?"

"American," came immediately, followed by a wary, "Is everything okay?"

"Epiphany." He laughed, hating how harsh it sounded. "I didn't know you'd been back to town while I was in Arizona. Was trying to be pissed off at not knowing. Trying to not be pissed off at the same time."

"I asked Andy not to tell you." She startled him with this pronouncement, and he glanced her direction, seeing her posture was straight and rigid, purse held in her lap, bloodless fingers tight around the edges. "I shouldn't have."

"Why?"

"Why...?" She cleared her throat. "He didn't want to. I should have listened to him." She paused and then softly added, "He's got such a good heart."

"No, why shouldn't you have? You don't owe me anything."

"Not true." Low and quiet, the words vibrated between them. "I owe you everything." She still hadn't called him by name, hadn't called him anything at all, and that apparent slight stung in ways he hadn't expected. Until the booze took over her life, she'd been quick with affectionate words, and he'd always been *my Benny*. "I don't have any secrets anymore. Anything," her voice broke, and he glanced over to see her looking out the window, "anything you need from me is yours."

Pulling up in front of the diner, he sat for a moment staring through the windshield. She was offering honesty on a level he hadn't expected, and what he thought he'd wanted now seemed frightening. Terrifying. "Do you think I'm weak?" Where in the hell had that come from? He glanced in the mirror, catching Mercedes' steady gaze. "You know what I've done, right? I assumed you knew everything."

"I know some. I still talk to Allen's mom, and I follow your band online. There's a riot on social media right now, rumors of new music on the boards." A soft laugh teased his attention, but he wouldn't let himself look, didn't want to see whatever emotion provoked the amusement. "I'm an OY groupie." This got his notice, and he whipped his head to find her studying him. She looked away in reaction as if their gazes held a way to repel the other's. *Polar opposites.*

"Took me off guard," he admitted. "You said 'Allen's mom' and I immediately thought Ruby, not GeeMa." The apple of her cheek curved up, and he knew she was smiling, even if he could only see the edge of her profile. "A groupie, huh?"

She nodded. "I came to one of your shows." The knowledge startled him, and he wondered immediately what kind of shit he'd pulled while onstage. "You're so talented." Pride rang through her voice, which startled him even more. "I was blown away."

"Good to know I can impress." He pressed backwards in the seat, lifting his arms and gripping the headrest in both hands, twisting side-to-side. "Look, Susan, I don't have an agenda. I don't have a series of questions." He hated the tension filling the car, wanting to cut through it quickly. "I'm looking for help wherever I can find it. I know what started me down this path, how far I sank and I think we've had similar experiences. I wanted to talk to you because it's part of the process, reaching out to those I've wronged." She made a noise but he refused to look, again not wanting to see what might be on her face.

"I trust my brother." Benny swallowed, squeezing the headrest before releasing it and resting his hands back on the steering wheel. "He reconnected and, I know you didn't see him before, but it healed something inside him. He went from...the emotions of before, to being good with having you back in his life. That's huge. See, he's very much a 'fuck me once, fuck you' kind of guy. At least, he was, but he let you back in."

Thumbs drumming on the wheel, he hated he was fidgeting like a little kid. Talking like this, it felt like he was circling an important fact, and he tried to dial in on it. Wrapping his hands around the wheel, he clutched it tightly. "I love he got that from you. What he needed. Because you were out. O. U. T. But you got back in. This means, if I fuck up bad enough to be out, he might let me back in. And if he can do that, if he can be that strong while I'm weak, then maybe I can be that strong one day." *Not quite there.*

"I want to be strong enough that he knows he can call me when he needs me, doesn't think twice about it, doesn't have to worry about what impact or effect it might have on me." *Nearly.*

"Like this meeting today." He gestured to the space between them. "He knew you were strong enough, didn't have any worries about you not hacking it. Just me. I want to know how you got to where it's real for him." *There.*

"If we're to have a chance at being a family again." *Is that what I want?* "And one of us is at risk, the weak link, then the whole thing can come tumbling down. I don't want to be the weak link." He paused, then nodded, affirming to himself this was what he wanted. "I want to make his life better, not drag him down a road he's spent far too much time traveling."

Throughout this, she'd been quiet, but not silent. Every so often she'd given little, hushed hiccupping sobs, but quiet. The atmosphere in the car had grown thick, heavy, weighing him down as he talked, now nearly suffocating while he waited for her reaction.

Her voice quiet, she began slowly, seeming to hunt for the words. "I never expected him to be so forgiving. I did the both of you so wrong, so many times. I knew I'd never be able to fix it, or change it...but he reached out. I didn't know then, but it was Ruby's doing. He pulled up in front of my house, and I told myself I was ready, ready for anything." Her laugh was full of pain, shards of it impaling him, causing a deep ache in his chest. "I never told him, but in the twelve hours between his call and him at the curb, I got in the car so many times I stopped counting. At first, I was trying to lie to myself. I'd only go to the grocery store. A quick run to make sure I had enough coffee and bread. What you don't know is the liquor aisle is situated between those two in the store. Then I thought that lie, the *'one'* lie, the one that has led to so many wrong decisions for me. Just *one*. I'd only have *one*. If I did buy anything, I'd only pour *one* drink. In and out of the car so many times. I got the shakes, threw up, felt like I was going to come out of my skin."

She paused, and he filled the silence because he knew exactly what she was talking about. The internal dialogue that could start the slip. The physical reaction to being denied what was needed so badly. "What did you do? How'd you beat it back?"

"Called my sponsor. He came over and helped me sort through the emotions that were driving me. Steadied me until I could get a handle on myself. Until I could stand on my little porch and welcome my oldest child, who I had betrayed in a way no mother ever should, and invite him into my home. Sober. The first time he'd seen me sober since he was sixteen. More than half his life had passed without me in it. That's what held me steady, what I told my sponsor. Knowing I'd missed out on too much, missed seeing him grow into the man he had become. Good, strong, loyal." She drew a breath that fractured in a half-dozen places, each scoring through him with shared pain.

"Not untainted by my mistakes, but somehow stronger in spite of it all." He twisted to look at her, seeing the tears flowing down her cheeks. "I kept telling myself I'd take whatever he needed to lay on me. My penance. I was ready for him to be angry, betrayed. Ready for him to take whatever pound of flesh he needed. Would have gladly taken a knife to myself, carved it out myself. Given him what he needed. Anything."

"Not Andy," Benny said, shaking his head, reaching out to thread his fingers through hers, pulling her hand away from the grip it still held on the purse in her lap. "He's got enough forgiveness inside him for ten people." The way she clutched at him was desperate, and he hated he'd made her feel that way. From what she'd told him about the visit with Andy, him calling her here would have laid her bare, opened her up to the same fears and terror, but still she came. Sober. "You were ready for the same thing today, weren't you?"

Wordlessly she nodded, and he squeezed her fingers in what he hoped was a reassuring way. "It's not that. I just..." He swallowed. "I don't know how to be sober. You seemed to have a lock on it at the wedding. I thought you could trade war stories with me, give me some of your mother's wisdom."

Sniffling, she laughed, lifting her other hand to wipe at her cheeks.

"No, I'm serious, Mom." The name slipped out without him meaning to give it to her, but once it hit the air, projected between them from his lips, it felt perfectly right. He knew what to say next. "I'm still your Benny, and I need you." Now his cheeks were the wet ones, and he felt the tears dripping off his jaw, soaking his shirt. "I need you."

Twenty-Four

Sitting on the couch in Jase and DeeDee's house, he marveled as his brother's friends rallied around him. As in *him*, not Slate. They knew the history; that much was clear. What they didn't know was how much of a trigger seeing his mother would be for him, and they were cautiously pleasant to her but pulled him close. One-armed hugs, pounding backslaps, tousled hair—they gave him the same affection they granted Chase, and seeing this, recognizing it for the first time, it warmed him. Sustained him in ways he didn't know he needed, but aware of the bonds he'd built here over the past weeks and months, he suddenly got it. He understood what drove Slate to be anything these men needed him to be.

Staring down at the cup of coffee in his hand, he was still trying to come to grips with this knowledge when the cushions at his side depressed, and he looked to see Mason settling into the corner. Arm across the back cushion, the big man was turned sideways, leaned against the arm of the couch, one knee cocked, and ankle on his other leg. Mason looked like he was there for the duration, and Benny was surprised to find this no longer filled him with a twitching fear.

With a nod, he acknowledged the man, following it with a quiet greeting, "Mason."

"Benny boy." Mason gave him an easy grin then tipped his head towards the kitchen where Susan stood talking to various women from the club. Ruby stood close, and the two women each had a fast-growing baby in their arms, Susan cradling her namesake, Danielle Susan. Benny hadn't learned the little girl's middle name for weeks; another thing Slate felt he had to buffer him against, not knowing how he might react. "How's it hangin'?"

He knew this wasn't a casual question, not throwaway words meant to be polite and fill the time; Mason didn't fuck around with things. If he asked it, he wanted a real answer, so Benny gave it to him. "Was a shit morning." Susan smiled, reaching out to cup Ruby's face and pull her in for a hug, the babies protesting as they were squeezed between the women, and he watched as they broke apart laughing, Ruby smiling at his mother. "A good day, though."

"I reckon so." Mason made a show of looking around. "No Lucia tonight?"

Benny smiled; that was another part of the day which had gone really well. "We stopped by Bear's earlier, so I could introduce Mom to Luce. Seeing her is always the best part of my day, never fails." Slate walked into view from the other side of the kitchen, stopping where he could slip an arm around each woman, tugging them into his sides and Benny watched their reactions, Ruby smiling up at him and their mom resting her head on his shoulder, her face relaxing. Benny thought they both looked like Slate had given them the world. "I don't know who was more nervous, her or Mom. But by then Mom and I had the real talk behind us, knew what we were both hoping to get out of this, and knew we could deliver."

"She needed to know if I could forgive her. And, until I heard her talking about Slate's visit, I didn't know I already had." He smiled as he watched Slate jokingly complain as his arms were filled with babies, and then pulled fountains of infectious laughter from each child as he blew raspberries into their necks in turn. "I needed to know she didn't hate what I'd become."

"What you *did*." Mason leaned in, put a hand on Benny's knee and squeezed until Benny looked at him. "You've never been anything other than Slate's brother. Susan's son." Thick fingers tightened, digging in. "My boy's friend. All that blond hair, you're a little lion man. Brave, fierce. *Loyal*." Leaning back, Mason released him, settling back into place. "You aren't what you've done, what you've lived through, Benny. You learn from that shit, pick your ass up and go forwards. You aren't what you've done." Abruptly changing topics, Mason asked him, "You know about Mica, up in Chicago?"

Benny knew the name and had heard stories about the woman the Rebels protected like they did DeeDee and Ruby, so he nodded. Mason said, "Couple years back, she got a tattoo."

"Good for her?" Benny had no idea where this was going and knew his questioning tone revealed his confusion when Mason laughed.

"Yeah, except I had to sit beside her and watch her flinch as they dragged that needle up the skin of her side, blood and ink oozing out. She about passed out. Pain ain't the point, boy. The tattoo is the important part. Hers says, without fear, there is no courage." Leaning in, Mason got close, holding Benny's gaze as he did so. "You're afraid of failing your family, your band, and your friends. You are so afraid, it bleeds from you. Just eat up with that fear, boy." The room was silent; the only noises were murmuring conversations from the kitchen, shouts of children's laughter from outside. "Gotta let it go. Trust yourself to be what you need to be, so you can move past this. You can't forget the past, no way to learn from it if you set it aside, but you have to let go the guilt and fear from your past decisions. Learn from the results, but give yourself a goddamned fucking chance."

Scowling, the big man leaned in another intimidating inch, and Benny held himself still, trying not to react. "Without fear, there is no courage," Mason repeated the words, then paused. "That's what you hold onto. Mica's ink. Courage. What you'll find on the other side of that fear eating you up inside. That's where you'll find your courage, little lion boy. Find it, hold on to it…feed it. Two things inside you: fear and courage. Feed what you want to grow."

He gestured around the room, and a dozen pairs of eyes turned their way. Benny knew Mason spoke for all of them when he said, "You are your brother's favorite person. Slate was scarcely a man when he took on the role he was born to, his brother's keeper. He's lived his whole life in service to others, including me, but you are one of the people who make his world richer. Now, seeing you through his eyes, I know your worth in a way I didn't before. You aren't what you've done, what's happened to you. You are what you became in spite of what life threw at you. In spite of stumbling and falling." Mason grinned, and in his smile, Benny caught a glimpse of the man Chase would become. For the first time, he was glad down to the bottom of his soul that his life had brought him here to witness this. "Like your shadow says, it ain't how many times you fall, Benny. It's how many times you get back up."

***

"Dude." Chase laughed as he whirled, walking backwards up the sidewalk towards the house his dad had bought. "You don't know, man, it could happen." Slapping his hands together, Chase made a sound like an explosion. "Out of the blue, like that. Come on, she's only here for a couple of days. I want you to meet my aunt."

"Chill, little dude." Benny was frustrated, but trying to not let his mood sour Chase's excitement. He'd gotten off the phone with yet another label earlier today. Their music was going great; actually, better than great. The demo they'd cut was rock solid, four songs, all original, each uniquely different, showing their range of skill. With every practice, they found new ways to fit together professionally.

The only downside was on the management side of things. Benny knew in his gut they needed representation. He could handle setting up and organizing promo pieces, but getting them booked onto a tour took connections, and every one of his had splintered over the last year. People in the industry changed jobs as fast as they changed underwear, and keeping up with who knew who when you spent half a year in rehab? Nearly impossible.

So he'd spent the last month working angles to try to get their music in front of labels that would be willing to leverage names and connections, sweet-talking them into taking a chance on the Occupy Yourself brand. *Not that there's much of a brand left*, he thought, watching as Chase continued to walk backwards, chatting with Luce like a magpie bird, endless noise with little substance. Chase was doing well, holding onto his newfound drive fearlessly, so Benny had put off the next call of the day. The boy was important to Benny and needed to know it, so when his aunt came to town, and the runt wanted Benny to meet her, he'd by God make time to meet her. He snorted, *By God? Thanks, GeeMa.*

His attention sharpened when he knew Chase had somehow gone wrong with his recitation of a story, watching as Luce glanced up at first Chase, then Benny, fear flashing across her face. He stared at her. Luce wore her feelings on the surface all the time. You could look at her and know what she was thinking, and after the time spent together, he knew these nerves weren't normal. Chase kept moving, so Benny didn't get a chance to ask what was up before they hit the door and were inside, Chase shouting the house down.

In the massive kitchen, Chase greeted his father and Benny gave a chin lift to Mason, watching the comfortable affection the man offered his friend. *Yeah, loves you more than you know*, he thought with a grin.

A petite brunette was walking into the room. Benny knew this feminine version of Mason had to be the aunt. Benny was still focused on Lucia but heard Chase laugh when the woman stopped walking to mutter something to Mason. Slipping an arm around Luce's waist, Benny pulled her close to him, wanting to settle her from whatever the mood was that took her confidence. "My Aunt Bethy," Chase introduced half of the equation, giving a wave. Bethy whispered something else to Mason, pointing at Benny and he wondered if he'd found a closet fan or a hater. Then she stuck her hand out, taking a step towards Benny.

"Mr. Jones, it's a real pleasure to meet you. I'm Bethany Taylor-Mason, a talent scout for Iron Indian Records." *Well, nice surprise.* He knew a little about Iron Indian; they were solid, mostly into rockabilly music, but they had recently signed a group similar to Occupy Yourself. *Hmmm.* Benny reached out and shook her hand, starting with a small smile, but allowing it to morph into his flashy, plastic grin when she gave him an impressed eye flare, letting him know he was right. Closet fan *and* a talent scout. *Time to work it a little bit.*

"Ms. Taylor-Mason." He tipped his head to one side, keeping the smile going, "Please call me Benny." Shoving his elbow into Chase's side, hard, he ragged Chase a little because he hadn't been primed to meet a representative. If the kid was going to be in a band, in the business, he needed to know what connections to leverage. "Little dude, you lose points for not telling me your aunt is hot." Luce gave his waist a squeeze and he grinned; she understood the schmooze routine.

"But I gain points because I remembered this." Chase dug around in the bag Lucia had on her shoulder. "One demo CD, coming up." Case in hand, he reached out and handed it to his aunt who first looked like she was about to have a heart attack, but then made a happy face at her nephew. *Definite fan.*

"I'll have to determine if I can clear some time on my schedule to give it a listen, Mr. Mason." Joking with Chase, she ruffled his hair before turning back to Benny, her gaze assessing. "Seriously, if you are looking for a label, I can guarantee you an audition."

Interesting. Tilting his head, Ben asked her, "How can you guarantee an audition if your label hasn't listened to the demo."

"Because I'm pretty sure 'my label' has already heard this in rehearsals." She laughed and stuck her tongue out at Mason. "After all, your rhythm guitarist is living with him." Benny skated a glance at Mason, then brought his attention back to Bethany.

Mason owns a record label. Hope had his heart thudding in his chest. This could be everything. *Our luck is changing*, he thought, then his mind skittered, echoes of Ruby on the phone from New Mexico ricocheting past, then a memory of Luce's hands stroking up his back as he heaved. *No.* His thought was sharp, like a knife's edge coming down on a string, severing bad from good. *Good change this time.*

Twisting, he looked at Chase. *All my work and we had a captive audience the whole time.* "You knew this." It wasn't a question. He could see in Chase's face he had known, and it was fast dawning on him that not telling Benny was very, very bad. "I've been bustin' my ass for weeks, trying to get our demo in front of the right people. You knew it, knew what I've been doing because I've bitched about it often enough." Chase stood there, frozen in place, staring, his face fixed in an indecipherable expression. Blank, looking as if he were entirely ready for a reaction that would wound him deeply. Waiting to be told he was failing at something, and Benny knew that feeling in his bones.

Fuck, make this right. Don't derail the progress the kid's made. "Probably a good call on your part, little dude." Teasing might get them through this, but Chase still looked like he'd been kicked in the teeth. "If she'd gotten an earful of your playing a couple months ago?" He mimicked the explosion sound Chase had made earlier, watched as one corner of the boy's mouth curled up. "Wouldn't have been good." A full smile testified to the success of his efforts. *Finally.*

***

With arms wrapped around Lucia's torso, Benny held his controller to one side, trying to avoid her elbows as she became engrossed in the firefight they were working their way through onscreen. Hilarious body

English helping her focus as she leaned side-to-side, twisting and grunting as her character moved. In his headset, he heard Chase say, "Delta sector is clear."

Lucia responded to him, distraction bringing out her accent and a mix of Spanish and English, "*Bueno*, Chase, good. *Este pinche cabrón's* gonna die here, too. *Un momento, por favor.*"

Benny grinned, pressed into her and found himself surrounded by the scent of her hair. *Danger*, he thought, watching her character onscreen forge forwards. It had become harder and harder not to take things to the next level between them. Body jolting, he quietly snorted at his internal *harder and harder* and she muttered, "Nearly there, *bebe. Un momento.*"

They were ass to the floor, him leaning against the couch and her leaning into him. He sat with knees cocked, thighs spread, and she nestled between his legs as if she belonged there. Totally focused on what was happening on the screen, she seemed oblivious to his physical reaction to her natural closeness even as he did his best to ignore his hardening cock. *Remember this is a bad idea*, he thought as his grip tightened around her, feeling the softness of her breasts resting on his arm, the soft curves of her ass right *there*.

They were alone in his apartment as they'd been a number of times, but tonight he couldn't seem to put his awareness of her aside. Last night, he'd again listened on the phone as she brought herself to orgasm and he wanted to be there with her, wanted to be touching, tasting...

Not helping, he thought, shoving the memories aside. She wanted more, he knew. Had wanted for a while, asked in her quiet, shy way more than once, but he'd put her off, touting the doc's words time and again.

The truth was, he was afraid.

It had been a long time for him. Probably the most prolonged dry spell he'd had since he was fourteen. A long time and things were different in his life now. He was sober for one thing. And Lucia, she mattered in a way no other woman ever had. His dreams about her wrapped around themselves in his head, but the overriding emotion was always fear. Fear he'd lose what he had of her, small as that was. Fear he'd fuck it up, and not make it good for her. So much fear, it was paralyzing. Like performing onstage, only a million times a million on the importance scale.

You got past the performance anxiety with the music, he thought. And he had. Taking a chance on the anthem for Jase's game was the first real step. Followed by a dozen baby moves on the stage at Marie's. Then the band had branched out, going to radio stations and doing on-air performances, booking into tiny bars and lounges, where the energy of the band felt like it had when he was first starting out with OY. Jazzed and excited, but wary. That was back when he didn't know how desperate playing places like that really was. Now he knew the truth and enjoyed seeing surprise in the faces of the patrons when the band didn't suck. Watched as the phones came out, friends were called to come out for a good time, and the place would fill up in a way the bar didn't anticipate. At least the first time. That felt good, but still held an edge of desperate.

Luce moved, shifting to one side as her character crept around the corner of a building. He pushed the joystick on his controller, running to catch up, getting there just as the sound of a blast filled his headphones, followed by her lilting curses. "*Idiota.* Sorry, Chase. I am dead."

Keying the mic on his headset, Benny said, "And I'm tired."

"Don't know why," Chase chimed in. "You didn't do anything that last round except stand around with your thumb up your ass."

"Hey, I'm tired," he protested, seeing Luce's grin reflected on the surface of the TV screen. "See you at practice in the morning. We've got a new song Bear and me been working on. I want to see if we can be ready to cut a demo soon. Book some studio."

"Okay, old man. You get some beauty sleep. You need—" Chase was cut off in midlaugh when Luce pushed the button on the console. She shifted to look up into Benny's face, and he knew what was coming. Knew what he should do, even as he knew he was giving in this time. He didn't have it in him to deny her. To deny himself any longer. *I want her so bad.*

"I'll lay down with you for a bit?" Couched as a question, the statement revealed the longing he knew she had inside. Something she wasn't confident enough to ask for, but the things she did ask about were tough to answer.

Tonight, he wouldn't put her off, wanted her as close as she could get. Standing, he reached out a hand to pull her to her feet, leading the way to the bedroom. "Love it, baby." Stripping his shirt over his head, he tossed it towards the closet. He then hesitated a second, hands hovering over the waistband of his jeans. With a half decision, he pulled his belt free from the loops, tossing it to the floor next to the bed. By the time he had crawled up the bed, turning to put his back to the mattress, he had expected she'd be already on her way towards him and the bed, but his gaze found her frozen in place.

"Come here, Lucia." He lifted one hand to her, pleased he could hold it steady as he waited for her to accept his offer. She broke from her stillness, her eyes holding his captive as she put a knee to the bed, sliding up to nestle into his side. "Love it." He sighed, curling an arm around her shoulder, feeling how she fit him. Cheek to his shoulder, palm to his chest, she curved into him. He twisted in the bed, shoving his arm underneath her, rolling them to their sides, facing. Holding her close, tangling his legs with hers. "Better."

He got a wordless hum in response and grinned, waiting. If she followed the usual script, she'd be content for about three minutes, then start pushing and pressing to see if he'd be interested in more. Of course he was interested, but the fear always crept in. In less than that amount of time, he felt her shift and take a breath, but then she stilled, and he felt the heat of her exhale along the skin of his throat. Both palms pressed to his chest, her fingers flexed, then didn't move again.

He bent his neck, pressing a soft kiss to the top of her head. "Comfortable?" Voice deliberately quiet, he waited, getting another hum in reply. "Can I have a goodnight kiss?" Wordlessly, she tipped her head back, lifting her lips to his. She moved as if to break the kiss, but he deepened the connection, angling his head, slanting across her mouth, the tip of his tongue stroking along her lips.

Fingers twisting in her hair, dark silk flowing across his hands and arms, he kissed her, teasing for entrance, nibbling and licking until she relented, opening for him, and he plundered what she offered. Tongue slipping inside, tangling with hers, he took her mouth, not breaking the way they fit together even when he pulled back, panting for breath. "God, Luce." He groaned, resting his forehead against hers. "You make it hard to be good."

Fingers moving restlessly across his bare chest, her touch was driving him mad, his mind imagining, wanting it everywhere. When she pressed close, the tip of her tongue flicking across his bottom lip, her words took a moment to register. "Then be bad, Benny. Be bad with me."

As if she'd lit a fire inside him, he felt his blood heat. His skin, already sensitive from her touch, became more so, and everywhere their skin connected blazed hot and fierce. He moved, rolling her, positioning himself so he was lifted on one arm, the other driving his hand up underneath her shirt, fingers and thumb honing in on her nipple as if guided there. *Be bad.* Through the lacy texture of her bra, he felt the pebbled surface perched on the peaks of her breasts, palming and plumping them as he caressed her. "God."

Rocking against her, he ran his mouth down her neck and across her shoulder as far as he could, exasperated when fabric interfered with his ability to retain access to her skin. With frustrated movements, he worked the shirt over her head, tossing it to one side, staring down in awe at what he had uncovered. *Be bad with me.* Ivory lace covered her brown skin, and he had a sudden, overwhelming desire to see if she had on matching panties. Fingers to the button of her jeans, he jerked it through and loose, then shoved them down, letting her help him remove them. "Beautiful," he murmured, gaze tracing up and down her frame.

Lace panties framed by the strength of her thighs, dark curls captured underneath. Her ample hips dipped to her waist, then flared out to her ribs, breasts on display except for the sheer coverage of her bra. His cock thudded behind the fly of his jeans, pulse pounding, rushing, and he was already hard as a rock, wanting to be inside her. "My Lucia." Nose to her cheek, he nuzzled her. *Slow down.* "*God*, baby. My Lucia. So beautiful. Gorgeous woman in my bed."

Gliding touches up her side, pad of his thumb brushing the curve of her breast, pulling a shiver and a soft moan from her. She curled her hand around his neck, pulling him close and he kissed her, delving into her mouth again, tracing all of her with his tongue. Groaning down her throat when her fingers trailed along the edge of his jeans. Pressing into her, trapping her hand with his hips, the movement across the covered head of his cock excruciatingly beautiful.

Breaking the kiss, pushing his head into her neck, he was focused on the sensation when her hand flattened, pressing against his belly before sliding into his pants, her fingers wrapping around his throbbing dick. "Luce," he encouraged softly, hips moving with her touch. "Yeah, touch me. *God*." His hand went down, curving around her hip and diving between her legs. Voice rough, gruff, rasping when he spoke, "Baby. Want that? Yeah? Want me to have that?" Shoving the gusset of her panties to the side, he found her wet, knew from the mewls falling from her lips she was wanting. Had been wanting for a while, as he made them both wait.

Wait for this time, he thought, *wait for me to be solid. Ready. Selfish, but she waited for me.* "So beautiful. You can't imagine what I see. The beauty, Luce." He groaned again, fingers sliding in her wetness, twisting his hand down, curling his middle finger in, deep, pushing hard as she cried out and moved against him. "So wet, *fuck me*. Wanting me. My baby." Her hand stilled on his cock while he finger-fucked her, kissing and biting her neck, feeling her arch against him, hips pushing up and away with his movements. "Yeah, God. Yes, Luce. Take what you need, baby girl."

Her head turned, mouth to his ear and he listened, waiting, and then she gave it to him. What he knew she had inside, how hot she ran. Comprehending none of what she said, those phrases she gave him in bed were nothing he understood, but spoken in her voice, in her fucking sexy-as-hell accent that grew thick when she lost herself like this, she could have said anything, and he would take it. "Ben, *te amo, tu eres todo para mi.*"

"Like that, baby?" He added a finger, teasing and tweaking her clit before slipping them back inside. "You like me? Like that?"

"*Jesucristo, tu no me gustas me encanta usted. Mi amor.*" He felt the edge of her teeth on his neck, and then her fingers tightened around his cock before releasing. She had one arm shoved under him, fingers playing with the hair at his neckline, ghosting across his skin, those finger touches so barely there they made him shiver. "Benny, please."

"Tell me what you need, baby girl. Tell me what you want." Cheek-to-cheek, he whispered to her, feeling her body as it moved under his hand, chasing her orgasm. She jolted beneath him when he tweaked her clit with his thumb, and he played on that response, rolling it under his touch, and then pressing hard, slipping up and down over the nerve-filled flesh.

"*Dios, deja perder el tiempo y besame.* Kiss me, please, Ben. Kiss me. *Dios,* just kiss me already." Her neck twisted and lips pressed to his, she kissed him hard. Her fingers paused in the act of unbuttoning his jeans, and he felt the wave moving through her, knew it blazed a path when she tightened on his fingers, when he felt the throbbing in her clit as she came. He worked her, thrusting in slowly, sweetly, watching as it peaked and slowed. Carefully, he slipped his fingers from her, then his pants were history, and he had a condom in hand, rolling it on while he knee-walked up between her legs.

"Lucia." Calling her name, he waited, watching her lids fluttering, hips still dancing in place. "Lucia." This got him a soft hum, and he grinned because this one was different from the last he'd heard from her. Sated, satisfied, filled with pleasure. Better. So much better. *Something I'll work to hear from her every day.* Throaty and sexy, the vibration rocked through him, and his cock pulsed in response. Bending, he put an elbow to the mattress next to her head, resting on her, covering her with his body until she was all he could see. Her face filling his vision, everything he'd ever wanted. His head tipped forward when her legs instinctively fell open in invitation. Welcoming him. Taking anything he would give her. Offering everything in return. *Fuck. I gotta do this right.*

Lacy bra scraping on his chest, corners of her lips tipping up, a flash of her beautiful browns as she blinked dreamily. Everything in him screamed to push forward, take her, make her his, but he needed to know something first. He knew she'd had lovers in the past, as young as she was. The life her family led meant she'd grown up fast. Far faster than she should have. But he was confident since he'd been in her life, she'd been holding tight. Marking time until he found his place. *Waiting for me, like I've been waiting for her.*

"Baby girl," his soft call finally captured her attention, and he asked his question. "You sure about this, Luce?" Once they took the plunge, things between them would forever change, and he needed to know she was ready for this. "I'm not pressuring, not pushing. All you. Your choice." Now his words were staggering, and he had to find a way to steady himself. "Want you to be sure, baby girl."

"*Si, mi amor.*" She chewed on her lip a moment, eyes flickering as her gaze moved up his chest and neck to his face, searching his eyes. Her fingers wrapped around his shoulders, hands sliding to the center of his back, pulling him down and over her. "Please, Ben. Love me."

"As my lady wishes," he quipped and saw a flash of something he couldn't identify before her eyes dipped closed. "I want you, Lucia." He slipped inside her, one inch at a time, holding his breath as she went stock-still beneath him. *Remember it forever. This moment, suspended in time.* "I want this, baby. Beautiful lady. Wanted this forever. Mine." Buried to the root, he held immobile, resisting the urge to start plunging deep, fucking her fast and hard. *Love her, her one request. All my life, if she'll have me.* "Want you. Need you. So much. I do, baby." He paused and then asked, "Do you, Luce?"

Her arms tightened around him as guttural Spanish fell from her lips, her gaze pinning him in place because whatever she was saying sounded profound. "*Sabes quien soy, sabes como me llamo, pero no cuanto te amo tu.*" Rocking her hips up, her eyes slid half closed as she gently urged him to move. "Love me, Benny."

Hotter and tighter than he expected, and he'd expected a lot, she moved with him as he slowly pulled out, and then slid back inside. "Like silk, baby. So sleek. Velvet all around me. So beautiful." Mouth to hers, he whispered his discoveries to her, finding words failing him. "Indescribable. We fit together, feel that? How you were made for me? Just mine?"

"*Si, bebe.* We fit. *Cuando estoy contigo estoy feliz que nunca he estado.* Happy. So happy. Happier than I've ever been." Their breaths mingling, he tried to slow the rhythm between them, but her hips lifted under him, drawing him deeper, offering him more. "My life. Benny, I've wanted you for so long."

Now. Finally, mine. He drove deep inside her where he'd longed to be forever. Since he first saw her, knew her. Wanted her.

Words poured into his mind, lyrics and phrases, thoughts, but he pushed it all aside to focus on Lucia in his arms. "Mine." Down to single words, he tried to express what this meant to him. "Lover. Woman." Mouth to her neck, licking and tasting her skin. "Only you."

Faster, he was chasing his, right there, out of reach. "God." She lifted her legs, rocking him deeper, wrapping her heels around his thighs, urging him onwards.

"I can't last, Luce. Too good." Grunting into her neck now as he slammed into her, sweat across his shoulders, the heat of her mouth there, lips touching, sucking, licking. *Love you.*

"Gonna…"

So long, he'd wanted this so long. *Want you.*

"God…"

"Go, Ben. Fly for me." Edge of her teeth now, raking fingernails on his back, but her words were what sent him over the edge. "I'm yours, Benny. Take all of me."

With a groan, he filled the condom, heat flashing around the head of his cock, her tight all around him, arms wrapping him up. Mouth to his ear, she whispered to him, holding tight, so fucking tight it was like she wanted to melt into him and he kept coming, sensations blazing up his spine so hard and strong he groaned again, pressing deep inside her, ass clenching hard, feeling his cock jerk and pulse.

"Honey." He murmured as it rolled over him again and then again; hard, a wave which stayed with him for a long time, throbbing in his whole body, echoed by his heart thudding in his chest. Her heart beating out the same rhythm. Anchoring him. Slowly coming down, he felt the tiny kisses she dusted up his shoulder and neck, across the hinge of his jaw. Felt her hands roaming his back, palms smoothing over his muscles, slowly stroking across his skin. Holding him to her, cradling him in her arms. Loving him.

I love you was on the tip of his tongue, but he bit it back as he had the last hundred times it wanted to slip out. Before, it was a promise he didn't know if he could keep, and now, he found himself not wanting her to think it was a heat of the moment thing, wanting to find the right time to tell her. Waiting.

"God, Luce. So good, baby. You're perfect for me." Saying things that were true, but the emotion they held only skimmed the surface of what he felt. "Perfect together. Sexy and smart, everything you do turns me on." He ran his hands down her sides, cupping her ass and lifting, gliding in, then out slowly, doing that again, feeling her so tight around him. "Best everything I've ever had, Lucia."

Leaning close, he brushed his lips across hers, chasing her tongue with the tip of his, grinning as she panted against his mouth. "Best kiss." Bowing his back, he dusted his lips down her neck and across her chest, sucking and nibbling at her nipple through the lace of her bra. "Best..." He nuzzled across to her other breast, loving how her hands clasped his head to her. "...ever."

Gliding in one final time, he eased out, hands sweeping up and down her sides again. Mouth to her belly, he kissed and sucked and licked and bit his way down her stomach. "Best..." Hand to his cock, he got the condom off by feel, tossing it to the floor beside the bed as he slipped between her legs. Mouthing the sensitive skin inside her hip, he trailed kisses from one side to the other, and then back again, angling down until he was exactly where he wanted to be. "Lover."

Fingers tracing between her lips, he teased her, dipping his mouth to glide his tongue up and across her clit. A gasp was his reward, and he held her open with his fingers, framing her and giving himself access to everything he'd wanted for so long. Licking and lapping across every inch of flesh, using every trick he knew to pleasure her. Fingers deep, twisting and plunging while he sucked her clit into his mouth, fluttering across it with the tip of his tongue. Covering her with his mouth, thrusting inside with his tongue, fucking her hard while he rolled her clit with his thumb.

"Best pussy." He hummed as he drew on her clit, then groaned when he lapped at the richness she offered. "So good, Luce. Tastes so good. Best I've ever tasted." Head to her thigh, he watched his fingers dipping in and drawing out, licking away what was delivered with every stroke. *Honey sweet, what she gives me.*

"Addictive." At the word, she stiffened, and he edged away from language that would describe what he felt. A high like he'd never known, her under him, him in her in all the ways he could be. Addictive didn't describe it. He would never get enough of her. *No OD in my future, just everything I need.*

"My baby feeds me what I need." Mouth between her legs again, his cock rocking against the mattress, rigid again as he ate her fast and hard, feeling her press up against his mouth, fingers in his hair. Pulling back, he grinned at her soft protest, then told her, "Want to love you again, baby. Get a condom from the nightstand."

Fingers still working her, he felt her legs quivering on his shoulders, felt the twitching of her muscles where her calves draped over his back. She moved, and he looked up her body, seeing her breasts arching up as she twisted to reach the drawer. "Other side, baby." She glanced down, her face soft and he saw her suck in breath as he thrust his tongue deep, teeth rasping across her clit, hearing her gasping reaction at the same time, feeling how she tightened and tensed. Twisting to the other side, she opened the drawer to find it empty, like he knew it would be. "Sorry, wanted to watch your tits move. Mmmm. Best titties, baby. Love those." *Love you.* He clamped the lid on the words, seeing her frown, pretending to be upset he'd fake her out.

When she had the condom in hand, he moved up, straddling her chest, knees to her sides, evidence of his desire right in front of her. Undeniably ready for her. For this. "Put it on me, baby."

"Okay, Benny." She grinned up at him, looking coy and before he realized what she was doing, the head of his cock was inside her hot mouth, lips tight around the shaft and for a moment, all he could do was feel. Hot, tight, sweet. *Lucia.*

"*Fuck*," he gritted the word out. Shaking his head at her, he shifted his hips back and muttered, "Don't be bad, baby." She pulled off him with a pop, and he felt the loss immediately, chill air replacing the unbelievably hot sensation of her mouth.

"Benny, *eres mi todo.*" Fingers tearing the wrapper open, she held his gaze with hers, the intensity of the look would have been unnerving if he didn't love her so much. "*Tu amor me inspira. El toque de tu manos me mueve y tus besos me hacen te quiero mas. Estoy enamorada de ti.*" Working his cock, she held on, stroking slowly. "Yes?"

"Lucia." Benny moved, lifting off her, settling in beside her, cupping her cheek with his hand. Still shying from those three words, he told her, "You gotta know, baby."

"I do, Ben." She lifted and pressed her lips to his, then turned to him, curving one leg over his hip as she reached down to guide him inside her. "You gotta know too, *si*?"

"I love you." Unable to hold back any longer, unplanned, the promise rose into the air between them, and he felt the swell of reaction from her, emotion boiling over along with her tears. A steady stream gliding down her cheeks, she wept as she tipped her hips and took him deep, even while his thumb futilely tried to sweep them away. Leaning in, heart racing, he kissed her, tasting the salt of her fears. "No. No, baby girl." *God, I fucked this up.* Murmuring against her lips, "Luce, honey. Don't cry, baby."

"I love you, too, Benny. *Eres me todo.* You are my everything. Since I met you, I knew you were the one for me." She set things to rights effortlessly, as she did everything else with him. Leaning her head into his hand, she took him in, hips rocking with his as they moved together slowly, softly, lovingly. Filling each other up with the emotions shared between them. Her quiet cries of completion bringing him up to and over the brink, crashing down with the knowledge that she was right there with him.

Hours later, he felt her hands on his shoulders, stroking across his skin. "*Papi*, what's wrong?" Heated breath ghosting from side to side as she pressed close, followed by a gentle pressure from her lips and a whispered, "Come back to bed."

He pushed the papers aside, shuffling through them to find the one he wanted. "Listen, Luce." He stood, taking her with him when he climbed into bed, leaning against the headboard. By the light of his phone, he silently read the words on the paper, tracing each line a final time as she settled against him. "Listen." Then he sang to her, and when she melted into him, he knew even before she uttered a word.

"*De muy bonito,* Benny. *Me encanta, de verdad*. So beautiful."

Twenty-Five

"Fucking shit, Slate." Benny cursed as he stumbled, again. This time cracking his shin on what felt like a low table his brother didn't even attempt to steer him around. His hands jerked up and he was about to pull the blindfold off when he caught a whiff of perfume. *Lucia*. A second later, he felt her hands on his wrists. "Luce?" She giggled, and he smiled at the sound. *Gorgeous*. "Gimme a kiss, beautiful."

Since the first night together, they'd spent only hours apart, today being one of the longest times. She'd left early this morning, scratching out a note and putting it beside the coffeepot, telling him she had things to do, would see him soon, that she loved him. He never got tired of it, how free she was with her affection, with telling him.

And how she spent her time showing him.

Her lips brushed his; gentle, slow, questing across his mouth with her tongue before pulling back. He groaned and pulled a face, pouting, hearing muffled laughter from both sides. People. *If she doesn't care who sees, then I surely don't.*

Luce giggled again and tugged on his wrists. Once she got him moving, her grip loosened and slipped until she held his hands. She was backing in front of him, making sure he didn't run into anything else on this fucking ridiculous trip with his brother.

Benny had woken this morning to a handful of frozen marbles in his bed; the frigid balls of torture rolling around, puddling everywhere he tried to brace himself. Hands. Elbows. Hips. Ass. Those little frozen bastards were everywhere.

This had been one of Slate's favorite ways to wake him when he was a kid, and once it stopped happening, he'd never missed it. Not once. Hadn't been pleased the frozen marbles were back today, but after tossing them one-by-one at his brother, he'd laughed hard at Slate pretending to shield his eyes when Benny jumped out of bed shouting...and naked.

That little treat was followed by a real one as Slate fixed him a hugely elaborate breakfast. One complete with a purchased blueberry muffin sporting a single candle. He'd looked a question at Slate, who laughed as he started singing, shocking Benny into realizing he hadn't even remembered his own birthday. Since things had settled so well with OY, and then with Lucia, he'd been busy, spending nearly every waking hour working or with Luce, and his birthday hadn't rated an ounce of consideration.

After breakfast, Slate loaded him into a truck and threw a bandana at Benny, telling him to blindfold himself. After making a show out of checking the fabric for obvious usage, he complied; the grin on Slate's face as he did so worth making a fool out of himself if that was what it all came down to. *Anything*, he'd thought.

That brought him here, walking blindfolded across an open space with the oddly-muffled noise of a large group of people all around, Lucia in front of him, knowing his brother was somewhere in the room. "Shhhh." The loud hiss came from an unidentifiable someone in front of him, right past where Luce was. He halted, and she stopped with him, her grip steady and strong.

"Can I take off the whisker-wiper, yet, bro?" His fingers curled and tightened, anxiety taking hold in the darkness. Luce would never steer him wrong, but this was starting to edge into weird. "I'm getting kinda freaked," he admitted and hated the emotion would be clear in his shaking voice.

"One sec, honey." This was Ruby, and he swung his head her direction, hearing a loud metallic sound followed by a muttered, "Fuck me." Butterflies eased by his brother's voice, knowing Ruby paired with Luce would have his back against any stupid birthday party tricks, he forced in a deep breath, waiting.

"Okay, shrimp." Slate's voice was full of pride. "Take off the blinders."

Luce's fingers got there before his and she pushed the tightly-tied fabric up and off his head, dangling it from her hand as he blinked in the bright light. *What the fuck?* His hand shot out, fingers wrapping around Luce's hand as he turned in a half circle, looking around in shock. There were amps, guitars, microphone stands, and a drum kit. The wall of glass in front of him revealed what looked like a sound room. Everything, down to the overlapping rugs on the floor pointed to one thing. The space had all the trappings of, "A recording studio?"

He faced Slate, taking in his brother's self-pleased stance, hands shoved in his pockets, rocking back on the heels of his black biker boots, a broad smile on his face. "You built a recording studio." Not a question, but he slowly felt his way through the words, his tone disbelieving. "A recording studio. I'm standing in a live room. In your house." Slate and Ruby had moved into a house a couple of months ago, not long after he moved out into his apartment. There was a huge outbuilding attached to their house via the garage and Slate had been cagey about what he intended for the space. Now Benny knew. He pointed to the walls of glass. "You built a recording studio in your house."

Stunned, he looked around again to see all the guys there, standing slightly apart from the bikers gathered around. As often as the band had played Marie's, and for all Mitty and Vic lived with Bear for a while, only Vic had gotten comfortable around the rough and ready men who made up the Rebel Wayfarers. Seeing the band there, he couldn't wait, words boiling out of him. "Sticks and strings? Wanna go? Try it out? See how she flies?" Bonnie was the first to move, and he mentally adjusted how he thought about the band. No longer all guys, she'd blended with them so well, it was as if she'd always played with them.

He told them what they already knew, the impossible thing Slate had handed him. "My brother built a recording studio in his house." No more scrimping and saving to get put on a list for studio time, no more stressing about the hours spent behind the mixing boards pushing faders, dollar signs ringing up with every sweep of the minute hand.

A thought hit him, and he turned to Slate. "I can use it, right?" A disbelieving headshake and grin were Slate's response, and Benny gave Luce's hand a squeeze before releasing his hold and striding over to Slate. Gripping the back of his neck, he stared into his brother's eyes, thrilled that the same love he felt was shining back at him. "Love you, brother."

"Love you, shrimp. Happy twenty-eighth. Promise to hang around a while, yeah?" His voice roughened near the end, and Benny barely heard his repeated, "Love you, shrimp." Pulling him in for a hard, back-pounding hug, Slate muttered, "More than you know, baby bro." Shared sentiments.

"Back atcha," Benny whispered, opening his eyes to find Mercedes staring at them, her gaze evaluating and after a moment, the corner of her mouth twitched and Benny relaxed. It was all good. Every bit of it.

It was hours later and they were still at it. Long after all the Rebel members had wandered away, going outside where a family barbecue was set up complete with kids running wild in the yard, jumping in and out of the pool, and babies napping in the nursery, music continued to feed out of the speakers. Slate was lounging in a chair behind the boards, while the OY members were scattered around the sound room, tuning and playing softly. They were trying to be patient as Vic messed with his kit for what seemed like the hundredth time that night already.

Staring through the windows at him, Benny waited until Slate cocked his head to one side, until he was certain his brother's focus was firmly on him, when he mouthed his thanks. Then, he strummed louder and began to sing, fingers flicking through an old advertising tune. "Oh my brother has a first name, it's A-N-D-R-E-W. My brother has a last name, it's D-I-C-K-H-E-A-D." Laughing, he watched as Slate lifted both hands, flying the bird on both of them, grinning widely at him.

***

Benny could hear Bethany's frustration when she spoke; over the phone, it even colored her laughter. She hadn't counted on dealing with this much of a challenge when Iron Indian took on OY, and found to her dismay the band's history dogged nearly every engagement she attempted. "Gonna crack this nut, Benny. Don't worry, babe. I have a hundred options in my bag of tricks yet."

As always, he was surprised she wasn't more pissed at how poorly he'd handled things last year, and the year before. Instead, she came off angry at the poor management they'd gotten from Benita, and furious at the venue owners and radio stations who called the band a has-been, pointing her towards booking the kind of dives they were already playing around the Fort.

Fortunately, those bars had turned into a groundswell of fan activity, and he loved seeing how they were packed, crowds standing shoulder-to-shoulder when OY was on the bill. The people enjoyed listening to the band, and since their last song in a set was guaranteed to always be as well delivered as their first, those folks hung around all night, which the bars loved. The real fans enjoyed their easy access to the band, crowding around between sets to ask questions and take selfies. The regulars at the bars had learned about Benny's path to sobriety, and now were as big a defender as Mercedes when it came time to deflect innocent offers from newbies.

Bethy had a broad knowledge of direct-to-fan promotions, and was a wizard at managing social media, so in addition to being their representative at the label, had basically become their general manager, too. Ten places in the Fort vied for eight shows a month. They could have played another eight, but Benny knew what he needed now, and for once, he wasn't afraid to ask for it, defend it if needed. Lucia helped, reminding Bethy of the three days reserved for group, and then the band needed practice time, so that filled the other two, leaving them Friday and Saturday for shows.

Every gig got them decent cash, and every performance brought Benny closer to where he needed to be in his own head. Looking out at the crowded floor in front of the slightly elevated stages, heaving with bodies moving to the music OY made, he would watch in fascination as mouths echoed the words back to him, learning every new song, feeding energy back to the band in a way they all needed.

But larger venues in the area were booked months in advance, and venues in other regions were understandably reluctant to take a chance on what was considered a relaunch band. Especially one that currently had limited airtime on syndicate, Internet, or public stations. They needed an in, and like Bethany, Benny knew all it took was one chink in the dam to pull the whole thing down. They hadn't found their *in* yet.

"You'll get this, Bethy," he gave her assurances he felt were needed, and she laughed.

"I know I will, Ben. This ain't my first rodeo." Warmth suffused her voice when she asked, "My nephew doing well? He never calls his aunt these days."

The smile faded from Benny's face. This was the one thing he didn't have a handle on. Chase. The boy was remote and surly by turns, making

Benny worry he'd started drinking again, or something worse, but careful questioning had only turned up the volume on the crabby without providing evidence for Benny's fears, so he'd backed off. Chase was short-tempered even with Lucia, someone who, next to Benny, was his best friend. He shook his head. "Boy's got something going on, Bethy. He's playing well, practicing all the time." He hesitated before offering, "Almost obsessively. I can't get a handle on him."

"He loves Lucia." Mercedes' quiet voice came from behind him, and he swung to look at her, a scoffed laugh breaking from him when she rolled her eyes at his shock.

From the phone, he heard a slow, drawled, "Maybe I'll talk to Mason." Bethy paused, cautious. "See what he knows."

Eyes to Mercedes, he answered, "Would be good, I think. His dad would know him best." He frowned at the face Mercedes pulled as she gave a little jump, settling herself on top of the desk in the corner. "Someone walked in, Bethy. I gotta go." Goodbyes said, he disconnected the phone and stared at Mercedes. With one contribution to a conversation she wasn't part of, she had provided a piece to a puzzle he'd been worrying about for weeks. He was incredulous he hadn't seen it before, and wanted to be sure of what she was saying. "What do you mean?"

"He's loved her as long as I've been around, probably as long as he's known her." She tipped her head, gaze moving to the doorway past Benny. "It's nothing you did, Lucia. The young man's done a good job masking it with the close friendship you have." Without turning, Benny held his hand out and, moments later, felt the heat of Lucia's grip as she snuggled into his back. He used her arm around his belly to pull her in front of him, folding her into his arms as Mercedes continued, "But he hasn't missed the change in this relationship,"—her waving finger indicated the two of them—"and he's now coming to terms with unrequited love."

Sadness stole across Lucia's features, and he leaned down, touching his mouth to hers in a quick brush. "You fucking see everything, Mercedes. I didn't see it," he said, angling his eyes to where Mercedes sat. "How did I not see?"

"He didn't want you to. You were vocal about your affection for Lucia." She grinned. "I'm not telling tales now. Luce knows exactly how you love her, but you never once hid what you wanted, except from her." With a shake of her head, she said, "Best guess? He wanted this for you, in an abstract 'I want my friends happy' way, because Luce, you weren't trying to hide what you wanted, either, so he knew his affection wasn't to be. But the heart wants what the heart wants." Another grin lifted her lips. "Woody was right. There's no logic."

"The cartoon character?" Benny shook his head, having a hard time following Mercedes, as usual.

She threw back her head and laughed, loud and long, corded muscles in her neck working. Without thinking, he dropped his arms and made his way to the desk, scrabbling at the surface for a paper and pencil. *Laughter ringing in the air, firm friendships forged in fire. Solid, holding tight. Memories of times we both share, strong faith because you inspire.* He made a face at the last line, shaking his head. *Fire. I could change that.* He underlined the word, then drew a quick line down to inspire. At laughter in the room, he looked up, startled, having lost himself in the words, which had been flowing fast and easy since he stopped fighting his love for Lucia.

"Allen." Mercedes' laughter rang in the room again because he was so clearly confused.

"What does my nephew have to do with anything?" It could be frustrating, how she jumped from topic to topic in a way it that made it hard to keep up, but from the beginning, she'd challenged him in ways he needed. Still did.

"Woody Allen," Lucia provided, and laughed, leaning her ass against the desk on the other side of Mercedes. He looked at her and shook his head. The two women had developed a close friendship since the night of the show at Marie's.

"What?" *Fire. Forged in the fire. Firm friendships wrapped with bonds of steel.* Bending to the paper, he reorganized lines, scratching through words and phrases nearly as quickly as he jotted them down. *My faith in you coloring all I feel. Coloring. Shading. Sheltering. My faith in you sheltering all we feel.*

"Let me hear it." That was Mercedes, and it was the same phrase she always used. Non-judgmental, patient, but demanding nothing less than his full participation. Always.

"Laughter ringing through thin air. Memories of times we both share. Strong, promises circled round with love. Solid, holding tight. Firm friendships wrapped with bonds of steel, Faith in us sheltering all we feel. Loving this, feels so right." He looked up to see two feminine sets of eyes trained on him, and he paused a moment, unreasonably nervous. With a shrug, he muttered, "Doesn't suck."

"No, Bibi." Mercedes reached out, gripping Luce's fingers tightly. The connection between these two women—women who meant so much to him in very different ways—was something he didn't understand but loved seeing. "That doesn't suck."

Twenty-Six

"Sounds good," Benny shouted down the hallway in response to a question from Mitty. They were setting up for a weekend run at Marie's. They'd played this stage enough the set-up could be done in their sleep, so he was letting Mitty run the load-in while Mercedes chatted with Gypsy out by the bar. This meant he was squatted in the staging room alone, going through the microphone flight box, slotting fresh batteries in the belt packs of the in-ear monitors they'd be trying out tonight. They didn't need them for Marie's, wedge monitors on the edge of the stage were more than the place really needed, but Bethy had upgraded them from the ones Danny had rigged three years ago, muttering about tools and artists, and Benny wanted to try them out. More sponsors were a good thing. Humming under his breath, he had worked his way through three sets and was grinning at the neon nail polish Bonnie had used to identify hers when there were footsteps behind him.

He shook his head. He knew Mitty could do this. He knew it, but Mitty was nervous because it was his first solo run, so he'd been checking in with Benny every few minutes. "Dude, I said it sounded good. Go with your gut, man. You got this."

When there still wasn't a response, he grinned down at the equipment in his hands, thumb snapping the battery cover into place on the wireless receiver. "Mitty. Man, you got this." He put one knee to the floor and twisted in place, grinning widely as he turned around to face the door.

His smile faded quickly when he saw it wasn't Mitty standing there, and every muscle in his body locked in place in unpleasant surprise at his visitor. "Benita." He hardly recognized his own voice, loud and angry in a way that shocked him, not realizing he had so much bottled up. With effort, he stopped himself from following those emotions, digging into his psyche to find out why she had so much power still, instead simply staring at her. "What the fuck are you doing here?"

"Hi, Benny." Fuck him, her voice was soft and small, uncertain in a way he used to like. He'd liked it when she was unsure of herself; it was the only time he felt he had the upper hand in their dysfunctional relationship. Now, with what he had found with Lucia, he knew needing to have the upper hand was a sign that dysfunctional wasn't even the right word for what he'd experienced before.

So different, what he and Luce had. They'd been finding their way through this new territory together, discovering things about each other and themselves which were good, and right, and held the promise of so much more.

"Don't fucking 'hi, Benny' me. You got no place here, and you know it. Made it clear when you called two months ago, you got no place. Why are you here?" A call Ruby hadn't been around to interrupt, but Mercedes had played bouncer, taking the device from his fingers and hanging up on Benita as soon as she realized who was on the phone. He pushed off his knee and stood, holding his ground with some effort when she took the first step towards him. "No closer, can't hardly stand your air from here, would rather it not choke me." Her flinch at his words caused him a moment of discomfort, but then he remembered everything that had happened over the past year and a half. The only parts she'd been present at were the bad ones, ones that were in response to shit she'd stirred up, so he tried to set aside his discomfort as he had the need to analyze his responses.

"Benny…" She trailed off, and he shook his head.

"What do you want?" She wouldn't have made this trip for old times' sake, so maybe asking bluntly what her end game was would pry the information out of her. "Know you, know you want something. What do you expect to get out of me?" She had taken two or three quick steps before he got his hand up, palm flattened towards her. "Said I didn't want you any closer, bitch."

This didn't get a flinch but earned him a scorching glare. She hated the word, hated the c-word even more, and being around the Rebels, he'd learned a number of very unattractive ways to refer to women when they were being bitches, and he'd pull every one of those out if needed to make her keep her distance.

"I understand OY is doing well. I believe you've got a twelve-show run lined up. Isn't that right?" Her head tipped slowly to one side, chin down in a way he figured she thought looked cute, but on her, looked like she was trying too hard. "Thought you could use a seasoned tour manager."

This was the first he'd heard about a tour, but he had skipped a scheduled call with Bethy that afternoon, not worrying about it since she knew about their gig here tonight, would know they'd be getting ready for the show. Benita kept talking. "Figured if I showed up, you couldn't say no. At least I hoped you wouldn't say no." Her eyes flashed, and she smiled at him. "I know how you like things, Benny. I can make everything easy for you."

Another two steps from her had him retreating again, finding the wall with his back, and then her hands were on him. Even through his tee, her touch on him had bile rolling up the back of his throat as every encounter with Benita flashed in front of his eyes.

"You…" He was panting for breath, trying to force down the vomit surging upwards, shaking his head even as his hands came up, gripping her wrists and tearing them away from him. "Goddammit." She twisted one hand free, and fast as a striking snake slipped it down the front of his pants, cupping his cock and balls with a firm squeeze that had the expected result.

Tipping her face up, she fucking smiled at him, the look one he remembered well, the one she wore just before she got whatever it was the spoiled bitch wanted. Took what she wanted from him, regardless of what he said. A sound registered and he looked up from Benita to see the door closing slowly, swinging shut on an empty hallway. This broke through his shock, and he pushed her away, hard, not giving one fuck that her nails scored him as her hand pulled free. Also not giving one fuck that she stumbled, falling backwards, reaching out with a hand to catch herself against the wall. "Benjamin."

At the shocked and scolding tone, her Wyoming accent harsh and flat, nothing like the lilt of Lucia saying his name in the Spanish way, Benny threw back his head and laughed. *I'm stronger than this, stronger than she made me. I've got Luce, and she's everything I need.* Shaking his head, he spoke through his laughter. "You got no place here, Benita. Don't want your brand of crazy, don't need it. I see now I never did. Don't you see? I never needed you." He felt his face twisting, memories of every hated thing she'd done nearly overwhelming him.

"Everything you did to me," she opened her mouth to object, but he blazed on, "and don't lie to yourself, cunt, you did things, showed me things I should never have learned. Surely not at fourteen. Not at twenty. The start of all my woes, I lay at your door." He took a step towards her, stopping when she cowered into the corner. "Never raised my hand to you unless you begged for it. Never fucked you when you weren't gagging for it. Never gave you anything you weren't forcing my hand on." Leaning in, he hissed, "And I remember everything, *bitch*. Every-fucking-thing.

Teeth grinding together, he told her, "I remember. Every line of coke you cut for me. Every goddamned drink you shoved in my hand. Fuck, woman, I didn't even have my driver's license the first time you roofied me, got me so fucked-up I couldn't hardly talk for two days, but you got your dose of my cock. You and your fuck buddies. I remember *everything*." He tapped the side of his head with two fingers, feeling like his blood was boiling through him, like his heart could jump from his chest. "Got it all up here, and I fucking hate it. I hate that you took all those things from me. My family. Stolen by your spoiled bullshit. Took my life, nearly." *Searing pain pounding through his body, his brother's voice, a broken question that echoed in his head, "He gonna die?"*

His breath hitched hard, hurting his chest. "My doc? Told her all the fucked-up shit you did. Every bit of it. Took fuckin' weeks to get that shit out, so fucking deep inside me, I couldn't hardly dig it out. Couldn't stand to say the words, have someone know what I'd done." His hands were shaking, and he clenched them into fists. "Know what she said? Would your daddy wanna know she said you raped me, not only my body like you tried to do five minutes ago, but you raped my mind in a way it will fuck with me my whole life. I was fucking fourteen, Benita. Fourteen goddamned years old, and you raped me.

"I have to guard against thoughts of you because the things you had me do, encouraged, forced...those things eat at me. Eat at me in a way it feels like it won't ever go away. Tearing little pieces of me free with every memory. Every thought of you. Killing me, it eats at me so bad. Used to see it every time I shut my eyes. Even sleep couldn't make me safe from you." Straightening, he swallowed, his throat raw, salt pouring down his throat from the tears streaming from his eyes.

"Fucking hate you in a way I never knew I could. You make me sick. You used me, and now I'm finally—*God*, fuck me—finally, free of you? You want to come back and try to fuck with me more? I'm sober, and you want to drag me back down to your level? Kill every good thing I've worked for? *Christ*, Benita! How do you live with yourself? How can you think you could slide back in and fuck with my life again? How did you think this was going to play out? Crook your finger, wrap your hand around my cock and give a tug, think I'd be headed up the hallway to the john so you could start back up? Or go down?

Throwing up his hands, he shouted, "I'm finally free of you. At last. Jesus, at *fucking* last. After my whole life, which you fucked up—I'm free. You think I'm stupid enough to want to go back? To you?" He was howling now, breath rushing out so fast with every word, pushing out the poison he'd had building inside him for so long.

"I finally have beauty in my life. Something so sweet and good you wouldn't even recognize it. Beauty so far away from what you've ever given anyone, Benita, swear to God, you never saw anything like it. Now when I shut my eyes it's with a vision of something I love more than anything. I have beauty and love, and you? Sad, man. So fucking sad. Your life. Jesus, will you just go away? Go away. You are an abusive bitch who needs to go find herself a new fucktoy. Go away." His eyesight blurred, and he had to swallow hard to get the next words out, wiping at his nose with the edge of one hand, futilely trying to stop the tears. "I won't give you another fucking moment. So fucking done with you, I can't even see you in my rearview. You're. Just. Gone."

He sucked in a breath and held it; the hitching sobs so painful they were tearing at his chest. Turning to the door, he staggered sideways when his eyes landed on the mass of men standing there. Slate, Bear, Gypsy, even Mason. More who he didn't know. They had entered the room while he shouted at Benita and now he couldn't control himself, knowing these men had overheard every word. *Slate* had heard. "*FUCK*," he screamed. His brother knew everything he never wanted him to know. "Fuck." All the shit that covered his life for so long, they tasted because he'd spewed it on the air. Like the dung beetle Mason once accused him of being, he'd spread his shit far and wide, covering every man in this room. "Fuck me." With his eyes squeezed tightly shut, he dropped his chin to his throat, "God, I'm so sorry."

251

"Fucking bitch." The force of emotion behind Mason's words shocked him, and he looked up quickly to see the men moving past him, towards where Benita stood. "You do that shit?" His tone bordering on brutal, Mason was speaking to Benita, but stopped beside Benny, reaching a hand up and gripping his shoulder. Pulling him around to face her again, Mason asked again, "Seriously, bitch. You do that shit to this boy?"

"It's not like that." Her eyes were huge in her face, gaze darting from side-to-side, taking in the wall of muscled men standing between her and the door. "We were…" Her voice trailed off.

Spreading his other hand, the one still firmly gripping Benny and holding him in place when he would have bolted from the room, Mason shook his head. "Edu-fuckin-cate me, bitch."

"It wasn't like that." Her whisper was scarcely audible, and Benny saw her lips were trembling, watched as two big tears slipped from the bottom of her lids and rolled down her cheeks. *Lies.* "I love him."

"Bitch, you don't fucking know what love is." Slate had stepped in front of Benny, putting himself between his brother and the woman. "Knew you were a fucking cunt the first time I laid eyes on you, buying a fourteen-year-old kid clothes so you could take him out with your friends without being embarrassed because he didn't have the flash you wanted. Made me feel like shit 'cause I couldn't give it to him. I didn't know how sloppy a cunt you were." Shoving his hands into his pockets, Slate rocked back on his heels. "See that shit now. Sloppy pussy. Fucking piece of lowlife gash right there."

"How do you want this to go?" Mason's question was directed at Benny, and he shook his head, not understanding. The hard grey eyes in front of him softened, and Mason took a breath. "She did that shit to my boy? I'd kill her. No joke, no bullshit. She'd not be breathin' his air. Told you, people don't fuck with my family." This was said flatly, without emotion, and Benny was shocked to find he didn't question the statement. "You're not my boy." Tipping his head to look around Benny to where Slate stood, Mason said, "But you're family, Benny." Slate nodded, and Mason turned his focus back to Benny, who didn't understand what had passed between the two men, but knew it was important. "You give the word, she's history. Like you said, not even in your rearview. You'll never have to worry about this kind of shit again. So I'll ask you again, how do you want this to go?"

"I...no." Now his breaths were coming sharp and short, panic setting in. They'd do this, for him. *For me.* Take this on themselves. Put them at risk. If they did anything, someone might pay. *For me.* "I won't ask...can't. What if...no. I...no."

Bear spoke for the first time from his place at Benny's shoulder, the position and his presence making a statement of support that didn't have to be spoken aloud to be true. "We can hold her a couple days, give you time to think about it. You don't have to decide today." Benny twisted his neck to look at the man who was staring hard at Benita. "You don't even have to decide this year. An offer like this? No expire. She pisses you off? Looks at you wrong? Shows up where you don't want her to be? Ten years from now, we'll still deal. We got you, little brother."

Benita gasped, and Benny turned to look at her. Ghost white, her stark red lipstick looked like a slash across her face and for a moment, he imagined her dead, a stripe of a different red across her neck. Mason's fingers squeezed when he shook his head this time. "No. I have to live with what she did. She doesn't get to take the easy road."

"Good enough," Bear said, then leaned close, speaking right behind Benny's head, his voice quiet when he said, "Lucia saw something, Benny. You need to go find my girl. Talk to her. I'll do the gig tonight, you take as long as you need to make her understand your demons, son. She's strong, Benny. Give it to her. Let her help you through. Don't let this damned bitch take *anything* else from you." Sick with the knowledge Lucia had run from whatever she'd seen, his mind remembering the door swinging slowly shut, he twisted from Mason's grip and quickly wove his way to the door even as the men at the back of the room stepped forwards.

As he hit the hallway, Mercedes swung into step beside him, and he heard his brother say, "I'm not as nice as my little bro, bitch. Let's have us a chat."

***

"God, Luce. Pick up the phone. Please, *God*. Talk to me." Benny paused to take a breath because his throat was so tight he could scarcely squeeze out the words. "Been everywhere I could think of. Baby, I can't find you, and you're scaring me. It's been hours, Luce. Please, baby. Please. Talk to me."

Ass to the hood of his car, he sat in the garage parking for the apartments. He'd gone to every place he could think of, called her friends, the few people outside of the band and Rebels he knew in town, and even contacted bartenders and managers at the places she liked to hang out.

He'd been to the library. A familiar location because they'd spent hours there, draped over adjoining chairs, her nose in a book and him flipping through music magazines, spending way more time watching her than absorbing information about new bass kicks, amps, venues, or marketing tactics.

He'd been to her Abuela's apartment, been to Bear's house, his apartment. Talked to Ruby and DeeDee, twice. No one at Marie's had seen her since she ran from the bar, her teary retreat the catalyst to Bear investigating what had upset her, his discovery of Benita bringing the club to stand at Benny's back while he faced her down. Now, Lucia was gone, disappeared, and he was about a hundred light years past freaked out.

With his phone pressed to his forehead, he closed his eyes. "Where did you go, baby? Where are you?" Mercedes made a noise, bringing his attention back. He had a thought and unlocking the phone, dialed Ruby again. Without even saying hello, he barked out, "Did you check the studio?"

"Yes, little brother. Checked the studio, the house. Even the backyard. Had to turn off the sprinklers and..." Benny was no longer listening, a memory of pure joy jolting him. One of the most perfect days they'd spent together had ended with them at the park, getting soaked in the fountains of the splash pad. "...go next?"

"I gotta go." Without waiting for a response, he disconnected the call as he jumped down. It was only six blocks; he could run there faster than he could take the car. Feet pounding the sidewalks, Mercedes ran beside him as he dodged around the few people on the street at this time of the evening. "Please let me be right."

Rounding the final corner, heart pounding in his chest, he pulled to a stop, gasping for breath as he swept the park, looking for Lucia. Not at the tables, not seated on the retaining wall, she wasn't lying on the splash pad in a recreation of their moment, a picture he hadn't realized his brain was painting, the carrot for his sprint to the park. "Fuck." Shaking with anger and fear, heart still thudding wildly, he spun in place, taking a long look at every person he could see. "*Fuck*." His shout pulled the attention of everyone nearby and a sudden, startled movement where he didn't expect it caused him to stare into the gathering darkness. "Luce."

Two strides across the grass brought him to the wall, and he jumped down, stumbling into a run again, watching as Lucia slowly stood from where she'd been sitting in the shadows. Wrapping both arms around her, he absorbed the feel of her along with the knowledge that she was okay. Telling her what she already knew. "You're okay. Thank God. You're okay. I've been looking for you. Couldn't find you, baby. Scared the fuck out of me." She was stiff against him, not holding on in return, not relaxing into his arms and his heart jolted to a faster rhythm again. "Luce, baby. I need to tell you what happened today."

"*No mames.* I saw what happened, Benjamin." She said his name in the Spanish way, her accent and voice thick with emotion. "*En serio? Mi corazon esta roto y tu quieres hablar?* No. I saw what I saw, Benjamin. Saw so much more than you wanted."

255

"No, baby. Let me—"

Head already shaking, she pushed against his chest, cutting off his words. "No. I don't need to hear." When he wouldn't release her, she twisted her head, facing away from him. "I *saw*. *Pinche puta's* hand in your pants, you so lost in what she does for you? You didn't even know I existed."

"That wasn't—"

Cutting him off again, she struggled against his grip. "I know what I saw."

"No, you don't," he said firmly, tightening his hold on her. "Lucia, listen. Please, please. *Listen*." When she stopped trying to escape, he released a breath he didn't know he was holding, and dipped his head, mouth close to her ear, already knowing where to start. *She's stronger than I could ever be.* "I lost my virginity at fourteen to Benita. Me a freshman, her a senior. She was five years older than me, and I thought I'd hit gold. Every boy's dream." Lucia stiffened, and he whispered, "Please. God. *Please*, listen." Nothing, no movement, no words, but no resistance, so he swallowed hard and began again.

"For the next eleven years, she owned me." Lucia jerked in his arms, and he pressed closer. "My first drink? Poured by her hand. My first line of coke? Cut on a makeup mirror in her bedroom. The first time I shot up? Her hand held the lighter to cook the spoon." Licking his lips, he paused, not sure how much to tell her, but then Bear's words echoed through his head, and he knew if he didn't do it now, their love would forever be in the shadow of what Benita had done.

"Every..." He paused when she moved and took a panting breath as Lucia's arms slipped around his chest, holding him to her. Holding on. *Thank God*. "Every sexual encounter I had, orchestrated by her." Turning his head, he pushed his face into her neck, muffling his words. "Until you. Every single thing I did for eleven years was dictated by her. I didn't even realize how controlling she was until rehab. Until Doc talked me through it, made me see how fucked-up my life had been." Her arms convulsed around him, squeezing hard, holding tight.

"Until I met you, I didn't know what love was. Until I met you, I didn't know what pure beauty was. What it was like to love someone and know they loved you back just for you, not for what you could do, or what your cock felt like, or the money you could make them. Someone who would go to bat for you, help you pick yourself up when you fell down, and still love you. Until I met you, I didn't know there was this kind of love in the world.

"Everything she did was ugly. It feels like everything I did with her colors me with the same pen and I hate that. Hate it with everything in me. Everything I want to be is at odds with what I was." Lucia's head was moving, shaking back-and-forth in denial.

"I did so many...so wrong. Because I..." His breath hitched, and he faltered for a moment, struggling to pick up the broken thread of his thoughts, trying to find the right words to say. "I don't even know why now. Stupid. I was so fucking stupid, and I'm sorry. What you saw today, Luce. I didn't know she was coming. I didn't want her there. Didn't want her hand on me. What you saw was yet another time she forced something on me I didn't want. Standing there, feeling that slimy touch, trying not to vomit on my shoes, I got away from her as fast as I could."

Her hand slipped up, fingers threading through his hair, cradling the back of his head, pressing his face into her neck. Comforting *him*. Him. *God, so sweet*. Holding him tightly, she told him everything he needed to know without saying a word, communicating her love through actions. Holding on.

"Fast as I could. But, like always, not fast enough because... *God*, I'm so sorry you saw. I never wanted anyone to know." Hiccupping, he felt like he was five again, bawling at his father's graveside, the sobs uncontrollable. "And now, everybody knows. Everyone who matters knows what I've done. So ashamed, Luce. I hate myself. Hate what she did. What I did. Don't leave me. Please. I hate it all so much. I'm so sorry." The last word broke in three places before he could get it out, but even over his ragged breathing, he heard Luce's barely-there whisper.

"*Estar en silencio*, Benny. Be quiet, *bebe*." She paused, and he felt her lips graze across his jaw. "Shhhh. I love you."

A moment passed, then another, and his sobs slowly faded. Darkness gathered around them, shadows giving them privacy while he pulled himself together with the knowledge that Lucia wasn't pushing him away. She was holding on. What she'd said registered, and he knew she needed to know it all, so he told her, "Baby, it's not that simple. I need to tell you—"

She pushed against his chest, gaining a few inches of space and then leaned right back in, tipping her face up and kissing him gently, silencing his words. Pulling back a fraction of an inch, her breath caressed his lips when she said, "It *is* that simple. I don't want to waste one second with you thinking any of that will matter to me. I will want to know, need to, but none of it changes how I feel. I love you, Benjamin Jones. Not because of anything you've done, or will do. Not because of anything other than the good man you are. Don't say to me different. The man in front of me is good. So good, *bebe. Te amo*, Benny."

She blew air out between her teeth, pulled back and stared into his eyes. Hers were flashing, and he knew why when she said, "*Dios! Estoy tan enojado con ella!* So pissed at her, I could spit. Little *fresa? Pinche puta* thinks she can put her hands on *my* man?" Palms flat against his chest, she made a face he thought was adorable, but he knew better than to say anything when she slapped his chest with both hands and yelled. "*Dios! Esa perra estupida de una mujer. Donde esta ella?* Where is she? *Puta* better watch her back."

"Luce, baby." She was nearly quivering with anger, and he realized this gave him something else he needed her to know. "Never had this, baby. Someone who cared so much they'd go to war for me." He remembered the men he left in the room with Benita and scoffed. "But, all this went down in the backroom at Marie's, and the guys got in on it. I left her there with Slate, Mason, and Bear." Lucia pulled in a breath, but he squeezed her and shook his head, cutting off what she'd been about to say. "She bought anything that happens to her. What you saw..." He swallowed hard, then said, "What the guys heard. They were...well...mad doesn't cover it."

"And they gave that to you today, yes?" He nodded and she smiled up at him, not a tip of the lips, but a full, broad smile, showing him she knew exactly what it meant. "You are well loved, Benjamin." Moving in, she pressed those beautiful lips to his, whispering just before she kissed him hard, the beautiful emotions evoked by her actions leading to his hands slipping down her back to cup her also beautiful ass. "Well loved."

Twenty-Seven

Lying next to a sleeping Lucia in his bed, Benny's fingers trailed over her shoulder, tracing an imaginary line down her arm. Using his fingertip, he slowly wrote out the words of his love song on her skin, singing along in his head.

If you'd told me I'd see her once and be hooked,
I'd laugh at you.
If you'd told me her beauty would call to me in the night,
I'd laugh at you.
If you'd promised me a lifetime of beauty like hers,
I'd laugh at you.

Knowing nothing
Nothing is as sweet,
Nothing is as pure,
As the promise of love.

There's a moment in time where your heart knows,
Mine beats for you
Never making peace with the hollow left behind,
My heart weeps for you,
Finding you again grants my dream come true,

It's always been you.

It's you for me and me for you.
Nothing is as sweet,
Nothing is as pure,
As a promise come true.

Be my promise, baby.
My promise of love.
True love come to me.
My promise come true.
Love me, like I love you.
Be my baby, be mine.
My baby.
Mine.

"Please, be my promise," he whispered the words into the stillness of the room. "My true love." Leaning close, he kissed her shoulder and then gently pressed his lips there, holding still, breathing her in. "My baby." Rolling so his back was to the mattress, he curled her into his side, bringing her beside him. "I love you, Lucia Foscan." Turning his head, he kissed her forehead, fingers sweeping dark hair back from her face. "My Lucia." Her nose crinkled as she made a humming sound, scrubbing her cheek against his chest and he grinned, whispering his deepest desire against her skin. "Lucia Jones."

***

"Benny," her voice called to him as from a distance, and he drifted slowly up from sleep. "Benny, wake up." He sighed and felt her hands gliding across his chest, up his neck, and then she cupped his cheeks. Exaggerating the movement, he pursed his lips in a silent request, making little smacking noises when she didn't immediately kiss him. "What do you want? Huh?" With the softly whispered question, her lips were on his. "Want this?" Her hands framing his face, she controlled the kiss, and he let her, opening when she stroked across his lips with her tongue, dueling with her softly. Taking everything she offered and letting her end it gently, she pressed her mouth to his again and again, and again, humming deep in her throat as she did so.

"'Mornin'," he whispered, eyes still closed, wrapping his arms around and holding her close. Cupping the back of her head, he pressed her cheek to his chest and kissed the top of her head. "Good morning, baby." He knew she could hear the smile in his voice when he said, "My Luce is fun in the mornings."

"I could be more fun." She suggested softly, and he brushed his lips across her temple. "So much more fun." Her hand grazed his stomach on a downward path, and he sucked in a breath. Her murmur was soft, threaded through with desire. "Way more fun, *Papi*."

"Yeah? You want more fun?" She nodded, hair rustling as it cascaded across his chest. He gave her a squeeze before releasing her and tucking his hands behind his head. He tipped his chin towards his throat so he could watch. "Knock yourself out, baby."

"Yeah?" She caught her bottom lip between her teeth and he had to stifle a groan. Her eyes were dancing with excitement, and he loved seeing it. Loved so much about this woman. "Whatever I want?"

"Go for it, baby." He gave her honesty and watched her breath catch in her throat at his words. "I'm all yours, Lucia. Always yours. Anything you want, anything I can give you, yours."

She shifted, and he watched as she selectively set aside the weight of those words, reaching for and recapturing the lighter mood with which they'd begun. Curling her hand around his hip, she trailed her fingertips across the hollow and towards his belly, brushing back-and-forth as his cock stirred, uncoiling, thickening. Her arm skimmed across in a move that could have been accidental, but when it repeated, he knew she teased him. "What if I want this?" Lifting to one elbow, she pushed the sheet just below his waist, exposing the head of his cock, and with one fingertip, she traced along the rapidly defining ridge of the crown. "If I wanted this,"—a fingernail lightly flicked the already-weeping tip—"is it mine to have?"

"Anything." Voice hoarse, he groaned when the heat from her hand engulfed his shaft in a loose grip, gliding slowly down to the root, tenting the sheet over his hips. "My Luce is playful." She wagged his cock to-and-fro, making little waves beneath the sheet and he smiled. "Aw, yeah, my Luce likes to play." Still under the sheet, he didn't have a visual of her hand as it moved but felt every change in grip, every nuance of difference as she shifted and her fingertips plucked at his sac. "*Jesus*, baby."

Benny tried to hold still, tried to let her play as long she wanted to, but when she moved down so her breath heated the head of his cock, he reached to gather her hair, holding it loosely clasped at the back of her head, to better see what she was about to do. "All yours," he urged as she hesitated a moment, eyes angled up. Her tongue darted out to lick across his tip, the corners of her mouth curling up. "Baby." He groaned when she took him in, her hand working the shaft in counterpoint to the movements of her head.

He held her gaze for a long time, watching the heat build as she loved on him. Sucking and licking, gently nibbling, she opened her throat and took him as far down as she could, then backed off, lips glistening wetly as she sucked the tip, jacking him fast in her fist. With her hair held away from her face, he saw the moment she lost herself in what she was doing. Lids sinking closed, she was entirely focused on his reactions, moving to counter every jerk of his hips, her other hand fondling and cupping his balls, fingertips sliding between his cheeks and back up, caressing firmly.

It was building, and he wouldn't be able to hold it back much longer. The heat, friction, suction, and—*God*—just watching as she took him in. His cock in her mouth and her obvious enjoyment of the intimate act, everything pushed him faster towards the end. "Baby." She didn't acknowledge his call, so caught up was she in the moment. "Luce, baby." Reaching down, he cupped her chin with one hand, the other holding her hair out of the way. Urging her to look at him, he waited until he had her eyes before saying, "Come here, baby."

She shook her head, closing her eyes and moving faster, head bobbing, strands of dark silk escaping his grip, trailing down her cheek to his belly. "Luce. I want..."

He lost what he was going to say when she took him entirely in, and he saw the side of her throat working to hold him there. "God." Her hand was stroking his balls, rolling and cupping, stretching out the sac and then rolling them in her fingers again. "Mmhmm. Baby. *No.*"

Jackknifing to a sitting position, he reached down and hauled her bodily up so she straddled his hips and he could feel the slickness between her thighs. Sucking him made her hot, and he knew it when she rocked against him with a muffled, sexy moan. Eyes at half-mast, there was a dark flush in her beautiful face, and he loved the look on her. *Mine.* Her lips were puffy, pouting, and he pulled her close, kissing her hard as he rolled them in the bed. In one movement, he was inside her and thrust hard, pushing to the root and staying planted. Nipping her bottom lip, he kissed her until they were both breathless and then started moving. Slowly. Deliberately. Feeling her all around him. "Hot. Tight, baby. Always so fucking tight." With a groan, he rooted himself again, every muscle clenching as he ground deep, feeling her hips tip up in response.

Sliding, pushing, rocking into her, she tightened around him. Threads of electricity pulsed up his spine. It felt like his skin was about to come off his body, as if every gasping breath unmoored him. Slipping a hand between them, he glided back, pressing his thumb against her clit. Rolling back and forth, circling as he swiveled his hips, thrusting hard with his cock while his fingers tweaked and teased, stroked and played. He kissed her deep, hard, and ate down each of her moans, feeling her legs lift, calves pressed to his sides. Her hips cradled him, holding him as close as she could, heels to his ass while he powered into her. Every sense heightened, he shivered at the sound of her musical whimpers echoing in the room, gloried in the feel of her hands on his back, watched as his fingers threaded through her hair. The taste of her lips under his, heat of her pussy wrapped around him, all of her holding him tight. *Holding on.*

He pulled his face from her neck to find her watching him, eyes wide, just in time to see her orgasm take hold, sweeping her eyes shut as it passed through her. It started deep, tightening her around him in a way that was exquisite pain of the best sort, making it impossible to keep the rhythm because he wanted to be in there, stay in there, feel it as she did. *With her, always with her. Forever.* Her arms wrapped tighter, her legs folded around him, her pussy squeezed, and breathlessly she called his name. "Benny."

My name. "Mine."

Fuck. "My Luce."

Face to her neck, he thrust deep, pushed hard, rocking into her and found it right *there*. Exploding, taking his senses as the orgasm stole his breath, making him gasp for air even as he grunted, hips driving wildly, then deep and hard, deep and rocking.

Mine. "Love you."

Always. "So much."

Holding on. "Lucia."

***

The brief phone conversation he initiated with Bear that morning hadn't settled his nerves much. A quick connection to see how things went with the gig last night, confirm to Bear that Lucia was good and then set a time that afternoon for Benny to show at his house for a chat. Something Benny didn't even understand why he needed to do, but he did. This wasn't a want; it was a need, nearly as compelling as the addiction. That time was now. He had hoped like fuck he'd figure it out before he opened the car door, but he'd been sitting at the curb for nearly fifteen minutes and wasn't any closer to sorting his shit.

Unfolding out of the car, he looked up at the Crews' new house. Big, spacious, it was a home for a blended family healing from something he couldn't understand. There seemed to be a lot more going on than he could put his finger on. Half the time, even with Slate, it felt as if he were skating around the edges of something. Shaking off his uncertainty, he started up the walk, but his steps slowed as he again cataloged the residence in front of him. Multi-level, multi-bedroom, big backyard, three-car garage, the house had a huge kitchen the family lived in half the time. Immense, roomy, and really fucking expensive.

Bear worked for the Rebels as a graphics designer and specialty mechanic, and Benny realized the man had to make a lot of money to buy this kind of place.

Benny had been pouring nearly all his money from gigs back into the band, replacing old tour equipment, paying for promotional shirts and other things out of pocket, so they'd have cash from merch sales at shows when they eventually hit the road again. Bethany had helped by getting comps from sponsors where she could, and sourcing things a lot cheaper than he could on his own, but it was still going to take a fortune to get things rolling again. If it weren't for his brother finding him the apartment in a building the Rebels owned, and then gifting him with a year's rent, he wouldn't have been able to do as much for the band.

Benny knew Lucia hadn't been raised in a house like this, but it didn't mean she didn't deserve it. Every good thing that could come her way, she deserved, and more.

I can't give her this. Halfway up the walk, he stopped, gaze dropping to the sidewalk. Broad, smooth, framed on either side by a sweep of brilliant green grass. A good life. Memories painted over what he saw with the cracked and busted sidewalk leading to GeeMa's house, the mud paths taking his resentful footsteps to the front door of so many of his mom's cheap apartments. *What if I can't ever give her this?*

"You're stuck." Twisting, he looked to the side and scowled at Mercedes. "Worrying about things which don't warrant the cerebral labor. She doesn't care about these things, other than to be forever grateful that her brothers will know a different life. Trappings don't matter to her. You do. Lay it aside, Bibi."

"How in the hell do you always know what I'm thinking?" He shook his head. "Weren't you going to wait in the car?"

"I was until my Bibi got stuck in his head. Now, I need to straighten him out before he fucks up bad." Stepping out of his sight, she got behind him and shoved hard, hands in the middle of his back. "Move it, soldier."

He set his heels, not moving. "This is a mistake." The words tore out of him, ripping pain thrashing through his chest. "Things can stay as they are."

"Nope, you made a decision." She shoved him again, and he twisted to frown down at her. A pink and periwinkle fauxhawk rode her head like the comb of a rooster, and even after spending nearly every minute over the past few months with her, he still wondered how she did it because she was never primping or fixing things, never hit the bathroom with bottles of product and never left streaks of color one might expect on the walls of the shower. She shoved, and he took an involuntary step, then another when she didn't relent.

"Is that new? Did you get a new piercing?" What looked like a new set of dermals glinted at him from behind her ear, on the soft, tender area behind the lobe. "That's dope." It was, the jewel colors beautiful against her pale skin. "When did you have time to get to a studio?"

"Walk, Bibi." Since he was moving, this time the shove against his back was less forceful, but Mercedes still made her presence known. "You are not making a mistake. You love her. She loves you. You need to make music, and she helps you do that." This was true. The music and lyrics were flowing like they never had before. He scribbled them onto scraps of paper everywhere, the leftovers of his creative efforts littered any area where he spent more than five minutes. Lyric ideas, thoughts for how to refine existing songs, changes in an arrangement for some of their long-standing tunes, he couldn't be still more than a minute without something taking hold of his mind. "Beautiful music, beautiful woman. Beautiful babies."

Babies. He hadn't worn a condom this morning. Or last night. A shitty move on his part, but she hadn't said anything, and he knew she knew. The idea of losing her had scored deep, scouring away any remaining doubts about what they were building together. The past two times he had made love to her, it had been her getting out of bed to clean up and him laying back, watching the show as she moved back-and-forth from the bathroom.

Her moods fascinated him. She could go from naked and confidently sensual, to being a little shy, grabbing his tee on her way past. Him getting to watch the hem of his shirt settle over her ass was nearly as nice as the view of that ass walking. The show on the way back to bed just as good, her face, hair, everything about her was everything he wanted. *Everything.* So the choice to not use condoms wasn't something they'd discussed, but when she didn't stop him gliding in bare the first time, the die was set. The feel of her pussy, slick and velvety at the same time, with heat from her all around him was something he'd never experienced before. Another first for both of them, together. Addictive. *Shit.* "I can't get a boner before I talk to Bear."

Musical laughter pealing forth, Mercedes patted his shoulder. "Then think of baseball. I understand it helps."

Coming to a halt in front of the door, he stared at the skull-shaped metal knocker set in the center of the surface. "I'm going to do this."

"Yes, you are, Bibi."

It was her hand that lifted, reaching past him to rap her knuckles hard against the door, eschewing the knocker. "Always a rebel."

She laughed again, saying, "Do not tell Mason. He might take offense."

"What would Mason take offense at?" Bear asked this as he opened the door and Benny stared at the man who had become his friend, remembering how he sounded yesterday in the room—*that fucking room*—with Benita. He had been certain Benny could fix whatever had sent Luce running, and then gifted him with the chance to make it right.

Without thinking, eyes stinging, he blurted, "You're one of the best men I know."

Shaking his head, Bear reached out and gripped Benny's shoulder, the feeling much like when Mason had held onto him yesterday. *Holding on.* "Bring it in, son. We don't needa do this in the door." A tug and Benny resisted, his feet stuck to the cement as if they were glued in place. "Benny, come on." Another tug and then a shove at his back and he was stepping over the threshold.

"I'll be in the kitchen with Eddie," Mercedes said, and Benny watched her walk away, wondering when she'd had time to meet Eddie. His train of thought was derailed when Bear put an arm around his shoulders, steering him towards a room at the back of the house.

"Talk to me, Benny." Bear released him, picked up a guitar and handed it over, pointing him towards a seat. Grabbing his own six-string, Bear sat on the edge of a nearby chair. "Tell me about last night."

"Fucked up my whole life." His hands were frozen on the strings, cold and bloodless, stiff with fear. "My entire life I've been the one who fucked up. The one who had to have his messes cleaned up, tidied up, and the one you could only count on not being able to count on." *Tell him something he doesn't already know, asshat.* He swallowed, hearing the simple melody Bear was picking out, his fingers sliding on automatic pilot to echo the chords. C, D, G, C, G, D, G. "I want to be someone she's proud of." Strumming gently, Benny leaned forward, hunching far over the guitar in his lap. "I want to be what she needs."

"You already are," Bear told him softly. "You aren't the same man I met more than a year ago. Proud of you, son."

"I'm scared out of my fuckin' mind," Benny confessed, eyes to the strings, following Bear's lead on the chords. A, A, A, B, D, C, A. "What if I can't do this, Bear?"

"Then you figure out what you need to change in order to do what you want." Back to the original chord pattern. Soft, soothing, Bear led him through the music, Benny's playing growing stronger every moment. "You love my girl?"

"More than anything." The words slipped out before he could stop them, and then, since it was out there in the open, he figured he should say what he felt. "Man, when I couldn't find her yesterday? Hours I looked and didn't find her, and I was losing my mind. First, I was scared she wouldn't talk to me. That she was gonna leave me. Couldn't stand to think of me without her. Then, I was scared to death when I couldn't find her. I decided that even if she never wanted to see me again, I needed to know she was okay." Bear threw in a minor change and then dropped an octave while Benny stayed where they had been playing. Their contrasting melodies wove together, different and beautiful apart, but even more so when blended like this, complimenting and lifting the music up, together.

"You didn't get drunk?" Benny shook his head, and Bear continued. "High?" Another shake and he glanced up to see Bear staring at him. "You even think about it?"

Benny held his gaze, his fingers stuttering on the strings, his playing faltering. Shocked because Bear was right, in his anxious rush to find Lucia yesterday, getting blitzed hadn't even crossed his mind. Hadn't ranked a single thought. "No." He said this slowly, still working to make sure it was true. "Nothing was more important than finding her."

"Benny, you are a good man." Bear's fingers stilled, the music resting in the air, then falling away, leaving Benny face-to-face with him in naked silence. "I couldn't choose better for Lucia."

Twenty-Eight

Leaning against the cabinets in Slate and Ruby's kitchen, Benny lifted a mug of coffee to his lips, watching as his brother made sandwiches for them. Coffee and tea his drinks of choice these days, and he'd drunk gallons of each since rehab.

Piling three kinds of lunchmeat on the bread already slathered with mustard, Slate was picking through different kinds of cheeses. Without looking up, he muttered, "Ain't got no Swiss. Shit." He sorted the packages again and then stood there, palms to the countertop, looking down. "Shit." Another pause, then a growled, *Fuck me.*

Slate's response to the lack of cheese was puzzling. Benny didn't remember him ever being particularly picky about his food. Jokingly he asked, "You that partial to Swiss?"

"No, but you are." Fingers walking through the packages again, pushing cheese and meats from side-to-side with a rustle.

"No, I'm not." Benny couldn't quiet the laughter that pulled Slate's eyes to him.

"Yeah, you are. You won't eat ham without Swiss." Lips in a firm line, Slate was not laughing with him, and Benny felt a stab of unease.

"I'll eat whatever you got." He set the coffee down and leaned over, picking up a package. "Provolone's good." Picked up another. "Cheddar." Dropping them both, he frowned. "I'm not hard to please, bro."

"You never eat ham without Swiss." Shaking his head, Slate picked up one of the packages and began peeling off cheese, placing the round, white slices on top of the piles of meat. "Never did, anyway. I remember Daddy driving from the ranch into town to buy Swiss so you'd eat a fuckin' sandwich."

"When I was what? Four?" Now he was laughing in earnest, unable to beat back his amusement. "I'm not a kid, bro. I outgrew that kind of shit a long time ago." He had to be careful picking up his coffee mug; he still shook with laughter. "I liked poking my fingers through the holes." The air in the room grew thick, and he glanced up to see Slate staring at him. "What?"

"What she said." Slate paused, and Benny froze because there wasn't any question in his mind to which "she" Slate was referring. "What she did to you." Brow furrowed, the hurt on his brother's face was hard to witness, and it set up a resonating ache in his chest. "So fuckin' sorry, Benny. I never knew that shit. Never knew." Chin to his chest, Slate stared down at the half-finished sandwiches. "My baby brother, and I never fuckin' knew anything because I left. Never shoulda left." There was a wide ribbon of bright pain in his voice, hard and edged with blades of self-recrimination. "Never shoulda left you like that."

"You didn't know. I never wanted anyone to know." Benny kept his eyes on Slate, waiting for him to look up, having to continue on without any clues how his words were being received when his brother stubbornly continued staring at the counter. "If I wasn't weak—"

Slate's roar startled him into silence. "You were fuckin' *fourteen*." His jaw hardened, and Benny thought he could hear the grinding of teeth.

"She's a fuckin' predator. No different from an old man with a bag of candy and you'd never hold a little girl in ridicule because she was little. No. I'm tellin' you, the bitch knew what she was doing. She groomed you, man. Groomed you and then used you for her own sick-as-fuck games. Fuckin' predator."

"I wasn't unwilling." Probably the worst part of everything because he hadn't been. "Every time she upped the game—"

"It left your eyes rolling backwards in your skull. Fuck me, of course, you weren't fuckin' unwilling. Why would you be? Fourteen? Gettin' off on having her hand in your pants. *Fuck me*." Head moving back-and-forth, Slate closed his eyes. "You still friends with Danny?"

The abrupt topic change left Benny reeling, and he snapped out, "Yeah, still friends of a sort. Been friends since we were kids."

"He spray painted my truck. Eight-years-old or so and fuckin' spray painted the word *whore* on my truck. Mom was such a waste back then." That sounded like another topic change, and Benny still hadn't caught up to why they were talking about Danny.

"I never knew he did that. We were friends. Why would he do that to you?"

"Why would he fuck up your life? He's an asshole. I traded him; and until right now, I was never proud of how I maneuvered him, but I did. Traded him an asswhuppin' against bein' your friend. Told him if he didn't make life easier for you, I'd make his miserable." Slate barked a laugh. "Another fine example of how me fucking with your life fucked it up."

"I don't understand."

"Even then I knew I'd be bailing on you sooner or later. I think it was a chance to see you got a friend to stand at your back. But I picked a loser. Fuck, Benny. My life is full of bad fuckin' decisions." Palms flat on the counter, Benny watched the muscles working underneath the surface of his brother's skin, the tattoos shifting and moving in response. Slate was working through some emotion tied up in him leaving Wyoming, but Benny couldn't figure out which way he was headed.

Reaching out, he rested one hand on the tattoo covering Slate's upper arm. Starting at the peak of the shoulder, the tattoo of a vengeful angel stretched halfway down his arm ending with the words 'My Brother's Keeper'. "You saved my life." *This is where it starts*, he thought. *Reparation. Because he didn't do anything wrong, and I can't let him live with that thought.* "Saved me. Was it the wrong decision?"

"No. But—"

He didn't let Slate get anything else out, talking over him and praying he could force his brother to hear him. "My whole life, you've worked to make it better. Was it a bad idea to try to do that?" He didn't give him a chance to respond, forging ahead. "No. It wasn't. It's never a bad decision to try to do right. You can't know what the outcome is going to be. Mason told me it's the intent that matters most, more than anything else. If you work and try to do what you think is right, then it matters most." Fingers tapping, he indicated the tribal band positioned below the angel. "This one, it's for me, too, even if you didn't know it at the time." Worked into the dark ink were the words 'The Past Is Practice.' "The only time we master life is if we're six feet underground, moving on to the next transformation. The whole time we're here, if we're doing it right, we're practicing so we can do better. Like playing music, you never stop learning." He leaned in, resting his chin on Slate's shoulder, whispering, "You saved my life. Nothing else matters."

The sudden tension under his hands gave him only a moment's warning before Slate exploded, shoving Benny away as his arm swept the sandwiches in an arc, sending them smashing against the wall. He roared again, and Benny made out the words, "You were fuckin' *FOURTEEN*," before Slate grabbed him, holding on tightly. "Fuckin' fourteen, Benny. I was fuckin' my way through the western states, and you were being fucked over by a fuckin' bitch. Goddamned fuckin' bitch. I left, and you were only fuckin' fourteen."

"You saved me." Benny wrapped around his brother and repeated his words. "Nothing else matters."

"I fuckin' left."

Benny squeezed Slate in his arms, wordlessly trying to tell him it didn't matter. "You're here now."

"Mom was a waste."

"Yeah, she was. She had to save herself. I was lucky. I had you." He swayed, and Slate caught him, holding him upright. "You saved me. I pissed away a thousand chances. Stole and lied to get what I wanted. Brought trouble to your feet and"—he squeezed tightly again—"you saved me. Fixed it all so I didn't have to worry about it and never asked me for anything other than to learn how to be a better man. I didn't have to look far to find the best example, Slate. Still don't because it's right in front of me. You are who I want to be when I grow up." This made them both laugh, and Benny heard a feminine chuckle too, looking up to see Ruby standing in the doorway, eyes on the two men standing in a man-hug in the middle of the room. "I love you, bro."

This got him a squeeze in return, and a gruff, "Love you, too, shrimp."

Releasing his hold and stepping back, he waited until he had Slate's gaze before he said, "You're not gonna clean make me that mess up, are you?" Laughter from two of the people he loved most in the world surrounded him, and he grinned at how good it felt.

***

"Are you trying to be nice?" Lucia's question startled him, and Benny blinked at her. He'd been watching her as she played and thought her focus on the game would keep her from noticing his scrutiny. "Because you're making me nervous. Do I have something on my face or something?"

Leaning forwards, he brushed his thumb up her cheek, sweeping his hand into her loose hair, threading his fingers in so he could pull her towards him. Pressing a gentle kiss to the side of her head, he released her and sat back, watching as her hair fell in a dark cloud around her face again. "No, I was thinking I wanted to kiss you but didn't want to bug you."

She cut a glance his way, then looked back to the TV. "Not buggin' me to kiss me." Lips tipping up, she said, "Like your kisses, *Papi*."

"I'm glad." Stretching out on the couch, he turned to put his head in her lap, grinning as she readily adjusted to the new position, lifting her hands and the controller so he could fit underneath. "I like kissing you." He waited a moment, then asked her, "Whatcha doin'?"

Her lips tipped again, mouth stretching into a soft smile. "Playin'." A pause, then, "Whatchu doin'?"

He turned his head, nuzzling under the edge of her shirt and kissed her belly, liking how it hollowed out at his touch, her torso jerking as his lips made contact. He drew a line of soft kisses, then looked up at her. No longer smiling, she had pulled her bottom lip into her mouth and was biting it hard. "Playin'," he repeated the word back to her and watched as that lip rolled out of her mouth slowly, glistening in a way which made him want to kiss her. *Not that I need an excuse.* Eyes still to the TV, she pressed her full lips into a tight line, and he decided to test her focus, turning his head to nuzzle into her again.

Lifting his hand, he curled his arm around her side, fingers drifting up her back underneath the fabric of her shirt, finding the edge of her bra strap and tracing along the line. "Benny." Soft and breathy, her voice wasn't scolding, even though he knew it was her intent.

"Hmm?" Raising his other hand, he slipped it underneath her thigh beside where he lay, curving his fingers around the bare skin, tickling the back of her knee gently. She didn't dress conservatively, but she didn't show much skin, either, always hitting a happy medium which meant he loved looking at her in whatever outfit she chose. Knowing, unlike all the other men who might look at her and see only what was hinted at, he knew what lay underneath. *The promise.*

Still breathy, she said, "Stop. You're gonna get me killed." He glanced at the screen. She was in solo mode, which meant she didn't really care. Shifting, he pulled his hand out from under her leg and turned his back to the TV, facing her. The hem of her shirt had lifted, baring a tantalizing strip of skin across her belly. Easing forwards, he moved until his cheek was pressed against her pelvis, lips brushing against her. Drawing slow circles with the tip of his nose, he crossed her belly, kissing as he went. "Benny." Breathless again, her voice trembled, and he felt the weight of her arm on his shoulder. Glancing up, he saw her eyes were closed, lips slightly parted.

"Gonna die, baby?" At his words, her eyes popped open, and she glared down at him a moment before looking beyond him to the TV. He rearranged his hands, sliding one underneath her thigh again, but up near where her shorts covered her ass, curving in and pressing against the seam in her crotch. Benny got to watch as her belly hollowed out at his touch again. Heard her indrawn breath, saw the tails of her hair dip, and knew she was looking down at him. Trailing a fingernail down the seam, he scratched and plucked at it, seeing her belly jerk again. *Wanna hear her moan.*

Lips to the fastening of her waistband, he worked and tugged, fingers getting in on the action to get her zipper down and then he slipped a hand into her panties, immediately shifting, frustrated at the angle. "Wanna eat you, baby." Nuzzling again, he heard a thud and looked up to see her empty hands sweeping her hair bac, fingers tugging on the elastic tie she wore on her wrist. "Leave it down." He liked her hair down. "Baby." She stared at him. "Lay back, Luce."

Shifting sideways, she edged towards the arm of the couch as he sat up and adjusted his hard cock in his too-tight pants. Sauntering to the door, he put the chain on and turned the deadbolt, turning to face her. Tiny socks on her feet, knees bent, heels together and tucked to her ass, she was lying with her head on a pillow. "Gorgeous." She was. Dark hair swirling around her head and shoulders, beautiful brown eyes bright, uncertainty warring with arousal on her face. "Stunning." The hem of her shirt rucked up, belly bare, red lace of her panties peeking out the 'V' made by the opened shorts.

"Continually amazed that you picked me." With one knee to the couch he curled his hands around her ankles, sliding up her calves and over her knees, thumbs between her thighs until he pressed against her still-covered pussy. "Looks like yours? Beauty you have inside you? You could have anyone." Fingers hooking in her shorts, he dragged them down her legs and off. Dark red lace covered her, darker in the center exposing things she didn't realize he'd see. "A thousand men would lay their hearts at your feet." Hands traveling the same path, he let her panties fall to the floor. "You let me in." Fingers loosely circling her ankles, he slipped her socks off. "Bringing all your beauty into my life." He leaned in, mouth against her skin. "In my bed. Letting me hold love in my arms, every day. Gonna kiss you every moment, tell you how much I love you. Always will. My heart is yours, Lucia." He lifted her hand, placing it against his chest.

Swooping in, he brushed a soft kiss against her parted lips. "Shirt off, baby. Bra too." Leaning up, she was occupied with his instructions when he stroked her gently, slowly slipping a single finger into her pussy, freezing her in place with the shirt half off. He went belly-down on the couch, pushing her legs apart, finding there was plenty of room to do what he wanted. He pulled one leg over his shoulder and leaned his head against her inner thigh. "Are you mine, Lucia? Do I hold your heart?" His question jolted her into movement, and her shirt went flying.

"*Si, Papi. Mi corazon.*" Dipping his face forward, he flattened his tongue against her, lapping at the sweetness which was all his. "*Ah, Dios.*"

"Mine," he murmured, mouth against her, knowing she felt every gentle breath. Hands under her ass, he lifted her to his mouth, watching as her belly did that hollowing out thing, imagining it rounded instead. "Forever." Licking and lapping at her, he fucked her with his tongue, slowly. What she gave him was deliciously sweet. "Always." Her body arched, hips tipping, hands running through his hair and he looked up at her to find her staring back intently. "I love you, Lucia." She nodded. "Keeping you forever, baby." Sucking her clit into his mouth, he traced across it with the tip of his tongue. "Never let you go."

"Never let me go," she repeated, hers breathy-soft where his had been raspy-rough.

"Never let you go." Fingers working her, hard and fast, curling and twirling inside her while he ate her like a starving man.

"Never let me go." Lips parting on a gasp, she changed the tune when she said, "Never letting you go, Benny."

"Don't let me go." His was a plea, but he prayed she didn't know, lost as she was in the passion he evoked in her. "Never let me go." Pressing deep, he covered as much of her with his mouth as he could, biting and sucking, desperate for what she gave him.

"Never." Moaning softly, lost in the emotions and feelings, still she knew what he needed. "Love you, *Papi*." Another moan and she tipped her hips, moving and thrusting up, seeking what he gave her. "Love you." Head back, he lost her eyes but got to watch her face as she came, seeing all the beauty she held inside. Thirty minutes later, she got to watch his as he exposed everything he thought he had hidden, making her love him even more.

Twenty-Nine

"Telling you, I'm not ready." Gaze fixed to the toes of his boots, he couldn't see Mercedes' reaction. Didn't want to, not like this, didn't want her to know how freaked out he was at the idea. "You can't go." The silence grew until he couldn't stand it anymore, looking up to see her staring at him.

"Bibi." Her gaze on him was considering, and he took that as hopeful, thinking maybe she saw the error of her ways, which meant she wouldn't do what she was threatening. "What do you need?"

The question surprised him because they'd moved past that kind of episode a long time ago. He hadn't seriously been tempted in what seemed like forever, but he knew by the exact count of days that he was only months into this sobriety session. Staring at his boots again, knowing he sounded like a sullen child, he asked, "What?"

It took several minutes, but she finally responded. "What do you need, Bibi? What will make it better?" *You not doing this*, he thought as he looked up, but didn't say. When she slowly shook her head, he knew she'd read it on his face anyway. "Bibi." Her voice was soft. "You knew this day would come."

"I didn't expect it today." Leaning back in the rolling chair behind the big mix board, he looked around the studio his brother had built. *For me.*

"I'm not talking today." Her voice was echoing through the room, coming into the control room over the speakers. She was in one of the isolation booths with the door closed, but he could see her through the glass. He'd gotten a text from her to meet here, walked in to find she'd separated herself from him by two glass walls in order to have this conversation. Another way Mercedes made her point. "But you're ready."

"What if I'm not?" Laying out his worst fear, that he would go slipping sideways again. "What if I fuck up?" Lose everything.

"Does it matter how many times you fall?" He stared at her. She'd taught him that. Taught him so much. Taught him to think instead of react. Taught him to believe in himself instead of feeding the pit of fear gaping open inside him. "You are so much stronger than you know."

"Don't go." His shadow for so long, threatening to separate from him and go dancing up the wall. *Time to grow up.* "I—"

"Bibi." She said nothing else, didn't move, merely held his gaze.

"I need you."

At this, she did smile, faint movement at the corners of her mouth, the crinkling at the corners of her eyes indicating deep amusement. "I need you, too." The backs of his eyes were burning, and his throat closed tight at those words, knowing what she truly meant. "I'll always pick up."

"Throwing me a bone?" Offering to stay connected, letting him have this, knowing he might need it. "You think I can do this?"

His question seemed to release her, and she stood to walk through the studio to where he sat. "I *know* you can." Small, waiflike, frail, quirky, and the strongest woman he had ever known. "My Bibi? He can do anything he sets his mind to."

"Mercedes Griffwaldo, I kinda like you." He intentionally mangled her name, as he had every time since the first day they met.

"My wife would appreciate it if you stopped doing that, Bibi." She reached out, brushing his hair from his face and bent to press her lips to his forehead. Benediction. *Love.* "It's pronounced grih-fith. G r u f f u d d. Grih-fith."

"Am I ever going to get to meet her?" In all the months Mercedes lived in his pocket, he'd yet to lay eyes on her partner, Slate organized her vacation when he could be around, but Mercedes never took more than a couple of days at a time. "This mysterious woman you love?"

"She will be my plus-one at your wedding."

Thirty

"Good evening, Indiana!" He shouted the words into the microphone, tipping his wrist sideways so they could see his full-on grin when they screamed the greeting back at him. "How y'all doin' tonight?" Another tip of the mic as he swept the crowd with his gaze, his smile broad and pleased. Nothing plastic, nothing fake about this, he was excited to be here, in Marie's, and ready to get the night started.

Glancing back at Chase, he saw his friend was loose and relaxed, wrist propped on the body of his guitar, fingers idly plucking out the fingering for their first song as if he could do this for hours. Glancing the other way, he grinned. Mitty was on the ego box at the side stage, getting a start on the set by lifting his hands overhead to clap, getting the crowd going on his side of the venue.

A look behind him caught Vic staring Bonnie's way, and he felt a sliver of worry dance in his belly. As far as he knew, Vic hadn't told anyone else about Bonnie, and she'd done such a good job hiding any feelings she might still be holding onto for their drummer, he was sure no one else knew they had a history. Vic's look said he wasn't past it, and Benny tried to tamp out the feeling he had. *Nothing I can do to change their lives.*

"Wisdom," Mercedes whispered in his ear, and he jerked his gaze to the booth where she sat with the front-of-house guy behind the boards. Her last show. He grinned. *And I have quite the finale planned.* "Don't do it." She lifted the microphone to warn him, her voice sounding alarmed for the first time ever. *"Bibi."*

Reaching up, he yanked off his in-ear headset, letting them dangle around his neck by the cord. "Marie's. Y'all feelin' any pain?" Another roar as he moved to the other side of the stage, ignoring the glare he felt coming his way. He reached out a hand, indicating the rowdy merrymakers on that side, the crowd roiling at his feet. "I didn't think so. Feelin' good? Are you ready for some rock and roll?" One more roaring response, and he grinned, twisting to give Vic a pause signal, letting him know not to launch into their first number yet. He got a puzzled nod in return and gave a thumbs-up. "Y'all ready for some Occupy Yourself?" Usually at this point in a bigger gig, he'd be pitching the main act, but tonight, as ever at Marie's, they were the entire show. *Headline run.* He smirked.

"Wanna introduce you to someone." He gestured to the knot of people standing at the side stage, giving a "come here" motion towards the tall blonde woman standing next to Lucia. "Raquel Gruffudd, she's the wife of a very good friend of mine, came all the way from California to see tonight's show. Rocky, come on up." With a tentative smile and a glance at the booth, she made her way to the stairs. "See, my friend is moving away. After a year of livin' with me, she's moving back home." A sympathetic sound from the audience made him grin. "Good for her, sucks for me, yeah?"

Raquel appeared beside him, put her hand on his upper arm and leaned close, holding up her phone so he could see the text as she whisper-yelled, "Put your ears in, Bibi." Shaking his head, he turned and stuck his tongue out in Mercedes' direction, then looked at the woman next to him.

Two weeks ago, after prying for hours, he finally got Raquel's number out of Slate, wanting her here for this. He also found out she was a closet fan, as well as a talented singer, and from that information crafted an idea. "Rocky, you need a mic." He held his hand out behind him, feeling the sting as Mitty slapped a wired mic into his palm. "Raquel's a singer, folks. Can you give her a warm welcome?" Applause and whistles filled the air, the energy from the people surrounding the stage starting to grow. Beating at him, urging him to get a move on while it was still building, before the swell fell, before the crowd would be past salvaging. Turning to Vic, he nodded and grinned as Raquel's fingers gripped his arm tightly. Handing her the mic, he leaned in, yelling into her ear, "The Promise of Love."

Vic counted them into the song, Bonnie's heartbeat thrum steady and strong underneath the melody Mitty laid down. Chase came in on the second round of the intro, and then Benny nodded at Raquel, grinning as they lifted their mics in sync. Her voice was good; he'd made sure of it via online videos before he put her on the spot like this. He'd never do something like that to Mercedes, put her wife at risk of embarrassment, but Raquel could belt it, had an amazing talent. Good enough that by the second verse, he could let her soar on her own, singing about love feeling out of reach.

Turning to the side stage again, he lifted his hand in invitation, eyes only for Lucia. Curving his fingers, he jerked his head, asking her to trust him. *Please, please God, baby.* She'd be hated by a thousand women after tonight, and when the video of what he was about to do hit social media, he'd be the envy of a million men.

Up the metal stairs, she carefully made her way across the jumble of wires and cables, sliding in to press close to his side when he curved his arm around her. His thumb flicked the mic off, and he reached to tuck it into his back pocket. "Luce." She smiled up at him. Hand to the front pocket of his jeans, he reached in and pulled out the ring that'd been burning a hole in his pocket for weeks, waiting for the perfect moment. Realizing that there would never be a better time than now.

He glanced around, seeing Mercedes splitting her focus between him and Raquel. Slate and Bear leaned against the barrier at the front of the stage, their patched leather vests granting a buffer of space around them few except their brothers breached. Vic, Chase, Mitty, all grinning like loons. Ruby perched on a stool by the bar, phone up in front of her face, recording everything. Mason standing near her, arms crossed over his chest, face impassive but Benny knew he was pleased with what he saw. Sober Benny, sober Chase, happy Slate.

He leaned in to kiss Lucia, watched her eyes heat then slip closed as she kissed him back. Lifting her hand, he broke the kiss, then pressed his lips to the ring on her finger. Grinned as her eyes widened, staring, then she looked up at him.

Raquel's voice softened, she moved to one side and as the crowd caught sight of Benny and Lucia they roared in approval.

> *My promise come true.*
> *Love me, baby, like I love you.*
> *Be my baby, be mine.*
> *My baby.*
> *Mine.*

~ *Fini* ~

THANK YOU FOR READING
$\mathcal{B}\!\mathit{orn}$ INTO TROUBLE

Benny's story started long ago in book #2 of the Rebel Wayfarers MC series, and he's been hanging around in the background since then. Waiting, not so patiently, for his shot. I hope you enjoyed his journey of recovery and self-discovery. If you are a recovering addict, you have my admiration and hope that things go well for you. If you are an addict, there is information below that I hope will help bring you peace. Everything is possible. I promise.

Benny's story deals with hard topics. Sexual abuse of a minor, that minor being a male, is still abuse, and can have long ranging repercussions. If you are an adult survivor of childhood sexual abuse, please know you are not alone. RAINN.org, the Rape, Abuse, & Incest National Network can help you find the resources to begin the emotional healing process. Many perpetrators of sexual abuse do so from a position of trust and power. In Benny's case, his abuser was an older teen; a girl with easy access to first alcohol, and then drugs. As a near-peer with great influence, she was able to steer Benny down that path with her until he was so mired in his addictions, he couldn't see any way out.

When you read *Born Into Trouble*, I pray you don't see a reflection of yourself or anyone you know, but if you do, please know that there is help, and hope. Among many available resources, both AA.org and NA.org stand out as beacons for people who are in need. If those organizations aren't a workable solution for your situation, then tell someone you trust and allow them to help you find what will work. Hold on. You can do anything, as long as you hold on.

For those who have never seen the face of addiction, the FBI released a movie that illustrates clearly how these dangerous behaviors are not restricted by economic boundaries, nor do they recognize sex or age as defining factors. I have a link on my website to the video, and you can find it at mldemora.com. Remember, addiction can reach into any family, through multiple vectors, and as with so many things, our first line of defense is knowledge. Watch, and learn, and pass it on. And above all else, *hold on*.

BENNY'S PLAYLIST

He's a musician, what do you want? I put together playlists of music both mentioned in the book, and used during writing and editing. Want a peek into the mind of me? Be sure of your decision, it's not always normal here!

Benny's playlist: bit.ly/oy-bit-playlist

ABOUT THE AUTHOR

Raised in the south, MariaLisa learned about the magic of books at an early age. Every summer, she would spend hours in the local library, devouring books of every genre. Self-described as a book-a-holic, she says "I've always loved to read, but then I discovered writing, and found I adored that, too. For reading...if nothing else is available, I've been known to read the back of the cereal box."

Also by MariaLisa deMora

Alace Sweets

A dark thriller, this book is not a light read. Filled with edge-of-your-seat suspense, this intense story commands the reader's attention as it drives towards the explosive ending. Alace Sweets is a vigilante serial killer, with everything that implies and is sure to trip all your triggers. Be ready.

At seventeen, Alace Sweets turned a corner in her life, taking the wrong shortcut home from school.

Resisting the harsh knowledge her attackers will never be made to pay for their actions, Alace takes a stand. Justice must be served, and if fate's scales are out of balance, she's determined to set things right as best she can.

When the laws of men fail, the rules of Alace prevail.

5-Star Reviews for Alace Sweets

"deMora has a superb story-line and exceptional character development. All of her characters have such depth that will intrigue the reader..."
~Turning Another Page

"Hot, sweet, dark thriller."
~Beth D

"It will keep you on the edge of your seat and give you chills."
~Escape Reality Book Blog

"Disturbing, haunting, sickly; yet hot, sexy and heart racing!"
~Amanda L

"From the first page [deMora] pulls you into the world she has created and you do not even try to escape..."
~Little Shop of Readers Blog

"A must read for all those dark, gritty romance fans out there."
~Sweet & Spicy Reads

"You will find yourself so drawn into the story that the outside world is blocked out and your locking the doors and turning on all the lights."
~Danena F

"Don't judge me for bonding with a vigilante serial killer, she's more than what she does."
~iScream Books

"Thrilling...chilling...full of suspense, nail biting edge of your seat excitement."
~Tracey H

"Every time MariaLisa deMora picks up her pen (or opens her computer), she creates characters you want to believe in."
~Gail S

"Intriguing dark storyline, beautiful love story and nail-biting conclusion, what more could a reader ask for?"
~Manda M

"This book takes you a dark and twisted ride that is gripping..."
~Renee Entress' Blog

"This book is dark and gritty and I literally had to take a day off from reading it because it's that intense."
~My Girlfriend's Couch

"This is my favourite book so far from this author ... I recommend this book if you enjoy dark romantic thrillers."
~Cheekypee Reads and Reviews

"There's not enough stars to give this book and 5 just doesn't really do it justice!"
~DeLane C

"I couldn't put this book down from page one! Tried to stop & go to bed but couldn't sleep thinking about Alace and got up & finished the book."
~Debbie M

"MariaLisa DeMora, wordsmith that she is, made this a story of the enlightenment of a woman and finding love in a life where she has had none."
~Kat W

"Whatever deep dark trench [deMora] pulled a character like Alace from should be revisited again and often."
~Confessions of a Serial Reader

ADDITIONAL SERIES AND BOOKS

Please note that books in a series frequently feature characters from additional books within that series. If series books are read out of order, readers will twig to spoilers for the other books, so going back to read the skipped titles won't have the same angsty reveals.

Rebel Wayfarers MC series:

Mica, #1
A Sweet & Merry Christmas, short story #1.5
Slate, #2
Bear, #3
Jase, #4
Gunny, #5
Mason, #6
Hoss, #7
Harddrive Holidays, short story #7.5
Duck, #8
Biker Chick Campout, short story #8.5
Watcher, #9
A Kiss to Keep You, novella #9.25
Gun Totin' Annie, short story #9.5
Secret Santa, short story #9.75
Bones, #10
Gunny's Pups, novella #10.25
Never Settle, short story #10.5
Not Even A Mouse, short story #10.75
Fury, #11

Christmas Doings, #11.25
Gypsy's Lady, #11.5
Cassie, #12
Road Runner's Ride, novella #12.5

Occupy Yourself band series:

Born Into Trouble, #1
Grace In Motion, #2 (TBD)
What They Say, #3 (TBD)

Neither This, Nor That series:

This Is the Route Of Twisted Pain, #1
Treading the Traitor's Path: Out Bad, #2
Trapped by Fate on Reckless Roads, #3 (TBD)

Other Books:

With My Whole Heart
Alace Sweets
Hard Focus

More information available at mldemora.com.

www.ingramcontent.com/pod-product-compliance
Lightning Source LLC
Chambersburg PA
CBHW070054030726
47506CB00002B/468